MERIT THE NAME

Reirin Miller

Merit the Name
Copyright © 2024 by Reirin Miller

Published by Long-Distance Beginner Press

Printed in the United States of America

Cover design: Paolo Skyrus
Book design: Clarity Designworks

ISBN 979-8-9897422-0-2 (paperback)
ISBN 979-8-9897422-1-9 (ebook)

Author's Note: This story does not intentionally mimic any real events. If you find this to be the case, delight in the whims of chance.

Mercy does not judge its own absence.
—Stephen Levine

CONTENTS

PROLOGUE

June 19,1987
Linda – Barcelona

I warned them about the bomb a full hour in advance. Using separate phone booths for each call, I notified the police, the newspaper, and the Hipercor superstore itself. If everything went according to plan, the bomb would detonate in Hipercor's garage, underneath fifteen stories of grocery, clothing, appliances, and housewares. Because of my advance warning, the department store would be evacuated long before the bomb went off—but things don't always go as planned.

First of all, it took some time to walk to each phone booth. Though plentiful in Barcelona back in 1987, phone booths weren't on every block. The calls took far more time to complete than I had expected. The minute I said the word "bomb" into the phone, I'd hear, "Please hold," and I was transferred, over and over again. When I called the police, they shuffled me around until finally someone who sounded half-asleep got on the line. I hung up on him when he started asking questions about my identity.

The same treatment happened at the newspaper: "...please hold...please hold...please hold." Finally, a raspy male voice answered. "You know, there's other ways of getting a man's attention. A short skirt, a low neckline—it's not that hard." I could hear laughter in the background. I hung up.

Lastly, I dialed the department store's number, went through the transfer maze, and finally got Hipercor's general manager. Again, I recited my warning. "A bomb will detonate at your location in one hour." I paused and checked my watch. I realized that one hour was, by then, inaccurate. They only had thirty minutes. But before I could say anything else, the manager snapped, "You prank callers are driving me nuts." He shouted at a secretary to get him more coffee, and hung up.

I walked to an apartment building a few doors down from Hipercor on the opposite side of the street, ensuring I was outside of the approximate blast radius. Going through the service entrance at the back, I accessed the roof, and settled in to monitor the store's main entrance.

Using binoculars, I closely observed the customers entering the store, hoping that I would see the same people running out any minute now. I preferred a calm, steady stream of departing shoppers, but a mob pushing and shoving each other out the front doors while screaming in terror would also be fine, just as long as they left the premises.

I watched a pregnant mother approach the entrance, trying her best to push a stroller while managing a daisy chain of two kids under five. An older boy held onto the stroller with one hand, and his younger sister was holding on to his other hand, pulling as hard as she could in the opposite direction. Her efforts had no effect on the forward progress of the family caravan, however. I wondered at first if the young girl was psychic, then I realized she had locked her sights on a pastry shop just to the right of the entrance. Who wouldn't want to be fortified with sugar before having to endure endless shopping inside a fifteen-story store? I didn't blame her. I could have eaten several donuts in that moment, myself. I tended to stress-eat in those days. But the mother wasn't having it, and in they went.

The afternoon sun was unrelenting, and there was no shade to be found on the roof. I couldn't take my eyes off the entrance. I felt hypnotized by the disconnect between what should be happening and reality. Another family approached the store, their school-aged kids clearly pleased about their imminent shopping experience as they rushed toward the doors—though they stopped abruptly when their mother yelled at them to step aside. She opened the door for an elderly lady trailing behind, whom I decided must be her mother-in-law. Despite the summer heat, the old woman wore a dark wool suit, a scarf, and a wool hat. She sailed through the door like she was Queen Isabella.

I lowered the binoculars to wipe my forehead awkwardly with the short sleeve of my polo shirt. Where were the police? Where were the bullhorns and traffic cones?

I looked closely at my watch. The second hand marched along, blithely ticking away in lockstep with the bomb's timer across the street. I imagined the timer's glowing numbers barely illuminating the outlines of the bomb, which was nestled under a tarp in the back of the Ford Sierra parked deep inside Hipercor's garage, underneath the store. Tick, tick, tick. I checked my beeper. It showed the exact same time as my watch.

Self-conscious and excited about their new bodies, two teenage girls pranced up to the store's doors like poodles then paused to confer. Their feathery bangs, their long permed hair, their black eyeliner, their midriff tops, their cutoff shorts—their style was carefully identical, as if conformity would keep them safe. One of them whispered in the other's ear; they giggled, then in unison they looked behind them to make sure no one had heard.

I started pacing. I could understand the police being totally incompetent, but what about the others? Wouldn't the newspaper, chasing the story, have called the store and the police by now? That would have made it obvious to everyone that this was serious.

Ten more minutes went by. No panic, no reporters, and no police. Far more shoppers were entering the store now, and almost no one was leaving. I swatted at flies orbiting my sweaty face. At 3:25 p.m., I finally saw two police officers strolling sedately towards the store's entrance, where they stopped, looking irritable and bored. They smoked exactly one cigarette each, then left.

Diesel fumes from a passing truck floated up from the street. I felt nauseous. I'd started having misgivings about this job from the minute José, The Galician, was assigned to our ETA cell. ETA stood for *Euskadi Ta Askatasuna,* a Basque independence organization. Bernard and I had given José the nickname, The Galician, as a joke. José was actually from Navarre, not Galicia, but he looked a lot like Francisco Franco (Spain's former dictator) who was born in Galicia. José was short like Franco, had Franco's bushy eyebrows that perched like sad caterpillars over his eyes—but the most annoying similarity to Franco? José's constant bragging about his previous exploits. Bernard and I found this to be in bad taste. What's more, it violated ETA's guidelines. We weren't supposed to know about other jobs done with other cells, in case one of us was later caught and tortured.

The bomb was supposed to have a small impact—a boutique bomb designed to cause only some minor property damage, nothing more. But as we prepared and planned the job, The Galician appeared to have different ideas, which we found confusing at first. We had thought he'd misunderstood the directive; José's dialect was different enough to occasionally cause some confusion. But no. Too late, we realized that The Galician was going rogue. He wanted to make a big splash.

"Only as powerful as it needs to be" had been our motto up until then. Bernard, our cell's bomb specialist, was a huge hairy bear of a guy who spoke as little as possible. I'd worked with him several times. We trusted each other. I myself didn't doubt that Bernard would build the bomb to spec, and it would detonate on time, because Bernard knew what he was doing. One time, he and I collaborated in Pamplona on a job where we had concealed one of his bombs inside a streetlight. That bomb exploded right at the moment a *Guardia Civil* vehicle was passing. The explosion killed a particularly energetic and well-known torturer of ETA members. The Guardia Civil—the Spanish Civil Guard—were like the FBI and CIA combined; a powerful, awful entity that had survived, despite the definitive end of Franco's regime in the 1970s, like a malignant cancer. We in ETA firmly believed we functioned as chemotherapy.

The point is, normally I had confidence in our work. But the day had gotten off to a bad start. Around 4:00 a.m., Bernard had quietly knocked on my bedroom door, and when I opened it, he whispered, "Bomb is different."

"Different how?" I whispered back, trying not to wake The Galician, who was sleeping in the adjoining bedroom.

"Too much," he said. But it was too late to fix whatever The Galician had done to it. We decided that perhaps it didn't matter that the bomb had a bigger payload than planned, since we figured the building would be evacuated ahead of time. So we simply agreed on a back-up plan.

My forearms were turning brick red. Sweat circles bloomed below my bosom. The flies had multiplied. When 3:40 p.m. came and went, I wondered if, when The Galician modified the bomb, he'd also messed up the bomb's timer.

I couldn't wait any longer. I ran across the roof and down the stairs, pulled my shirt up over my nose and mouth as a makeshift mask, and dashed across the street to Hipercor's entrance. I stopped short. I wanted people to leave the building. But how could I make them leave? If I was caught, the Guardia Civil would surely torture me, thus exposing Bernard and all my other ETA contacts, who would in turn be arrested and tortured as well.

I didn't know for sure if the bomb would actually detonate, either. Who knows what else the Galician had messed up? I turned away from the store. I hurry-walked down the street, pulled out my pager, and sent an emergency code to Bernard to activate the backup plan.

At the next corner, I caught a taxi. This was easily done, because Meridiana Avenue was a main thoroughfare that led straight to the train station. At the station, Bernard was waiting for me behind the wheel of a hired car idling in a loading zone. I had just opened the passenger door and was about to get in when I heard a deafening roar. I thought the ground was shaking too, but no, it was just my legs turning to jelly as I collapsed onto the passenger seat and shut the car door.

We took off and managed to get on the autovía before the police blocked all transportation and roads leading out of the city. I looked in the rearview mirror and could see a giant plume of black smoke forming in the sky.

I pointed it out to Bernard, who said again, "Too much."

"Too much...property damage?" I asked.

"It was wrong. Like napalm," he said, shaking his head.

We ended up hopping a freighter bound for Cuba. On the freighter, I managed to snatch a newspaper that a sailor had left behind in the head. Splashed across the front page were photos of the destroyed department store. The article reported that the Ford Sierra at Hipercor had been filled to the brim with ammonia, gasoline, and soap flakes. Innocent people carrying their groceries to their cars in the parking garage were asphyxiated by the bomb's toxic fumes. Those people might have survived if the bomb hadn't been radically modified. The bomb's explosion opened up a crater in the ground and created a ball of fire that blew through the garage's ceiling.

Bernard and I never spoke about that day again. Not during the freighter crossing. Not in Cuba, where our ETA contacts helped us procure a rubber raft that got us to Mexico. There was certainly no chitchat while we made our way westward, hiding under burlap on top of a pile of manure, in the bed of a rickety truck.

There was no boundary between the manure and me, because I felt dirty inside. I imagine Bernard felt the same. We came to appreciate our bed of shit for two reasons; the first reason became apparent during our cross-country road trip. The Mexican highways were pitted with potholes, and as we bounced along what felt like the surface of the moon, the manure helped cushion the ride. We didn't discover the other reason until the end of our journey.

In Puerto Vallarta, our ETA contacts outfitted us with new identities. Posing as janitors, Bernard and I boarded a cruise ship bound for the US. Two days later, we disembarked in San Pedro, California, and hopped a freight train that brought us directly to the center of Los Angeles—to the City of Merritt—where we've lived ever since.

The second benefit of spending eleven hours hiding in manure was that we had lost all aversion to unpleasant odors. This turned out to be extremely helpful when it came to living in Merritt.

Even though we were reborn into our new American identities, and we had managed to avoid torture and lengthy jail time in Spain, we still felt permanently incarcerated with self-loathing and regret. We never spoke of what happened in Barcelona in 1987 because it had swallowed all of our words. We were afraid that if we weren't careful, we'd lose ourselves along with them.

Twenty-two years later, all that changed after we set fire to this lady's house.

DUTY TO WARN

Losing her job at AFA Foods meant that Meredith would never set eyes on the City of Merritt again. As she started her commute home, she tried to focus on this happy fact, but the banker's box of her desk items reproached her from the passenger seat, reminding her that she'd have to find a new job immediately. During a lengthy stop in traffic, she hefted the box out of sight into the back seat and let the army of home tasks fill her mind, like soldiers goose-stepping down the boulevard of her developing migraine. She had to make dinner. She had to feed the cat. She didn't know which of her husband Grillo's many volatile moods would be in play.

As she pulled into her driveway forty-five minutes later, a large orange tabby was sprawled in front of the side door, sunbathing in the ninety-degree afternoon sun. Meredith usually arrived home after nine in the evening, and at that time, she could count on the cat yowling with the same entitlement as a fat mustachioed banker at a steakhouse. But at four in the afternoon, it couldn't care less about her arrival.

From the back seat of her car, Meredith grabbed her bag and wrestled out the box, balancing it on one hip while she shut the door. She heard a horn sound repeatedly, like something out of a cartoon. She looked up the street and saw a man pushing a repurposed, fully-loaded shopping cart with one hand, while honking a bicycle trumpet horn with the other. Various pushcarts selling snacks canvassed Los Angeles's sprawling grid with regularity during the day, but it had been a while since Meredith had seen one up close.

In perfect synchronization with the cart's arrival, a boy slipped out the front door of the house opposite hers and crossed to meet the vendor, who stopped directly in front of her driveway. She didn't know the boy, even though he was her neighbor. She had never met his parents, either. She'd only lived in Atwater Village for three months, which was long enough to get to know the neighbors, but this was LA, where most people preferred the opposite.

Without speaking, the kid gave the vendor a five-dollar bill. The vendor, a Latino man with high broad cheekbones and muscular, tanned forearms, gave the boy his change. The boy appeared to vibrate in anticipation as the vendor prepared and handed him corn on the cob, mounted on a stick.

Meredith's stomach growled. She couldn't remember when she'd last eaten. She watched the boy joyfully munch his corn, stray kernels sticking to his tawny face like he had come down with yellow chicken pox. He wore his hair cropped short on top, with a skin fade on the sides. Meredith herself kept her hair cut very short as well, because it was easier to manage. She realized she'd probably have to let it grow out, to save on the cost of haircuts.

The cart vendor turned to look at Meredith, raising his eyebrows to form a silent invitation.

As she hesitated, the boy called out to her, "You gotta try it." She put down her things next to her car, fished out her wallet, and walked down her short driveway. The boy said, "My mom doesn't let me get ice cream from the other cart. That cart comes around 1:00 p.m. But she lets me have this, even though it's close to dinnertime." He held up his corn and waved it at her for emphasis. "I call this a 'cornsicle' because it's like a popsicle, as long as you forget how popsicles taste."

"*Elote?*" said the cart vendor to Meredith.

Meredith nodded and paid the vendor. Using tongs, he pulled an ear of corn out of a large stockpot, and jabbed a stick in its end. He proceeded to slather the corn with mayonnaise, butter, parmesan, and a squirt of lime, finishing it off with a sprinkle of cayenne pepper. He handed it over to Meredith with a flimsy paper napkin.

"Gracias," she said. It was the workhorse word in her limited Spanish vocabulary.

"De nada," said the vendor. He continued pushing the cart down the street and turned the corner, the horn fading into the white noise of the city.

"Yum," said the kid to Meredith. "Yours looks so good. My mom says I have to get the sweet corn. No mayonnaise or butter."

Meredith moved to stand under the shade of a Chinese elm growing in the sidewalk median. The boy trotted after her, talking all the way in between bites of corn.

"I always wondered why your house has blackout curtains," he said. Kernels shot out of his mouth like sparks from a fire. "You don't look sick," he said.

Meredith bit down on her corn with firm commitment. She closed her eyes in appreciation while she chewed.

"Why are your curtains always closed?" the kid asked again.

Meredith looked up at the house she rented, swallowed, then said, "My husband prefers it that way while he works. The sun distracts him. He's a conceptual artist."

"What's that?" asked the kid.

Meredith said, "Conceptual art explores ideas, often emphasizing process over results."

The kid stared at her blankly, then his big brown eyes narrowed. He said, "Are you messing with me?"

Meredith shook her head no, and took another bite. The elote was satisfying and disgusting at the same time.

The boy said, "We went to the natural history museum last week and I saw a painting of a dead rabbit lying on a table covered with a white tablecloth. It was bleeding all over the table, next to a bowl of fruit. The guide said that people hung up paintings like that right next to where they ate dinner!"

Meredith smiled and said, "The dead animal was a symbol of their prosperity, I think."

"What's prosperity?"

"Like, having a lot of money."

"Oh. Was the picture a concept art?"

Meredith said, "No...conceptual art is more like a practical joke but is usually dead serious."

The kid frowned, then shrugged, and said, "The dead rabbit with a fruit bowl could be a practical joke, right? Maybe it was a joke and not about prosp—being rich."

Meredith considered the boy's theory. She'd majored in art history in college, but that was long ago. Her husband Grillo was usually the one in charge of art exegesis, not her. She said, "If the painting was a full-sized installation of a dining room, and the rabbit was human-sized and seated at the table...and let's say the footmen serving it were human-sized fruit—"

Excited, the kid finished for her, "—serving tiny humans! On a plate!"

She nodded. Was this inappropriate content for a boy his age? She wasn't sure.

"Whoa," said the boy. "That would be cool. I'm going to build it. A diorama!"

Meredith said, "OK but…you might want to check with your parents?"

"My mom is okay with dioramas. She won't let me use the computer or play video games, so what else is there to do? She says I can get on the computer when I go to middle school. But that's three whole years away." The boy flipped his denuded cob into the air and caught the stick. He looked at Meredith expectantly. She stared back, munching her corn. A grease slick had spread across her lower face. Her thin napkin was fairly useless.

"Watch this," the kid said. "Are you watching?"

Meredith nodded.

The kid threw his corncob up in the air again, made a fast pirouette, and caught the stick before it hit the ground. He looked at her again, waiting for a reaction.

She said, "Yes, you did it." She wondered if she was supposed to say, "Good job." She was out of her depth.

The boy asked, "Was my trick a conceptual art?"

"Not quite…"

Abruptly he changed the subject and asked, "Why are you home so early?"

Taken aback, Meredith said, "How do you know that?"

"My room faces your house." He pointed to the house opposite. He continued, "I never have my shades down. I like the light. See? I'm the opposite of your husband."

Meredith nodded as she finished off her corn. She thought the boy was actually very similar to Grillo, but didn't say so. They both had outsize demands for her attention.

The boy said, "My mom doesn't understand that even though I'm nine years old, I can't go to bed at 9:00 p.m. It's too early. She says that when I'm ten, I can go to bed at 10:00 p.m. So I stare out the window at the street until I get sleepy. It's really boring. The squirrels are asleep. The dogs have been walked. No pushcarts. That cat sleeping by your door? It paces back and forth on your driveway right before you get home, then when it hears your car, it jumps up on the stoop. Then you come home. It's usually about fifteen minutes after my mom says goodnight."

Meredith said, "I'm sorry that you have trouble going to sleep."

"Why are you home early today?"

"I was fired."

"Why?"

"Because of pink slime."

"What's that?"

"You don't want to know," said Meredith. Her cell phone rang. She waved goodbye at the kid with her corncob as she walked back toward the car, answering her phone.

"Meredith James," she said as a greeting. She looked over her shoulder and saw the boy running back to his house.

"I've been trying to reach you." It was Dr. Stein, Grillo's therapist. She stopped at the trash can perched on the far side of her driveway and threw away the cob.

"Hello, Dr. Stein," Meredith said. "I'm so sorry, I meant to call you back, but work was really busy today." She had planned to return his calls during her lunch break, but she ended up not eating lunch because that was when the worst PR crisis of her career had commenced, ending her career just a few hours later. Calling Dr. Stein back had completely slipped her mind.

Dr. Stein said, "When a patient poses a threat to himself or others, it's my duty to warn family as well as the authorities," He sounded like he was reading a warning label on a pack of cigarettes. Switching to a more natural tone, he added, "I don't believe he's serious, though. You know how dramatic Grillo can be."

"Duty to warn—? Did Grillo—? What threat? I don't understand." She turned around to pick up the box sitting by the side of the car, and saw Grillo standing in the kitchen doorway, his face red with rage. He wore a vintage smoking jacket over striped pajamas pants, and an eye mask was pushed up onto his forehead. He looked like an angry child dressed up as a superhero.

The sleeping cat at Grillo's feet opened its eyes, jumped on all fours, and scrammed down the driveway.

TOPA CAFE

Wednesday, August 19, 2009

The day after Meredith was fired, she got up early to go for a run. The angry summer sun hadn't fully birthed itself yet, but flowers had already opened up for the day, like retail shops.

She returned and showered. Because Grillo generally didn't get up until around noon, he was still asleep. When she opened the bathroom cabinet to get her deodorant, she noticed that Grillo's prescription medications, prednisone and oxycontin, were missing. She made a mental note to request refills from the pharmacy, but first she needed coffee.

Coffee and energy bar at the ready, she opened her aging laptop to conjure up a new job. An urgent priority. An *immediate* priority. She estimated that unemployment benefits would cover only half the rent, and she was fully on the hook as the sole bread-winner. Grillo had not yet achieved financial success as an artist. Fifteen years ago, they'd agreed that Grillo would dedicate all his time to his art and Meredith would cover all expenses. It had worked out well for a couple years, but then Grillo developed severe artist's block.

She logged into LinkedIn to update her profile and noticed that she had a few new unread messages. Most were spam, but the most recent message was anything but.

Meredith, it was a pleasure to see you again at the last Merritt business mixer. I'd love to discuss urgent opportunities in PR on behalf of the city. Time is of the essence. Please contact me at your earliest convenience.

–Vern Page, Community and Public Relations Officer
  City of Merritt

The City of Merritt. Just the thought of it made her ill. She reminded herself that she couldn't be choosy. It was difficult recalling details of the mixer, which had been held two weeks ago, because she attended events like that all the time as part of her job. They tended to blur together. At the mixers, she easily navigated the clumps of business people wearing business casual, who spoke mostly in business jargon, who *pinged* and *synergized*. They sounded like cicadas buzzing in atonal unison.

She couldn't associate Vern's name with a face, but she messaged him back anyway, composing something sufficiently chirpy, and making sure to include her cell phone number. She moved on, updating her LinkedIn profile, editing her resume, emailing recruiters, and applying to job listings.

She realized it was already one in the afternoon. She felt guilty about her enjoyment of the quiet house while Grillo slept. She made a quesadilla and was sitting down to eat it, when her cell phone rang with a call from an East LA area code.

"Meredith James," she said.

"It's Vern Page. I received your message." There was a pause. He prompted, "City of Merritt."

"Oh of course! Nice to hear from you," said Meredith.

"We need someone with expertise in PR immediately, to help with some urgent matters. It's short-term. Perhaps you could squeeze it in as a side gig, since I'm aware you're full-time at AFA Foods. I was thinking if you had some vacation time accumulated, we'd probably only need you for a week or two."

"I'm actually freelance now," she said. "I'm no longer at AFA Foods."

"When can we meet?" Vern said. "Do you have anything today?"

"Today? Oh! Let me check my schedule," said Meredith, continuing the charade. "Yes, I have a one-hour window at 2:30 p.m. A client cancelled at the last minute. Does that work?" Vern gave her the address of Merritt City Hall and hung up. When Meredith left the house thirty minutes later, Grillo was still asleep, so she left him a note on the kitchen table.

1:30 p.m. was an excellent time to go anywhere in Los Angeles. A commute that was arduous at rush hour transformed into a breezy joy ride. As she flew down the freeway, she wondered about Vern Page and whether this gig would be as satisfying as her job at BVD, where she had worked before AFA Foods. BVD was a plumbing distributor that sold parts specifically for repairing backflow valves, which she'd never heard of before she started working at BVD. A backflow valve kept grey wastewater separate from clean water, thereby preventing mass death from diseases like cholera and typhoid. It was a genius invention that no one outside of plumbing and construction had ever heard of—not at all sexy, but completely essential. She'd learned a lot about backflow valves during the five years she'd worked at BVD.

As she cruised up the freeway, she reminisced about the time she'd shot over thirty training videos for the BVD website. On camera, BVD's owner, Jim, explained how to disassemble, repair, then reassemble various backflow valves, often including fun facts about the manufacturers who'd produced them, going back fifty years or more. The fluorescent lighting drained his face of color, but he had endless energy and patience. He'd been very sure that educational videos would be the ticket to cornering the market. And he had been right.

The videos were useful and stood for everything that was the opposite of entertainment. She could imagine the hapless plumber at the other end of the continuum, staring at a broken backflow apparatus. She pictured the plumber somewhere in the Inland Empire, an enormous area east of Los Angeles, originally called the Orange Empire until all the orange trees were replaced with endless warehouses, strip malls, and bedroom communities. The heat beat down on him like a sledgehammer. The broken backflow valve was mounted prominently in the insipid curbside landscaping of a strip mall, painted the customary red and blue, surrounded by shrubs. The plumber had got the thing open and was staring at a spring, a diaphragm, and an o-ring, and he thought, *Jesus Christ, now what?* Maybe he wasn't even sure which freaking valve manufacturer made it. Maybe he was thinking to himself, *Dammit, I shouldn't have been such a stoner in high school, but I had dyslexia and it wasn't easy.* Then here comes Jim and his repair videos to the rescue.

That job was a cakewalk.

Why had she left? She could see now that it had been a stupid career move, though at the time, she thought she was being strategic. At BVD, her job covered marketing, PR, and advertising. She had to make up her title depending on whatever task was at hand. At AFA Foods, she had only one title, Communications Director. She learned too late that titles were meaningless, and that simplicity had nothing to do with happiness.

She tried to focus on the meeting with Vern Page. When she'd heard his voice on the phone, it jogged her memory. LinkedIn had depicted a confident, smiling black man in his 60s, but it was his voice that allowed her to connect his face with the whole person. His outfit had stood out. Other mixer attendees always favored a neutral pallet of dark blues, grays, and browns. Vern, however, wore a pink button-down shirt and green plaid pants. She remembered feeling relaxed after talking to him, as if he'd given her a temporary reprieve from the effort of appearing professional, savvy, and competent to strangers with short attention spans. How had he done that? She couldn't remember.

According to LinkedIn, Vern had worked in media relations for several years. His career started in the army, then he'd worked in PR at several large corporations, all of whom had a presence in Merritt. She guessed that's how Vern had jumped to City Hall. He'd been a Merritt insider for a while.

Under his profile, several people had posted recommendations. "Need it solved yesterday? He's your man," said one. Another admirer cryptically gushed, "I had a brief conversation with Page last year mentioning a business slump. Since then, we've seen double-digit growth. I don't know what he did, but it worked. I love doing business in Merritt!"

Sometimes LinkedIn profiles included hobbies and other outside interests. This part of Vern's profile, as with Meredith's profile, was blank. Meredith didn't really have time for anything besides work and Grillo. Even if Vern had left that section blank by mistake, Meredith decided she liked him more because of it.

She arrived a half hour before the appointment time, which was far too early—she'd look like she had nothing else to do. To kill time, she headed to Topa Café, a few blocks away on Leo Boulevard. Sometimes when her car was in the shop and she needed a ride, Grillo would pick her up from work, and he always wanted to stop at Topa before going home. They both were amused by the design of its interior, with its homey '60s kitsch that wanted to be part of the future.

Although impersonal white, boxy buildings dominated Merritt's visual landscape, the owners of Topa Café had made a little more effort. To the left of the front door, overgrown bird of paradise plants pushed up against a gridded iron pergola. A few had poked through, reaching out like prisoners' hands through the bars of a jail cell. She parked and went inside, where, just to the left of the entrance, padded pleather stools guarded the three sides of an empty bar. Beyond slatted wood screens enclosing the bar space, the restaurant dominated a large open area, featuring white tablecloths and large brass chandeliers. Along one wall ran a long formica coffee-shop counter with attached vinyl seats.

The last time they'd visited Topa Café, Grillo had said, "I love the schizophrenic interior design of this place. Is it a deli? Is it a private club? Is it a steakhouse? It can't decide." He tried to order a pastrami-flavored gin cocktail, but the bartender simply stared at him, his unamused patience quickly withering Grillo's mockery. Abashed, Grillo had rubbed his bald head with one hand while he collected himself, and had contritely ordered a beer. Meredith had ordered sangria. When the bartender was out of earshot, Grillo continued to eviscerate the establishment's aesthetic. His large brown eyes came alive in his thin pale face, and as he pointed out the many design failures, he raised his hands, opened his palms, and splayed his fingers, like a traveling preacher uplifting the unsaved. Meredith had laughed. He could be funny, sometimes.

After several drinks, they'd giggled over the inscription on the overlarge bronze plaque, which was mounted on the front of the fireplace's copper hood. Unlike other historic plaques, it contained nothing about the historic or architectural significance of the restaurant, only noting the full name of the city's founder and the year, which seemed odd to place in the middle of a restaurant. They'd tried to figure it out. Wasn't City Hall a more appropriate place for something like that? Unless the plaque was in every restaurant of the town, as a mandate? (But what other restaurants were there? Meredith didn't know of any.) Merritt was so weird.

Now, as Meredith perched on the first barstool closest to the unlit fireplace, she noticed that the restaurant was completely empty. It was a little early for happy hour and too late for lunch; she figured that must be why. The bartender came out of a door behind the bar, saw Meredith sitting there, and said, "Sangria, right?" She was shocked he remembered. It had been over three months since her car had been in the shop.

"Sangria? That sounds good, but I'm not sure," she said. "I have a meeting—"

The bartender shook his head. "That's the trouble with people nowadays. They're so nervous. Back in the day, people knew how to relax."

"I am a bit nervous, I guess. My meeting is at City Hall."

The bartender shrugged and looked at her, like a dog straining at a leash. His serious expression belied the bouncy, playful letters of the restaurant's name embroidered on his baseball cap.

"Yes, okay," she said. "Sangria it is." He sprang into action, grabbing a chilled glass and a pitcher from the bar fridge, filling the glass with ice, pouring in the sangria, adding a slice of lemon, and placing it on a napkin on the counter in front of her.

It looked inviting, but she was still unsure. She said, "Sangria's mostly fruit juice anyway, right?"

The bartender shook his head. "There's absolutely no fruit juice in our sangria."

"Really?"

"Nope."

Meredith took a sip, tasting the acidity of the wine mixed with an elusive sweet flavor not unlike licorice. She said, "Maybe that's why I like your sangria so much." The bartender nodded in approval while he sliced more lemons, then put them in a storage container.

She said, "Sorry to bother you. Can I have a Coke too? You know. To be sharp for my meeting."

The bartender said, "You don't need a Coke because Coke is in the drink already. Red wine and Coke. It's actually called *kalimotxo*. Classic Basque aperitif. We renamed it 'sangria' because no one would order it otherwise."

"Oh!" Meredith said. "Red wine and Coke. It does sound a bit—unpleasant. But it's very good. How do you say it again? Kali—"

"Kalimotxo. It's Basque. Some executives from Alabama came into the bar once and were all in my face about how the correct name was 'Jesus Juice' because that's what they called it in the South. As if. We couldn't wait for them to leave."

"That is a horrible name for a drink."

"I know."

"If you have to call it something more recognizable, 'sangria' wins the day, for sure. What's the ratio of Coke to wine?"

"Sorry, no can do. It's a secret recipe. Kalimotxo allows you to stay sharp and at the same time, feel relaxed. Perfect prep for your meeting. Plus, it's on the house. We're closing permanently next week."

"That's a shame," said Meredith.

The bartender shrugged as he put away the container of sliced lemons. "In the past, our customers liked our heavy-wristed pours. Now everyone wants to work, work, work." He gestured at the empty restaurant. "The food isn't what people want anymore, either." He looked off to the side, momentarily pausing constant movement, and sighed.

"Did you work here for a long time?" Meredith had planned to use her time before her meeting with Vern to do more research, but she felt sorry for the bartender. His quick execution of unnecessary tasks, like wiping the already-clean counter, was useless without customers.

"Since the '90s. Back when Leonata still ran the place."

"Leonata?"

"Mayor's wife."

"It's an unusual name," said Meredith.

"It's a nickname. The mayor's name is Leo Mendebal. This street is Leo Boulevard, and the plaque over there is about J.B. Leo, the founder of Merritt." He shrugged. "One night, a long time ago, the staff got drunk after work and we gave each other nicknames that started with 'Leo.' Leonata's real name is 'Gaxuxa.' She's Basque. But the nickname stuck, I guess. No one ever calls her 'Gaxuxa.'"

"What's your nickname?"

"Shitbird." He lined up the glasses on the shelf behind him, making sure they were evenly spaced.

Meredith choked on her drink and coughed.

The bartender picked up a glass, held it up to the light, decided it had water spots, and proceeded to wash it in the bar sink.

Meredith said, "But there's no 'Leo' in your nickname. Unless it was a nickname for your nickname? Like, was your nickname originally, I don't know, *Leo-shitbird*?"

The bartender turned around, drying the glass with a towel. "My nickname had already been set in stone before that night. I started out working in the kitchen." He smiled. He clearly loved telling this story. "I had a crush on this beautiful waitress. I couldn't take my eyes off her, so of course I burned the rotisserie chicken. Big fire. Lots of smoke. I thought I'd lost my job for sure that night, and Leonata was furious, but she didn't fire me. Instead, she reassigned me to the bar, where I've been ever since."

Meredith tried to imagine Bob, her former boss, reassigning her elsewhere at AFA Foods, instead of screaming at her and firing her.

The bartender continued, "'Shitbird' became my nickname, and it stuck."

"Did that ruin your chances with the waitress?"

"The opposite. She's my wife now. She calls me Shitbird too. But my name is actually Emile."

"Meredith James. Nice to meet you, Emile. What'll you do next, now that the place is closing?"

Emile shrugged. "I'll go over to City Hall and be a security guard or something. The mayor will take care of us. For decades, on the days he was in town, he ate all his meals here. He knows us well."

As Meredith watched Emile wipe down the clean counter, she couldn't imagine him as an immobile security guard, but she didn't want to sound negative. She said, "The mayor sounds very generous!"

Emile shrugged. "He has no choice really. We know too much. Lots of deals went down here over the years. Have another?"

Knew too much? Deals? What did he mean? Meredith pretended that she hadn't heard, and said, "No, thanks. I really have to get going." She left him a large tip. On the way out, she grabbed some matchbooks for Grillo from the large urn placed at the unmanned hostess desk. Grillo would enjoy dissecting the matchbooks' clumsy graphics.

When she arrived on time at City Hall, she found Vern Page pacing the lobby. Vern wore a yellow button-down shirt and chartreuse pants. All he needed was a sun visor and he'd be ready for eighteen holes.

They shook hands and exchanged greetings. Vern led her down the hall to his office. After he seated himself behind his desk and gestured for her to sit in a chair opposite him, he said, "Your LinkedIn profile was very impressive. A gold Stevie award at the age of twenty-five, a Drum award a few years later. That's unusual."

"Thank you. I worked with an amazing team in both cases, of course." Meredith always felt ambivalent towards the awards she'd received early in her career. Recognition meant that you weren't invisible, but invisibility was pre-cisely what the best PR people strove for.

She tried to change the subject. "How can I help you?"

"I'm sure you've heard already."

"Could it have something to do with PR?" said Meredith, faking an innocent look and smiling. She felt both alert and relaxed from the kalimotxo.

Vern chuckled mirthlessly. "It has to do with Leo Mendebal."

"The mayor?" She was grateful for the conversation she'd just had with Emile. Though she'd worked in Merritt for three years, she had no idea who the mayor was until thirty minutes ago.

Vern sighed and said, "You've read the articles in the *LA Times*, right?"

"The *LA Times*? I just read the business section, it's all I have time for. Was this front-page stuff?"

"No, thank God."

"I'm very focused on my work. I read business and industrial food trade publications mostly," Meredith said. "I've had my hands full with pink slime lately, for example." The pink slime fiasco had slaughtered AFA Foods. She was pretty much certain that they'd have to file Chapter 11.

Vern nodded thoughtfully. "I heard about that."

"There's no such thing as negative publicity—," said Meredith drily. Someone might pivot AFA's reputation. But it would not be Meredith.

Vern nodded, saying, "Go in H.O.T., as they say." Meredith nodded knowingly at his acronym for the guideline of appropriate PR crisis protocol: don't Hide, don't Overreact, don't Threaten.

"Right. Then clear it A.S.A.P.," returned Meredith. A.S.A.P. stood for: Apologize, show Sincerity, Amplify advocates, and be Positive.

"No acronym is strong enough to crush a stubborn reporter with a vendetta, unfortunately."

Meredith said, "Are you sure that Merritt's bad press is a liability? You can't reframe it somehow?"

"Not this time. The Mendebals own a large percentage of Merritt's land and lease it to the corporations that operate here." Meredith scanned the five-mile-wide expanse of Merritt in her mind. Warehouses, processing plants, and manufacturing lined up opposite each other, up one street and down the next. Fortune 500 companies.

"Impressive," said Meredith cautiously. "Mr. Mendebal is the mayor as well as the landlord. That could be concerning."

"Take a look," said Vern as he pushed a stack of news articles toward Meredith, brushing against a framed photo. The photo depicted a regal black woman posing with two smiling young men who looked like younger, carefree versions of Vern. Vern righted the framed photo, stared at it, then placed it face down on the desk.

Meredith glanced through the headlines of the articles that shouted about voter fraud and indictments. She said, "I see. Still, I'm sure it's solvable. I have some great relationships with journalists at the *LA Times*." Her relationships were with the Business section's staff writers, not those working at the City Desk, but Vern didn't need to know that. She asked, "Can I keep these articles?"

"Yes, if you're taking the job. But you'll have your hands full with that goddamned reporter. He really has it out for us."

Meredith glanced at the bylines on the articles and saw they were all written by the same journalist, Gil Girron.

Meredith said, "Investigative journalists do require kid gloves, but I have a proven track record for placing press releases successfully; they rarely need much editing, and they're newsworthy. Most importantly, my contacts in the press trust me."

"Impressive. Explain how you pulled that off," said Vern.

"The usual, but I'd say persistence and consistency were key components too. They realized that they never had to bother with detailed fact-checking. When I had to occasionally spin a topic in a slightly different direction, they didn't question it. The Business staff, of course, is a bit easier to deal with than the City Desk. They'll probably be more thorough. It just means all our ducks have to be in a row. If we provide the data to support what we're trying to convey, they'll bite. It would help me if you could summarize all the immediate goals and deadlines. I also need to know about any obstacles or concerns, besides—" Meredith glanced down at the journalist's byline again. "Gil Girron."

Vern nodded, but didn't answer immediately. She assumed he was still unsure about hiring her, so she tried to close the deal. She said, "Please feel free to be candid. I'm the soul of discretion. I can sign any NDA you might have handy. I have very reasonable rates, and Crisis PR is of particular interest to me. Do you have a Crisis PR Plan?"

"The City Council had other priorities."

"I happen to have AFA Foods' Crisis Plan right here, if you'd like to take a look." AFA Foods never approved the plan. The board had repeatedly postponed its review and approval, other priorities always coming first, but Vern didn't need to know that. She pulled the inch-thick plan from her bag and slid it across the desk to Vern. As Vern flipped through it, color infographics and charts flashed by, interspersed with narrative bullet points.

Meredith asked, "Can I take a look at Merritt's Crisis PR Plan?"

Vern opened a drawer and pulled out a sheet of paper. As he handed it to her, he said, "Your plan is very impressive. I should have included more infographics."

"Thank you. It's a lot harder to get in front of a crisis without a plan already set up, isn't it? It's like an evacuation. With a plan, you know where all the emergency exits are."

"Right," said Vern, handing AFA's plan back to her. "Otherwise, it's a bunch of hysterical people running around in circles in the dark, bumping into each other and screaming." They both laughed. Vern's laugh was like a big hug. Meredith leaned into the sound.

She said, "Yes, and then—all the injuries." Vern nodded. She asked, "What's the most important goal that you'd like me to accomplish?"

· "We have only two weeks before the state of California votes to de-charter the City of Merritt, at which point it will be absorbed into the City of Los Angeles."

Meredith blinked. Two weeks. That wasn't much time. She said, "Can you be more specific as to why that's not a desired outcome? I suppose Merritt's civil servants would lose their jobs, but how would it affect the businesses operating here?"

Vern quickly rattled off the reasons why Merritt should remain a separate municipality. Clearly, he'd had a lot of practice. "Merritt offers business-friendly infrastructure— high-speed internet, for example. We have our own power plant, which provides inexpensive electricity. We have our own police department, staffed with thirty-eight officers for only a hundred residents. LA, on the other hand, has 9,000 cops for 4,000,000 residents. Then there's our fire department. We have two fire stations for an area that is just five square miles. The inevitable industrial fires that pop up here and there are always contained immediately. I could go on, but those are the highlights."

Meredith said, "I can see why Merritt's motto is, 'An Industrial Paradise.'" She had seen this below the City Hall sign on the building's exterior right before she had gone inside.

Abruptly, Vern said, "I assume you have other clients. We need someone full time. I knew it was a long shot, but I heard about that PR app you invented, so I thought it was worth a try. If you aren't available, Merritt can make you a very good offer to purchase the app, though obviously we'd prefer to throw everything you have at this."

The PR app? Meredith wasn't sure what he meant.

"I'll clear my schedule," she fibbed. "This is far more important than my other clients. They'll understand. Let me get back to you later today after I've had a chance to reschedule my other projects and get up to speed on yours. Don't worry. We can solve this."

400 INHALERS

Wednesday, August 19, 2009
Senate charter vote in 14 days

Leaving City Hall, Meredith felt like celebrating. A signed contract with the City of Merritt guaranteed that her homelessness had been temporarily postponed, but the feeling evaporated when the heat of late afternoon smacked her in the face as she went out the door—smoggy, muggy heat that made her feel like she was stuck in the clogged drain of a gas station's stained bathroom sink. In fact, "The Basin" was a colloquial term for central Los Angeles, an area hemmed in by four mountain ranges and the ocean. Merritt's geographical location was exactly where one might locate The Basin's drain. A dirty drain that smelled.

She abandoned further development of yet another extended metaphor for her renewed, deplorable location of employment. Extended metaphor was how she had tried to come to terms with her aversion over the years. Ashamed at how quickly her gratitude for winning the contract had turned into disdain, she reprimanded herself, and headed to McDonald's, trying to feel insouciant. Like an employed person might feel. Rolling down her window at the drive-through to order a McFlurry® shake, she noticed a heavy scent of boiling hot dogs. The Farmer John meatpacking plant, across the street from McDonald's, huddled behind a high cinderblock wall that obscured the source of the smell. Even though she couldn't remember the last time she'd eaten a hot dog, they still smelled good. Which made her feel dirty.

The Farmer John property spanned the entire city block. The ten-foot wall surrounding it was covered with a mural depicting wall-eyed caricatured pigs, rendered in pink, brown, and black. They were looking especially lively today.

McDonald's milkshake machines were chronically, notoriously out of order. McDonald's milkshake-addicted customers were painfully aware of this fact, but to Meredith's delight, today the machine was working. She reached up from her window to accept the McFlurry® from the drive-through attendant's hands, temporarily feeling like she was a character in a Titian painting. In college, she'd written her thesis in art history on Titian's use of arm gestures—of supplication, protection, or prayer. A lifetime ago.

She tried to leave the parking lot, but rush hour was now in full swing despite it being only 3:00 p.m. After many cars inched by, with drivers avoiding eye contact, a dented green Corolla finally took pity on her and stopped, allowing her in. She waved thanks to the Samaritan, her raised-arm gesture signaling gratitude. Titian would have approved. By then, she'd almost finished her McFlurry® and a sickly-sweet metallic aftertaste coated her tongue.

While she sat in gridlock, inching along past Farmer John's mural, she was grateful for something to look at. The mural depicted a bucolic cartoon fantasy of stylized hogs in rolling green fields. As she slowly crept along the street, the mural changed. Its foreground depicted black and pink pigs frolicking together in a racially-integrated mud pit, segueing to a drunk farmer snoozing under a tree, while a curious squirrel perched on his belly. At the end of the block, pigs gazing down at her from a barn's loft. It faintly reminded her of Diego Rivera's murals, but the hogs' exaggerated cartoon eyes jumped genres into the realm of Bugs Bunny. The mural's depicted sky was infused with an intense Prussian Blue hue, and was dotted here and there with puffy clouds. It nestled just below the real sky. The real sky, though massive, was haggard and anemic; bled out by pollution.

Grillo knew all about the mural artist, Les Grimes, because he kept track of artists whose deaths had been unusually grisly or poignant. Apparently, artists had a higher percentage of such deaths than people in other professions. In 1957, Les Grimes, a scenic background artist for movie sets, asked Farmer John if he could create this mural, and they agreed. Les Grimes didn't realize he'd be at work on it for the next eleven years, nor did he expect to fall to his death from a ladder while putting the finishing touches on a puffy white cloud he had painted on the side of the plant itself, thirty feet in the air. Meredith wondered if he fell on a Thursday.

Not for the first time, she was glad today was Wednesday, not Thursday. Merritt smelled awful on Thursdays. She'd hated Thursdays the entire time she worked at AFA Foods. Merritt, a tiny municipality surrounded on all sides by the vast behemoth of Los Angeles, was just five miles east of Downtown LA—yet it was still considered Slaughterhouse Central. When cattle arrived on trucks on Mondays, any animals that were dead on arrival were saved for processing on Thursdays. As a result, the smell that day was always paralyzing. The stench always stuck to the back of her throat like peanut butter.

As she inched closer to the freeway entrance, she could see the San Gabriel Mountains in the distance, but only as an uncertain mirage. Today the smog was thick. The mountains looked like they were coated with plastic. Once she was past the complex downtown freeway interchange, which reminded her of a taffy winder on the fritz, she whizzing along at a somewhat steady twenty-five miles an hour.

Meredith began to feel anxious when she realized she hadn't heard from Grillo all afternoon. On any given weekday, she was accustomed to getting several calls from him at work. She always answered, except during meetings; and when he called during a meeting, she became rattled and unfocused, because she knew he'd be angry she hadn't picked up. Bob had written her up for it several times. She restarted her phone just to make sure her voice mail was working, but no notifications or messages appeared.

Poor Grillo. She felt bad for him. First there had been the wood-fired pizza restaurants that had sprung up around the corner from where they had owned their first house, in Silver Lake. They had loved Silver Lake at first because it had a grimy, artistic soul, but in came creeping gentrification, and with it, pizza-oven smoke that drifted in through their open windows, aggravating Grillo's asthma. They had sold that house at a loss in 2008, then they moved to a rental in Echo Park.

The Echo Park house had rat shit in the crawlspace and attic, but the rats themselves were gone, so they figured they would be fine, especially since no wood-fired pizza places were nearby. Nevertheless, after they moved in, Grillo quickly developed a skin reaction all over his body, little tiny red dots that itched like crazy. He became emaciated from constant anxiety and lack of appetite. After going through several doctors who accused Grillo of psychosomatic fantasies, they finally found a specialist who guessed that it might be rat mite bites. Apparently, mites will jump ship when their rat hosts die, and if humans are around, they switch species. So Grillo and Meredith had to move again. And again. The prednisone and oxycontin prescriptions for his skin reaction and pain followed them from house to house. It seemed like every house they rented had some kind of rat problem, and the mites were everywhere, though they never bothered Meredith. Just Grillo. Their latest rental, in Atwater Village, had, so far, been free of mites, rats, and wood-fired pizza oven smoke. She hoped they wouldn't have to move again.

Traffic halted again without any explanation. She swore loudly, a small grace of being stuck in traffic. No one cared how loudly you swore or sang or cried, as long as you didn't dilly-dally, as long as you efficiently closed up the gap between you and the car in front of yours in stop-and-go traffic syncopation. She'd forgotten to call in the prescriptions to the pharmacy, but she was pretty sure Grillo still had a few pills left of each; she could easily pick them up tomorrow.

In addition to oxycontin and prednisolone, Grillo also took Valium. Meredith had no idea if he'd run out of that as well. It might explain the fight they'd had the night before. Grillo always apologized afterwards; he was often the one who apologized first. If he had never apologized, it might have been better, because then she could probably see things for what her mother claimed they were: that he was just living off her and trying to drag her down. When her mother said this to Meredith, it made her angry. It felt like her mother was belittling Meredith herself, by association, and really, it was none of her business.

Maybe Grillo hadn't called because he was finally working on the last art piece he had started four years ago. He had gotten the idea from the wood-fired pizza smoke: he planned to build a smokeless wood-fired pizza oven that was entirely fueled by asthma inhalers. He'd sketched out a design—this had taken a year. Then he ran into trouble with the funding. Approaching several pharmaceutical companies for donations of inhalers had taken him another year, resulting in only a small batch of defective inhalers from a company that made him sign multiple NDAs and releases of liability. They weren't nearly enough. Instead, he saved up all his old inhalers. He decided it didn't matter so much if the inhalers didn't actually provide fuel for the pizza oven, because they were symbolic of the conditions imposed on him by gentrification. He hot-glued his inhaler collection to the exterior of a large wooden box he'd made to represent the oven, adding to it whenever an inhaler ran out of juice—though this decoration barely covered one side of the box. He had hot-glued about fifty-four inhalers, all told; but he needed about 400 more.

Juggling her satchel, a bag of groceries, and her keys, Meredith unlocked her kitchen door and was momentarily blinded by the gloom. She dumped her stuff on the floor by the breakfast table and made her way directly to the bedroom. She stood quietly in the doorway, letting her eyes adjust to the dimness. It appeared that Grillo was still asleep in bed, so she didn't turn on the lamp. Wasn't that the exact position he had been in, when she'd left a few hours ago?

"Grillo?" she said softly. It smelled like he'd been farting again. He had bad gas attacks, though usually he farted while he was up and around, not while he was asleep. Today's farts were especially pungent; they smelled a little like paint combined with the acrid smell of...fireworks? Though he was, technically, an artist, paint was not his preferred medium, but maybe he'd started working again—in a new medium. But fireworks? What the hell had he eaten for lunch?

Opening some windows in the bedroom, changing out of her business-casual outfit into something more comfortable—she did all this in the semi-darkness, feeling her way around the room in the low light of dusk. She didn't want to disturb him. She returned to the kitchen, and as she started making dinner, she decided she'd wait to wake Grillo up—when the food was ready. She wanted to extend the peace just a little longer. While he slept, he looked so calm and integrated—he almost looked dead. She used to hold up a mirror to his mouth, checking for the fog of his breath, because he was so quiet. When he awoke, she never knew what would arrive with his consciousness: candor, contrition, perhaps curiosity; maybe even deep understanding and affection, sometimes.

Grillo still didn't know Meredith had lost her job, but now she had a new one, and she ought to bring him up to date. She wasn't sure what his reaction would be. Though he hated the companies she worked for, either because they were boring or evil or both, he was fully aware that she supported him financially. If she didn't talk about her day, then he'd fill the conversational void with aggressive grievances delivered with zeal, his purpose being to get her to agree that people sucked and LA sucked and there was no hope. He was like a southern preacher, thumping a bible and railing against sin. Except he was an atheist.

She'd planned tacos for dinner. Marinating shrimp, dicing tomatoes for salsa, grating cheese, and shredding cabbage—the textures and colors of the ingredients soothed her. She even made some tortillas from scratch, though several didn't survive the process—she was still getting the hang of the tortilla press. As she swept the deformed ones into the trashcan, she noticed two empty bottles of vodka. *Two.* That was excessive, even for Grillo. Maybe that was why he'd slept late—though it was *very* late at this point.

Beans. Too late to soak them, certainly, which had to be done overnight—so she heated up the contents of a can of pinto beans and doctored them with a little salsa and some bacon fat that she had saved in a jar in the refrigerator. Rice? She got out the rice cooker. Why did cooking dinner always start out as a simple affair and then evolve into a banquet? She preferred not to confront the answer to this question and kept working. An hour later, she finally went to wake Grillo, feeling her way again without turning on the lights.

"Grillo," she said softly. Then louder. "Grillo. Grillo?" He was turned away from her, sleeping on his side. How had he managed to stay under the covers in this heat? He usually was a thrasher. She pushed on the rise his shoulder made under the covers. His shoulder felt stiff to the touch and his whole torso shifted, as if it didn't have joints, tendons, and fascia.

"Dammit," she said out loud. She went to get a hand mirror from the bathroom, and finally turned on the lamp by the bed. She leaned over him, holding the mirror up to his mouth. But the reflection remained clear.

She pressed a finger to the artery in his neck. His neck was cold to the touch. There was no pulse.

She dropped the mirror. Her legs moved her back out of the room. A feeling of being pursued and attacked. Back in the kitchen, the tacos huddled together on a serving plate. Arms swept them into the trash, the food landing on the tortilla casualties and empty vodka bottles. Knees bent, sitting her down. Knees straightened, standing her up. Down. Up. Down again. Her eyes puzzled over the crack in the wall above the kitchen table. All the LA houses they'd rented had cracks in the wall. The shifting clay soil made cracks ubiquitous. Her brain told her that, uselessly. The next time her eyes were capable of notification, it was dark. The sun had gone down, which meant she'd been sitting there for a while. Her left hand wiped her forehead. Her right arm reached up and behind her, and her right hand flipped on the lightswitch. Legs propelled her to her bag in the foyer, then returned her to the kitchen. Right hand reached into her bag and grasped her cell phone. Left hand fished out Vern Page's business card. Right hand dialed his number.

He answered on the first ring. "Vern Page."

She had planned to leave a message but her mouth wasn't working as well as her legs and hands.

Vern said, "Hello? Meredith?" Caller ID had already announced her.

"Are you—are you still at work?" asked Meredith.

"Wrapping up," he said. "What did you think of the articles?"

"I haven't—something has come up."

There was silence on the line. This would normally make Meredith anxious. She hated mid-conversation silences and often had to restrain herself from babbling and making a total fool of herself. This time, however, she had no words to fill in the gap. She matched her breathing to his. In. Out. Finally, she said, "I can't take the job. My husband's mirror isn't foggy."

"His mirror—?"

"I held it up to his mouth and there was nothing. Clear mirror."

She paused. She could hear Vern breathing. Was he waiting with patience or impatience? She usually cared which one it was, could sense it immediately, but now, she neither knew nor cared. She continued, "And also? No pulse. In bed, I thought he was sleeping. But he wasn't sleeping? I thought he was, when I came home. After our meeting."

There was another pause.

She said, "But he wasn't. Sleeping. I don't know what I should do."

Vern said, "What's your address? I'll be right over."

"What? It's kind of far—"

"Address?"

"I was just calling to tell you I can't do—"

Vern said, "Never mind that. Address?"

"214 N. Landis Street, Atwater Village."

"Just sit tight." He hung up.

LINDA: GRILLING SARDINES

I was grilling sardines when Vern called. I hadn't done any special projects for Vern in a while. The last interesting one happened a few years ago, when the convicted treasurer of East Gate tried to hijack the City of Merritt's mayoral elections. A couple of his cronies came to Merritt, squatted in an empty office building—thereby establishing residency—then, one of them declared himself a candidate for mayor, running against Leo Mendebal, the incumbent. Mendebal had been mayor of Merritt since 1974. The *LA Times* reported that the city of Merritt hired private detectives to shadow, harass, then run these interlopers out of town.

The paper got some things wrong. We weren't PIs, for one thing. I preferred the term "black ops." Bernard, on the other hand, called us "goons" because he watched too many mafia movies. Officially, we worked for Merritt Police Department, in a separate division called Security Services.

"Private investigators." Give me a break. One thing was for sure. Whoever leaked the story to the *LA Times* had no clue as to the true nature of what Bernard and I actually did; however, no one should know what we in Merritt Special Ops actually did, so I tried to feel grateful for the inaccuracies.

As former ETA members, Bernard and I had plenty of experience with extra-legal projects. What's more, no matter how egregious or urgent, none of Merritt's projects had ever stressed us out. Not even close. Also, the salary and benefits were excellent.

I told Vern to hang on a second, then pulled the sardines off the grill and went out the front door of my studio apartment to get a better signal. It was still hotter than hell outside, but it was beginning to cool off. Not a moment too soon. The only thing I missed about my country was the weather. It was almost always overcast or raining there. That was rarely the case in Merritt.

Vern said, "I need a clean-up at 214 N. Landis. Atwater Village." I was a little surprised to hear he wanted us to work a job outside Merritt's city limits. Atwater Village wasn't an area I could recall ever visiting, either, though I'd lived in LA for twenty years.

"How many?" I asked.

"One. I've surveyed the scene. It appears to be suicide."

"Suicide?" I didn't understand why a suicide needed cleaning up.

"Merritt's charter vote is in two weeks. I need access to the surviving wife, Meredith James. She has something. An app. Peck thinks it will fix all our problems." Chuck Peck was Merritt's city manager. Short temper. Lots of power. Also, Vern's boss. Vern continued, "As if an app can solve this crisis. But we gotta do what Peck says, and I don't have any other options at this point. I also don't have time to wait for LAPD to do their forensics, hold the woman, take her statement, have her identify the body—it's all too time-consuming. The LAPD bureaucracy? Forget it. Speed is not their strongpoint. Could be weeks of obfuscation. They might even decide she's a suspect. Who knows. They can, legally, hold her for 48 hours. We don't have 48 hours. It would be stupid to consider the woman a suspect, but LAPD is not necessarily known as not stupid—"

I was fluent in English, having lived here for over twenty years, yet I still struggled with double negatives. I think he meant that LAPD was stupid. Or were perceived that way. Why not just say that? But he was still going on about it, so I tried to refocus.

Vern finished with, "Even though she has an alibi—she was in Merritt, meeting with me. And even though the husband left a suicide note—sort of—it looks like an overdose, clearly, anyway—these are white folks, after all." That part was clearer to me. White people's cases got white-glove treatment. Therefore, a proper investigation would be *de rigueur*, as they say in France.

"All right," I said. "We'll be there at the usual time."

Vern said, "No. It needs to be now. ASAP." Vern generally wasn't impulsive, and he knew protocol as well as I did. Protocol for clean-up jobs dictated 3:00 a.m., when only the 24/7 manufacturing operations in Merritt were active. At that time, all the rest of the Fortune 500 employees had gone home to various distant neighborhoods. Merritt's citizens— less than one hundred people—were all asleep.

"It's 9:30 p.m.," I pointed out. "Can we at least wait until 11?"

"You can make the final arrangements at the usual time, but there's one area of concern that requires your immediate attention. You'll see when you get here." He hung up.

Final arrangements, areas of concern—the man had veered away again from plain speech into the syntax of public image control, like he was speaking into a microphone at a press conference. Like he forgot who he was talking to, and was instead rehearsing a speech for when shit really hit the fan.

I paged Bernard with a meet-up code, then went back inside my apartment. I sprinkled some minced parsley and lemon zest over the sardines along with a little extra virgin olive oil and ate them on toast. Usually I just open a can and give them the same treatment, but earlier in the day I had found a restaurant food distributor in Bellmar Gardens who stocked fresh sardines. As luck would have it, the fish were delivered directly to me—even though I don't own a restaurant—when one of their trucks broke down around the corner from Merritt Police Headquarters. I helped the driver coordinate roadside assistance and told him that since I was with the Merritt Police, I could stand guard and make sure nothing was stolen while he went inside to use the facilities. That's when I spotted the flat of sardines on ice in a Styrofoam box, peeking out of the crack in the truck's misaligned roll-up door. I slid it out and into the trunk of my vehicle, which I had parked half-in and half-out of the adjoining lane in order to protect the stalled truck from further damage. Traffic was backed up for at least five blocks because of my parking job, but I couldn't help that. Horns blared and people were getting pretty pissed off. I placed a portable red beacon light on the top of my unmarked vehicle to make it clear that I was police. That shut them up.

By the time the truck driver had returned, he was none the wiser about the sardines, and he thanked me for helping him out. The sardines were still chilling nicely on dry ice when I opened up the container later at my apartment. It was a special treat to eat them fresh instead of canned.

I washed up, changed my white polo shirt for a black one, then went down to the parking lot. Bernard walked up to the car as I was changing the license plates on my minivan.

"Clean-up job," I said by way of explanation. He grunted and got in the car. As we drove over to Home Depot to pick up some supplies before they closed at 10:00 p.m., I thought about how difficult this would be for the wife, after we'd made the body disappear—even if it made things easy for Vern and for Merritt. The wife would have to wait seven years to declare her husband dead. And because of that, any joint assets would be frozen. And because of that, she wouldn't be able to sell her car, refinance her house, or close any joint bank accounts. It was a simple matter to make a body disappear. It was not a simple matter for a law-abiding citizen, however, to survive the financial ramifications of a disappearance, not to mention the usual uncertainty. Grief and bereavement limbo. Must be horrible. But we had orders.

To make the body completely disappear meant that we had to be thorough. We liked to be thorough, and, at the same time, temper that with our old ETA motto: *only as powerful as it needed to be.* It was a tricky balance, but we prided ourselves on our work. When Vern told me to get rid of those squatters from East Gate, Bernard and I busted open water pipes in the office space they had turned into a home. That flushed them out quickly. Then we ran them out of town. The flood created a huge mess, as designed; they weren't able to squat there again.

Later, Mayor Mendebal complained to Vern about the damage. Mendebal owned the building, and he couldn't lease it in that condition. We didn't crave recognition for our work, but we were disappointed with his reaction. After all, he'd won the election—his seventh term—and it was only because Bernard and I had been thorough. What's more, we both felt that we'd devised a scheme that was *only as powerful as it needed to be.* Not only did we feel disappointed, we also felt confused. Technically, leadership didn't know about us or what we did. If we were invisible, there was nothing to criticize. You can't have both, it seemed to me. Acknowledging us meant you could criticize us, but not acknowledging us by definition meant you couldn't criticize us. I am probably too logical in my dealings with people. That has always been one of my personality flaws.

At Home Depot, the Latina cashier took one look at me and spoke to me in Spanish. She assumed that I was from Latin America. I did know Spanish, so I conducted the rest of the transaction in that language. Though the misidentification bothered me, I couldn't complain. After all, Bernard and I came here to disappear, and being mistaken for people from the wrong continent meant that our cover was still intact.

When Bernard and I need to communicate without anyone knowing what we're saying, we spoke Euskera. The Basque language. We've found that most people don't recognize it at all, let alone speak it. No one in twenty years has ever butted in on our conversations, brief as they may be.

I dislike admitting that Euskera is obscure, because the Basque people have been through a lot. Why are we not as well known as Kim Kardashian, who, from what I can see, has no special skills besides self-promotion? She's not really my type. The cleavage and the big butt leave me cold, but she has wonderful skin. The American media often finds her new outfit or hairstyle newsworthy. That's about it for Kim Kardashian. The Basques, on the other hand, have been fighting for secession from Spain for centuries, but no one here seems to know anything about their struggle. Except for other Basque immigrants, of course.

It's surprising how many Basques live here. Merritt's Mayor, for example, is Basque, though he's third generation. The mayor's wife is Basque—she emigrated in the '50s. Other Basque families have lived here for many generations, spread out all over what the TV news calls "The Southland." Basque festivals are often held in Bakersfield, a couple hours north. At these events, you might hear a lot more Euskera, and that must be nice, but Bernard and I avoided them, in order to keep a low profile. Anyway, though our conversation on the way to Atwater Village was minimal, it was in Euskera, which gave me a warm, cozy feeling.

When we arrived at the address Vern had given me, we parked around the corner. Bernard commented, "Getting rid of the trash early," as we unloaded the supplies from the back of the minivan. He was referring to the incorrect time of day for this type of work.

"Vern said there were 'areas of concern' and insisted," I said. Bernard raised his bushy eyebrows, then shrugged. This meant, "It's alway important to someone, but not important to me."

"Agreed," I said. We pulled out gloves, face masks, extra heavy-duty trash bags, a body bag, and plastic sheeting. We walked over to the house, where we saw Vern sitting with a thin white woman on a landing in front of a side door. She looked dazed.

Vern stood and walked a few steps toward me, meeting me at the base of the driveway, with his back to the woman. He shook my hand while passing me a piece of paper, like we were movie spies. He gestured with his thumb over his shoulder and whispered, "In the bedroom." I nodded, putting the paper in my pocket. I assumed it was more details about the job; I planned to read it when I had better light available. Bernard and I went inside.

We used flashlights to make our way through the kitchen and then the dining room, which contained several pieces of heavy antique furniture. The table, chairs, and sideboard were almost as oppressive as the hulking ornate European stuff I grew up with, back home, but these pieces were of a different, simpler style—a California style. I recognized it from the reality house-fixer-upper shows I sometimes watched on TV. Green & Green, they called it. The style was intended as a rebuke to industrialization, come to think of it. Very anti-Merritt.

But I digress. As we made our way toward the back of the house where the bedrooms were, a rank odor became stronger. The stench was surprisingly similar to how Merritt smelled on a Thursday: an acrid top note of chemicals merged with a pungent base note of rotten organic matter. It didn't bother us. We walked up the hall toward the bedroom, where we found the body.

Since there were black-out shades covering the windows, I felt it was safe to switch on a bedside lamp. On the bed, a small dead white man in his forties was curled up on his side. There was some vomit on the sheet near his mouth. His right hand was tucked under his head, cradling it tightly, like he was trying to keep his brain from liquifying and draining out his ear. His head was shaved. His delicate, pale skin contrasted with dark stubble lining the jaw of his face. He might have been handsome, if he gained a few more pounds and got a little more sun. And wasn't dead.

Rigor mortis had stiffened the body, so it was fairly easy for us to move it onto plastic sheeting. Bernard stripped the bed and stuffed the bedsheets into a trash bag. While he was doing that, I found the linen closet, pulled out fresh sheets, and we remade the bed. We'd take the soiled sheets with us back to Merritt, where we'd burn them in an oil drum on a weedy patch overlooking the LA River. We favored that spot for clean-up jobs because it had a lot of privacy. It was tradition. I brought marshmallows sometimes and we roasted them on sticks over the fire.

Marshmallows are one of those foods that exemplify the American sensibility. First of all, they aren't real marshmallows which, I read on Wikipedia, come from the mallow plant. They're actually made of corn syrup and gelatin. Real marshmallows were made by Victorian doctors for patients with sore throats, and originally it was more like marshmallow juice. I really like Wikipedia, because it explains weird

American things like marshmallows to me. And there's a lot of weird American things to make sense of.

Somewhere along the way, candy manufacturers used a tiny amount of marshmallow juice in production of these squishy white sugar squares. It was less work to make, and more people would rather eat sugar than take medicine, even if the medicine was basically tasteless. And that's my point. Americans like to make things more enjoyable. They also like to make things. What is the result? A sweet soft pillow you pop in your mouth, or burn over a bonfire.

After we had put the body into a body bag, and put the body bag into an extra-large, extra-sturdy trash bag, Bernard slung it over his shoulder like Santa Claus, and carried it out to the minivan. The body was small; light enough for Bernard to handle without my help. As he walked up the street, I scanned the rest of the houses to check that we weren't being observed. In some of the living rooms, the lights were on. I could hear the babble of TVs through several open windows, a rowdy cacophony that covered the noise of our activities well. Just before I turned around to go back inside, I thought I saw a slight movement in a darkened window on the second floor of the house opposite. I stopped and watched it for several minutes, but I didn't see anything more.

Vern had parked his car right in front of the dead man's house, which did not follow protocol, and he hadn't changed his license plate, which was even worse. But it was too late to do anything about it.

I went back inside the house. I wanted to look for spatulas, to see if there were any unusual ones. I like to collect them. They weren't hard to find. The woman kept them in a big old-fashioned pewter mug. The mug contained several utensils that were of no interest, but there were three different types of spatulas. Motherlode!

There was a slotted fish turner (great for crepes also), a nylon turner for shitty nonstick pans, and a spoonula, which was a spatula with a curved concave head. I took the spoonula and shoved it in my backpack.

Collecting spatulas was a hobby that I tried to enjoy in order to remind myself of my vow, a vow that I made after I left Barcelona—during the transatlantic freighter trip from Spain to Cuba. Back in Spain, sometimes I felt it was necessary to retaliate personally for unacceptable transgressions. For example, all of my comrades in ETA who were arrested by the Guardia Civil were then tortured. In a display of so-called parity, the Spanish government indicted the most notorious torturer of all. He was sentenced to 75 years, but was quickly pardoned, because he was depressed. Depressed, can you believe it?

I was so angry that the depressed torturer got off almost scot-free, despite his heinous crimes, that I took it upon myself to adjust the outcome. This was entirely outside of ETA's guidebook. They did not instruct me to do so. I have a knee-jerk reaction to certain forms of injustice, and the depressed torturer reminded me of my uncle, who assaulted me when I was thirteen, and who, incidentally, had also complained of depression, as if he was the victim not the attacker. Suffice to say, both my uncle and that depressed Guardia Civil fucker are now short two gonads. The vow I made to stop interfering with gonad ownership was necessary to ensure that I didn't blow my cover. If my cover was blown, then Bernard's cover would be blown too, so I amended my hobby. Instead of gonads, I collect spatulas.

Maybe this guy we had just taken care of, the dead guy in the back of the minivan, had been depressed too. It was pretty clear he had died by his own hand—the to-do list in my pocket detailed a grandiose suicide with multiple backup strategies. I wanted to believe the dead man had been simply depressed and was not also a torturer, but some of the to-do list items were decidedly not suicidal. They were homicidal.

I didn't feel too bad about what I did to my uncle, the torturer, and others. They had weak characters. They had it coming, and besides, you can get fake gonads now, so I hear. Just like marshmallows. They don't have to be real. It's not like gonads are central to intimate experiences, or so I hear. On the other hand, with boobs, not only are they rather essential in contributing to a pleasing intimate experience, there's generally a huge difference between real ones and fake ones. To be clear, I like all kinds of boobs, real or fake. Change your boobs, if you want to. It's a free country.

I've always enjoyed boobs. At some point most people realize who they are and what they want, though it can be variable as to when that happens, and whether they even notice that they've noticed. For me, it was crystal clear when I was nine. I developed a huge crush on my schoolteacher. She was an atypical nun, being both sweet and young. Despite her full-length habit, she was totally hot. I imagined all kinds of boobs nestled inside that habit. On the other hand, I was never curious about how gonads looked inside men's pants. When I did have to set eyes on them in order to help a man lose a few ounces of gonad weight, I always had to control my gag reflex.

LINDA: TO DO LIST

We had planned to wait around until 3:00 a.m., which was when we'd be able to dispose of the body back in Merritt, so after loading the body into the minivan, Bernard suggested we drive to the Burbank airport, which was a few miles away from Atwater Village, to watch the planes take off.

We hadn't done that in a while, and preferred LAX for this activity, but LAX was too far away. We liked to park on a street that intersected the end of the runway, right where the planes left the ground. It was more thrilling than you'd think. First there was the fugue of the engines. The interwoven exchange of total noise. Then there were the planes themselves, massive, yet seemingly weightless as they left the ground, ascending into darkness, buoyed by the halo of the runway lights below them. As they became airborne overhead, they looked like celestial great white whales with wings.

I almost agreed to this plan, but then Vern called me.

Vern said, "I'm taking the woman back to Merritt. She'll be in apartment #101. Make sure to pack some of her clothes and drop them off. Don't forget, we need full access to the woman and her app. No LAPD. She's instrumental in pulling Merritt out of the shit, and we have no time to waste."

"Okay," I said.

"Again, to reiterate. We can't have LAPD detain her for a wrongful death investigation. I left the keys to my car on her kitchen table. Drive it back to Merritt. I'll give further instructions tomorrow. I take it you've read the note. Follow up." The line went dead.

I pulled the note out of my pocket, skimmed it, then passed it to Bernard. I watched his bushy eyebrows knit together, then crawl up his forehead in dismay. His eyebrow semaphore conveyed more than words, as usual.

"There's a bomb in the attic?" Bernard asked.

"Is it checked off?" I asked.

He nodded. "But item five, 'Activate bomb,' is not checked off."

"That's a relief," I said.

Bernard said, "Item three says: 'Banksy stencil of suicide note.' What is a Banksy?"

I said, "Graffiti artist. Must be the reason for the chemical element in the stench inside the house. Did you notice?" Bernard shook his head no. I continued, "Maybe there's freshly painted graffiti somewhere? I don't know. I didn't see any graffiti. Did you?"

Bernard shook his head no again. He read out loud, "Item seven: 'Hook up noose to bomb to improve aesthetic activation.' What is 'aesthetic activation'?"

"Is it checked off?" I asked.

He nodded.

I shrugged. "Maybe the dead man wanted to make some kind of Rube-Goldberg suicide contraption. This to-do list is both extremely thorough and extremely chaotic. It's all out of order. Some items not being checked off—it's not methodical. I suppose it might be difficult to follow a to-do list if you were ready to...end your life?"

Bernard shrugged.

I asked, "Did you happen to check the attic?"

He shook his head no. He gave me back the list as he recited, "Item 9: 'Troubleshoot bomb timer.'"

I read down the list until I found the entry. "That's not checked off either," I said.

"This is bad," said Bernard, who cleared his throat judgmentally. "'Only as powerful—'" he started to say.

I finished it for him, "'...as it needs to be.' I know." Our old motto from our ETA days. He meant that if the man wanted to commit suicide, why didn't he just overdose and be done with it? There was no need for theatrics. No need for *bombs*. I knew Bernard was thinking about Barcelona, as was I. Just how big was this bomb?

I said, "We'll watch the planes land some other time. Let's go back to the house." After we got out of the car, we walked up the street. I noticed that most of the houses were now dark, which was helpful.

Vern had left the kitchen door unlocked. Inside, I grabbed his car keys and put them in my pocket, then I found a duffel bag in a closet and went to the bedroom to fill it with the woman's clothes, as Vern requested. Bernard went up to the attic to take a look at the bomb.

After stuffing some clothes into the bag, I looked carefully around the bedroom. Nothing was out of place. I then checked the second bedroom, which appeared to be an art studio. In this room, the windows didn't have black-out shades, so I didn't turn on the flashlight. The streetlight shining in through a front window allowed me to make out a strange assemblage of wood in the center of the room. It was about the same size and shape as a pizza oven, with a domed top and square sides. It even had an opening to slide a pizza inside. Along one side facing the window, the streetlight illuminated around forty asthma inhalers hot-glued to the exterior.

The paint smell was prominent in this room, but I saw nothing on the walls but various schematics and illegible drawings tacked up here and there. There was an empty easel in one corner. In the dim light, dried-out brushes in a paint can looked like a bouquet of dead pussy willows.

It was a strange art studio, if that's what it was, because it contained no art.

Finally, I looked up at the ceiling. There, I identified the source of the fresh paint odor. Several large Banksy-style stencils had been applied using red paint. At first, I couldn't make sense of it. I thought it might be the kind of art where you aren't supposed to make sense of it—but then I could make out the subject: a man was seated on a toilet. A necklace—no, it was a *noose*—was around his neck. An emergency plastic pylon perched, slightly askew, atop his head, like a dunce cap. In his right palm, he held a ball. No—it was a *bomb*—an old-fashioned cartoon bomb—with a burning wick.

This self-portrait of the man committing suicide in several concurrent ways on the ceiling of the house would become evidence that he hadn't simply skipped town, gone to Tijuana, or similar—that he hadn't just disappeared. In that case, Vern's fears would come true—there would be an LAPD investigation. Then Vern wouldn't get his hands on this app that our boss was obsessed with.

Bernard came in, almost knocking over an open gallon can of red paint with his big feet. I pointed to the ceiling. He squinted at it and shook his head like a mother who has discovered that her toddler has puked on the furniture— dismayed yet stoic.

He reported, "Bomb in attic had enough C4 to blow up the whole block," while holding up several ivory-colored blocks of said C4, duct-taped together. "Detonator was also set. But incorrectly. Safe now."

I nodded, somewhat relieved that neither we, nor the rest of the block would be blown to bits. I gestured toward the ceiling, saying, "We don't have time to paint this white again. And where do we get the paint? Everything's closed now."

"Plenty of paint in Merritt," Bernard pointed out. He meant that we could easily 'borrow' some paint from one of several paint manufacturers located there.

"We don't have enough time. Drive back to Merritt, steal the paint, drive back here, give this ceiling at least three coats, then return to Merritt again by 3:00 a.m. to dispose of the body? There's no way."

"And tomorrow is Thursday," said Bernard, as if I needed to be reminded.

After a pause, he said, "Modify the bomb. Make a small fire in the attic. Just powerful enough. Burn down this house. Not the whole block." The attic was immediately above the art studio. And if anyone knew how to make a bomb with such a specific, small payload, it was Bernard. He would also know how to cover up the source of the fire, in case there was an arson investigation.

At that point I wondered: was it a bit excessive to burn down the house? The last time we were accused of being too thorough was when we'd unleashed that flood to get rid of the mayoral interlopers in the last election. But in this case, I didn't think we had much choice, so I agreed. Bernard went back to the attic to make the adjustments. I took the duffel bag of the lady's clothes to the kitchen, picked up her laptop and slipped it into the bag, then went out the kitchen door and set it down on the driveway, bending over it to zip it up.

I heard a child's high-pitched voice behind me say, "I saw you, earlier. And I saw a big man with a big black bag walking up the street and another man with the white lady who lives here, who looked sad. She always looks sad, though. But this time she looked really, really sad. You almost caught me watching you through the window earlier. See that house?

That's my house. Across the street. But I hid. I didn't move the curtain one little bit and the next time I looked out the window, everyone was gone. I couldn't go to sleep. I tried to tell my mom but she just yelled and said she wasn't having it and she grounded me for the rest of the week for being up past my bedtime. Way past. Where did the man take the lady? What's in the duffel bag?"

I stood up and slowly turned around. A young black boy wearing spaceship pajamas shivered in the driveway, hugging his sides in the slight chill of the evening. He looked amped up and tired at the same time.

Here was a new complication. But I wasn't too worried; I was comforted by the knowledge that no one believes kids when they talk about anything out of the ordinary. For example, no one believed me when I tried to report my uncle after he raped me, but admittedly I didn't really have the words to describe it correctly until I was older, and by then, it was too late.

"There's a laptop and some clothes," I said. I proceeded to itemize every last clothing article in the bag, because the kid looked like he needed a lot of detail, and I thought maybe it would distract him from the other, more difficult question he had asked me.

I said, "Four pairs of socks—running socks, white, mid-ankle; running shoes, Nike, dark blue, slightly worn. A couple of t-shirts, some sweats. Two pairs of running shorts, black. Two pairs of dry-fit tops, fluorescent green. Five white blouses: two v-neck, two button-down, one short-sleeved. Fabric is variable: polyester, rayon, silk, and linen. A black work blazer. Gabardine. Black work slacks, three pairs. One's linen, the others are gabardine." While I listed off the many details, I observed the kid. By the end, he looked a bit bored, exactly what I'd hoped for.

"What's gabarderdeen?" he asked.

Lucky me. My father had been a tailor. "Gabardine is a fabric. Originally, it meant 'cloak.' It was a special cloak, worn by knights—when they weren't wearing their armor, and needed to travel without detection."

"Ohhh. Ninja knights!"

I nodded. Leaving the duffel bag on the stoop, I started walking slowly down the driveway as I continued explaining about goddamned gabardine. The kid trotted along next to me, his mouth slightly open, eating up my facts like they were candy.

I whispered to the boy as we approached his front door, "Explorers wore gabardine when they discovered the South Pole. Napoleon's army wore it when they conquered Europe."

The boy looked a bit sleepy, but he was not done interrogating me. "But what about the big guy with the trash bag, and where did the other man take the neighbor lady?" he asked, his voice trailing off as if he was trying to honor his over-focused brain but didn't have the strength to follow its immediate directive. I kneeled down in front of him. "Listen. You must help me to help your neighbor. You know how you said she is always sad?"

He nodded.

I said, "We're rescuing her. From sadness."

"Like sadness is a tower she's locked up in?"

This was getting very existential, but I went with it. "That's right. Like a tower. My mission is secret. Because I am a ninja knight. You must make a vow to secrecy, too. Then you can be part of the mission."

"I vow! Do I get a sword?"

"You must be our lookout. You must stand watch for the dragon."

"Then I'll be a ninja knight too?"

I whispered, "That's right." I opened his front door and pushed him gently over the threshold.

He could barely stand up, he was so tired. I whispered, "Now give me a strong handshake and your word of honor. 'Euskaldun Hitza' is the promise of the knights in my country." I held out my hand to shake his.

"Hitza," he said, his little hand gripping mine firmly. He closed the door. I turned and went back across the street to try to warn Bernard—we needed to delay activation of the bomb for a little longer, at least another half hour, to make sure the kid didn't see anything else exciting, like a bomb going off—though I was pretty sure the kid was exhausted.

Unfortunately, I didn't get to Bernard in time. He met me by the kitchen landing, duffel bag in hand. He shook his head when I tried to argue and he turned me away from the house. As we walked down the driveway, we heard a small pop behind us, which sounded like the perfect amount of combustion to start a small attic fire. We parted ways at the bottom of the driveway—I, to drive Vern's car, and Bernard, to drive the minivan.

As I got into Vern's car, I looked over my shoulder at the house—the bomb hadn't even shattered the glass on the the attic window. A faint light glowed from within. I surveyed the other houses on the street. Unlike other more recently-developed areas of Los Angeles where homes crowded close together, Atwater Village was different. Probably it was developed back in the twenties, at a time when people spent more time outside, in the famous California sunshine. The houses were much smaller than their lots, in other words; ample open space surrounded each home. What's more, the palm trees lining the street were twice as tall as the houses. Their combustible palm leaves hunched high above, like sad, pouting clowns, silhouetted against the LA night sky, where not one star was visible because of light pollution. I didn't think there was much chance the palm trees could catch fire easily. There was absolutely no wind, not even a breeze—another good omen.

We caravanned back to Merritt to finish things up. As I drove, I reflected that no job ever goes off without some tiny hitch. As long as the hitches didn't add up to total failure, I was usually satisfied with our work. Tonight, though, was different. I felt a little bit uneasy, which is unlike me. Maybe I was getting too old for it.

LINDA: RENDERING

Some of the smaller, independent rendering plants in Merritt had very lax security. Over the years, we'd figured out which ones had security system codes that we knew weren't ever changed. Bernard kept track of the list of addresses and codes.

After I dropped off Vern's car at Merritt City Hall, Bernard picked me up. We drove the body to Best Coast Rendering on Indiana and Bandini, because we knew they didn't run a twenty-four-hour operation. We let ourselves into the processing area, then we selected one of the large bins, one that was only two-thirds full of 4D raw materials (animals that were Dead, Dying, Diseased, or Disabled, so not destined for your steak dinner). I found a stepladder and leaned it against the bin, holding it for Bernard while he climbed up and threw the body in. Using a shovel, he covered it up with some of the animal parts already in the bin, burying it. Tomorrow the bin's contents would go through the grinder.

Rendering went on every day of the week, but Thursdays were different. On Thursdays, meat processors rendered meat that had become 4D on the journey to the plant, creating a tidal wave of nauseating odor that blanketed Merritt and surrounding areas, all the way to Boyle Heights. The smell was worse than the stench of my uncle's balls, while he had them.

"Been a while," said Bernard as he climbed down the ladder. I nodded. We didn't have to do this sort of job too often, which was good, because with every year that went by, there were more and more security cameras in Merritt. Soon we would run out of places to dispose of bodies so easily.

We then drove two miles to our apartment building behind the Leo Power Substation, going to our separate apartments to change clothes. Then we headed over to our weedy patch of land by the LA River. We threw our discarded clothes into an oil drum, along with the linens and the clothes from the body. Bernard set it all on fire.

"We should have brought marshmallows," I said. I was hungry. It had been several hours since I had eaten the sardines.

Bernard shook his head. "Not enough heat to make the tasty burned bits," he said. I pulled out a thermos of kalimotxo from my backpack, and we passed it back and forth, watching the flames in silence until they died out.

I thought about how much longer we'd be doing these jobs. Twenty years performing services for Merritt was a long time. Mayor Mendebal's wife, Leonata Mendebal, helped us flee Spain after the Hipercor disaster. When would we feel that our debt to her was fully paid back?

Mrs. Mendebal used to manage the main Merritt restaurant, Topa Café, though she and Mendebal lived in the ancestral mansion over on Hudson and Sixth Street, in Hancock Park, on the other side of Downtown LA. Ten years ago, she turned the management of Topa Café over to her nephew, and stayed home to enjoy her retirement and her grandkids. I could understand her preference. There was no rendering done in Hancock Park. Beautiful old trees lined its streets, whereas in Merritt, there were very few trees to speak of.

After Mrs. Mendebal saved us, Bernard had gone from being my ETA brother to my MPD partner, a transition that felt very natural. It was the one thing about moving here that wasn't difficult. We had a shared history and we understood each other.

What Bernard lacked in conversation, he made up for in brawn. The Basque have an old story about a woman and a bear getting it on. I think Bernard could easily pass as the mythological offspring of this pairing: he's got this big bristly beard, hairy arms, and big meaty hands. The Basque also have an origin myth that they were descended from a race of giants, despite the fact that most Basque are a bit short, like me. Tall ones like Bernard give us a lot of pride.

Despite the fact that he was a man, Bernard's quiet company fit my needs perfectly, like the knife that I always had strapped to my calf. I rarely had to use it but I liked that it was there, snug against my skin.

Bernard and I drove back to the apartment building where we lived. He lived in #308, and I lived in #201. They were identical tiny one-room apartments that suited us just fine. At #101, on the floor below mine, I dropped off the duffel bag for the white lady, putting it just inside her door. She was sound asleep.

The city owned the building, and kept #101 empty but furnished and ready for occupancy as a way to prove that elected officials actually lived in Merritt, even though most of them didn't.

Scandals about Merritt's leadership were stacking up. First, the city attorney had distributed a report to the city council about Chuck Peck's problematic activities, ranging from his use of petty cash as his personal ATM, to his expensing of limousines, groceries, and golf memberships. Instead of firing Peck, though, the city council fired the city attorney. There were multiple voter-fraud allegations involving Mayor Mendebal, and last but not least, the attempted coup by the East Gate treasurer-convict. It was Vern's job to manage Merritt's reputation through these crises, and he was overwhelmed.

When the mayor got arrested, the evidence came out in court that his residence was not, in fact, located in Merritt. The address he used on his voter registration card, his official Merritt residence, was a two-bedroom apartment around the corner from a cement processing plant, in The Leo Building. As noted, he actually lived in a four-thousand-square-foot mansion in Hancock Park. A bedroom in his Merritt apartment still had Raggedy Ann and Andy wallpaper from 1974 decorated for his son Michael, who was by now thirty-nine years old and had his own unlived-in apartment up the street.

Instead of reform, the City of Merritt made damn sure that the next time they had to prove an elected official actually did live there, it would be believable. Even though unit #101 was just a small studio apartment identical to mine, it was well-appointed, with a sleek dinette set, a full bed, and matching nightstands. The apartment was cleaned regularly and the kitchen was always fully stocked, courtesy of City Hall Janitorial Services. I should know. Whenever I ran out of milk, I'd go over to #101 to get more.

Aside from one or two of these "unavailable but unoccupied" apartments, Merritt's rentals were otherwise rarely vacant, and preference was given to City Hall workers, their friends, and their families. Merritt was almost entirely industrial, by design. You would think no one would want to live there. It didn't have a laundromat nor a grocery store. You had to drive to Huntington Park for most shopping errands. But in fact, everyone who worked for the city wanted to live in Merritt-owned housing, despite the lead in the water, the hydrocarbons in the air, the rendering stench, and the freight trains, because renting here was practically free. You could nab a one bedroom for $400/month. In the surrounding cities like Bellmar Gardens, that shithole southeast of us, the average rent was $1200.

When I got back to my apartment, I texted Vern to let him know the job was complete.

He texted back immediately, *You didn't wake up the woman, right?*

I replied, *She's sound asleep.*

Vern texted, *I gave her a Valium when I dropped her off.*

I commented, *Final-final job. Must be important.*

He replied, *Merritt is a mess. First Mendebal, and now Michael. We have no time to lose.*

Michael had also been indicted for voter fraud. Participating in the family tradition, Michael didn't live in Merritt, but he voted there. In his own fake Merritt apartment, he had never bothered to unpack his mattress, though at least the walls there weren't covered with nursery-room wallpaper. When the Los Angeles District Attorney's office searched the place, they found that Michael's mattress was still wrapped in plastic. Obviously, it had never been slept on, contrary to what Michael claimed. What a joke.

After a pause, Vern texted, *If we get her ship-shape, we can weather all of it. We need her. She has this magic app called The Model. The Model will turn everything around.*

Our relationship was not based on curiosity. I didn't need to know what The Model was, and he didn't ask me about the body or how we'd made the job final-final. He told me to check on the lady in a few hours, so I set an alarm for 9:00 a.m. and went right to sleep.

COFFEE & TOAST

When Meredith woke up, the first thing she saw was a popcorn ceiling. She was mystified by this. Grillo would never live in a house with popcorn ceilings, because this type of ceiling, though sealed, was full of asbestos. Also, the mattress was firmer, offering more support than the squishy one she shared with Grillo. The sun streamed in through a window. No blackout curtains. She heard a freight train that sounded so close, she thought it might come right through the front door. She waited for Grillo's answering protest; there was none.

As she looked around, she realized her bedroom was also the living room and kitchen. Its mass-produced Ikea furnishings bore no relation to the Craftsman-style antiques at home. Grillo had carefully sourced all the antiques they owned, except for the mid-century modern couch her mother had given her during a bout of redecorating. When Meredith had moved the couch into the living room, it looked like it might float away; the rest of the heavy rectilinear furniture closed ranks around it like bullies. It had surprised her that Grillo never objected to the couch, since he was always against incoherent interior design, but maybe this had been different, because he didn't want to cross her mother.

She thought about the night before. She could only remember pieces of it. Why had she called Vern, of all people? She had meant to tell him she couldn't do the contract PR job he had offered now that...

On the phone, what had she said? Something about the mirror being clear. God. That made no sense. How unprofessional, she thought. It didn't matter. She couldn't work for Vern, now, obviously. She should call the police; she should get back home. Call her mother. Or maybe not call her mother, just yet. But the police, yes, the police needed to know.

Those people that showed up at her house after Vern got there—a tall man and a short woman. What were they doing inside the house, while Vern sat with her on the back steps? Why did they go out of their way to help her? It seemed to Meredith that Vern could have easily found some other PR freelancer to resolve his crisis. She looked around and saw her bag on one of the dinette chairs, bulging with the newspaper clippings Vern had given her, still unread.

The day before, Vern said to her, "You shouldn't stay here tonight."

"I don't know," Meredith said.

"Come on. You can't stay here tonight and you know it."

Meredith didn't know how to let people help her; it made her uncomfortable, and she might have been in shock, but she was not so far gone that she wasn't going to put up a fight. She said. "I couldn't possibly come to your home, that would be—"

But Vern cut her off. "My home? No, ma'am, that's not what I had in mind. Nor would my good wife of twenty years agree to that sort of arrangement, either. I assure you, she is a kind, generous person, but she doesn't like things to be last minute. Unplanned. She runs a tight ship. I suggest you let me take you to one of the Merritt city-owned apartments. They're clean, furnished, and comfortable. Linda lives in the same building."

"Linda?" said Meredith.

"One of the people helping out."

"Helping with what?"

"Arrangements. A passing of this kind. It's a lot on your plate. This must be distressing."

Meredith was confused. "But I can't do the work."

"For what?" said Vern.

"The PR work for Merritt."

"This isn't about that," said Vern. "I know what you're going through. Let me help you. Come on."

He didn't touch her, but the timbre of his voice felt like an embrace. She said tentatively, "I could get started sooner on the PR stuff then, I guess? If I didn't have to—" What? Didn't have to live with what had happened? Didn't have to do whatever it was you did after what had happened? She couldn't even think the words to herself to be more specific than that. Work would soothe her, it was her refuge. If she was unable to process what had just happened, she might as well work. But that was crazy, wasn't it? Irresponsible. She felt confused.

Vern asked, "Can you drive?"

"Drive?"

"Your car. You'll need a car tomorrow. Hmm. I'll drive you. Can I have the keys?"

"I don't need to—I shouldn't. I'll be fine," she said, standing up and facing her closed back door. She put her hand on the doorknob, but then she was unable to open it. She froze.

"Here, come with me," said Vern, as he took her elbow and led her down her steps to her car. He opened the passenger door and waited until she got in. Before he closed the door he said, "I'll have Linda bring over some of your things."

That's all she remembered. She got up. She recognized her duffel bag on the floor by the front door. She unzipped it and found that it contained her laptop along with some of her clothes. She got dressed. In the bathroom, there was a brand-new toothbrush, along with toothpaste and dental floss. She brushed her teeth and threw water on her face. She had to go back to Atwater Village, but then what? She didn't know. Maybe call the police or something? Call a funeral home? She had no idea. She had just finished buttoning her blouse when there was a knock and the front door opened. A short, slightly heavy Latina woman poked her head in. The woman from last night. She was wearing sunglasses. Her thick, dark hair was pulled back into a bun.

"I'm Linda," the woman said. "I live in the unit above you. Vern asked me to check on you. Can I borrow some milk?"

"Milk?" said Meredith.

"Thanks," said Linda, who was already walking past Meredith and over to the refrigerator, sliding her sunglasses to the top of her head. She grabbed milk out of the refrigerator and turned to face Meredith. "I'm making coffee at my place. You want some?"

"You have a key to the door?" asked Meredith nervously. Why was the refrigerator full of food? Meredith realized she hadn't eaten since the McFlurry® yesterday afternoon. And that wasn't food. Her stomach grumbled.

"Toast too," said Linda. "Coffee and toast." Without pausing for an answer, the woman walked back to the door, and turned. "Coming?"

LINDA: HICCUPS

I made some coffee the way I liked it, Vietnamese style: you pour water over dark roast sitting in a Vietnamese metal filter that fits atop a coffee cup. While I waited for it to brew, I got a text from Vern.

The Model. Find out.

I know, I texted back. I looked over at Meredith. She sat at my tiny kitchen table, looking around my studio apartment, a deer in the headlights. She was very fair. I suspected she burned easily in the sun. I myself never have to wear sunblock, though they're saying now that everyone should. I wasn't sure how old she was, but I felt older.

We need it, texted Vern.

I know, I thumbed back.

Tendrils of the earthy, maternal odor of brewing coffee encircled us. I toasted some bread and slathered it with Nutella, and placed it near Meredith on the table. Nutella goes straight to my thighs. Good thing I don't care.

"Coffee takes time," I said, "But it will be very good."

She nodded and picked up a piece of toast, but didn't eat it. She just looked at it. Then she put it down.

I said nothing and gave her some space. My cell buzzed again. When Vern was anxious, he had trigger-happy texting fingers.

Any chance you can get ahold of her laptop? Maybe The Model is on there.

In texts Vern had sent me earlier that morning, he had choppily explained that he wanted The Model for some mysterious PR plan to save Merritt from disincorporation. Whatever that was. But even if The Model was on the laptop, would he know how to use it? It sounded sketchy to me.

I thought of how I could placate Vern so as to stop the endless tide of anxious texts. I thought of what the Goop lady might say. Sometimes I watched her infomercials on You-Tube. I found them instructional about being American. Like marshmallows.

I texted back, *I'll install a Trojan.* I added, *Take deep breaths.*

I was met with a series of angry symbols. I turned my phone off.

"Cream?" I asked Meredith.

"Just black," she said. I nodded to myself in approval. I placed a coffee cup by her elbow and sat down opposite her. She took a sip and her eyes got bigger. Then she chugged the whole cup in one go.

I took a bite of toast and sipped my coffee.

She seemed so fragile, like a wild animal I might scare off. I said, "How do you know Vern?"

"I met him at a Chamber of Commerce mixer; I feel bad, I don't remember it too well." She took the cup to the sink and washed it.

She went on, "I'm supposed to help out with Merritt's image, Crisis PR stuff. Get the press on his side. Do some data modeling. I remember I had a glass of sangria on an empty stomach right before the meeting. Except it wasn't sangria, it was like, wine and Coke mixed together." She looked at me and continued, "Really professional right? I guess he didn't notice. Oh my God. There's also the State Senate vote on

Merritt's city charter in two weeks. Two weeks! I called him last night to tell him I wasn't in any shape to help. To tell him he needed to find someone else. Because my husband—" She looked away and stared at my poster of frolicking dachshunds on the wall opposite the table.

She said to the puppies, "...Because of what happened. Because...What's Vern going to do now? I feel bad." She trailed off and stared at her coffee cup again.

This was a high-functioning mess of an explanation, and I would say I "felt bad" for her, but I signed off on that kind of shit ages ago, when my uncle raped me. After that, whenever I thought I might blame myself for other people's bullshit, which, except for Barcelona, never happened, I would just decide whether the balls needed to come off. Because more often than not, it was a question of whether some man needed fewer balls, and not about whether I should feel bad. I thought about my spatula collection, in order to calm myself. The spoonula was quite a find.

I said, "Perhaps you do not count your knowledge enough. You're too young to see." I was a little out of my element here, so I sipped my coffee and finished off my toast. Was she going to eat hers? I gazed at it as if it might give me permission.

I thought about the many text messages building up on my inactive phone. Vern was totally different when he was at work; but since it was 7:00 a.m., he wasn't at work yet, he was at home. I think he used his phone as a shield against his wife, who was pretty formidable, from what I could tell. I had met her once or twice while dropping Vern off after other, shall we say, successful conclusions of difficult projects.

"I'm forty," said Meredith.

Forty. Just nine years younger than me. She looked good. I said, "I'm sure you have skills of great value. Vern always knows." I was trying to find a way to ask her about The Model, but without any warning, she started crying.

This made me very uncomfortable, so I got up, moved to the kitchen, finished the last of my coffee, and put the cup in the sink. I returned to her side and offered my handkerchief to her, without looking at her. "Here," I said. I always carry a handkerchief in my pocket. My allergies are hyperactive here in East LA. It's a toxic wonderland.

She didn't take it. She just kept crying. "It's clean," I said. I put it on the table by her plate and went to make her more coffee.

I tried to distract her. "It's Thursday," I said. "Thursdays in Merritt are difficult. Best to stay inside, unless the Santa Ana winds are blowing. I don't believe they will, today, unfortunately." I looked through the kitchen window at an intrepid oleander growing along the back fence. Not a leaf stirred on it. "There is a bad smell," I said.

Meredith said, "DOD Rendering Day, you don't have to tell me. I know all about it." She blew her nose. Then she started hiccuping. Post-weeping hiccups are so cute. I'm a sucker for that. I focused on the coffee. Drip, drip, drip. Damn, those Vietnamese are a patient people. Who can wait that long for coffee? But I liked how it forced me to slow down. Everything keeps speeding up these days. Nothing teaches us that there could be alternatives. I had all the time in the world, as long as my phone was off, as long as this woman, Meredith, sat at my kitchen table, hiccuping.

WORK HEALS ALL

"Thank you for the coffee," Meredith said. "It was really good."

Linda said, "It's nothing. You should go home and rest yourself. I have to go to work. I'll come tomorrow to check on you, yes?"

Meredith nodded, admitting defeat. Normally, there was no way she'd admit she needed someone to check in on her. But nothing was normal anymore. "Yes. Thank you. Sorry to keep you from work. I hope you won't be late."

She took a deep breath, opened Linda's front door, and dashed down to the first-floor apartment, exhaling finally when she was inside and the front door was closed. Pacing the studio, she felt amped up. Things had to be done, but which thing came first? Her father had died while she was away at college—he was much older than her mother—and her mother had handled the details after his death. By the time Meredith flew back home, everything had been taken care of. Her mother had been weirdly calm throughout the entire ordeal, graciously receiving guests at the small gathering at home like she was holding court. Meredith had been in a fog the whole time. She felt the same way now, as if the borders of her body had been washed away. She couldn't feel where it started and ended.

She picked up her phone, intending to call her mother, but she couldn't do it. Meredith wanted control of the situation. She didn't exactly know what the situation was, though; therefore, she'd be unable to defend herself in her mother's inevitable interrogation.

Who else could she call? She hadn't talked to her best friend in a couple of years, or any other friends recently, for that matter. They'd all fallen by the wayside because she could never make it to dinner or other get-togethers. Or maybe it was because they had felt frustrated that she wouldn't leave Grillo.

She googled the LAPD station listings, to find the one nearest to her home in Atwater Village. She stared at the map on her laptop screen, marked with a red pin where the neighborhood station was located. Above it, a small speech bubble displayed, containing the station's number and address, as if the station was a comic book character urging her to act. The speech bubble, however, failed to include exactly what she should say to the police.

How would the conversation go exactly?

"Hi! I would like to report a death."

"Address?"

"214 N. Landis. Atwater Village."

"Name?"

What then? Meredith could claim it was an anonymous tip. Didn't she need a payphone for an anonymous tip, not a cellphone? Where was a functioning payphone?

Didn't the police rule out foul play first, even if suicide was a foregone conclusion? Wasn't the spouse always the primary suspect? How long would the police hold her for questioning? Which was fine really, but how would she explain Vern, Linda, and that big guy to the police? She had noticed the big guy carrying a large heavy garbage bag down the street. She was mad at herself for letting all these people come into her house and take things out of it, while she was busy crying on Vern's shoulder.

Meredith didn't think she was normally this stupid, but the shock had done its job.

She tried another tack and googled "cremation services." Part of Grillo's recurring monologue was his declaration that after he killed himself—he had threatened this many times, but had never followed through, until now—his wish was that his body be cremated and dumped in the LA River. Meredith always rolled her eyes at this point. The LA River, at least the parts of it that she'd glimpsed from the freeway, was totally dry most of the year; its banks were solid concrete. Even the parts that did have enough water to be a proper river were polluted, and often had off-the-chart levels of *E. coli*. Grillo's ashes wouldn't accelerate the river's actualization as a toxic drainage ditch much, but it wouldn't make things better, either. Maybe that was the point.

She thought about the fight she'd had with Grillo the night she got fired. Was it really just two days ago? There was the call from Dr. Stein, Grillo's reaction, then her attempts to de-escalate his tantrum, which only backfired. On repeat. Guilt made her throat close. She tasted acid from her contorted stomach.

She stared at the listings for cremation services. Grillo hadn't been superstitious or sentimental, and he certainly hadn't been traditional. This included his views on the afterlife. Cremation seemed like a tidy solution, but she hesitated. She probably needed to call the police first, not a crematorium.

She was back where she had started. If she called the police, this might cause trouble for Vern, who was already struggling to contain his PR Crisis. She didn't want to make things worse for him. He had been very kind to her. Linda had been kind, too. She was so gruff and unapologetic. Brusquely sweet, if that was possible. "Perhaps you do not count your knowledge enough," Linda had said to her.

Her accent—Meredith couldn't quite pin it down—was endearing.

She felt bad about Grillo and felt bad about blowing off Merritt's PR crisis. As if the next steps for each problem were mutually exclusive, she felt stuck, suspended in amber like a bug.

Meredith has a sinking suspicion that her husband's body had been in that large garbage bag. What else could it have been? It was so strange that they'd remove it, though. What else would it be? She really should drive back home and see where things stood. But the thought of returning and finding his body gone—or just as bad, finding it there—made her feel faint. She had to lie down.

She stared up again at the popcorn ceiling. Its stippled surface reminded her of dirty cottage cheese. She decided that until she had the emotional stability to deal with Grillo's death, she would work. She would work for Vern and fulfill the promise she'd made to him. She would solve his PR Crisis problem in time before the charter vote in two weeks. She couldn't leave Grillo's body mouldering at home for two weeks, but she didn't even know if the body was, in fact, still at home. Maybe the big guy with the garbage bag had in fact been carrying Grillo, in order to transfer him to the morgue. They were, after all, police. The morgue, unlike her house, would be refrigerated. If that was the case, Grillo's body could wait until after she kicked things off for Merritt. If he *was* at the morgue, like she hoped. She would ask Linda.

The clock was ticking. It was Thursday. She had all day to get a new project set up in The Model, while she waited for the stench outside to dissipate. She got out of bed and pulled out her laptop.

In the space of ten minutes, she had gone from feeling terrified of being alone with emotions that she knew would annihilate her if she allowed herself to feel them, to being grateful that she had the whole day to herself. She could get a lot done in one day. While her laptop booted up, she opened a can of mixed nuts that she found in one of the kitchen cabinets and opened a bottle of water she'd found in the refrigerator. The only thing that put the nightmare in a box, a box that she could close tight and stick at the back of her brain closet—the only thing that helped her forget anxiety, uncertainty, grief, and guilt, was to work, work, and work some more. And running. Running helped her recover from work, so that she could work more.

She read the press releases as well as the articles that Vern had given her during their meeting and took a few notes. The press releases told the story of the benevolent and experienced city council and the mayor, Leo Mendebal, who had led the city for decades—Merritt citizens always voted for him and he always won by a landslide. His grandfather had been mayor before him, also for decades. The press releases further mentioned Merritt's quick response to 911 calls—cops showed up within ten minutes of the call, any call, unlike LA where it could take up to eight hours for someone to show up, if at all.

As Vern had summarized during their meeting, the press releases touted Merritt's self-sufficiency. The city had built its own electrical plant, and had vastly superior high-speed internet service. This odd five-square-mile-wide city-state, squatting outside of downtown LA, sandwiched between freeways, the LA River, and the train tracks, hemmed in otherwise by the sprawl of Greater Los Angeles, was almost completely independent in every way. Meredith remembered how smooth internet service had been at AFA Foods. She rarely experienced the spotty internet coverage that was the norm at home in Atwater Village.

The press releases quoted a few local businesspeople, emphasizing their desire to keep current leadership in place.

One testimonial byline stood out: Bob Hawley—her old boss at AFA Foods.

Bob's endorsement was flush with his typical whiny cadence, authenticating it. "Everything works well here. Nothing impedes business from getting the work done, which is, let's face it, the priority. Merritt provides the services we need at reasonable rates. I could care less where the mayor lives. Why take down an efficiently run city that has always been very clear about its mission? It's a place where business can make money without a lot of red tape. We have enough to worry about, what with keeping our shareholders happy and improving profit margins, than having to also deal with disruption in essential services."

Meredith could picture him saying that, with his paunch, bald spot, and vitamin D-deficient complexion. She didn't miss his bad breath nor the off-putting smell of his antiperspirant that left a chemical odor in his wake. It was the kind of antiperspirant that men wore because they didn't want to leave behind pheromone clues about their true nature. In the hallway, by the coffee station, en route to the network printer; in all these places, she could scent him like a rabbit fleeing a wolf, and she gladly went the long away around to avoid him.

Though Bob had no time to do a PR Crisis Plan, he clearly had enough time to be quoted for Vern's press releases. How had Vern managed that? Completely uninterested in public perceptions of the company's image, Bob concerned himself solely with logistics, statistics, and revenue cost analysis. But here he was, quoted at length in this press release, all bright-eyed and bushy-tailed, ringing the bell for the City of Merritt—a press release she'd never seen, even though it had been her job to support and review all PR-related activities, including those of AFA Foods executives. She made a note to follow up. She doodled a concentric spiral next to the note, not totally done with her hate-reverie. As she added horns, body, and a tail to the spiral, she fantasized about sneaking back into AFA Foods at night to prank Bob. She'd put some pink slime in a bucket and balance it on the top of his office door, so that when he opened it, all the goo would drop on his face, satisfactorily transforming him into a bad horror movie extra.

She decided to see how well the Merritt press releases had landed with journalists, and whether they showed up at all in some cannibalized form in published articles. She checked the *LA Weekly*, *Curbed LA*, and the *LA Times*. She got tons of results from the *LA Times*. All the articles were written by Gil Girron, the journalist that Vern had mentioned. Vern's dismay at the dogged, continual, negative press had been laced with the timbre of a man mourning the dead. None of Girron's articles had utilized Merritt's press releases, except to highlight discrepancies and inconsistencies in Merritt's version of events.

She googled Gil Girron but there was almost nothing online regarding his personal life. How did anyone, nowadays, manage to avoid an online presence? Especially a journalist. He'd grown up in Boyle Heights, which adjoined Merritt on the north. Maybe Girron didn't like what "business as usual" in Merritt was doing to Boyle Heights. It must be incredibly unhealthy to live next door to Merritt—not only the putrid stench of the slaughterhouses, but also, there was lead in the soil. She'd read about the Exodus plant in the business section of the *Times* just last week. It was going to be a superfund site. If Merritt lost its charter, Boyle Heights' residents would be ecstatic.

Meredith made some more notes, itemizing possible ways to ameliorate the situation. *A large grant to Boyle Heights' after-school programs from the city of Merritt. Free concerts at the Merritt electrical plant. (Brightly lit at night, but maybe not perfectly safe for a concert? What with the transformers and high wattage.) Hire in some Boyle Heights mariachis, create a new "Historic Merritt Industrial Festival."* But there wasn't much time. Instead, she would try to connect with Gil Girron. She added a couple of reminders to her calendar, and kept reading through the rest of the articles.

Needing a break, she stretched her arms over her head and yawned, then got up from the tiny kitchen table to look out the kitchen window. She had a fine view of the backside of a fire station, where a dilapidated campanile stood: paint peeling, sinister. She supposed new recruits used it for training exercises. The tower reminded her of the Disney film *Dumbo*, specifically the scene in which Dumbo is poised at the edge of a window on the top floor of a tower, engulfed in flames. Poor Dumbo. She remembered how terrified he was, ridiculed by the mean clowns on the ground below, who were dressed up as firemen. Dumbo had no choice but to jump, falling into a giant pie, not realizing yet that he had the power to fly.

Next to the tower was a large swimming pool. Meredith loved swimming, though she didn't have much opportunity. A tall retaining wall topped with barbed wire made it clear to anyone with a view of the pool from the apartments that it was not available to the public. Tall retaining walls topped with barbed wire repeated themselves consistently across the streets of Merritt. What was available to the public, in Merritt, besides Topa Café? She made more notes. *Merritt library? Suggest founding a Merritt Boys & Girls Club?*

Meredith cranked up the A/C, then went back to work.

The newspaper articles made it clear that that Mayor Mendebal and Merritt were in deep shit. The last mayoral election, a fiasco, had unraveled like something out of a hard-boiled crime novel. The 'private detectives' mentioned in another article sounded more like mafia thugs. A third article had reported that the city manager, Chuck Peck, had been indicted for misappropriation of funds.

How could Mayor Mendebal think he'd get away with fake ballots? Was there in fact a mafia presence in Merritt? Thinking back to what Emile, the bartender, had insinuated to her yesterday, Meredith wondered if there was such a thing as a Basque mafia. She checked online, but didn't find anything, though there was mention of "ETA" which was some kind of separatist group in the Basque Country of Spain. She googled "Leo Basque" and learned that Calabasas, a town about forty-five minutes west, where the Kardashians lived, was originally a ranch owned by Jean Leo, a Basque immigrant. Drilling down, it appeared that Mendebal was related to him.

Trivia-ridden rabbit holes were her downfall. She tried to refocus. It didn't appear that Girron had found anything damaging about Merritt's actual governance. The election issues, however, couldn't be whitewashed easily because Mendebal didn't live in Merritt and was hiding it poorly. It was always the cover-up that was the kiss of death. Mendebal's mansion in Hancock Park had been in his family for over a hundred years. Of course that's where he lived.

In his articles, Girron kept harping on the fact that around ninety people actually lived in Merritt—the other 45,000 people only worked there, commuting in from distant areas. As a former member of Merritt's white-collar workforce, Meredith knew that working in a windowless air-conditioned office meant that you could be on the moon or up in the Andes, for all the difference the outside world made. It was fine as long as you could leave at the end of the day. (Even if leaving in rush hour sucked, you could still leave.) But living there full-time?

She was surprised to find it oddly peaceful—even on a Thursday. But was that because she had fled from—she refused to finish the thought and typed harder at her keyboard, googling *voter fraud*. Apparently, if you didn't live in the jurisdiction that you governed, that was a felony. She tried to find parallel situations in other towns, but there weren't many. Apparently, mayors didn't usually get indicted for voter fraud, they got in trouble for assaulting their secretaries, for bribery, tax evasion, or embezzlement. The normal stuff. There was one article about corrupt cops in a city in Arkansas. Most of the policemen lived in adjacent towns, and because of this, relationships with those they were charged to protect and serve were tenuous at best. Similarly, if the mayor of Merritt didn't live in Merritt, how could he know what the issues were that affected people who did live there? Remedying that gap could be Merritt's way out of this mess.

She opened the door of the refrigerator and surveyed the options: some bread, some lunch meat, yogurt, an unopened jar of mayonnaise, sliced cheese. She could make a sandwich, but instead she grabbed a canned soda and fished an energy bar out of her bag. She opened the front door thoughtlessly to get some air, but quickly closed it again. She forgot it was Thursday.

Trapped inside, Meredith returned to her computer and tried to log into the marketing database she had used for demographic research at AFA Foods. The login still worked, which was no surprise; the IT department at AFA Foods had barely remembered to ask for her key card on her last day there. She already had a script written to import data from the marketing database into The Model, something that had taken her many hours to set up back at AFA Foods. She didn't want to start from scratch with whatever Vern might send her way. There wasn't any time to waste. That's why she spent the next hour downloading voter information from the last census, merge-purging it with the demographic info from the database, and massaging her spreadsheet with sorted results. In the end, she knew where Merritt's citizens lived; how many people were in each family; their ages, their education level, and their ethnicities.

She expected Vern's data fairly soon. She planned to cross-check it against what she had already come up with, to catch any corrections or omissions. No database was one hundred percent accurate, but it was a start. She had confidence in the process as long as it was rigorous. She liked having control over the finer details, improving the data, cleaning it up. It relaxed her. It allowed her to forget other things, like what happened the day before. Like the fact that she was now a widow.

LINDA: TAMALES

Friday, August 21, 2009
Senate charter vote in 12 days

While Meredith was in the shower, I snuck into her apartment, found a file called "TheModel" on her computer, downloaded it onto a thumb drive, and then installed a Trojan. I returned to my apartment, where I then emailed the file to Vern.

I thought I'd done what he asked, but I received a text message back from him a half hour later. *WTF? Meet me at City Hall in 10.*

As I was leaving, Meredith caught me on my way down the stairs.

"Hey Linda—" said Meredith. I arrived at her floor as she continued, "I was wondering if you know how early Vern gets into the office? He's supposed to send me some city data, and I'm ready for it. I need to do a merge-purge with some basic Census stuff."

"I'm on my way to meet him."

"Oh! Could I get a ride with you?"

"Sure."

On the way over to City Hall, Meredith filled me in on all the work she'd done the day before. It was impressive. When we arrived, I badged-in ahead of Meredith, who needed to go through security. I noticed she stopped to talk to the new security guard, Shitbird, the former bartender at Topa Café. Shitbird and I were acquainted, ever since that one time I came to the aid of a waitress he had a crush on several years ago, who was now his wife. Long story. They often asked me to cook-outs at their house, but I usually declined, because matrimonial bliss is annoying. Also, I had to keep a low profile. It was nice of them to offer, though.

When I got to Vern's office on the second floor, I found him hunched over his laptop. He was stabbing at the keyboard, alternating with mouse clicks in an erratic syncopation.

I waited. After he was tapped out, he pushed the laptop away in disgust and said, "You have to figure this out. The Model. How to use the damn thing."

"Not my area."

"Have Meredith show you."

"Why don't you ask her? She's downstairs. I'll get her."

"Downstairs?" said Vern.

"She's talking to Shitbird right now. She wanted to see you about data you were supposed to provide? She's ready for it. She said she was also going to the mayor's office to make an appointment."

Vern stared at me. "Why?" he asked.

"She wants to talk to everyone. The mayor, everyone on the city council, the parking tickets cashier, the janitor, admins. It's research, she said."

Vern's stomach gurgled and a long, slow moan emanated from it as if it was haunted. He was flushed.

He said, "Dammit. All we needed was The Model."

I didn't ask him why we needed The Model because it was not my place. I simply nodded and said, "I see."

Vern said, "She's doing the right thing, if we had all kinds of time. But we don't. A grieving widow who was just fired is not going to help the City of Merritt avoid losing its charter in two weeks by talking to every single person who works at City Hall."

I said, "Was she fired or laid off?"

"Fired, laid off, who cares? It was probably because of pink slime."

"What is pink slime?"

"You don't want to know. Ever since the last business mixer, Chuck has been nagging me to hire Meredith as a way of getting our hands on the Model. The gossip in this town is unbelievable. I tried to get him to switch his focus, but he was like a dog with a bone. Then pink slime handed me this golden opportunity. The PR person always takes the fall in situations like that. I checked around and sure enough, she'd been let go. I contacted her immediately. I just wanted—"

"The Model."

Vern said, "Take your time, I haven't got anything better to do." He pulled the laptop closer and assaulted the keyboard some more.

Vern was rarely sarcastic. He was a good boss overall. His directives were typically clear and concise. I had long admired his self-control and social grace. He could really connect with people, no matter how powerful or intimidating. Countless times, I had witnessed him gliding in, his voice relaxing his subject like a hypnotist, getting what he wanted, then gliding out and away. What's the expression? "Like grease." (Or was it butter? Something like that.) They never knew what hit them. This Vern Page sitting in front of me was a different person. I'm not generally affected by other people's frustration, but I was feeling emotionally muddy.

I realized my problem with him was not how he was treating me, but how he was casting aspersions on Cutiecups. Meredith. I had started referring to her as "Cutiecups" in my mind, because she was cute, and because of her weepy hiccups the day before. I said carefully, "It seems to me that this lady has more to offer than you think."

He looked up and said flatly, "Really."

"Yes."

"Like what?" said Vern, swallowing a yellow pill with some coffee.

"She reads a lot."

"Great."

I said, "All the documents you gave her? She's already done with them."

"All of the *LA Times* articles by Gil Girron?" asked Vern.

I nodded. Vern had asked me to take care of the Girron problem back when Girron first started writing hit pieces about Merritt—not a 'final-final' solution; he was too high-profile for that. I wasn't ultimately able to do much, however, because I had nothing with which to inspire fear-driven cooperation. He didn't have a wife or kids. He was totally clean. After a month of shadowing him, Bernard and I had nothing to show for it besides four new washcloths that Bernard had knitted during our stakeouts. Bernard liked to keep busy.

Vern said, "Meredith mentioned that she might be able to persuade Girron to write more positively about Merritt. But he's the last person who would ever support Merritt's retaining its charter. Good luck with that. What else?"

"She downloaded the census data on Merritt residents from some marketing database."

Vern stared at me, waiting for me to continue.

I said, "On the way over here, she told me that she put every single name, address, and phone number into The Model."

"That wasn't in the file you gave me."

I said calmly, "The file I gave you is called 'The Model', right? That's the file you asked for. Perhaps she made a copy to work with Merritt's data. Do you want that file too?" I settled back into my chair. I reminded myself that I was comfortable with aggression, and I was comfortable with sarcasm. This new version of Vern Page wasn't impossible for me to handle. Just different.

The pinkish tone blooming across Vern's face and neck was turning darker, like rare roast beef. "Obviously," he said. "What's she up to? I mean, all this useless chitchat at City Hall—if we only have two weeks?"

I shrugged. "She said it's the first step."

"Of what?"

"She said she wants to talk to all the residents, the civil servants—"

"One and the same."

I said, "Right. She wants to create a focus group, but there's not enough time; so instead, she will conduct field interviews. She said, 'The environment of the field interview is almost as useful as the interview.' Something like that? Then in The Model she will do a merge thing."

"Merge-purge?"

"Yes. That."

Vern thought about this, then said, "I want to know her every move—online and offline. You're never to leave her side, and you need to get her to wrap up this interview shit immediately."

"You want me to be present for all the citizen interviews?"

"If you can't get her to stop, then goddammit, yes."

"That may cause difficulty," I said.

"Why?"

"Some do not approve of our methods."

"Just do it."

I found Meredith talking to the city clerk's admin. When she was finished, we left City Hall and went to Boyle Heights together. She wanted to buy some tamales for Girron. Apparently, PR people—the good ones—did stuff like that.

She thought that if we brought Girron his favorite tamales then he might be willing to write about Merritt's honorable aspects instead of its nefarious ones. I was extremely doubtful that a dozen tamales would win him over. After all, Vern had failed to move him. I guess some people were immune to Vern's powers of persuasion. Bernard's light sabotage on Girron's car, my harmless pranks staged at his apartment—these also had no effect. Girron was either totally unafraid, or we were too indirect. I mean, it's not like we could come right out and tell him that we were harassing him on behalf of the City of Merritt.

But what did I know about PR? Absolutely zero. Meredith said, "Connecting with journalists isn't easy. The results aren't reliable, but the payoff can be huge."

"This tamale scheme? It shows initiative," I said encouragingly, grasping for something nice to say, but feeling baffled. "Everyone likes food."

As I pulled up to the bakery, Meredith said, "When I was young, I rode in the car with my dad all the way across town to get tamales from this place. He bought them for the series of women who cleaned our house over the years." The bakery hid behind bars on its windows, and the building looked like it could use a new paint job. Nevertheless, a line of customers snaked out the front door and down the street.

Meredith continued, "The women who cleaned for our family were in constant rotation from different Central American countries: Guatemala, Honduras, El Salvador. They had three things in common: they had no experience, they spoke no English, and they were extremely homesick. Each country had their own way of making tamales. My dad always tried to get the right kind.

"Some of the women who worked for us were really young, barely eighteen or so—though I guess I didn't know that until I grew closer to them in age. Cleaning our house was usually their first job here, because though my mom didn't pay much—maybe because of it? Anyway—she didn't require previous experience, either. Sometimes I could hear them crying in the bathroom."

I said, "I can confirm that homesickness is difficult. My partner Bernard suffers from this. But the tamales—I'm confused. Your family could not afford to pay better wages?"

Meredith sighed. "My mother needed to do things her way. My father stayed out of it. This was his way of trying to make up for it."

"Your father sounds nice," I said.

She nodded. "He passed away a few years ago. He *was* nice, though I didn't see him much—he worked long hours. My mom says that's where I get it from—working too much. He loved to bring people food as gifts. He'd go to Winchell's Donuts with me every Saturday morning. And sometimes on Sundays, in the late afternoon we'd head over to 31 Flavors for ice cream."

It was a wonder she wasn't 300 pounds. I certainly would be that fat, with a father like that. My father died when I was ten and I never forgave him for abandoning me. If he had lived, my uncle wouldn't have dared to touch me. I know my father would have kicked his ass so hard he'd need a special ass brace that he'd have to wear for the rest of his life.

After we found the end of the line and joined it, I noticed a large mural adorning the facade of a small market directly opposite. The mural was so much better than Farmer John's back in Merritt, though I wasn't sure why. It depicted a caballero who had no legs because his bottom half was made of smoke floating up from a brass lamp that was actually a cornstalk. Seeds were nestled in the palm of the man's giant hand, which was overlarge, as large as the man himself. Ants carried more seeds to the giant hand. With his other hand, the caballero held an Aztec torch that was bent sideways ninety degrees in the middle. The torch reminded me of the snake in the *Busy, Busy Town* children's book that I had when I was very young. I mostly looked at the pictures since it was in Spanish. I wasn't forced to learn Spanish until I was sent to school. Fortunately, there were tons of pictures in that book. The worm with the little green hat was my favorite. His car was made out of an apple and sometimes it could fly.

I asked Cutiecups, "The mural over there. What do you call it when that hand with the seeds feels like it's in my lap? Not flattened out, like the Farmer John pigs? Are you familiar with the Farmer John mural?" I asked, and that's when I grabbed her hand, pretending to pull her away from some pedestrian traffic. She didn't flinch, which made me happy.

"Yes, this one's quite different. Its strong use of perspective creates depth," she said. "Grillo would know exactly how to explain it. Which I've been meaning to ask you. His body? Which morgue did you take it to?"

Morgue? Meredith had come up with a pretty logical explanation for what we had done with her husband. I didn't plan to set her straight anytime soon. I said, "The mural over there has an inscription in the corner. I wonder what it says? I'll go find out. Be right back."

I jaywalked over to the mural, pretended to read the quote at the bottom right with great interest. The print on the plaque was big enough to be readable from where we were standing in line for tamales, but I needed to deflect her question. By the time I returned, Meredith had forgotten all about the morgue, and was thumbing through something on her phone, but she put it away when I brushed her elbow. She has the whitest arms I've ever seen, with sprinkles of light brown freckles. Precious.

She said, "OK, Girron likes queso and green chili tamales the best." In all my stakeouts, I had never seen Girron buy tamales, let alone knew what kind he liked. Meredith really was extraordinary at research.

I said, "This is a very long line. The tamales here must be worth it."

We both fell silent as the line slowly inched forward. I thought about the inscription on the mural, which had said, "La tierra es de quien la trabaja con sus propria manos." Loosely translated, it means, "The earth belongs to the people who work it with their own hands." This was similar to what we believed and fought for in ETA, that the Basque Country belonged to the Basque people and not to Spain, no matter how many Spanish landlords moved in and bought up the land. The Basque people still worked the land and were there first. I felt an affinity for these California Latinos and their efforts to maintain their identity in a town that wasn't interested in anyone's identity.

After we purchased two dozen tamales, one dozen for Girron and the other dozen for us, I drove Meredith downtown to the *LA Times* building. It was only 2:00 p.m. but traffic was awful, as usual. I took back streets all the way, cruising over the old 1940s bridge that spanned the railroad and the LA River, zigzagging through the Arts District, the Garment District, then past Skid Row. I pulled into a red zone in front of the *LA Times* at First and Spring. Meredith grabbed one of the bags of tamales, and was about to open the door, but then she hesitated.

"What is it?" I asked.

"It's just that it might be better optics if you dropped them off."

"Why?" I already knew why, but I wanted to see how terrible this was going to be. As I watched her rosebud lips open to speak, I felt my heart beat a little faster than normal.

I didn't want to stop calling her Cutiecups. I didn't want to stop rooting for her.

She said, "Because I don't look like a Latina. I'm not Latina."

"Neither am I," I said patiently.

"I didn't assume—I mean I didn't know—I'm just talking about appearances. I mean, I sort of wondered? But your accent is different from other Spanish-speaking folks? I'd like to know, but only if you want to tell me, and I respect your privacy." She stopped talking abruptly, horrified at the hole she had dug for herself.

It killed me how Cutiecups could go into a tailspin so quickly. Of course, I wanted her to get as far as she could to solve Merritt's crisis; I wanted her to feel successful, even though I was pretty sure that she'd fail, no matter how excellent she was. She had no chance at all. I've always been a sucker for the underdog.

"That's OK," I said. "I'd be happy to take in the tamales. And for the record, I am Basque. Not Latina."

"Basque! That's so cool! I went to school with this girl who was Basque—"

"Should you write a note?" I assumed I wouldn't get past the security guard, and would just drop the tamales off like I was a delivery person.

Meredith scribbled a note and handed it to me. It said, "I was in the neighborhood—just following up on my email yesterday. I'd like to call you tomorrow to discuss Merritt's recent innovations and improvements along with testimonials from its citizens. It's the People's Choice! Best, Meredith." She had this beautiful handwriting that was more like elegant printing, with evenly spaced letters that linked together, compressed and uniform. Sort of like the way she talked.

"'People's Choice?'" I said, amused.

"I'm trying to amplify the fact that the citizens of Merritt like how they've been governed—"

"Good idea," I said. "But you haven't actually interviewed citizens yet?"

"True," she said. She crumpled up the note. As she finished off writing a new note, she said, "Merritt citizens must be fairly happy. The cheap rent alone makes living there worth it. You could actually save for retirement."

"If you survived the—"

"Olfactory pollution!" she said.

"Other kinds of pollution, also. Too many to list."

"Yes—but I sleep really well there! It's weird." She fished out a business card from her bag and paper-clipped it to the note. I'd given her a set of business cards that morning. These contained her name, an official merritt.org email address, and the title "PR Consultant." Below that, she wrote out her personal phone number—I could tell from the area code. That was a lapse. I'd forgotten about getting her a business phone. It had completely slipped my mind. As she handed the note and the bag to me, she said, "Thank you SO MUCH." Her hands felt like little lacy doilies, light and delicate.

I'd noticed by now how Meredith's thank you's were always very emphatic. I personally avoided thanking people unless it was unavoidable. It's cultural. Americans thank the waiter, the bank teller, the cashier, every damn person remotely related to the service industry. I have news for Americans: They're all paid to do it, surprise! They aren't doing it out of the kindness of their hearts. There's no need to thank them. But no, Americans thank, thank, thank, all the live-long day. Where I come from, no one expects thanks for a paid service. What's more, they'd think you might have some kind of mental illness. But Meredith's gratitude was different than the American robotic thanking I've observed. She meant it, every time. She was genuinely grateful for every little small thing done for her, no matter what. It melted my heart.

I got out of the car and went into the *LA Times* building. Inside, there were more murals, granite floors, and a big statue of an eagle who looked angry that there were no rodents to devour.

"Delivery for Gil Girron," I said to the security guard, who "looked Latino." He sized up my boobs. They never fail to distract men, who often appear to have misaligned nerve pathways that gather and send information to their loins, instead of to their brains.

"Bueno," he said. "¿Puedo tener tu número de teléfono?" He got right to the point, at least. He held up his hand to his ear in the international gesture for phone call, and winked at me. Then he smiled sheepishly like he couldn't help himself.

I fake-laughed. "Claro que sí!" I exclaimed. On the sign-in sheet for visitors, I wrote down the number of the rendering plant where we had dumped Meredith's husband's body. Then I left the bag of tamales, Meredith's card, and her handwritten note with the man-toad and sashayed out of there. Just kidding. Obviously, I did not sashay. I walked.

A heavyset male meter maid in a three-wheeled electric vehicle was double-parked next to the car, writing a ticket. Meredith was standing nearby, wringing her hands while she pleaded in vain. I walked up to him and flashed my badge. He immediately put away his ticket book and moved on. No one ever looks close enough at my badge to notice that I'm not with the LAPD—even meter maids.

"That was amazing!" said Meredith as we drove off. She was easily impressed.

Driving back to Merritt, I thought about how I'd never really been involved with anyone romantically for longer than a few weeks. In Spain, I had been too busy with ETA to have a relationship, though I enjoyed some casual flings here and there. In ETA, I had to be more of a badass than my male compatriots, not only to earn their respect but also to teach them proper boundaries. After all, cutting off the balls of every member of my squad would hinder ETA's strength as a whole, so that wasn't an option. So I trained and trained and trained some more.

Then, after Barcelona, I couldn't really handle anything emotional. I gave up on looking for my soulmate because I wasn't sure of the qualities I wanted in a partner anyway, though as a baseline, I preferred someone who could at least take responsibility for their actions. I'd never encountered anyone like that, until now.

MARTINIS

Saturday, August 22, 2009
Senate charter vote in 11 days

Meredith fired up her laptop, plugged in a thumb drive containing Vern's city data, merged it into The Model, then updated individual listings with tags and keywords to improve cross-demographic searches and analysis. Once the data was in better shape, she created projections, pie charts, and bar charts. Lastly, she wrote up a few short summaries of the interviews completed to date.

The day before, when Meredith and Linda had arrived at City Hall, Linda told Meredith she'd catch up with her after a meeting with Vern, then disappeared. At the security station, Emile, the bartender from Topa Café, was running the X-ray machine for the walk-through scanner by the front door.

Emile wore a security guard uniform. His khaki cap was embroidered with the city's crest—at least that's what Meredith assumed it was. Emblazoned on a 10x10 sign across the building's exterior, the city crest retained some coherence, but on a baseball cap, the crest scaled down to nothing more than a murky ball of black thread. It was a branding problem. She made a mental note to mention it to Vern.

When it was Meredith's turn to be scanned, Emile nodded at her and said, "Meredith. You're back. Your meeting last Wednesday must have gone well."

"*Sh*—Emile!" said Meredith, closely avoiding calling him "Shitbird." "Did Topa Café close already?"

He nodded his head yes. "A little sooner than I expected. Put your wallet, phone, and purse in these containers. Make sure nothing is in your pockets. You can keep your shoes on."

Meredith complied and walked through the scanner without incident. As she gathered her things, she said to Emile, "I was wondering about something you mentioned Wednesday...something about how the restaurant staff knew a lot about what went on here at City Hall? I'd love to get more concrete details."

Emile scanned the room and said, "I'd like to keep this job, if you don't mind."

"I'm sorry. I'm not necessarily looking for anything sensitive. Any background info at all would really help me with this special project I'm doing. It's for Vern Page?"

Emile raised his eyebrows in recognition.

She continued, "I'm helping to improve Merritt's image and I think the best place to start is with its citizens. You live here, right?"

Meredith regretted that last remark. She shouldn't know that Emile lived in Merritt, but she did, because he was in The Model. There was only one "Emile" in the list.

Unfazed, Emile said, "Ah, 'An Industrial Paradise' is finally wearing thin, is it?" He looked about him again. Employees scattered here and there were involved in their own morning conversations. He said, "If the cocktail quirks of the barflies I served are at all relevant to Merritt's image, I'm your man. You're welcome to come by my house for some kalimotxos Sunday afternoon. We have cookouts every week unless it's raining. This cookout is a special celebration, though. My wife had jaw surgery a month ago—her jaw was wired shut. After her doctor's appointment today, though, she'll be able to eat real food instead of smoothies. Do you have any pictures of cats? My wife really likes cats."

"Oh! I have a cat! Or I did have a cat, sort of. It's a stray. A big tabby—" Meredith had no idea how the cat was doing, but she was pretty sure it had adopted several families, and it was probably doing just fine. She couldn't recall ever taking a picture of the cat, actually. Meredith looked down, embarrassed and then overwhelmed by the other urgent home-related matters that she hadn't handled yet. She was at a loss for words.

She heard a cough behind her. She looked over her shoulder and saw that several people had lined up, waiting to get scanned in.

As he turned back toward the X-ray machine, Emile said, "Great! My wife and I live over on Mallory Place, just behind City Hall. 505 Mallory Place. Sunday, don't forget. Come by any time after 2:00 p.m. If you also bring some cat pictures, my wife will be your new best friend."

After Meredith took her leave of Emile, she located the mayor's office and spoke with the mayor's admin, who was very friendly but apologized, explaining that the mayor didn't work Fridays, but he was available the following Monday. Meredith then headed to the office of the city manager, Chuck Peck.

Chuck Peck's admin was a pinched, unsmiling woman named Gina. Meredith's chit-chat overtures went nowhere with her. If anything, the woman became even more surly than she already was.

"Mr. Peck won't be able to meet with you until Tuesday, September 1," said Gina, scanning a full calendar.

That was more than a week off, but it would have to do. Meredith said, "Oh, great! Thanks so much for fitting me in."

Gina looked at her blankly. "Is there anything else?"

"What a nice plant that is," Meredith said, pointing to a sad spider plant behind Gina. They were unkillable but this one looked to be on its last legs.

Gina ignored her and turned to her computer to end the exchange.

As she went out the door, Meredith wondered how Gina could be teased out of her hostility. Maybe it was better to focus on folks who were more willing to connect, like Emile. Besides, Gina wasn't on the list of Merritt residents, so her feedback about the city didn't apply.

Meredith then located the general admin assigned to the rest of the city council, and found that none of them maintained offices at City Hall. She set up several phone appointments scattered over the next few days.

She stopped by Vern's office, but his door was closed and his light was off, so she walked back to the apartment, which was only a few blocks away. She worked the rest of Friday from the apartment, then went to bed early. The next morning, even though it was Saturday, she worked on fine-tuning collateral materials and adjusting The Model data until four in the afternoon, before calling it a day.

Meredith drove a couple miles north to the nearest liquor store and picked up ingredients for martinis. She felt she needed to repair her politically incorrect stupidity regarding Linda's ethnicity the day before, and besides, she could really use a martini. It was Saturday, after all.

She returned home and ate a peanut butter and jelly sandwich, with an ear out for Linda's step. When she finally heard someone's footsteps on the stairs, Meredith stuck her head our her door and saw that it was Linda.

"Would you like a martini?" Said Meredith.

Linda looked surprised. "That sounds very nice," she said. "I'll be right back."

Meredith couldn't find a cocktail shaker, so she poured a lot of ice and martini ingredients in a pint glass then upended another glass over it, shaking the contents carefully. There weren't any martini glasses either, so she poured the drinks into coffee cups. She set the cups out on the table along with some olives and roasted almonds.

When Linda arrived, she was wearing her hair down and what appeared to be lipstick.

Meredith gave Linda a martini and they clinked cups. In the ensuing silence, Meredith chugged her own drink a little too fast, which gave her hiccups. "Dammit," she said, as she went to get some water. "I really need to slow down. Hiccups are so annoying. I seem to be getting them a lot lately."

Linda covered her mouth and coughed slightly before saying, "Maybe drink out of the glass backward, I hear that helps to stop them."

"Great idea." As Meredith leaned over the glass of water and drank from the outside rim of the glass, she realized her loose top had fallen open and revealed a bit too much, so she straightened up. Her hiccups were gone.

Linda looked a little flushed. She blinked, took another sip of her martini, and said, "Very strong."

"I've had a lot of practice," said Meredith.

"I like the sour taste."

"That's the olive juice. Dirty martini."

"Ah," said Linda.

Meredith asked Linda, "So you're Basque, right?"

Linda nodded.

Meredith got her bag, which was sitting on the floor near her, and rifled through it. "I grabbed this matchbook from Topa Café right before they closed," Meredith said, handing it to Linda. "See there at the bottom—*zazbiak bat*? What's it mean?"

As Linda took a close look at the matchbook's cover, she tried to tuck her hair back behind her ears but her hair was too thick to stay put and it immediately sprang forward again. She said, "It's a patriotic Basque slogan. Difficult to translate."

Meredith said, "I knew this girl in grade school. She talked a lot about Basque folk dancing. Our school put on an 'International Day' once a year, and the girl always wore her Basque outfit: a bright red skirt with three rows of black piping, a white shirt with puffed sleeves under a black bodice, and a white kerchief on her head."

Linda nodded without much enthusiasm. "Yes, all the girls had to wear something like that and perform dances at festivals. I liked the boys' dances better. They used swords. Much more fun."

"I'm sorry for insinuating you were Latina yesterday."

"It's nothing. Long forgotten. What did *you* wear for International Day?"

"Not anything nearly as interesting! We're from Canada. We're Jewish—nonpracticing. We moved to LA when I was four because my dad got a job working for Mattel."

"Mattel?"

"A big toy company. I had all the Barbies."

"Barbies?"

"A doll—never mind. I hated International Day. There was no way to dress up as a Jewish Canadian, unless, I don't know, come as a moose? Bullwinkle?"

Linda said nothing and sipped her drink.

Meredith said, "*Rocky and Bullwinkle* is a cartoon about Canadians, sorry. One year my costume was a headscarf with a maple leaf design—I wore my regular clothes with it. My mom tried her best, I guess. She was busy selling real estate and didn't really have an interest in creating special costumes for school. I need to call her. I'm way overdue. It's just that my mother...my mother's calls require so much energy and time."

"She sounds complicated."

"She *is* a lot. And...she's kind of a grudge-holder. And she doesn't like it when we remember things differently, like *really* doesn't like it—but how can anyone remember things the same way?"

"That sounds very unsatisfying. Why call her then?"

"Well. She's my mother. I mean, I have no choice."

Linda shrugged. "Do you not? My mother died when I was born, and my father is also dead."

"Oh my god, I'm so sorry!"

"Canada was settled mostly by people from England, is that right?"

"And France...my family tree is just—a void. They could have come from anywhere. I don't know. My grandparents on both sides of the family died before I was born."

"It is strange that neither of your parents explained to you about your origins."

"It *is* strange! My mother didn't want to dwell on what she called 'humble origins.' As for my father? He was really confusing. He would switch his identity depending on whoever he was talking to; he might say he was Hispanic—he did speak Spanish, but never explained how he knew it—or he might say he was Catholic. It wasn't until I worked at an event company after college that I was finally able to pin down the exact 'kind' of Jew he was, when one day I described to a colleague my father's weird shape-shifting. He immediately knew what I was talking about. That's when I first heard the word *Sephardic.*"

"But how did he guess?"

"Well, because he was Sephardic too. He said they all act that way!"

"Ah," said Linda. "Your origins are the same as mine, then—from Spain."

"How?"

"The Sephardic Jews are all originally from Spain. They lived there before the Inquisition. You probably know the rest." Linda looked at the bottom of her coffee cup with great interest.

As she prepared another round of martinis, Meredith said, "I wonder if that's why hiding their identity was part of the Sephardic culture? It makes sense. This is really exciting, to put together one more piece of the puzzle! The way my father was so shy about who he was, or you know, making his identity into whatever he felt like? Maybe that's why I felt uncomfortable when I was around the Basque girl. She was so proud of her Basque outfit...and she would practice Basque folk dancing at recess sometimes. I worried that she'd get teased."

Meredith's phone rang. She picked it up and looked at the caller ID. "It's my mother," she said. "Her ears must have been burning."

Linda started to rise as if to leave, but Meredith said, "No, you can stay. This shouldn't take long."

LINDA: RUSES

I was admittedly a little bit inebriated. I usually didn't drink, except for the occasional kalimotxo. Also, I didn't expect the martinis to be so strong. In Spain, a martini is mostly vermouth; but Meredith's martinis were composed almost entirely of gin. I wouldn't have been surprised if Meredith had used an eyedropper to measure out the vermouth.

While I could still see straight, I observed Meredith talking to her mother. It didn't look good.

"Hi, Mom," said Meredith into the phone. As she listened, she hunched forward and contracted like a boiled shrimp. She said, "I'm really sorry. I had to work. I'm on assignment for the City of Merritt."

Meredith's face got smaller and tighter as her mother talked. She said, "You know them?"

I wondered why she continued to listen to a person who was making her uncomfortable.

"Who?"

She turned away and walked to the kitchen sink to stare out the window, then turned around and looked at her fingernails. She brought a finger up to her mouth and started chewing on a hangnail.

I watched her face. Her normally open and inquisitive expression had disappeared and what replaced it reminded me of the doll heads I used to make out of dried apples when

I was a kid. I would stick the apple heads on sticks, then stage swordfights. The winner was the doll who hadn't been decapitated.

Meredith's mother had a lot to say. Did Meredith really have no idea how to get off the phone? I resolved to help her, so I got up and went to the front door and knocked on it loudly. Meredith looked up and cocked her head. She smiled at me and shrugged. I opened the door then slammed it. I mouthed, "Make an excuse to hang up," but she didn't respond.

I called Meredith's number from my phone. She heard the beep for an incoming call, but didn't recognize the number, and even though I pointed to myself with the phone to my ear, she didn't notice. She let my call go to voice mail. I hung up.

Her mother kept talking.

I went out the front door, walked over to the fire alarm, and set it off. It was very loud. There was no way any conversation could continue, in person or on the phone. Sure enough, when I returned to the apartment, Meredith had hung up the phone.

We left the building along with everyone else who lived there and stood around in the parking lot, waiting for the fire department to arrive. Most of the other residents worked at City Hall, though I spotted one lady who worked in police department administration. A few others worked at the electric substation next door.

A fire station backed up to the rear of our apartment building, so a fire truck arrived almost instantaneously. Much to my chagrin, Bill Ochoa jumped down from the rig along with a few other firemen, who went to turn off the alarm and to survey the building for signs of fire and smoke. There were none, of course. No one would own up to setting off the alarm, either. The other firemen ended up chatting with the residents, whom they all knew well. Before I could escape back to my apartment, Ochoa spotted me.

"Vasco," said Ochoa. "You're in deep shit this time, my old friend."

I hated the guy. Ever since he sexually harassed that waitress at Topa Café and I had intervened, Ochoa and I had not been on good terms, and that was years ago. What was he doing here? He was supposed to be assigned to the other Merritt fire station. I had ambushed myself by trying to help Meredith get off the phone. I didn't care.

"I have no idea who made the false alarm, if that's what you mean," I said, smiling, trying to walk some distance away from Meredith, who looked at me, mystified. I waved at her as if to say, *I'll get back to you after I dispose of this nuisance.*

"I'm not talking about that. I'm talking about Atwater Village. You should be pissing your pants right about now."

"Oh yes, I am very frightened," I said. "Like when a bear is about to eat the honey. Very frightened."

"You should be," said Ochoa. "Apparently there was an arson job in Atwater Village and evidence is pointing right at you."

"Backwater Village?" I said, pretending confusion.

"*Atwater.* Someone called a tip in to LAFD. A lady. Said her son saw two people go into a house there, right before it caught fire. LAPD CCTV picked up a partial license plate that they think may be registered to Merritt City Hall. They're asking a lot of questions."

"Isn't this part of your job?" I asked.

"It's my job to put out fires."

I said, "This is also a fire to put out, is it not? I do not see what the problem is."

"The problem is that I'm done lying to LAFD. It's a violation of the fireman's code."

Oh my God. Suddenly this douchebag had a *code.*

I had meant to get rid of him quickly, in order to get back to Meredith, but I couldn't help myself. I said, "Are you sure there is nothing in your firefighter code that says, perhaps, to keep your hands off women's asses when they walk by? Just curious."

He glared at me. "That was a long time ago and thanks to you I was permanently banned from Topa Café."

I shrugged. "It's closed."

"Yeah, and for how long was it that I couldn't get a decent meal or a drink in this town? I always had to go to Huntington Fucking Park. I couldn't ever party with my brothers after our shift ended. They always wanted to go to Topa Café, so I was left out. Every. Fucking. Time. That's because of you."

"OK, Ochoa, whatever you say," as I started walking back to my apartment.

"I know you pulled that fire alarm," he called after me. I waved him off as I walked away.

BALL BEARINGS

Sunday, August 23, 2009
Senate charter vote in 10 days

Meredith went for a run first thing Sunday morning. Jogging through the deserted streets, she marveled at how peaceful it was. Only a few businesses ran a 24/7 operation. 30,000 employees were gone, and Merritt's residents had the five square miles of the city to themselves—that is, any stretches of land that weren't behind barbed wire.

Her route took her past the fire station around the corner from the apartment building. Merritt's power sub-station dominated most of the rest of the block except for four duplexes squeezed between them. These were "ranch-style" single-story boxes painted in earth tones or classic white. Each property included a narrow strip of lawn and a detached garage.

From there, she jogged up Boyle Avenue to Leo Avenue. There she passed a building with its name, Leo C. Mendebal Building, stenciled in large letters on its windowless side. Some people liked to see their names in big letters, others preferred the opposite. She was definitely part of the latter group. Meredith liked to be invisible. It was safer that way.

From the Mendebal building, she crossed 49th and ran up Santa Fe. She slowed down to a walk to take in a small church. A sign said, "Church of the Deaf." She could hear organ music. Through the gaps in a tall wrought-iron fence surrounding a tiny courtyard, she glimpsed a small statue of the Virgin Mary, about three feet tall. Towering over it was an eight-foot-tall sign affixed to the side wall of the neighboring building, announcing the product the business sold: ball bearings. The sign made the Virgin Mary look even smaller than she was.

Meredith continued on. Around the corner, she turned right on Mallory Place. This was a half-block of small single-family homes, identical in style to the duplexes. The block dead-ended into the windowless rear wall of the City Hall building, like a flea hidden in the hard-to-reach fur on the backside of a dog. Six spindly tall palm trees lined the stubby block, and like most palm trees, they provided almost no shade. Their long skinny trunks towering far above the street made the houses look smaller and more exposed than they already were. It reminded her of the ball bearings sign dominating the Virgin Mary statue at the church.

Doubling back, she caught sight of Emile, who was taking out the trash in front of a light blue home. He waved and said, "Don't forget the cookout later! Any time after two is fine. Bring cat pictures."

She waved and continued on her way. It might be a good idea to take Emile up on his offer; a barbecue was the perfect opportunity to extract more information about Merritt without seeming too nosy or confrontational. But she wasn't sure she could handle it. She was tired. Maybe Linda would come with her. Meredith felt more effective when Linda was around. And she made things more fun.

Meredith rounded the corner and ran up to East Merritt Avenue to the last two homes she'd identified in her research. These were also simple single-story ranch-style homes with detached garages, each sporting a small patch of front lawn. Behind and to the left of the homes crouched a water tank, twice as wide and twice as high. In front of the tank, a pink one-story building, not much bigger than a shed, perched near the street. A sign over the door announced that this was the Merritt Water Department.

With these last two homes accounted for, she had finished her tour of residential Merritt, for the most part. Aside from a councilmember's two-story home that she hadn't managed to fit into her running route, the rest of the population lived in various covert accommodations: a hastily added-on in-law, a small office building converted to lofts. These blended into the industrial milieu like military tanks painted with camouflage, distorting the sandy landscape of a foreign oil-rich country's forever war. Meredith wondered if it was by design. Perhaps these residents preferred not to be easily found. She could relate.

She jogged down Downey Street. After a few blocks, she arrived at her apartment building. She wasn't sure how long she'd be in Merritt, but at least she'd found a good jogging route that was easy to follow. She liked following a familiar route when she jogged, so she could let her mind wander. She liked to go over to-do lists, as well as let miscellaneous thoughts arise, without getting lost in the process. She wanted to keep an eye on the tiny homes, too, as if they needed her protection.

LINDA: COOKOUT PROXY

I was talking to Bernard about Ochoa in the parking lot of our apartment building when Meredith returned from her run. She was all sweaty and flushed. She looked like a delicate rose, kissed by the morning dew. My feelings were cutting off my oxygen and my breathing became shallow. I tried to collect myself. I glanced at Bernard to see if he noticed, but he was frowning over the latest news I'd just told him about the Atwater job. We would be in serious trouble if Ochoa stopped covering for us.

"Meredith, hello!" I said, as she ran up to us. "This is Bernard, my partner. Bernard, this is Meredith."

He looked down from his impossible height at Meredith and nodded hello. Meredith looked up at him, momentarily agape, then said, "Hi! You—you were there that night. I remember." I watched different expressions chase each other across her face: sadness, anger, and resignation. She looked down and said, "Never mind." Then, turning to face me, she said, "Linda. Do you think you can come with me to a barbecue over on Mallory Place later today? Last Friday, the security guard from City Hall invited me. I thought he was just being nice, but today I ran into him on my run. He appears to be very serious about including me, which makes me feel a little uncomfortable because I don't really know him well. But it might be a great opportunity. It's the perfect setting to casually sit down with residents, and you know, prep them for the surveys I was going to do this week. If some of them knew me already, it might pave the way for the rest."

Bernard said, "Shitbird?"

Meredith turned to him and smiled. "Yes! But I call him Emile, since I'm not from around here."

Bernard nodded. "Kalimotxos."

"Yes, they are quite good," said Meredith. "What do you say, Linda? And Bernard! Do you want to come too? I mean, I don't know if bringing two people is okay or not. I just feel a little awkward, going by myself?"

"Unfortunately, I am busy this afternoon," I said. "Bernard? Do you want to go to Shitbird's house with Meredith?" I would have loved to be Meredith's plus one, but Shitbird's wife, lovely as she was, talked too much, especially about cats. I detested cats.

Bernard nodded and said, "I can bring cat pictures."

"You're a life-saver!" said Meredith. "That was my biggest worry—Emile was very specific about that! And I have no cat pictures, unfortunately. Would you like to come by around two and we can walk over there together?"

He nodded.

She said, "Great! I'm in apartment #101. Just knock. I'm sorry to be abrupt, but I'm really thirsty, and desperately need a shower. Bernard, see you later. Linda—don't work too hard!" She jogged over to the door of her studio, and let herself in.

Bernard said to me in Euskera, "It's OK for me to go to Shitbird's house?"

"Once in a while, why not?" We tried not to socialize with Basque people, because they gossiped too much and it might blow our cover. "You'd be doing me a huge favor, too. Vern wants me to watch Meredith 24/7. She's moving really fast and I'm supposed to be there every step of the way."

He nodded. "What about Ochoa?"

I sighed. "If you go to Shitbird's with Meredith, I can deal with Ochoa. I'll have to check into the LAFD investigation, and see how much intel they have. I also need to get Meredith a new phone and new license plates for Vern."

Bernard shook his head. "LAFD is Ochoa's job."

"Not anymore, apparently."

"I can sit on him," offered Bernard.

I laughed at the image of Bernard literally sitting on little Ochoa while he squealed in pain. I said, "If necessary. He's like a mosquito. All buzz, buzz, buzz, but in the end, what can he do? He works for the same people that we do, ultimately. MFD always thinks they're somehow above it all, but they're not."

EMILE'S BBQ

As Meredith walked with Bernard to Emile's barbecue, she noticed that his droopy eyelids made him look permanently sleepy. His gait was like that of a tired hockey player who was weighed down by protective padding, exhausted from playing a game his team had just lost. She had resolved to ask him about Grillo's body, but first she tried making small talk.

"What do you like best about working with Linda?" Meredith asked.

"Trust."

"The worst?"

"Old mistakes."

"In Merritt?"

"No. Before."

"Where?"

He looked at her with a tortured expression.

"Sorry. I can be a little nosy." They walked in silence for about a block, passing several businesses devoid of signage and landscaping. The anonymous homogeneity of the buildings made Meredith feel lost, though they hadn't gone far. She had a weak inner compass and preferred to navigate using landmarks. It was a good thing that Merritt was mostly a straightforward grid, except for the flamboyant Pacific Avenue, which curved gracefully from north/south to east/west, then changed its name from Pacific to Merritt

Avenue after the curve. She had studied that street closely on a map, to make sure it didn't throw her off when she went running.

On the next block, they passed four mature bottlebrush trees lining the street in front of a wholesale business's twelve-space parking lot. Hugging the one-story building on the opposite side of the parking lot were two twelve-foot tree trunks whose branches had been lopped off, as if they'd been beheaded for daring to grow too close to the building.

A block of silence was all Meredith could take. To assuage her anxiety level, she tried again to make conversation.

"Do you have a cat?" she asked.

"No."

"But you're bringing cat photos to Emile's, right?"

"Yes."

"Can I see them?" Bernard handed her several photos. She stopped to peruse them in front of Randall Farms, which wasn't a farm but a business featuring a nondescript commercial building, asphalt, power lines, and sleeping semis. The photos did contain cats, but the cats appeared to be photobombing whatever was the real subject, though the real subject was difficult to determine. One photo featured a cinderblock retaining wall; another, a close-up of the ungraffiti'd, stuccoed side of a building; in a third, the primary subject was two commercial steel roll-up doors, closed tight and locked.

Meredith asked, "These photos—did you snap them for work? Like, for evidence?"

"Sometimes."

"For fun, too?"

"Sometimes."

"Can you tell me more about this one?" She showed him the photo of the rollup doors. A black cat's tail and back legs could be seen in the bottom right corner, mid-sprinting out of frame, as if to flee the banal subject matter.

Bernard said, "Weak spots for force calculations."

Meredith looked at him blankly. "Force calculations? Merritt's police force really goes above and beyond. Do the businesses here know just how much their city strives to protect them?"

He shrugged. Meredith felt like she was on the outside of the roll-up doors in the photo, trying to get in, and he was inside, having a cup of tea, oblivious of her efforts. Conversation usually created connections. But with Bernard, it felt like the opposite.

The normally crowded intersection of Soto and 50th was so empty, they crossed against the light. She decided to cut to the chase. "Bernard, can you tell me about that big black bag you carried out of my house last Thursday night?"

Bernard raised his eyebrows in surprise and some alarm.

Meredith persisted. "Was my husband's body in that bag?"

He nodded and then appeared to give an unusual amount of attention to the Merritt Generating Station across the street. It was a massive structure containing what appeared to be an impossible tangle of transformers, arrays, and wires.

Meredith asked, "Did you take my husband's body to the morgue?"

He shook his head.

"Where did you take him?"

Bernard rubbed his right eye with a fist and said, "Not to worry."

He said nothing else. They walked in silence for another block and with each step, Meredith got more and more uncomfortable.

Meredith tsked in frustration. She said, "It's just that, I need to take care of things and I can't really do that if I don't know where my husband's body is."

Bernard sighed and said, "Linda will help you."

She couldn't get anything else out of him. They walked in silence. Meredith always fought silence with questions. People usually liked answering them because people usually liked talking about themselves. But not Bernard. She decided to test out some citizen interview questions on him, to get a sense of his opinions about Merritt, but his answers were brief, neutral, and noncommittal.

At the barbecue, Bernard handed over some cat pictures to Jeannie, then he sat near Emile, who was minding the grill. Emile gave them each a kalimotxo. Meredith nursed it slowly. She had to be on the ball for her interview with Mayor Mendebal the next day.

Emile served little snacks he called "pintxos" (she asked him to spell it for her)—toasted baguette slices topped with cheese, tomatoes, and shrimp. He also grilled a whole sea bass that he served with lemon slices and capers, which ended up on the ground when he showed off his tray-balancing skills. Everyone laughed and drank more kalimotxos.

Meredith had hoped that at the barbecue she'd be able to get some background information on Mendebal, Peck, or anyone else in Merritt leadership, but every time Meredith tried to guide the conversation in that direction, Emile's wife Jeannie effectively steered it back to the subject of cats. Five cat photo albums in, Meredith was sure that she had seen enough cat pictures to last a lifetime, yet Jeannie seemed to have an endless supply.

"That's Shitbird's cousin's cat," said Jeannie, pointing to a piebald cat that was on its last legs. "Isn't she so beautiful? Those eyes really get me. And look how the couch, the pillows, the blankets, all the accessories match the cat! She's ready for the camera. Her name is Cream Puff. She's a rescue. Shitbird's cousin's daughter's boyfriend couldn't keep her because he was moving. It was a terrible situation, no one could take her, until finally Shitbird's cousin agreed to do it.

He doesn't even like cats, or so he thought. There she is with Shitbird's cousin in a little kitty backpack. It's amazing what you can do for a cat now. Take it camping or to the park. They even have cat leashes! Look at Shitbird's cousin's big smile."

Jeannie went on like this for two hours. Was there really that much to say about cats? Apparently, there was. Granted, the woman had just recovered from a month of not being able to speak. Jeannie's words crashed down on Meredith like water bursting through a dam. But the woman was so full of joy that it was impossible for Meredith to feel annoyed. Jeannie was really nice.

While Jeannie talked about cats, Meredith thought about how her mother always admonished her to "be nice." This didn't mean "Be joyful." Her mother would say, "Be nice," right at the moment when Meredith was about to blow a fuse. As a result, any time Meredith wanted to express a not-nice emotion, she didn't. Instead, her throat constricted, like someone was strangling her. But Jeannie? She freebased being nice, without effort.

The conversation with Meredith's mother the night before hadn't gone well.

"Why haven't you called me? It's been weeks," her mother had said.

"I'm really sorry. I had to work. I'm on assignment for the City of Merritt," said Meredith.

"Merritt? That nasty city that the Mendebals own?"

From Meredith's research, she knew that the Mendebals apparently did own about half the property in Merritt, but certainly not all of it—as far as she knew. The rest of the property titles were in the names of a mixture of corporations. It would take a lot more time and research to figure out exactly how many of these entities were tied to the Mendebals, and ultimately, it didn't matter in terms of what she had to get done. Meredith didn't have that kind of time. Maybe her mother was right. Maybe the Mendebals did own all of Merritt; but it was more likely that she was exaggerating.

Regardless, the fact that her mother, of all people, was a good source of information on Merritt surprised her so much, that she couldn't understand what Linda was signaling to her; she seemed to be trying to get her attention in various ways. Meredith felt bad that she was being such an impolite hostess. At one point she noticed Linda standing near the front door of the studio apartment after knocking on it, opening it, and slamming it closed. Maybe she was testing that the door was secure?

Her mother had continued talking, ending with, "You went to grade school with Marie, don't you remember?"

"Who?"

"Marie. You rode the bus home together."

"Oh." An incoming phone call had beeped on Meredith's phone. She dismissed it.

Her mom had continued, "That whole cheating scandal. Unbelievable."

"What?"

"You don't remember? You were both accused of cheating on homework on the bus. I didn't believe it. That wasn't how I brought you up, and anyway, you didn't need to cheat on homework. You got straight As with your eyes closed."

Marie was the girl who liked to dress up for International Day, the one who bragged often about being Basque. It had been so many years ago, Meredith had forgotten Marie's last name. None of Meredith's research on the Mendebal family and their role in Merritt politics had turned up anything on their daughter, though she had seen a brief mention about Mrs. Mendebal organizing a charity event for the Church of the Deaf, with the help of her daughter.

But the cheating scandal? Meredith did remember that well. It had happened a month or two after Meredith had skipped grades from fourth to fifth. That had been harder than she had expected. The fifth graders didn't know her, and she was painfully shy, so it felt impossible to make new friends. She'd had a solid group of friends in fourth grade, but after she skipped, she had none at all. The fourth graders regarded her as a traitor, and had stopped speaking to her. Except for Marie. She still talked to Meredith on the bus, after the others had all gotten off at the previous stops. Theirs had been the last two stops on the forty-five minute bus ride home.

Her mother continued talking about the cheating scandal, saying, "It's a good thing your father set the school principal straight."

"Yes, I remember now," Meredith had said. "It was just a misunderstanding." It was true that Meredith had done homework side by side with Marie on the bus, but they were in different grades by then. It never seemed like cheating, more like tutoring. "So, uh, what else is new? Still playing tennis?"

Her mother had said, "Seriously? 'Am I playing tennis?' You suddenly have this new job and who knows why. You had a perfectly good job at AFA Foods.'"

"They restructured."

"You lost your job and didn't tell me?"

"It happened just a few days ago."

"You weren't actually laid off, were you? I always know when you're talking slightly left of the truth. Are you going to tell me what really happened or not?"

"It was all because of pink slime," said Meredith.

"What's that?"

"You don't want to know." The call had ended abruptly when the fire alarm went off—Meredith had no choice but to hang up. The martinis and the noise of the alarm were fertilizing a growing headache, so she resolved to call her mother back when she felt better. Perhaps the next morning. She turned off her phone.

At the barbecue, Meredith was shaken out of her reverie when a passing freight train caused Jeannie to shout loudly, "I love these new photos, Bernard! They make me smile, each and every one of them. I just want to hug and kiss each little kitty. But I don't know, they all seem to be lost?" The freight train finally receded and Jeannie adjusted her volume down automatically, without missing a beat. She turned to Meredith and said, "Look at this one! So full of mischief! How do they balance like that? Like walking a tight-rope. You can see Gavina Coffee in the background. I love the coffee bean smells that drift over when the breeze is blowing just right, don't you? And here's another kitty in front of Bonne France Bakery. Looks like that kitty is hunting a mouse. Oh, I just love their danishes! I want to hug this tortoise-shell beauty. Look at those green eyes! And this little cutie is peeking out from behind a trash can. It looks a little scared." She turned to Bernhard and asked, "What do you think, Bernard, do we need to track these kitties down and make sure they have forever families?"

Bernard shrugged.

Jeannie kept going. "Gosh, the weather has been so hot this week. But at least the muggy, thick air is gone. I like dry weather myself..."

Meredith and Bernard finally took their leave. On their way back to the apartment building, the silence between them had changed. The two of them now inhabited the quiet contrails of Jeannie's chatter. Meredith was surprised to find that she didn't mind the silence. On the contrary, she found it soothing.

As they passed a series of parking lots full of semis arranged in neat rows, Meredith decided that Bernard's silence felt comfortable because he seemed to be listening, though nothing was being said. He had this innate presence. Amplifying it with speech was unnecessary. She realized that for most people, it was the opposite. Look at Jeannie. And Meredith's mother. As for herself, which category did she belong to? Meredith supposed that since she never felt fully present, neither speaking nor being silent made much difference.

After Bernard dropped her at her apartment, she watched him lumber up the stairs to the third floor, where he apparently lived. Resolving again to discover the truth about Grillo's body, she dashed up to Linda's door and knocked. No one answered.

LINDA: HEELS

On Monday morning, I met with Vern to give him a status report. During our conversation, his phone kept ringing. One after another, every city councilmember called him to complain about Meredith's phone interview appointments coming up, and they were terrified. They wanted Vern to give them an out.

After getting off the phone with one of them, Vern sighed and shook his head. "Councilman Sanders just tried to convince me that we should organize a City Council week-long retreat in Cabo—starting tomorrow! Can you believe it? The city is about to lose its charter and his solution is to have Merritt pay for a vacation in Mexico."

I shook my head. I never took vacations, because I wasn't really that interested in going anywhere. My last big trip was my escape from Spain. It killed almost all desire I may have had to see the world. Any wanderlust I still harbored was satisfied with having the best TV on the market. I liked watching *The Biggest Catch*, obstacle-course competitions, and nature programs. Once a year, I'd drive to San Pedro, park by the harbor, and watch the giant cranes load shipping containers onto flatbed train cars. Then I'd drive over and under the tangle of bridges leading to Long Beach, dip my toe in the water, and watch the seagulls. It was usually enough of an outing to tide me over for another year or so.

I explained to Vern the situation with Ochoa and the LAFD investigation. Vern said, "MFD is technically a separate entity. If they stop playing along, I cannot force them." I was surprised. I'd never seen Vern withdrawing from an opportunity to wield his influence. After all, this was what he was good at: getting people to do what he wanted, usually without them realizing it.

He thought about it some more, then said, "Requisition a new phone for Meredith, and destroy the SIM card from her old one." He pulled out a requisition form and signed it, then handed it to me.

I said, "Meredith's mother called her personal phone Saturday. It appeared to be a distraction."

"That's what mothers do. I should have given Meredith a new phone last week after she signed the contract." He shook his head, angry at himself.

I said, "There's still the issue of your license plates."

"What issue?"

"You forgot to swap them out for fake ones."

Vern juddered his hands as if he wanted to swap out the plates right then. "Shit," he said. He reached for his blood pressure pills.

I said, "This is making the LAFD case a bit more difficult to erase."

"How good is the photo evidence?"

"Partial."

Vern said, "I'll swap out the plates and make sure the paperwork is in order. What's the update on The Model?"

"Here's the new file." I handed him another thumb drive with a copy of the file that Meredith was using to build and triangulate Merritt's data.

"Did you figure out how to use it?"

"There seems to be no magic trick," I said. He appeared to crumple from within.

"I gave you one simple task—" he started to say, but I cut him off. He'd given me more than one task, and none of them were simple.

I said calmly, "You thought The Model would solve problems. This is not the way. Meredith believes she can win. She's working hard. She meets with Mendebal in—" I checked my watch. "—ten minutes."

Vern laughed. "That'll be harmless."

I nodded. Vern's phone rang again—another councilmember. He sent it to voice mail.

I said, "Gina told me that Meredith made an appointment with Peck next Monday."

"That'll be savage," said Vern. "I'd feel sorry for her, but she asked for it. All right. I'll take care of the license plates first, then I'll look at The Model. Maybe it'll make more sense than that other one. Check in with me tomorrow." He got up and I followed him out the office door.

As we left Vern's office, he walked towards the elevators. I walked in the opposite direction, to see if I could catch Meredith going into Mendebal's meeting. Even if Mendebal was harmless, Vern wanted me to stay with her as much as possible, and yesterday I had been unable to accompany her, because of Ochoa.

That afternoon, I had tried to figure out what evidence LAFD had, and how much of it I could make disappear. I had even called Ochoa to find out more, but that had gone nowhere. He was very committed to opting out of Merritt shadow work. Not only that, he had started asking for hush money. I hadn't told Vern this part, because, honestly, I didn't believe Ochoa really meant it. He was just as guilty as the rest of us, with a long history of not exactly legal acts, ones that he performed when Merritt's fire department had collaborated with the police department on some difficult cases. He was shooting himself in the arm. Or was it the foot? He was shooting his arm and his foot. I decided to give him a few days to calm down before I tried to talk sense into him. If he still wouldn't budge, I'd enlist Bernard for more extreme measures.

When I got to Mendebal's office, his admin said the meeting had already started. I decided not to interrupt, since I hadn't been invited anyway. I went back up the hall to the elevator, and as I approached Chuck Peck's office, I saw a small blond woman in extremely high heels exiting his office. She wasn't exactly walking calmly though. Someone just inside the door frame had pushed her very hard, and there was shouting. It sounded like Chuck. She stumbled a little bit, but quickly caught her balance again. It wasn't an elegant exit, and I myself would have wound up on the ground, especially in those heels. But not this lady. She adjusted her white business blouse, which was slightly crooked, and with a disgusted look on her face, said to whoever was just inside the door, "My predecessor may have gone along with this, but I—"

Chuck's louder bellicose voice overrode hers, drowning her out with expletives. Then I heard the door slam. As I walked by, the woman pretended not to see me, and I pretended I had seen nothing. Feeling like you have a shred of dignity is important when you are humiliated. Also, it was none of my business.

Peck was the overlord of Merritt's intertwined relationship with the businesses who operated there. Like conjoined Siamese twins that shared one brain, it was difficult to separate the city from these businesses without one or the other dying off completely. It was my good fortune to rarely work directly for Peck on any jobs. Peck was legendary for his tantrums, yet always acted like an obsequious servant when he interacted with anyone with more power than him. It was helpful to Merritt that I didn't work directly under Peck. Getting his balls cut off would have interfered with his deals, and my job was to protect Merritt's interests, not sabotage them. Vern, despite his recent grouchiness, was vastly preferable than Peck as a boss.

EASY PEASY

When Meredith arrived at City Hall for her appointment with Mayor Mendebal, she exchanged glances with Emile, who smiled at her weakly. He looked like he was still waking up. He processed her through the scanner without comment, and waved her on benevolently when she thanked him for having her over to his house the day before.

As she waited for the elevator, Meredith thought about how, at the barbecue, she'd failed to get some additional background information on Mendebal, Peck, or anyone else in Merritt leadership, though she now knew a great deal about the local stray cats. Still, she had won over Emile and Jeannie, and she hoped that word would quickly get around that Meredith was someone safe to speak to. This would give her an advantage when she came knocking on people's doors in the week ahead to interview them about their impressions of Merritt.

When the empty elevator arrived, she entered and pressed the button for the fourth floor. As she drifted upward, she tried to map her free-floating anxiety back to its source. She wasn't anxious about the interview with the mayor, but she was anxious about Girron. She had hoped to hear back from him by now. Maybe the tamales had been the wrong approach. If that was the case, she'd have to come up with another gambit.

She was also anxious about the impending Senate vote. She had nine days to swing opinion in the opposite direction. It was a ridiculously short time window.

As she exited the elevator on the fourth floor, she turned and watched the doors close behind her. She pretended that she'd left her anxieties back in the elevator and imagined them descending down, without her, to the ground floor. The image helped her clear her mind.

She walked down the hall to Mendebal's office suite. His admin said she could go in. When she opened the inner door to his office, he greeted her from his seat behind an enormous desk, saying, "Hello! Step right up," like he was a carnie at a rigged ring-toss booth. An older man in his late seventies, Mendebal was balding and wore thick glasses. Several liver spots dotted his forehead and pate. Framed family photos took up most of his desk space, which was otherwise clear of paperwork. There was no computer.

Mendebal put his hands on his desk and struggled to push himself up and out of his chair.

"Please don't get up on my account," said Meredith, crossing the large office to shake his hand. She introduced herself.

"Pleasure to meet you," said Mendebal, falling back into his chair. "Please make yourself comfortable. How can I help you today?"

Meredith explained her special project for Vern.

"I'm at your service," said Mendebal. "What do you want to know?"

"I'm curious as to why your grandfather chose the name 'Merritt'?"

"Great question! I wish people asked me that more often. Two reasons. My grandfather was from southern France, close to the border of Spain. When he arrived in Los Angeles, he noticed the locals' mangling of Spanish names given to various streets here. 'Loss Feeliss' instead of 'Lohs Fey-LEES' for example. 'La See-EN-egg-a' instead of 'La See-en-Eh-ga.' And so on. But the main reason was to make it more attractive to American businessmen from the Midwest and back east. These Spanish names were too exotic. That translated to 'unmeasurable.' Businessmen prefer what's known—what's measurable."

"Did his strategy work?"

"Look around—what do you think?"

"Your grandfather sounds like he was extremely savvy."

"He was. I took what he made and improved upon it. I'd love to see the next mayor improve it even more." Mendebal frowned and said almost to himself, "He won't be a Mendebal, I guess."

Meredith nodded sympathetically. She knew Mendebal was talking about his son Michael, and how he would not be Mayor of Merritt, ever. Michael had voted in Merritt's elections along with Leonata, Mendebal wife, though all three of them lived in Hancock Park. Michael's indictment had been different from Mendebal's and his wife's indictments, though. In addition to voter fraud, Michael had also been charged with far more sordid crimes.

Meredith changed the subject. She said, "I'd love to get a better understanding of your role as Merritt's mayor. Specifically, how do you work with the City Council? It wasn't clear to me how decisions and planning got done."

"Chuck takes care of all that," said Mendebal.

Meredith said, "Chuck Peck? The city manager?"

Mendebal nodded. "I attend all the council meetings, of course, if I'm in town, but Chuck handles all the details. Good man, Chuck. I've known him since we were both kids. We used to go up to my family's cabin in the Angeles Forest and hunt together. See that photo?" He gestured to a brown sepia photo of two teens with guns, straddling a dead deer. "That's us. 1946. I remember it like it was yesterday. We went our separate ways, him and I, after high school. I was in the Korean War—" He gestured to a photo on his desk depicting a younger, thinner version of himself in uniform. "Chuck got a law degree. After the war, I went to college, then I worked at a bank. The Bank of Merritt! I started out as a messenger and worked my way up. But what were we talking about?"

"Chuck Peck?"

"Yes. We ran into each other many years later at the Jonathan Club. I managed to persuade him to come work for Merritt. Things have been going great ever since."

Meredith said, "It sounds like Mr. Peck is invaluable to Merritt. I look forward to speaking to him. To clarify, are you saying that you aren't really involved with the daily operations here?"

"Of course! I'm the mayor!"

Meredith smiled. The conversation was beginning to feel a little circular. She tried another approach.

"Is this a photo of your daughter?"

"Yes," Mendebal said. "She was born here, you know."

"Really!"

"Yes, so was I."

"There's no hospital in Merritt, correct?"

"Nope."

"Were you both—delivered at home?"

"No. It's more like...were born here *in our hearts*."

Meredith cocked her head to one side. "You're saying, just to be clear, that you weren't technically born here, but you have an emotional attachment that makes you feel as if you were?"

"That's right! The truth of the heart is just as important as the actual facts. More important, sometimes."

Meredith briefly considered using this in Merritt's PR campaign—portraying the mayor as a man who governed with his heart. She was enchanted by how the same idea, applied to her own life, it might justify otherwise stupid decisions. Her friends had argued with her several times over the years, pointing out that Grillo was abusing her emotionally and that she should leave him—yet she had stayed on. Why? Because she had to be true to her heart. Measured in this way, she could perhaps escape eternal regret.

She nodded at Mendebal and said, "It's a beautiful way to look at things. I appreciate that"—even though she was fairly sure, in the end, that it was an irrational defense against voter fraud, and ultimately not a good philosophy for governing a city. "Do you mind me asking about the voter fraud charges?"

Mendebal shrugged. "Oh that. I'm not worried at all. Merritt has always been my primary residence."

Meredith said, "Are you saying that the papers aren't reporting the facts accurately?"

"They just want to sell papers."

"But you do live in Hancock Park, not Merritt, right?"

"Like most people who own several properties, I don't live all the time at one place. What's more, I hate traffic and I love Merritt, so I live in my Merritt apartment during the week. On the weekend, I might be in Hancock Park, or I might be in Huntington Beach, or I might be at the cabin."

"Huntington Beach. Isn't that where Mr. Peck lives?"

"Correct. I have a beach house there. Peck and I play golf there every other week."

"I see. But what about your wife Leonata and your son?"

"Leonata? What about her?"

"She voted in Merritt but wasn't a resident."

"Leonata spends time at all the properties we own, just like me. I don't have her on a short leash." Meredith smiled a little. She wished that her marriage had been like that. Mendebal continued, "We've been married for over fifty years."

He gestured toward a wedding photo. A beaming young Mendebal with thick dark hair embraced a small woman who peered at the camera suspiciously, as if the camera flash might somehow cause her wedding dress to disintegrate. The photograph's colors, with their deep hues and high contrast, made the couple look like they were part of a butterfly collection, with needles stuck in their backs. That's always what Meredith imagined the '50s were like. No one could move normally in tight clothes that had to be perfect.

Mendebal said, "Isn't she beautiful? I met her at a picnic, you know. A Basque picnic. She'd just arrived from France. She didn't know much English. It was love at first sight."

"That's so romantic," said Meredith. "Is it your impression that the DA doesn't have a strong case?"

"Nah, it'll blow over. There's no mischief going on. They've tried to frame us before. It's always some dummy who suddenly doesn't like how things are going. Maybe his bonus wasn't big enough. He creates a stir, gets everyone riled up. And then? Bogus charges—easily dismissed. You'll see. This will turn out fine, too."

"So in your opinion, Merritt isn't experiencing a crisis? What about the charter vote in less than two weeks?"

Mendebal shrugged and smiled. "You worry too much. I mean, it's great that you're gonna, what, help Merritt with marketing to businesses, get them to move here? That's all we really need. I wouldn't worry about the rest. In a few days, I'll play a few rounds of golf with Chuck and some friends in the State Senate. Easy peasy. You play golf?"

"No, unfortunately I don't."

"Golf is a very valuable skill. If you want to get anywhere in your life, learn how to play golf."

"I know how to play tennis. At least I did, when I was young."

"Nope. That won't work. It's gotta be golf. Look. I've been doing this a while. In election after election, the City of Merritt chose me as mayor, because they wanted me, and not some knucklehead from East Gate. Even the ex-fire chief once tried to run against me. He felt bitter that he couldn't form a union even though Merritt's firemen received the highest pay in the state. Unbelievable. He lost, of course. I've been reelected, I don't know, ten times? Something like that. I've lost count. Hey, maybe you could contact the Guinness Book of World Records? I can see the headlines now: 'Mayor sets new world record for getting reelected.' Now that would be something that sells papers. It's a lot more fun to read about than, 'Oh no, two or three people voted in Merritt elections that shouldn't have.' Give me a break!"

Meredith said, "Your positivity is infectious. I will definitely do what I can to get the papers to pivot." She had no intention of pursuing this strategy with Girron, however, because she was sure it would just create more negative coverage.

Mendebal said, "Just tell them that there's nothing but opportunity here. It's an industrial paradise! Make sure you include that in your press releases."

Meredith nodded and pretended to take down some notes.

As he put his hand on his protruding stomach, Mendebal grimaced, then said, "It's time for my morning rounds. I like to walk the hallways of City Hall every day, make sure people know who's mayor. My doctor also told me I had to do it. Doctors! Nice to meet you. Let us know if you need anything that will lead to new commercial property leases!"

LINDA: SHADOWING

As I was exiting City Hall, I saw Meredith sitting near the rock monument in front, making some notes. The monument was an oddity to me. Instead of a statue of, say, J.B. Leo, the founder of Merritt, the monument in front of City Hall was composed of three large boulders, which looked like several gonads cut from the nether parts of giants, stacked on top of each other in a precarious pile that defied physics. The boulders had something to do with the Mexican-American war, which I found amusing. I mean, if my countrymen saved boulders from every battle fought there going back millennia, we wouldn't be able to walk down the street, there would be so many boulders blocking the way. The other odd thing about it was that it didn't fit in with other monuments in Los Angeles, which usually celebrated wealthy landowners. No knights, no kings. Just white people who'd arrived here first and staked a claim.

Meredith looked up as I approached. She smiled and said, "Linda! How are you? Sorry we missed you yesterday at the barbecue. Were you able to take care of that extra work you mentioned? Too bad you had to work on a Sunday."

I smiled and said, "What did you think of the pintxos? Good, right?"

"Yes!"

I said, "Shitbird is a wonderful cook. Just don't let him near the rotisserie chicken."

"I heard about that," said Meredith, which surprised me. How he came to have his nickname was not something that Shitbird would tell just anyone. He must have really liked Meredith. Or, more likely, Meredith had a way of getting people to talk.

I pulled out the Blackberry I'd requisitioned for her from my breast pocket. "Here, have this," I said. "Vern wanted you to have a work phone. He figured you'd max out your cell plan pretty fast and Merritt should pay for it. The number is on the back."

"A Blackberry!" Meredith laughed. "I used to have a Blackberry attached to my hand at the job I had before AFA Foods. It took me forever to get the hang of the Android that AFA gave me instead," said Meredith, sliding it into her bag. "It does help to separate work from personal stuff. I have a Nokia and mostly it rings with anxious calls from my husband. Or used to ring." Meredith looked stricken. She said, "His body—Bernard said I should talk to you. Are you—"

"I myself have trouble separating work from personal life," I said. "Maybe I should get a second phone like you. It's a very good idea." I didn't mention that at the next opportunity, I would slip a dead, unrechargeable battery in her personal phone and remove the SIM card. A dead phone would protect her from unwanted LAFD inquiries. What's more, they couldn't track her using her phone's GPS.

My phone chimed with a new text from Vern, in addition to the three texts he'd already sent me. They all asked about The Model. Apparently, he still didn't understand where the magic was. Because there was no magic. I shut it off and put it in my pocket.

Meredith frowned, like she was aware that I'd deflected the question she tried to ask about the whereabouts of her husband's body, but was unsure of how to escalate. I took advantage of her hesitation and asked, "How was the interview with Mayor Mendebal? He reminds me of my father. When I see Mendebal at city events, I feel as if my father is still alive, for just a moment."

"Oh, Linda, that's so sad. I'm sorry."

"And the meeting?"

"It was a little strange," said Meredith. "He kept contradicting himself. I get the feeling he likes the idea of being mayor without actually doing the job. But what is the job, exactly? I never did learn how the various leadership roles work in concert with committees and so forth. I guess I'll try to find out more when I talk to the council members and Mr. Peck."

I tried to suppress a laugh. Meredith's assumption that the city council worked in concert with various people in leadership positions was logical, but imaginary. Over the years, Peck had taken on almost all of the active leadership roles. It all fell on Peck, and by extension, Vern's shoulders, and that was unfair. As Peck took more and more liberties with the city's finances for his own personal gain, it fell to Vern to ensure everything looked legitimate. It was no surprise that Vern had high blood pressure. As for the city council, they'd been making themselves scarce. The last council meeting had been held over two months ago, even though the Senate vote was in only nine days.

Could Meredith somehow coax Peck into telling her things? I wondered. He was the most irascible person I knew, and I've known a lot of hotheads in my life.

"Some advice about Peck," I said, "Try to find a way to make him understand that you have more power than him."

"More power? But I work for him, indirectly."

"You have power. You don't see it. If he understands that you have it, then he will be less forceful."

Meredith said, "I wasn't planning on getting into a fist-fight. I just have a few questions."

"I should not tell you how to do your work. You know a lot about the public information relations. I do not." We walked together toward the parking structure, which offered some shade. "Care to eat an early lunch with me?"

"That'd be great." We headed over to Rage Café, ordered salads, and sat down.

"What's on your schedule this afternoon?" I asked.

Meredith said, "Interviews. The Zazueta residence is first on the list. Do you know it? That yellow house around the corner?"

I nodded. "Of course. It's the only two-story single-family home in the entire city."

"Yes. Zazueta is on the City Council. She lives with her father and a teenage daughter. Zazueta works full-time at the power plant in addition to being a councilperson. I'll be speaking with her by phone on her lunch break tomorrow. But I'd like to also talk to the teenager and the father. Anyway, I figured that the first interview needs to be an easier one, you know? I'll still be finding my stride. I might as well start with a councilperson's family. They'd be more open and willing to talk. Like a rehearsal for interviewing residents a little farther away from City Hall, emotionally and physically, if you know what I mean."

I struck a thoughtful pose, and said, "Would it make sense for me to attend your interviews as well?"

"I don't know, I'm sure you have plenty to do. You had to work on a Sunday."

"Honestly? I don't like cats," I said, and winked.

Meredith laughed. "I totally understand! But I still don't see why you'd want to bother."

I said, "Do you speak Spanish?"

Meredith said, "I am nowhere near fluent, to be honest. It's terrible. I do understand more than I can speak."

"That's how Bernard is," I said. "He understands a lot more English than he can speak. Same with Spanish. He favors Euskera—the Basque language—but almost no one knows it."

"That's really interesting! It explains why he's so quiet, yet seems to be very attentive."

I nodded. "He's a good one. Anyway, I could translate, in case the person doesn't speak English."

"Around eighty percent of Merritt citizens speak Spanish as their first language, actually." Cutiecups was crazy about statistics. She paused to consider my offer, then said, "If you're sure you don't mind? That would help a lot."

"No problem," I said. I was not comfortable with carrying out Vern's order that I be involved with the citizen survey. Not only did I dislike attention of any kind, I especially disliked being ID'd by people who may have experienced collateral damage during some of the jobs I'd executed over the years on behalf of Merritt. But Vern had been very explicit when he ordered me to accompany her, and he was still my boss.

AMONA

After lunch, the two women went their separate ways to catch up on work, agreeing to meet up later, around 5:00 p.m., to interview the first batch of Merritt citizens. Although it would have been easier to survey Merritt's residents by phone, door-to-door canvasing was Meredith's preferred mode of contact. She wanted interviewees to see her face. She wanted them to see that she wasn't trying to sell anything, that she was a friendly person who only wanted their honest input. How people went about their lives as residents of Merritt was also of great interest. Everything was data. Meredith planned to fall back to phone calls or text messages only if she absolutely had to.

At the Zazueta house, Meredith and Linda walked up to the door just as a surly teenaged girl opened it, on her way out. She was dressed in black, wore a nose ring, and had plucked out her eyebrows and drawn them back on in dark eyebrow pencil.

The girl said, "What the—not you people again." She pulled out a huge cross pendant. It hung from a chain around her neck that resembled a dog's choke collar. "I'm Catholic. I will not give up my birthday, Christmas, and Halloween, just because you think Jesus was a holiday hater."

Meredith said quickly, "No, I'm sorry, there's been a misunderstanding. We're not Seventh Day Adventists. We're conducting a Merritt citizen survey. Take a look." Meredith handed the girl a flyer with the headline, "Merritt Life Improvement Project (MLIP)."

From within the house, they heard a phlegmy cough. A rasping male voice then shouted, "That's the woman Shitbird told us about. Talk to her, Lydia."

Meredith said, "Lydia Zazueta?"

"No. My name is *not* Lydia. It's Prolithia Ploth. I've changed it."

Linda raised her eyebrows but said nothing. Not missing a beat, Meredith said, "And how long have you lived in Merritt, Prolithia?"

"I was born in this shithole."

"No palabrotas, Lydia!" shouted an older male voice from the interior of the house. A coughing fit ensued.

"PROLITHIA!" Lydia shot back over her shoulder.

Turning to them, the girl rolled her eyes. This was effective because she had so much dark eye makeup on. She said, "All right. Shitbird said you'd want to know how I like living here. I wasn't born here, obviously, because there's no hospital. But I've lived here all my miserable life. It's boring. It smells. It's not dark enough at night. That's the whole story. I gotta go." Slamming the door behind her, she pushed past Meredith, but stopped short in front of Linda, who appeared immovable.

Linda crossed her arms and said, "I think you have more time to speak to the lady, yes?"

Prolithia made a sound like a frustrated horse. She stomped her foot, but said, "Fine." She turned back toward Meredith and said, "What do you want to know?"

Meredith confirmed Prolithia's age, which was fifteen. Because she wasn't a voter yet, and because her irritation made Meredith uncomfortable, Meredith asked just a few questions.

"What would make living here better for you, Prolithia?"

"Better? Having my own place. Far away."

"OK, but until you get your own place, what would make it better? A park, maybe?"

"A park? What am I, a toddler?"

"Sorry, no, of course not. Perhaps a roller rink?"

Prolithia glared. "I have no idea what you're talking about."

Meredith smiled. "I'm sorry, I can see you're in a hurry. Thanks for your time anyway."

Prolithia nodded and started walking off, but then she paused, turned back around, and said, "Something like Universal Studios would be mega. Like, if it had rides based on horror movies. *Zombieland. Friday the 13th.*" Not waiting to hear their response, she disappeared into the garage, and in another few moments, they saw her ride off on a black bicycle.

Meredith looked at Linda. They both started laughing.

Linda said, "Teenagers. They think everyone wants to—" she paused, then slammed her fist into her other palm. "Smash them. Maybe they are correct."

Meredith shrugged. "I so rarely talk to anyone under the age of thirty these days, they're like aliens." She thought about her neighbor, the boy that she'd talked to last Thursday, who was so curious about conceptual art. That brought up painful thoughts. She chastised herself: *stay in the present.* She turned to the front door and knocked again. No one answered. She made notes about Prolithia's feedback, even if it hadn't been that helpful. She'd have to return another time to speak to the coughing man.

As they walked a few blocks south to Fruitland Street, Meredith said, "You really need to tell me where my husband's body is."

Linda said, "I apologize for not telling you sooner. But now you are working. It is better to focus on the interviews. I can explain tonight. Do you agree?"

She didn't answer at first, but looked at Linda with frustration and ambivalence. Linda returned her gaze with aplomb. Meredith broke the stare-down first, then looked ahead, saying nothing. Meredith was sure that if she knew what had happened to her husband's body, she would snap out of it, but why would this make any difference? Was she actually prepared to handle the answer, whatever it was?

"All right," she said. The buoyancy of avoidance was stronger than the weight of guilt.

When they reached Fruitland Street, Meredith knocked on a couple of doors, but the occupants were either out, or didn't answer. For each house, she pulled out a flyer, crossed out her personal phone number, and wrote in the city phone number that Linda'd assigned to her Blackberry. Then she pushed it through the mail slot.

At the third house on Fruitland, a lady in her late sixties answered the door. She was about five feet tall. She peered up at Meredith with annoyance.

"I am Catholic—" the woman started saying.

"I'm not a Seventh Day Adventist," said Meredith.

"You're dressed like one."

Meredith looked down at her outfit. The lady was right. Meredith's work clothes—a white blouse with black slacks and sturdy black walking shoes, were just like the standard uniform of male Seventh Day Adventists and Mormons.

Embarrassed, she said, "You've done me a huge favor, pointing that out. I'm actually from the City of Merritt. I'm conducting a survey of all citizens to get their input on residential life here, with the aim to make various improvements."

Meredith handed the woman a flyer, who looked it over before responding, "Jeannie mentioned you'd be by."

Meredith was pleased that looking at photos of cats for two hours was already paying off. "Yes! Jeannie is so nice. Can you tell me—"

As Meredith spoke, the woman peered around Meredith and spotted Linda, who hovered a few steps away, checking her beeper, which had just gone off.

The older woman's expression soured and her eyes narrowed. She hissed, "Is it you? You were the one who—my *amona*—it was because of you!" Meredith didn't understand why the tiny woman was talking about ammonia. Was she in the middle of cleaning? She couldn't smell any ammonia. She made a mental note to run it through Google Translate later; maybe "ammonia" meant something else in another language.

When Meredith turned toward Linda, she caught Linda gesturing with her hands, as if to say, *Calm down*. Linda realized Meredith was looking at her, so she turned and walked away a few yards, to a dehydrated and asthmatic tree growing in the corner of the neighboring house's lawn. Linda's beeper went off again. Linda squinted at the code displayed on the beeper, rushed down the street, and disappeared around the corner.

Meredith heard the door shut behind her; the woman had gone back inside. Though Meredith knocked again, no one answered. Feeling a little stunned, Meredith walked back to her apartment building, just a couple of blocks away.

She logged Prolithia's interview notes into The Model and updated the records of the other houses she'd need to return to. She then pulled up Google Translate. After plugging in different languages to see if "ammonia" was a recognizable word, she failed to get anywhere, but then she tried dropping the extra "m" from "ammonia" to see if other spellings would improve the results. Google Translate liked this modification and provided a close match. Amona was the Basque word for grandmother. She pulled up the lady's name in The Model and added a note: "Speaks Basque. Angry about her grandmother, Linda involved? Follow-up."

Early the next morning, on her run, Meredith popped over to the lady's house and slipped an envelope into the mailbox. The envelope contained several items. First, there was a handwritten note that Meredith had written.

I'm so sorry I bothered you yesterday! I am an independent contractor hired by Merritt's PR department to do research. I'm conducting a survey of Merritt citizens to gather information on wellness needs, satisfaction with the local government, and anything else you feel is important to note. I believe you knew the woman with me, who accompanied me on my visit solely to help with translation, if necessary. She has no other role in this project. I hope I hear from you soon. I will ensure that your valuable input for this survey is completely private and anonymous. *My personal email address is not connected with Merritt in any way. You can tell me anything. Attached please find a signed confidentiality agreement stating that every-thing you tell me is private."*

The envelope contained the confidentiality agreement that she'd downloaded from the internet along with a flyer. On the flyer, Meredith wrote out her personal email address at Yahoo. She didn't change the phone number to the new work number. She wasn't sure why, but it felt necessary.

LINDA: POLICE CHASE

It was just a matter of time before we'd run into an awkward situation. The Ogia Onena Bakery job was the first black ops job I had to do for the city. Though it had been years ago, that woman, the granddaughter of the deceased owner of the bakery, knew me immediately. Fortunately, I was called away in the nick of time.

My pager displayed several emergency codes: code 3, code 8, code 20. My phone was still off; I'd forgotten to turn it back on after I'd cut off Vern's rapid-texting, earlier. As I ran back to my car, I turned the phone on, but I was passing through a dead cell phone reception spot. The beeper was worth carrying around for situations like this.

I got to my car and radio'd in. Dispatch said to get over to the corner of Bandini and Soto as backup for the LAPD. They were in active pursuit of a fleeing vehicle that was coming through Merritt in the next fifteen minutes, that is, if the LAPD didn't catch them first.

I wasn't overly worried, but the beeper codes were urgent enough to require immediately attention. Los Angeles high-speed police chases often ended in Merritt; the fugitives thought that in order to avoid traffic on the clogged freeways nearby, they could just take a shortcut through Merritt. They were wrong.

The Merritt police department had no druthers about setting up several obstacles that usually ended the chase, because the city had the perfect geography. It was hemmed in by the LA River on one side; several different freeways canted and blocked off its other boundaries; and together with street traffic, it all conspired to be one giant trap. With some extra effort to set smaller traps inside the bigger trap, it was no problem to take most hotheads down.

Despite the frequently televised vehicle chases that LA is known for, the fact is that the LAPD preferred pursuit of suspects by air, using their huge fleet of helicopters. Pursuit, patrol, backup: they used helicopters for almost every situation. That's why the nights were so noisy. If you had any sensitivity to sound, which I do not, you'd be an insomniac in this town. Streetside, they didn't have the manpower for the massive territory they had to patrol. It was usually a pleasure to help them out, and besides, it meant they would then help us too, when we needed it.

I met Bernard at the rendezvous. MPD officers had already diverted traffic to the side streets. Many of the side streets had no outlet, so commuters were standing around in the heat, pissed off and angry that they couldn't go home. Bernard and I helped the other officers set up spikes and tack strips.

As we waited in a strip of shade that we'd taped off for our exclusive use, ignoring the glares of overheated commuters who had to stand in the sun, Bernard said, "I miss the ramming."

Ramming, also known as the PIT maneuver, was another excellent technique to curtail a fleeing suspect's journey. You simply rammed the violator's vehicle with one of yours, preferably one fitted with a bullbar. This either functionally damaged the suspect's vehicle so that it was no longer drivable, or scared the shit out of the suspect, or both. Bernard liked ramming because it could lead to a healthy explosion, and he loved explosions, which was understandable, given his background. The MPD Chief, however, had to remove ramming from allowable procedure because one time, a suspect's car caught fire next to a chemical plant. That hadn't ended well.

I said, "These days, it's hard to have any fun. But everyone is safer."

Bernard said, "Seatbelts, car seats, helmets." He shook his head.

"I doubt the jackass they're pursuing is wearing a seatbelt, but wouldn't it be funny if he was?"

Bernard smiled. "I will take a photo." He pulled out one of the new micro cameras that fit in a pocket. He had a lot of hobbies, unlike me.

Farther down the street, officers had set up a roadblock. After a few more minutes of waiting, we saw the entourage come screaming up Soto.

The driver of the fleeing vehicle was a female, who was, in fact, wearing a seatbelt, but the passenger, a male, was not. We ducked behind a car when we saw the passenger lean out the window with an enormous silver pistol in his hand. He discharged several rounds aimed at his pursuers. The gun had an extra-long barrel. Did this guy think he was a cowboy in an old Western movie? Instead of riding a horse, he was riding shotgun in a silver Prius. Like that expression, "High Low Silver." Or something like that. I would have laughed, but that ridiculous gun had real bullets. It got a bit more serious when my colleagues returned fire. The cowboy slumped forward against the dashboard. The Prius hit the spikes, crashed into the bollard blockade, and that was the end of that. The driver, covered in blood, surrendered. Poor woman. She obeyed commands relayed to her over a loudspeaker, allowing her to exit the car without getting shot to death. Finally, she fell to her knees in the middle of the road, with her hands behind her head. Her face was covered in the gunman's blood.

Bernard didn't take a photo. He hated the sight of blood. We heard later that the gunman had forced the woman, his ex-girlfriend, to drive him to a liquor store. Then after he robbed it, he forced her into an even worse mess—fleeing the police. And now here she was, in handcuffs and covered in blood. I thought about dropping by her holding cell later to suggest she consider the knife-gonad solution in the future, but I figured she would be too distraught to comprehend good advice. I wondered why the heck she'd helped the guy in the first place. I suppose, with nothing to defend herself, she had to be nice. Being nice, especially to an ex, especially to an asshole ex, just got you jail time and a smashed-up Prius that probably wasn't totally paid off. What a ripoff.

In all the excitement, I forgot about the bakery lady and what she had said to Cutiecups. This lapse came back to haunt me later.

LINDA: PICNIC

Tuesday, August 25, 2009
Senate charter vote in 8 days

In addition to in-person interviews with citizens, Meredith had also conducted several phone interviews with city councilmembers. I had listened in on a few. I was annoyed by how they answered her questions with ellipses and bland generalities. I was impressed, though, by how quickly they warmed up to Meredith. They often became less opaque and almost genial, which was impressive.

When I wasn't eavesdropping on her calls, I researched the best way to get Ochoa to play nice again. I tried to dig up some dirt on him, but aside from his long-term committed relationship with porn, I didn't really see an angle I could use to neutralize him.

It looked like we'd have to resort to a physical intervention, which was Bernard's area. Showing up with a baseball bat in one hand and a frown on his face was often all Bernard needed to get a target to cooperate. While this method worked well on outsiders, Ochoa was on the inside. I wasn't sure whether Ochoa knew that Bernard hated violence. Merritt was a small town. Of course, we all knew each other; but *how well* was what Bernard and I sought to control as best we could by not socializing too much. I'd have to ask Bernard if he had better ideas.

That night, Meredith called me and suggested a picnic. "We could have kalimotxos and pintxos," she said. "Am I saying that right? But I don't know where we could have a picnic. There's no public park in Merritt. The Church of the Deaf has a sweet little courtyard, but I'm not sure if it's open to the public."

I didn't really feel like dining under a giant sign promoting ball bearings, myself. What's more, I'd left the Church when I was eleven. My aunt tried to force me to take my first communion, but she backed off after I cut up the frilly white dress she'd made me into tiny little pieces. Then I set fire to it. As if I'd do anything she wanted, after what my uncle had done to me.

I said, "Your accent is perfect. The elementary school is an option. They have closed for the summer. I have the keys to the playground."

We arranged our picnic in a cozy area abutting a jungle gym under a large tree—the most mature, healthy tree in all of Merritt. It provided plenty of shade. Meredith had brought a thermos of kalimotxo for us to share, along with fixings for pintxos—or rather, pintxo-like snacks. These were technically not pintxos, but I admired her imagination. She had made toast with two different kinds of toppings: peanut butter and bananas; cream cheese and smoked salmon. Capers kept falling off the salmon and rolled over the kid-friendly prefab outdoor padding upon which we'd settled ourselves.

"Dammit," said Meredith. "I should have put the capers on first, before the salmon."

"It's no problem," I said. "This is a wonderful idea. I can't remember when I last had a picnic."

"Me either," said Meredith. "Oh—I remember. I went on a picnic with Grillo at the Tar Pits after we'd gone on a tour of mimetic architecture around LA."

"What is 'me-it' architecture?" I asked.

"Sorry. I talk too fast. Mimetic architecture is when the building is shaped like the product sold by the business that owns the building. Tail o' the Pup was shaped like a giant hot dog. Raymond's Doughnuts wasn't shaped like a donut per se, but it has a giant chocolate donut with sprinkles, about fifty feet tall, straddling this tiny little shack. We also visited one of the Brown Derby locations, which was, of course, originally built in the shape of a large brown hat."

"A derby is a hat?" I asked. "I thought it had something to do with horses."

"Yes, that's true."

"English always tricks me."

"It's understandable."

I said, "I don't remember seeing a building in the shape of a hat in all the years I lived here."

Meredith had taken a bite of the peanut butter-banana pintxo. I watched her as she tried to get the peanut butter unstuck from the roof of her mouth. She looked like a little kid. The peaceful playground made me feel a little bit like a child myself. It was a nice feeling.

I gave Meredith the thermos so she could wash down the peanut butter with some kalimotxo. I had already noticed that unexpectedly, they tasted great together.

She said, "Developers built a two-story shopping center around the dome of the Brown Derby—the main part forming the hat—in the '80s, and painted it pink. It looks like an alien's egg, surrounded with a tacky tangle of stucco and steel, like a giant nest. It's terrible."

She looked sad. I doubted it was because of ugly architecture. More likely it was because she was thinking about her dead husband. I tried to distract her.

"Is there actually tar at the Tar Pits? You know, where you went on your other picnic?" I asked.

"Yes," she said, brightening. "We had to watch our step, and we avoided sitting on the grass. We sat at picnic tables instead. I remember poking an oozing black puddle of tar in the grass with a stick. It smelled bad. I think it causes cancer? There's methane explosions sometimes, too, over in that area. LA is such a weird place."

"It is not for the unconscious of heart."

Meredith looked confused.

"What is the expression about not having courage?" I asked with humility.

"Oh! It's not for the faint of heart!" She laughed. It didn't feel like she was laughing at me. At least I hoped she wasn't.

She said, "Your take on English expressions is often so poetic. Don't ever feel embarrassed. It's like you've rescued them from banality."

I looked blankly at her.

She explained, "It's like you've made them fresh again. They've been reborn."

She smiled at me. I smiled back. I blinked. I wanted to bathe in her smile and let it wash off all the dirt of my hopeless cynicism.

Meredith gasped and said, "What if Merritt was mimetical?"

"Merritt?" I asked.

"They make all the things, right? Scissors. Tape. Party favors. Hamburgers. Hot dogs."

I said, "Leather jackets. Lingerie. Couches. Paper cups. Lipstick. Toys."

"Cheese. Cigars. Rivets. Ball bearings."

I said, "Medical waste processing. Slaughterhouses. Rendering."

"Maybe not *every* business here is appropriate for my idea, but yes! It would be a great way to make the city more family-friendly. Remember Prolithia Ploth?"

"Lydia?"

"Yes. Remember how she wished there was a Universal Studios here—but for horror movies?"

I frowned with distaste. "I disapprove of those movies. If people only knew what real horror looked like."

"Agreed. But remodeling some buildings to use mimetic architecture would not only be family-friendly, it would also emphasize Merritt's rich traditions."

"Merritt has traditions?" This was new to me. Did I somehow miss the folk dancing festivals in the last twenty years?

"I mean like the Bandini manure mountain."

I felt lost yet again. I took a swig of the kalimotxo to cover up my bafflement.

She said, "The Bandini manure mountain existed when I was a kid—before you moved here. It was located at Bandini Fertilizer—where the Exodus Battery Plant is now."

"The superfund site?"

"Yes. I watched a lot of TV when I was a kid. Sitcoms. I thought they could tell me something about how to live. Ridiculous idea. Anyway, the local TV commercials were often more entertaining than the shows they sponsored. The Bandini commercial was the most versatile. Actors posed as athletes who surfed, skied, or hiked a 100-foot mountain of fertilizer. 'Bandini Mountain,' they called it, or 'BM' for short."

"Did this mountain actually exist?" I asked.

"Yes. We had to close our car windows when we passed it on the 710, on the way to see my grandmother. Because of the smell..."

"It sounds like a bad job."

"What?"

"The actors who come to Hollywood to be famous, and this is where they end up. With elbows in manure." It reminded me of the eleven hours Bernard and I spent buried in manure during our road trip across Mexico. How strange it was that manure kept cropping up in my life.

Meredith said, "I never thought of it that way." She looked up and tried to stare down a crow perched overhead in the tree, complaining in a manner difficult to ignore, but it wasn't deterred. She gave up. She drank from the thermos and passed it back to me. She said, "I still remember the jingles and gimmicks from the other local commercials, like the ones for Pete Ellis Dodge, or Cal Worthington."

"Let's hear."

Meredith started singing the jingles perfectly, like a catechism. In one, repeated driving directions to a car dealership in East Los Angeles dominated the lyrics for eight measures of melody. The crow stopped shrieking and listened. When she was done, I clapped energetically.

"You have a beautiful voice," I said.

"I always wanted to learn how to sing. I just never got around to learning."

"You must put it on your wish list," I said.

Meredith smiled. "Do you mean 'bucket list'?"

"Yes. That's right." I changed the subject. "This mimetic architecture tourism idea is exciting. Do you really think it could work?"

"It could spawn an entirely new revenue stream. The mayor would like that! We could bring back the Bandini Mountain, maybe. Though I think we'd have to figure out how to do it safely. On windy days, the manure blew everywhere."

Meredith looked thoughtful. The crow started screeching again, but she didn't seem to notice. She said, "We could create a Map of the Makers, like the Map of the Stars that they used to sell on Sunset Boulevard across town, in Beverly Hills. I always wanted one of those maps, but my mother never stopped to buy one." She pulled out her notebook and started writing notes.

I said, "Did you know that two doors down from this school is a fireworks business? I wonder how they will change such a building into fireworks?" I thought about how happy such a structure would make Bernard.

Meredith wasn't listening. She was very focused on her idea, which was very creative, though I had some doubts. Businesses in Merritt didn't like too much attention. They wanted what Merritt wanted: to be left alone in order to focus on one goal: profit. Sweat, widgets, and punchcards. Swing shift, graveyard shift. I was grateful I'd avoided that kind of job, even though I hadn't prospered due to my own bad choices and some bad luck.

She said as she closed her notebook, "I need to gather business leaders in a meeting of some kind, as soon as I can, and get them on board. Then that would motivate City Hall to approve it. I don't suppose you have a chamber of commerce, do you?"

"No, but I can easily put a list together. We're familiar with all of them. In regular contact, for various reasons."

"There's so much to do! It could be a great solution... Thank you, Linda! You're so inspiring."

No one had ever said that about me. I blushed. It was probably the second time I've blushed in my life. The first time was last Saturday, when Meredith had leaned down to pick up something and her shirt fell open, allowing me a glimpse of the twin treasures within. What was happening to me?

THROWING KNIVES

The next evening, Linda and Meredith met up again, this time over martinis. The distraction of work wore thin at night because by then, Meredith was exhausted. But not working meant her responsibilities regarding Grillo's death should therefore be at the forefront of her mind. Drinking and chatting with Linda prevented the seams of her avoidance from becoming unravelled.

"I can't believe how easy it's been to access citizens for this survey," Meredith said, bringing a third set of martinis in coffee cups to the kitchen table, even though Linda hadn't yet finished her second one. "And I know that drinking martinis mid-week isn't exactly professional, but tomorrow is Thursday. It's a good thing there's only ten interviews left."

Linda sipped her martini daintily, like it was a cup of hot tea. She said, "It's true. It isn't possible to be outside on a Thursday, in Merritt, at least for most people. The stink doesn't really bother me, though."

"The forecast says the Santa Ana Winds will be blowing all day, though. By 6:00 p.m., my guess is that any remaining stink will be gone by then. 6:00 p.m. is the perfect time to catch people at home."

Linda popped an olive into her mouth, crunched it, then washed it down with the rest of her martini. Meredith's third martini was already half-gone. This was unlike her, to drink so fast. It reminded her of her cat back in Atwater Village. The cat had been attacked by the dog down the street; afterward, it arrived at Meredith's house, drank all the water in its bowl in one go, then took a nap under the car.

Linda said, "Let's go throw knives. I know a decent spot a few blocks away, by the LA River."

Meredith considered Linda's cryptic offer. She said, "Throwing knives in a river. Might be tough to keep afloat."

Linda said, "Near the very top of the cement foundation for the river, there are a few small trees. Also a wood power line pole. Decommissioned. I like to use it for target practice. The pole was inaccessible until recently, because of a homeless camp. MPD cleared and sanitized the area last week. Let's go."

The sun was setting as they walked to the river. The weakening light that smog filtered into a golden glow made Merritt look almost celestial. Celestially industrial. They picked their way through some scraggly underbrush to a chain-link fence. The fence had already been neatly breached with a wire cutter. Linda led Meredith through, making sure her clothes didn't get snagged. They crossed the train tracks and hiked up an embankment. There, Linda found a second break in another chain-link fence, and after crossing through it, they found themselves looking down the steep, graded cement banks of the LA River. The embankment they stood upon was at least thirty feet above the bottom. The cement channel was designed for giant flash floods that might quadruple the river level, though this rarely happened. The river was almost totally dry, with a skinny strip of green brackish water at the center of the giant channel, which still retained the heat of the late afternoon, though evening was falling quickly, and with it, the temperature.

"The glorified storm drain known as the LA River," said Meredith.

Linda unsheathed her knife and showed it to Meredith, who could barely make it out in the gathering gloom. The moon was full but hadn't hit its apex yet. It did offer some light, but Meredith doubted it was enough to conduct target practice, of all things. But she didn't really care, either. The martinis were circulating in her bloodstream. She felt relaxed and playful.

Linda said, "My uncle taught me how to skin squirrels with a knife like this one. Squirrels. He roasted them with salt and parsley." She turned and threw the knife into the darkness. A faint thunk indicated a direct hit.

Meredith giggled. "Wow! You hit that tree twenty feet away in the dark! Wait. What were you saying about squirrels? Your uncle eats squirrels? That seems wrong, like eating Bambi. Does it taste like chicken?"

Linda eased the knife out of the trunk of the tree and walked back toward Meredith. "Sort of," she said. "He doesn't eat squirrels anymore—he's dead."

"I'm so sorry!"

"I'm not. Squirrel tastes bad. Like thick string. I didn't go near it because I hated my uncle. He later got the disease from eating too many. Like the cows."

"Mad Cow's Disease?"

"That's it. The Disease of Mad Squirrels. My uncle loved to eat the thing that killed him."

"It's like cats and mice," said Meredith.

"How?"

"Toxiplasmosis."

"What is this?"

Meredith explained, "It's a virus that the mouse gets. Humans can get it too, if you're exposed to cat feces. For the infected mouse, though, instead of running away from the cat, it runs toward it. It has an urge; it can't stop itself even though it means certain death."

"The mouse falls in love with the cat," said Linda.

"Yeah. The mouse acts like it's hypnotized."

"Interesting."

Meredith watched Linda demonstrate throwing the knife a few more times. Then Linda turned to Meredith. "Your turn."

"Oh, I don't think…"

"Yes. You hold the knife like this," said Linda, and she held up the knife showing Meredith how to grip it. In the darkness it looked like the knife was an extension of Linda's arm. "Then you just need to throw it with a loose wrist. Be flexible. But also have the control to know when to let go—"

"How do you know when to do that?"

"It's a feeling. You'll know, if you keep doing it." said Linda. Meredith tried throwing the knife at the tree but it failed to catch and fell to the ground. Linda walked over to the tree and rooted around in the weeds until she found it. Walking back toward Meredith, she asked, "What happens to the mouse?"

"The mouse?" said Meredith.

"When it runs toward the cat."

"Oh. The cat eats it, I guess."

"Here. Try holding it like this," said Linda. She placed the knife in Meredith's hand, then cupping Meredith's hand in her own, Linda flexed it back towards her wrist. She moved behind Meredith and reached around her left side with her other hand. Slowly with both hands, like she was spotting a gymnast, she mimed the action Meredith needed to take, showing when to release the knife for optimal effect. Meredith could feel the heat of Linda's body against hers and the curve of her fairly large bosom, which felt strangely exciting. Her mother never stood behind her like that, and didn't have a large bosom. Her mother used that word though: "bosom." You'd never hear her say "tits" or "breasts." "Bosom" reminded her of those carved wooden ladies decorating the prow of a pirate's ship, their heads and *bosoms* on display, cut in half at the waist, their lower torso and legs replaced with the prow of the ship. Figureheads.

She was getting goosebumps. The night air was becoming chilly.

"It would be nice for once," said Meredith, "To be the cat, not the mouse. How did the disease affect your uncle?"

"His brain turned to mush."

"I'm so sorry."

"I'm not. It was the end of my life as a mouse and the best thing that ever happened to me, until now."

Linda pulled Meredith's knife-holding hand across her body, turning Meredith so they were face to face.

"Until now?" said Meredith.

"Until now," said Linda. She took the knife from Meredith and threw it backward over her shoulder, where it planted itself firmly in the power pole. Linda cupped Meredith's chin in her hand. Her fierceness had disappeared; her large brown eyes looked mournful and innocent.

Meredith felt like she was in a trance. Linda's small fingers felt calloused and rough, so different from Grillo's soft hands and long tapering fingers. Linda said quietly, "Can I?"

Meredith didn't know what she meant, but she nodded anyway. Linda leaned in to kiss her. At that moment Meredith knew what the hypnotized mouse might have felt like— not bad at all.

The next morning, Meredith pulled out her Nokia to check her personal email. It was a tiny, awkward little screen to use for reading email, but she liked that it was physically separate from her laptop, which contained everything related to work.

The phone was dead. She plugged it in and waited for it to charge while she picked up the apartment and washed some dishes. Somewhere floating around in the back of her mind was the memory of Linda's kiss down by the LA River the night before. It was the part of her brain she used to file anything that didn't pertain to work, because she functioned better that way. Sometimes, like now, that kiss floated out of the deep freeze area of her brain locker to the surface of her consciousness and defrosted there, causing her to have to deal with it or insist that it return to sub-zero conditions again, where it shared cold comfort with Grillo's death, and all the other things she didn't want to examine for fear she would disintegrate into a puddle of confused guilt. Her brain was unreliable. She wished she could handle these uncomfortable thoughts and feelings with the same swift dispatch she brought to handling business emails.

She again tried to turn on the phone, to no avail. She finally accepted that she'd need to use her laptop.

As Meredith logged in and then went through Yahoo's hoops of approvals and offers, she thought about how nice Linda was. Very nice, but...all that attention, Linda's *very kind* attention, made Meredith a little uncomfortable. She was used to being invisible, and when visible, to be found lacking. And then there was that *kiss*. She found it thrilling, but she'd drank too much. It felt unreal, like she'd dreamt it. She resolved to skip the martinis for the immediate future.

There were three messages from her mother that she didn't read, and another one from an email address she didn't recognize, with "be careful" as the subject. Meredith opened it. The message said:

Dear Mrs. James,

My daughter wrote this for me because I don't understand the computer. My family's bakery, Ogia Onena, was our only source of income. Then twenty years ago, I found my grandmother lying unconscious in a pool of blood on the floor of the bakery. I could see she'd hit her head. There was so much blood. I couldn't revive her.

Yesterday when we spoke, I saw a police officer standing a few feet behind you. I recognized her. After my grandmother's death, I gave that police officer evidence that proved the death was not an accident. The officer never returned my phone calls. When I went in person to complain, the police told me it had been ruled an accident and the case was closed.

My grandmother was the only one in our family who knew the secret recipe for our bakery's famous sourdough bread, and it was lost with her death. We were forced to close the bakery. I'm telling you this in strict confidentiality. Be careful.

LINDA: SOURDOUGH

I was grateful that Cutiecups hadn't asked me about the woman who, during her interview, had become distraught after she'd caught sight of me.

I remembered that bakery job like it was yesterday. It was a job that I'd executed successfully, though it had turned out to be an untidy affair. I still felt some regret, though generally I don't believe in regret. Because what could you do about the past? Not much. What was done was done.

I tried not to think about the Ogia Onena Bakery fiasco like I tried not to think about Barcelona: the end was an unwanted outcome that I couldn't prevent, although I was, admittedly, the cause.

I'd hoped that Meredith had forgotten about it, but the morning after we conducted target practice with knives and lips, she brought it up. I had made her some coffee and some toast. When we settled down to eat, she was very quiet. I figured she was hungover, so I let her wake up in peace. I drank my coffee. I ate my toast.

I asked her to show me how The Model worked. I figured it was the least I could do for Vern. Peck was still pressuring him, insisting that The Model was the magic cure for all of Merritt's problems. Calmly and professionally, Cutiecups showed me the endless columns and categories, as well as their significance. Every single Merritt citizen was documented. She updated a few records, and added notes. Meticulous, detailed work. I didn't understand what she would do with the results when she was done, but before I could ask her, she pulled up the bakery lady's record and switch her status from "follow up" to "closed." Meredith pointed to the entry and said, "Linda, this lady said she knew you."

Perhaps too quickly, I said, "Everyone knows everyone else, a little bit, in this town. It's small."

"She said you were the lead on an investigation into her grandmother's death, but it never went anywhere." With all my careful monitoring of her computer movements, I had failed to notice this exchange. I had slept in.

"When was this?" I asked.

"The investigation? Like, twenty years ago?"

I said, "I've been involved with a lot of investigations in the last twenty years." Technically, that was the truth.

Meredith said, "During the investigation, the woman said she'd pointed out damning evidence to you personally, evidence indicating that her grandmother was murdered. She could never get ahold of you, there were no arrests, nothing. No one on the police force would help her!"

"How strange," I said. I wondered if I could improvise at the same time as not lying. I didn't want to lie to Cutiecups anymore. It felt wrong. After a pause, I said, "The Merritt Police Department was incompetent when I joined. Let me try to remember." I closed my eyes to buy myself time. I opened them. There she was before me, waiting patiently, wanting very much to believe whatever I told her. Little frown marks had formed between her delicate eyebrows. I brightened as if I had suddenly remembered something.

I said, "I shared a desk with Bernard. It was before the new City Hall was built and we worked in a very small office. Reception usually left my messages somewhere on my messy desk. I don't like paperwork. Perhaps Bernard spilled coffee, threw the message out by mistake. It wouldn't have been the first time. He's kind of clumsy." I felt terrible about throwing blame on Bernard. He wasn't clumsy. He was extremely dexterous, which was critical for making bombs. He was also a dexterous knitter. His stitches were always even and regular. No mistakes. One time he tried to show me how to knit, but the result was a ragged clump of yarn, gnarled and ugly. I called it "My Soul."

Meredith wasn't satisfied with the weak excuse I'd made. She said, "The woman said she left you many messages—not just one."

"I don't know what to tell you," I said. This was the truth.

Meredith looked askance at me and wrinkled her brow in this cute, pensive way that made her prettier, if that was possible. She said, "It seems weird that Vern would ignore something big like a dysfunctional police department, especially since he's the public liaison."

"Vern didn't work for Merritt yet. My boss was this guy named Jerry."

"Really?" said Meredith.

I nodded. "Jerry was the mayor's second cousin. He was in charge of handling 'difficult situations.' But in reality, he used city resources for personal projects, which then created the difficult situations." I added, "Later, he died of an overdose."

"Oh my God!"

"They hired Vern at that time," I said.

Meredith's laptop dinged at her. She opened up the email notification.

"Wow!" she said. "Gil Girron just emailed me!"

"What wonderful news," I said, silently grateful for the distraction.

Girron had agreed to a phone call appointment. While Meredith was composing her reply and nattering on about tamales and the personal touch, I poured myself more coffee and thought about that first job I had to do for Jerry.

Cousin Jerry had lost a substantial sum in a high-stakes poker game with the owners of a commercial bakery named Stagecoach, whom he'd met at a Basque get-together.

As usual, Jerry didn't have the cash to settle his debt. Jerry suggested that to make things right, he could help take down Stagecoach's number-one competitor in sourdough bread: Ogia Onena Bakery, which was conveniently based in Merritt. Jerry assigned the problem to me.

I cased the bakery for a few days. From the second-story fire escape of the building opposite, I had a clear view of the bakery kitchen. At the early hour of 3:00 a.m., I observed through binoculars the entire process of Ogia Onena's sourdough bread production. First, an older female and her staff mixed and kneaded the day's batch of sourdough dough. After placing the dough balls in individual baskets, they then put the baskets on a high shelf where the dough was left to rise.

All this was a bit weird for a commercial bakery, but then it got even stranger. The old lady dismissed everyone for a couple of hours. After they left, I could see her going up and down that ladder every fifteen minutes, checking the dough's progress, adjusting the thermostat of the kitchen's heating unit.

She was a control freak, if you ask me. Sure, sourdough needed a very narrow temperature range to rise properly, but this was ridiculous. I knew of several bakeries in Merritt whose commercial proofing ovens worked great. I knew, because I'd toured their facilities. Merritt leadership assisted many businesses operating here with passing state and county safety inspections. In return, these same businesses made large donations to the Merritt General Fund, in cash. Some of the business owners thought it prudent to pretend I was touring the facility, to make my visit look legitimate.

The point is, I knew my way around a commercial bakery. But this bakery was different. Her process was so old-fashioned, it broke practically every food safety rule in the book.

After I was done casing the place, doing the job was easy. During one of the amona's bathroom breaks, I snuck in and substituted a ball of concrete in place of a dough ball in one of the baskets. Fifteen minutes later, I watched again through binoculars as she returned from the bathroom, went up the ladder, and checked the dough. She could immediately see that something was wrong with one of the baskets. She reached to pick up the basket to get a closer look, but its unexpected weight threw her off balance, which caused her to fall off the ladder and crack her head open on the edge of a sink.

I didn't expect my sabotage to cause her death, I just wanted to put her out of commission for long enough so that Ogia Onena couldn't satisfy open orders, and supermarkets would start buying more Stagecoach bread instead.

As it happened, because no one else at Ogia Onena knew the secret recipe, it died with the amona. It was unfortunate. This paranoid attitude towards baking is a classic quirk of the Basque. There are so many secret family recipes back home. I'm sure if they were compared side-by-side, they'd be almost identical. In the case of sourdough bread, however, maybe it does matter how you make it, because after her death, the bakery tried other recipes, but they were never able to recover their lost customers. They closed shop.

Jerry was thrilled. I found the whole affair completely depressing. I consoled myself that it was a job done more throughly than planned. It had, after all, been an accident. That at least was true.

The lady who had slammed the door in Meredith's face had been the same person who had reported the incident to the Merritt police department. She had found her dead amona and also the incriminating ball of concrete.

I was first on the scene before other detectives arrived, to take photos and gather forensic evidence. Naturally, I was first on the scene—I had never left the scene. I watched from an unmarked car, a safe distance away from the bakery, as the lady dialed 911. Then I counted to thirty, put the siren on the roof of my car, and hauled ass to the front door. The lady immediately showed me the ball of concrete as proof her amona had been murdered. I nodded sagely and bagged it up as evidence, labeling it carefully and using surgical gloves, to make a good impression. I kept it safe while the other officers taped off the area, took photos, and bagged more evidence. Later, I threw the cement ball into the dumpster behind my apartment complex.

After a few days, the lady called the Merritt police department to ask about the status of the case. They had no idea why she was ranting about murder. They didn't have anything checked into evidence resembling a ball of concrete. When the woman tried to escalate her complaint to the chief, she mentioned my name and badge number. The chief knew immediately that this was a "special ops" job. He then notified Cousin Jerry, who told Bernard to keep her quiet.

I was surprised that the lady had been willing to talk to Meredith at all. Back then, Bernard's outsize girth and serious expression had thoroughly subdued her, in that special way he has with people who need to be subdued. He'd sweetened things by also guaranteeing her rent would be controlled at the 1991 rate for as long as she stayed there. That's probably why she was still living in Merritt. It was just about the only perk we could offer people who actually lived in Merritt, when we needed their cooperation without resorting to physical methods.

When the lady spotted me behind Meredith, her angry expression made it clear that a twenty-year-old injustice was as fresh as if it had happened yesterday. Typical Basque. They never let go.

In all these years, I'd managed to avoid the woman, because I kept to myself, and because she'd never reported another incident or needed MPD detectives for anything. Until the citizen interviews this week, I had maintained a pretty good cover, considering. Not anymore.

SPECIAL K

Late in the afternoon, Meredith and Linda visited the last ten citizens in order to complete the city-wide survey. They were relieved that the Santa Anas had blown most of Merritt's Thursday odors out to the ocean. Not one person who answered the door was suspicious or surprised to see them. In fact, at one residence, the occupant asked them what had taken them so long to show up. Apparently when Jeannie and Shitbird had news to share, it traveled fast.

Despite their overall enthusiasm, two of the interviewees had acted oddly. Meredith had tried to go along with the idea that the bakery lady might have been an outlier, but now it seemed like a trend. It didn't sit right.

At one bungalow, a man had answered the door. He was a dead ringer for The Dude from *The Big Lebowski* if The Dude had been Latino. He greeted Meredith cheerfully, noticed Linda and said, "Hey! I didn't expect you until next week. I'm good for now. Unless you have some Special K?" He looked hopeful.

Meredith turned to Linda with one eyebrow raised. Linda shook her head. "That's not available. Ms. James would like to ask you some questions."

Meredith explained the survey and wrote down The Dude's feedback about living in Merritt.

His responses were glowing and disjointed: "Great! I love it!" "Five out of five!" "What's a little odor now and then? I personally don't smell like a rose myself, most of the time!" "The lead in the soil is a bummer, but I used to make mud pies when I was a kid growing up just a hop, skip and a jump from the harbor, and I'm sure whatever brains I was born with were turned to mush long before I moved here! Did you know there's a giant DDT repository buried in the ocean just off the coast there? Yeah, I probably got all kinds of stuff in my system that can't be good!" "Are those Nike 990s? I got plantar fascitis and it's killing me but I would love to start running again! I'm a size 9 too, can I try them on?" "Oh right, women's and men's sizes don't correspond. Crazy! My bad."

And so on. Meredith extricated herself. Linda followed her down the path.

"Special K?" asked Meredith, as they starting walking back to their apartment complex. It was early evening. They passed the gates of a dark commercial building, whose gloom stood out in Merritt's brightly lit nighttime environs. Beyond the gate, a security robot rolled silently by on the other side. Meredith had read about the new security robots in the food trade publications she had subscribed to at AFA Foods. Robot security guards could record video using infrared; lights were unnecessary.

"Did you see that white object on wheels?" said Linda after they passed the gate.

"I saw it. Security robot. Don't change the subject. Why did that guy ask you about Special K?"

"Ah...he was just talking about cereal."

"Cereal."

"He has colitis. He used to be with MPD but had to go on disability."

"They have you buying this guy cereal in addition to performing your duties as a police detective?" Linda didn't answer. Meredith sighed. She waited for a stoplight to turn green, then said, "I'm sorry, Linda. I really want to believe you but I don't think I can."

Linda looked down at her shoes. She put her hands in her pockets. She looked away, then back at Meredith, squaring her shoulders. "You're right," she said. "It's not cereal. He referred to the other Special K. Ketamine. But I don't give him ketamine because it's very addictive, as you may know."

Meredith just stared at her blankly, then said, "I know nothing about ketamine."

Linda looked at Meredith seriously. "I so admire your ethics and integrity, Meredith. But please don't ask me to explain too much. From now on, I want to tell you the truth. I don't think—I don't think it was ever as important as it is now."

Meredith looked at her, perplexed. How do you base telling the truth on the kinds of questions someone asks you? As if the context could constrain the truth? That didn't sound truthful. But the way Linda looked at her was undoubtedly genuine. More than genuine. It was like Linda couldn't live with the idea that Meredith might think badly of her.

It was so odd how Linda could flip the switch on her demeanor just like that, as if Meredith had unwittingly carved a tunnel past the layers of brusque no-nonsense cynicism to the vulnerability that it shielded. Linda reminded her of a scallop. Scallops had eyes all along the edge of their shell, watching in all different directions. Linda's scallop shell was usually closed tight but whenever she looked at Meredith it was like all one hundred scallop eyes closed at once and the shell opened. And inside was the softness. It made Meredith feel calm and blendy. She was touched by the transformation. Grillo never seemed to change, regardless of Meredith's presence, or lack thereof. Meredith never felt like she herself was capable of change, for that matter. But Linda? Linda was different.

"I think you should tell me anyway," said Meredith softly. "If I'm going to straighten out Merritt's reputation, I need to know what else Girron might use against Merritt in his ongoing reporting. You know, get out in front of it. Right?"

"Yes," Linda said, scratching her ear and looking uncomfortable. "That man does have colitis. I provided him with marijuana, for the pain and for digestion. I helped him for many years while it was illegal. But now it's legal. He can buy it himself, but he forgets."

"That's from the marijuana too," said Meredith. "That's one thing I do know about. Grillo used to smoke several joints a day, but when his asthma became more severe, he had to start taking medical marijuana pills, instead. He'd forget a lot of stuff, but always remembered the things that he thought people were doing to him...anyway. What about that other citizen we met four door-knocks ago? The short guy with the mole on his chin. Benitez. He said, 'You promised that if I did what you said, my family would be safe and I'd never have to see you again.'"

"Flu shot, definitely," Linda said too quickly. "But then one of them reacted and got sick. You can't have a flu shot if you're allergic to eggs."

"Linda," said Meredith. "Try again."

"I need more practice..."

Meredith waited and said nothing.

Linda cleared her throat and said, "That was the former fire chief. He ran for mayor against Mendebal many years ago. I really don't know the specific source of his paranoia. Really. You could ask Vern. I don't do everything 'special' around here. Bernard helps out too. That's the truth. Whatever happened, in the end, he withdrew his bid and Mendebal ran unopposed, as per usual."

Meredith shook her head. They had arrived at their apartment complex. "Maybe I will ask Vern. I just might do that," she said, as she walked up to the door of her apartment. She didn't linger. She had a ton of work to do to get ready for her call with Girron the next morning.

Nothing was ever clean or simple, that's why companies hired PR people to begin with. PR was intended not only to help clients communicate with their target audience, which in Merritt's case was really the California State Senate who planned to revoke its charter, but PR was also intended to help get clients back in touch with their own mission. Communicating that mission to their target audience was then much easier to do.

Meredith didn't know why this was always the most difficult part: getting stakeholders to recommit to their mission statement. It was the first thing you needed to do if you were going to make amends for a mistake. Everyone made mistakes, but the longer they remained unchecked, the worse they got. She saw that at AFA Foods. She'd seen it throughout her career, all the way back to her very first job after college when she'd worked for a nationwide PR agency who handled a food company that sold canned beans. They were famous for their refried beans in particular, which contained lard, but the lard was clogging up people's arteries and causing heart attacks. Meredith helped focus consumer attention on their line of vegetarian refried beans, which didn't contain lard, with the ultimate goal of improving their image and disconnecting their company's name from any immediate associations with death.

It was supposedly much more stressful to work at a PR agency than it was to be in-house PR, but she couldn't really tell the difference. Looking back over her career, she guessed it was because she was such a workaholic. At any rate, successful PR always came down to the client understanding themselves first. And that, for some reason, was the hardest thing of all to accomplish. She should really dig out her New Client Questionnaire that she had developed when she worked at the PR agency. She'd had the plumbing distributor fill it out in her first month of employment with them, enabling her to match initiatives and campaigns to their needs, and helping them to understand why it was important. Then, at AFA Foods, they ignored the questionnaire. God forbid they should step back and really look at what the whole point of AFA Foods was, besides making a profit.

She berated herself for forgetting about initial screening procedures for new clients. It was because of Grillo's death. She needed to shake herself out of her fog. She made a note to find the New Client Questionnaire and work with Vern on it at their next meeting. It was a little backwards, to do the questionnaire after she had already established a crisis plan for Merritt, thought up a PR campaign to turn around their reputation, and had even gotten Girron to engage, but better late than never.

PIE CHARTS

After running macros in The Model and compiling results, Meredith stayed up late to crunch data. She created pie charts and timelines, trends and forecasts, and added them to a ten-page PowerPoint presentation. Even though Friday's call with Girron would be nothing more than an informal introduction, she wanted to be ready.

The next morning, Meredith called Girron at the appointed time.

He answered tersely, "Gil Girron."

"Hi there! It's Meredith James. Is now a good time to talk?" They had agreed on the time in advance, but Meredith always led with this question.

Girron said, "Yeah, now's good. Thanks again for the tamales. That's my favorite place."

"Mine too! What's your favorite filling?" Meredith asked, even though she already knew the answer.

"I favor the queso over the pork, without question. it's probably because I love the combo of masa and gooey cheese. With that little spark from the green chile? Yeah. Those were gone pretty fast. I had to put them in a lock box in the fridge here at the *Times* just to make sure no one raided them."

"Really?" said Meredith.

"Nah, just kidding."

"Oh! Haha!"

Girron said, "So what did you want to talk about? I know this has to do with Merritt based on your note. I'm not actively pursuing leads on stories having to do with Merritt these days. Maybe after the Senate revokes their charter, I'll write up something about it."

"That's not a sure thing though!"

"...Oh really." She heard muffled snickering.

Meredith's voice went a little higher and she spoke faster than normal, if that was possible. "I have some new data gathered that I thought might be worth bringing to the public in the interest of, you know, balanced reporting. Your articles were amazing, by the way—I found out so much I didn't know about. It's so important to make information available when it isn't absolutely transparent. I have no intention of interfering with your investigative reporting, but—"

"You're doing PR for Merritt, correct?"

Meredith said, "I'm an independent contractor. I have a lot of autonomy. But yes, that's correct. The city spokesperson asked for my help in improving Merritt's image. Transparency is part of their goal, because it might help them keep their charter—"

"That's what Vern Page told you?"

"Yes, that's right. How about those preppy plaid pants—crazy, right?"

Girron said, "Never met him in person."

"Oh."

"Vern didn't strike me as someone striving toward transparency." Girron sounded detached yet curious, like he was dissecting a frog and explaining where the kidneys were.

"Well, maybe your terrific reporting surprised him—"

"I asked him for comment. He had none, though come to think of it, he did lead me down a complicated conversational path that made it difficult to stick to the topic."

"The dynamic has shifted since you last spoke with Mr. Page, I believe. I've been able to convince him to pivot his approach. After reviewing some hard data, he changed his mind. In fact, anyone's mind would be changed if they saw what I've compiled. If you have time, I'd like to explain." Vern hadn't seen her presentation, technically. She wasn't lying so much as believing very much in the preferred outcome of her meeting with Vern later that day. She was still doing everything backwards.

"What data?" asked Girron.

"I interviewed all the people who live in Merritt, getting their take on whether they felt they had been accurately and fairly represented by the city council and the mayor. For example, did they feel their best interests were always top priority with leadership and—"

"The citizens of Merritt. About 62 people?" asked Girron.

"One hundred and twelve, or thereabouts! The results were quite revealing. Can we set up a time to go over the summary conclusions? I have a PowerPoint ready and would love to share several interesting revelations. For your next article."

"Revelations?"

"Yes, 97.8 percent of Merritt's population have reported being entirely happy with city leadership and they were definitely satisfied with living conditions. Even Boyle Heights, though it has always been a strong community, didn't come close—"

"Boyle Heights isn't a chartered city," said Girron.

Remembering that Girron grew up there, Meredith said, "Boyle Heights is so culturally distinct and interesting. My husband and I used to visit Mariachi Plaza when we toured the beautiful murals there. We loved the music and the elegant charro costumes." Meredith said.

Girron said, "My mother would always request 'Sin Ti.'"

"I love that song."

Girron abruptly said, "But it doesn't matter if the population of Merritt approves of how their city is run."

"It doesn't matter?" Meredith was thrown. If only she could get her presentation in front of him. People loved pie charts.

Girron continued, "Because voter fraud is illegal, and I don't care how benevolent Mendebal is, you can't harass squatters until they leave in order to avoid an open democratic election. And why was Mendebal so worried? Presumably, if everyone in Merritt was happy with him as mayor, he wouldn't have any concerns about the election outcome, right?"

Meredith said, "But the other candidate was backed by a convicted felon, isn't that right? The ex-treasurer of East Gate managed it all from his jail cell. It seems to me that Mendebal was genuinely trying to protect the city from being run by thugs."

"What makes you think it isn't already run by thugs?"

"That's not fair. I interviewed Mayor Mendebal this week and he was anything but. Mendebal is around 80 years old. He's running a city that is full of Fortune 500 companies who demand immediate results."

"Businesses are not citizens. That's also my point. What, or rather, who, does he think is more important?"

The sparring was a challenge, but Meredith had done her research and now it was paying off. She said, "Cheap power benefits citizens and businesses alike. Mendebal founded the Merritt Power Plant. He also made sure that Merritt has the best internet service in the entire LA Basin. Nothing is earmarked for businesses over residents. They all get equal access. That includes outstanding, immediate response to distress calls from Merritt's fire and police departments. Mendebal has accomplished a lot during his long tenure.

There were solid reasons why the electorate chose him as mayor time and again. What's more, he told me he was on speaking terms with every resident." Meredith assumed that last bit was true. In a town this small, how could he not know everyone? He had eaten lunch at Topa Café almost every weekday for the last forty years, until it closed. Naturally, he knew everyone.

Meredith ended with, "It's a fairly large number of people to keep in touch with. I mean, I can't seem to find time to talk to my own mother more than once a month."

"Shame on you!"

"I know!"

Girron laughed. "All right, Meredith, I have to go. Email me the PowerPoint. But you should look closely at the city manager."

"Chuck Peck? Yes, I'm meeting with him in a few days. Before you go, can I schedule another call with you on Monday? The PR campaign I'm planning is not only going to be fun, but exciting—"

"I have a deadline. Goodbye." The line went dead.

Meredith sent an email to Girron to thank him for his time, ping him about Monday, and to make sure he had her new Merritt phone number. She ended the email with: *Newsworthy changes in Merritt are afoot!*

Later, at City Hall, Meredith met with Vern. She planned to kick off the meeting with the Client Questionnaire, even if it was a little late for that. At her very first internship, her manager had told her, "You can skip steps, but you'll end up doing them anyway, when it's too late for them to be useful, and at a point where it's damaging. By then, you'll find yourself drowning in difficulties you could have avoided. It's better not to skip anything."

Meredith sat down in the seat opposite Vern, who sat behind his desk. He held a cup of coffee, but didn't offer her any.

"Thank you for taking the time to meet with me," said Meredith. Today, Vern wore a lime-green Ralph Lauren button-down oxford shirt and khakis, accessorized by a pink and blue striped belt. The grim look on his face was out of step with his resort wear.

"I've had my hands full," replied Vern. "Officer Vasco has kept me up to date. I've concluded that since the State Senate votes on our charter in six days, we hired you far too late to be of any practical benefit. I think it's time we called it a day."

Meredith had not expected this at all; nevertheless, she persevered, saying, "There's a lot that I've uncovered though! I've already developed—I have a lot to share with you. I brainstormed the perfect strategy to create a new image for Merritt. And it's a new revenue stream, too. However, I wanted to make sure we were on the same page first, Mr. Page—no pun intended!"

"Vern is fine," He wasn't amused. It was obvious he'd heard that joke many times.

Meredith said, "Sorry. I make bad puns when I'm surprised. Your decision is a bit of a shock. I urge you to reconsider it. Look. I brought a New Client Questionnaire with me. We could go over it quickly to make sure I haven't missed anything and then—"

"There's absolutely no time for that. Either you explain The Model to me now, or I'm going to have to terminate your contract."

This was a whole new Vern. He wasn't nearly as kind or fatherly as he had been that night he swept in and made her old life disappear. "I'm sorry?" said Meredith. "What does The Model have to do with—"

"Can we stop pretending? I'm well aware of the successes this app has given you, which is why I wanted to hire you in the first place. I honestly just needed to gain access to The Model, learn how to use it, then get moving on whatever it said we needed to do. But I couldn't—did you not hear me earlier? We have SIX DAYS." The echoes of his raised voice reverberated off the hard surfaces of his office.

Meredith's mouth dropped open a little. She felt the blood drain out of her face. She looked down at her laptop, which was open to the Client Questionnaire. She silently explained to the questionnaire, *He only wanted The Model. Not me.* Vern thrummed the desk with his fingers impatiently.

Meredith realized how, up until this meeting, the Vern she thought she knew was only a PR persona. She should have recognized this for what it was, since her default was to do the same thing, even if for different reasons. His PR persona was black-belt level, considering how good he was at obscuring his intentions. He appeared kind and authentic, fully available, with a sidecar of advance forgiveness by default—since everyone always felt ashamed about something. In reality, his PR persona was just how he got people to do what he wanted, or got them to tell him what he needed to know, or both.

Her own PR persona was similarly useful, though it was different. Through baseless cheer and diligent fact-finding, she could distance herself from her life.

She filed away her emotions and met Vern's eye, determined to further her cause. She said evenly, "With all due respect, sir, I've already employed The Model in order to gather data about Merritt's citizens, then crunched it against historical trends, then banked it all against data sourced from other small cities of the same size and demographics in order to come up with what I think is a game plan that we could easily implement. I'd like to present the results, a really fantastic PR campaign that would turn this place around immediately, if you greenlight it. I had hoped that the Questionnaire would confirm what I already know about Merritt and its issues. It was just a formality. You're right, there's not much time. As you noted, that's not my fault, but it would be a waste of a lot of work and analysis to give up now."

Vern sighed and said, "I don't like being rude. I really don't. That's not how I was brought up. It's Merritt. It's this town. Everything feels tainted. The taint is in the air, then it gets into your pores. And now my wife split—"

"Oh my God, I'm so sorry!" said Meredith.

Vern said, almost to himself, "It's like a mushroom cloud blooming behind you while you wash the dishes and assure everyone that there's nothing to see here. 'It's being handled.'"

"I'm sorry?" Meredith was not following.

Vern said, "My wife decamped to Puerto Vallarta two days ago. Never mind." He looked at Meredith thoughtfully. "Fine. Do the dog-and-pony show. I'm listening."

Meredith silently explained to the Questionnaire, right before she closed it and pulled up the PowerPoint, that if she could outrun diesel fumes when she went jogging, she could outrun Vern's splintered pessimism, too. She focused on the task at hand.

As she went ahead with the PowerPoint presentation, she tried to ignore his resentful expression. What mattered was that Vern was listening. It was a small miracle when the client actually listened. An hour later, Vern's demeanor had dramatically changed. But not in the way she had hoped.

When she finished, Vern said, "So you think that the solution is *transparency*?" He gripped his coffee thermos with both hands. A vein stood out on his forehead.

Meredith said, "It's been proven that this is the only effective PR strategy for the kind of crisis Merritt is facing.

If you want to save the city, you have to be completely transparent. Look at Tylenol. One hundred percent successful—"

Everyone in PR knew about Tylenol: the 1982 PR disaster that resulted when a maniac randomly laced the painkiller with arsenic. Seven people died. The killer had never been caught.

Vern rolled his eyes. "It took ten years for Johnson & Johnson to recover from that! We have six days!"

"I've already discussed some of this with the *LA Times*—"

"Gil Girron? That motherfucker who started everything?"

"Is that accurate? It was his job to expose—"

"Spare me. FUCK. I cannot believe this." Vern gulped down the rest of his coffee.

Meredith was silent. She shut her laptop and put it in her bag.

"Is there a reason why transparency is a problem?" Meredith asked.

"No, of course not! I mean. Well. It depends on how you look at it."

"That might be the root of Merritt's problem."

"What do you mean?"

"Merritt is a chartered city. It's supposed to abide by the tenets of its charter, by the laws of LA County, by the laws of the State of California, and so on. There's no way to spin that. Did Mayor Mendebal, his wife, and son all vote in Merritt's elections even though they don't live here, or are we really supposed to believe that wealthy people are hobos with no fixed address?" Meredith remembered how Girron urged her to look into the city manager. She said, "And what about the allegations concerning Chuck Peck?"

Vern glowered and said nothing.

She closed with, "These questions are easily answered by someone in your position. If you want me to help you—excuse me, if you want *The Model* to help you—you have to be candid about what's really going on here."

Vern coughed. "All right, Meredith. I'll give you until Monday."

"I'll have total access to all parts of the government and its records, correct?"

Vern's phone rang. He picked it up. He raised his eyebrows and said briefly, "Great news, Chuck. How—" He looked out the window at the pastel sky and his shoulders relaxed as he listened. "Ah. Yes. No doubt Mendebal is crowing about the wonders of small talk and eighteen holes." He looked over at Meredith, then said into the phone, "Yes, I'll take care of that." He hung up and leaned back in his chair.

He said, "The charter vote has been postponed a week. They moved it to September 9th."

"That's fantastic news! That gives us something like seven extra days?"

Vern glanced at a calendar hanging on the wall to his right. He said, "Yeah. I still want results ASAP."

ASAP was a word that Meredith loved to say. Hearing Vern say it made her feel like she had renewed a connection to the Vern from last week, even if that Vern wasn't real.

"Thank you," she said. "I'll give you twice-daily reports on progress. I sincerely believe that I can get Girron on our side—yes, even Girron! And if we can turn him, we can turn around public opinion, and no one in the State Senate will want to go against that unless it's all beyond repair. The *LA Times* is the key to everything. We just have to make them a partner. If you could also find out whether Merritt's building code would permit the freedom and creativity that mimetic architecture requires, then it would be a slam-dunk. Just think: businesses showing their product in the form of their buildings is a beautiful consummation of Merritt's new transparency campaign. Think of the tourist attractions, the public support from far and wide, not just from Merritt's citizens. Look at Tail o' the Pup. Twenty years after the entire hot dog stand was carted off to storage because they lost their lease, people still complain about it being closed down. It didn't matter whether the food was good or not because ordering cold fries and a bad hot dog from a man behind the counter of a giant hot dog was *fun*. People need fun. Fun will make them like you. The same could be done for City Hall—I'd wager all this would easily allow Merritt to keep its charter."

"Fine, whatever," said Vern. "I'll look for your report Monday morning." He turned to his computer monitor and started clicking his mouse. The meeting was over, apparently.

She left Vern's office, went straight to the women's bathroom, entered a stall, and locked it. She took off her glasses and put them in the side pocket of her bag. She stared at the stall door up close, the nubby texture of its painted surface covering up layers of graffiti, faint outlines of pen marks in different colors bleeding through the paint here and there. A palimpsest. She thought she would cry because she'd wanted to cry in Vern's office. But now she felt nothing. She should have felt satisfaction at having succeeded and relief that the vote was postponed. Maybe the emotions were there somewhere, but she couldn't recognize them. They were like the graffiti on the door: all painted over with stray bits poking through.

WHO ARE THE PLUS

After Meredith left City Hall, she inched along in Friday traffic in the direction of her apartment building, only a few blocks away. She had driven to her meeting at City Hall instead of walking over, because her laptop was old and heavy, and she didn't want to show up with sweat spots under her arms. The Santa Ana winds were in full force, hot gusty winds blowing east from the desert.

Solid and dependable, the gridlock felt almost comforting, the way it slowed down time and forced her to look around, though Merritt offered nothing to look at. Not yet. She was determined to change this.

What had happened to her active loathing of traffic? It was probably exhaustion. She had driven in rush-hour traffic for too many years to feel enraged about it anymore. And she was smart enough to know that shortcuts could just as easily lead her in a circle that took her back to where she began.

She looked forward to her destination: the tiny apartment she'd lived in for a week. Already, Meredith had grown to love the studio, because it was spare and anonymous, and she liked that it was in the same complex as Linda's apartment.

She thought about their drunken kiss two days ago. What had they been talking about, before it happened? Something about killer squirrels. The next day, she'd found scratches on her legs from the underbrush, but had trouble piecing together what had happened, exactly.

She glanced at her face in the rearview mirror. Had Linda's kiss changed her? Her lips didn't look any different than they usually did. She had thin lips. They weren't voluptuous like Linda's lips. But maybe not so thin as to be a disaster. It seemed to her that her lips were always in need of a little more color. She wore lipstick the same way blond women always darkened their eyebrows or used mascara. It was a necessary application that she never skipped, otherwise she felt washed out.

She had been too tipsy that night to notice if she had smeared lipstick on Linda's face after they kissed. Not tipsy—too *drunk*. She hated using the more accurate word, but maybe it was time to stop conning herself—she had to stop the constant angling for a more optimistic view, and instead face unpleasant facts. These ongoing crises that found her so easily—did she seek them out on purpose? They made her spin like a top. Stopping the rollercoaster meant having to comprehend what was actually happening; continuing the ride meant she never had any real grounding or insight, because there was always the next wall to bounce off, the next obstacle that seemed to appear out of nowhere, resulting in her feeling chronically, existentially dizzy. It was simple physics. Inertia leading the way, without purpose. Without end.

She said out loud in the car, with gusto, "I was *shitfaced*." She laughed. It was embarrassing but also ridiculous. She didn't know if Linda had scratches on her legs too. Had they rolled around in the underbrush, kissing? She was pretty sure they had not. But there had been a kiss.

Linda probably did have Meredith's lipstick smeared across her face that night—she probably had looked like an insane serial killer. Meredith thought about Linda's expressive lips. She didn't need lipstick. Her lips were just the right color, a ruddy red that set off her olive skin.

Did Linda usually kiss women? Linda was a woman, but she was a different kind of woman. Maybe she was a lesbian. Meredith didn't like to jump to conclusions. When people bragged about their "gaydar" she was offended. Meredith felt that a person's identity was up to that person, and if it was something to know about, that person would tell you. It had become more complex lately, though. Twenty years ago, there were fewer letters in the LGBTQ+ acronym, but simpler didn't mean better. Meredith was happy they included a plus sign on the end of LGBTQ now. The plus referred to all the other identities that didn't get a letter assigned, but it was also like a bonus, like extra cash at the end of the year for being superlative, rather than superfluous. A celebration.

It seemed like sexual identity was becoming more elusive. *Genderqueer.* Linda was sort of like that. And what about folks who, for whatever reason, never seemed to have any romantic relationships at all? Linda seemed like one of those people.

Meredith had known of at least two people who lived happily without romantic relationships. One of them was a colleague of hers, from three jobs back, when she worked for an event company in the late '90s. Jimmy Iha. Jimmy loved to drink giant Diet Cokes until he heard the news that it gave you cancer; then he cut back from six 32-ounce cups a day to two. He got them from the convenience store near work. Meredith never touched the stuff because it made her pee all the time and it tasted weird. She drank water instead. When she was a kid, all the canned soda bubbles hurt her mouth. Then as an adult she just drank water. You could never drink enough water in LA, because it was basically a desert covered with cement, tarmac, blacktop, and more cement.

Her mind was wandering. Jimmy Iha, that colleague who had no apparent love interest in his life, seemed happy enough. He knew more about marketing than anyone she had ever met. He said he had gotten turned on to marketing by one of his professors in college who explained how perfecting communications, in a way that connected people, was the basis of all marketing. This professor made marketing seem like a higher calling. Meredith didn't understand Jimmy when he explained it. All these years later, she wondered if he still felt that higher calling. Now, marketing was all about Big Data and selling out privacy so that marketing could drill down and customize the sales message perfectly for each person, to improve the bottom line. How was this virtuous? How did that mean anything?

She had mostly appreciated being in PR, not marketing, but lately she had doubts. Was PR any better than marketing, if what you were doing was trying to convince people that your spin on the facts was the absolute truth? It was easier to believe that what she did was meaningful when the company she represented was trying to do the right thing, but since she had always worked for corporations, where was the virtue, exactly?

She missed Jimmy, with his giant soda and his frequent giggle—she missed how sweet he was. Maybe he put all his romantic urges into marketing, and wanted connections only on a purely abstract level.

Linda wasn't like Jimmy. She was more passionate, yet she was patient, too. Linda didn't mind if Meredith worked too much, which was remarkable. Linda was also quiet in a way that didn't make Meredith feel like she had to fill the silence with something, either—this was even more remarkable. Was this what ease felt like? She treasured the feeling and wanted more of it, but then she thought of the "amona" lady and her cautionary email, and all sense of ease quickly evaporated.

Linda had another side to her, one that Meredith didn't want to know more about. But she should try.

Meredith was terrified of everything, not just the kiss. It was too soon, she was still in shock, she didn't know what she felt about anything. She just wanted to work.

Linda must have known that it was too soon for Meredith, too, because after the kiss, she had backed off, saying, "Don't worry. I can wait."

Wait for what?

As Meredith parked her car in the parking lot of the apartment complex, she stared out the window at the haze that occluded the mountains at the end of Merritt Boulevard. She had lost Jimmy, and would never know if he had found love, or if it ever mattered. She knew him before social media was invented. In those days you had to make a serious, continuous effort to stay in touch, on both sides. She doubted that he thought about her at all these days. It had been over fifteen years since she had lost touch.

She wondered if someone as nice as Jimmy secretly hated everyone, deep down. She usually felt like that. She doubted it. Jimmy's niceness was the real deal. Meredith pulled her key out of the ignition and said to herself, *Face it, Meredith. You were always working too much to bother keeping up with him. You didn't even try.*

The sun was still hotly contesting its inevitable decline, zinging her in the eye with light that penetrated the protection of sunglasses. Soon, the particulate matter blown in from the open desert by the Santa Ana winds would produce a beautiful sunset. It almost redeemed their negative effects on LA's population (the murder rate always went up when Santa Ana winds blew). As the air quality plunged, the colors in the sunset deepened. Pink and red streaked the sky in a vibrant last gasp of the day.

Once inside the apartment, Meredith tore off her shirt, which smelled of nervous sweat, and threw it in a basket in the corner of the tiny closet that contained her meager collection of corporate clothes—navy blue slacks and white tailored blouses. She hoped this uniform created a non-threatening, approachable effect, even if, apparently, she always looked like a Seventh Day Adventist on the hunt for lost souls. She didn't ultimately care.

She thought about how she didn't really need any of the other clothing she'd left behind, which led her to think about the giant responsibility of sorting out Grillo's death. She'd made almost no progress on gathering information about it. She still hadn't notified the authorities. Her attempts so far had been weak at best. If she was honest with herself, she had to admit that she never wanted to go back to her real home. It felt so nice to not be attached to anything, to not be weighed down by anything, to just be immersed in the work, without anyone pushing or pulling at her or telling her she must do better. The critic inside her head was loud enough on its own.

LINDA: WASHCLOTHS

Almost every day this week, around 6:00 p.m., I'd dropped by Meredith's place to check in on her, which then often turned into a tête-à-tête. I'd begun to look forward to my 6:00 p.m. visits. I'd begun to crave them. Being with Meredith made me feel as if I'd been let out of a cage. She was a rope that I clung to, in shock and surprise, as I gaped at how vast the world actually was.

On Friday, Meredith cancelled on me; she said she was exhausted. I tried not to show my disappointment. I didn't blame her. I realized I should probably catch up on correspondence, something I loathed. What's more, it had become difficult to respond to texts while shadowing Meredith, in addition to my regular police duties.

I scrolled through multiple texts from Vern sent earlier in the day. The last one was timestamped right after his meeting with Meredith: *Charter vote postponed to 9/9.*

Maybe Meredith would have a chance, after all, to promote her quirky architecture idea. I was doubtful about her being able to advance on her campaign, even though it was brilliant. But who knew? If their stock price wasn't affected, maybe Merritt businesses might actually agree to remodel their building facades into giant toilet paper rolls, bottles of hot sauce, and blowtorches—as long as they didn't have to pay for it. Businesses were simple to deal with. It was all about money. People, on the other hand, were more difficult.

I'd also received a few stupid texts from Ochoa around noon. These were mostly full of feckless threats and nasty physical comments about my person. It was clear he was still mad about the cocktail waitress.

Bill Ochoa was one of many reasons why I never frequented Topa Café. One night about two years ago, I was sitting at the bar, minding my own business, drinking a kalimotxo. Bill was a few stools away and very drunk. I observed him as he slapped the waitress's ass every time she walked by. She would turn and glare at him but there was only one way to get to and from the tables she served, so she was unable to avoid Bill and still do her job. I suspected Bill regularly perched on this very stool, taking advantage of her impossible situation.

I fully admit that on that particular evening, I had one too many kalimotxos, because I lost it and punched Bill in the face. Busted his nose. Then I left, while he whined and screamed in my wake, suddenly the victim.

I waded through Ochoa's garbage texts and found a few that were actually important.

> *horse wants me 2 meet LAFD abt Atwater*

> *horse wants special oops there*

> *Haha oops—that's you, a big mistake.*

> *wheres page?*

Ochoa's "oops" play on words was pathetic. One of my favorite Basque traditions by far was the Basque duel of insults: each insult was improvised, rhymed, and delivered as a song. I'm confident that if he were to take part in such a contest, he would be disqualified in about five seconds flat. The insult didn't bother me. What bothered me was that Ochoa was still not doing his job; that is, to provide LAFD with plausible alibis. With Ochoa sitting on his hands, and his boss, the fire chief, out on vacation, LAFD must have gone up the chain of command to involve Chuck Peck as well.

I wondered how angry Peck had been upon learning that he was now personally involved with a clean-up job on behalf of a lowly contractor, exposing him even more than he already was. I texted Vern: *Heard that Peck now involved with Atwater investigation—fireworks?* I stared at my phone, waiting for his typically immediate response, but got nothing in return. Vern was the Peck Whisperer. He always knew how to calm Peck down. But if Vern had also told Peck that The Model wasn't the silver bullet Peck had hoped for, and if that, combined with Peck's over-exposure, had pushed him over the edge—what then?

It was too bad that Peck was so obsessed with the idea that The Model would fix everything. Vern knew that a city's reputation couldn't be mended with an app. He was no dummy. But if Peck was pushing Vern to get his hands on it, Vern would have had no choice but to comply.

If Peck now knew that The Model was a dead-end, he wouldn't want to keep Meredith around. Meredith, however, hadn't been fired. I worried that Vern had been fired instead. Vern himself had said last week, "The PR person always takes the fall."

It was just a twenty-minute drive to the LA Fire Department's Arson Squad office near Dodger Stadium. Carpooling with Ochoa was out of the question, however. I knew my knife would be itching to see the light.

I texted Ochoa back. *I'll meet you there at 10:00 a.m.*

I beeped Bernard. He came down to my apartment. I caught him up on the latest developments.

Bernard said, "I can sit on Ochoa now?"

"No," I said. "I'm a big girl. I can handle that squirt. But Meredith is driving to Hancock Park to interview Leonata and her daughter at the same time, and I was going to go with her. Can you go in my place?"

Bernard looked stunned.

"You remember Marie, right?" I asked, fully knowing he absolutely remembered her.

He nodded. Poor Bernard.

It had all started right after we'd arrived from Spain. We were doing security for a fundraiser dinner that Leonata and her daughter had organized to benefit the Church of the Deaf. It was a quiet dinner, because most of the people attending were, of course, deaf. Bernard and I didn't know sign language, nor did we know much English. We scanned the crowd, watched the doors, and tried to look less traumatized than we felt. Barcelona was still fresh in our minds.

We'd been standing at the exit doors for a couple of hours with no breaks—we didn't yet know about mandatory work breaks, because there were no breaks in ETA— when a young woman in a modest black dress walked up to Bernard and offered him a bottle of water. I could hear what she said, even though I was stationed opposite him on the other side of the dining room. She spoke to him calmly in Euskera: "Thirsty? Please sit. Water." She then turned and walked over to my station, offering me water too. I accepted the bottle from her, but said nothing.

Leonata had helped us settle in after we arrived here from Spain. Since she'd emigrated too (though probably not via a truck full of manure), it made sense that she spoke Euskera perfectly. It didn't make sense that a random stranger spoke it, however. After the benefit wrapped up, Leonata introduced Marie to us as her daughter.

A couple of days later, I noticed that Bernard had taken up knitting; about a month later, he gave me a couple of knitted washcloths. I didn't use them for a few years, not knowing what to do with them. Later, when I got hooked on Goop, the Goop lady talked a lot about exfoliation. That's when the washcloths came in handy. I liked how I felt after I exfoliated. I liked to pretend that I was wiping away shame and regret along with dead skin and dirt. I felt pure, if only temporarily.

Three months later, Bernard and I handled security at the Mendebal's Hancock Park mansion for a large pool party they'd thrown for key Merritt businessmen. Bernard and I weren't aware of the donation system we'd later be tasked with enforcing (the payoffs). We'd just been made detectives in order to help out in that area, but had yet to fully grasp the system.

The pool party was full of middle-aged white men in their version of casual wear—polo shirts and chinos—with a small number of females who accessorized the men. Bernard and I watched the exits and oversaw the general flow of traffic, making sure evacuation paths were clear. Making sure everyone was safe.

Marie was at that pool party. She wore a one-piece sea-green bathing suit with a long filmy wrap skirt to match. As she moved through the crowd, her long skirt swirled around her legs, like the waves of the ocean. She looked like a curvy little sea nymph. The other women at the party wore dresses, not bathing suits.

Her mother spotted Marie and moved quickly to her side. Words were exchanged, then Marie stomped into the house. About fifteen minutes later, she came back out, wearing a boring white dress with a high collar and long sleeves.

She sat glumly near Bernard's station by the east gate, with her arms crossed.

Bernard inched toward her, then bent down and offered her a stack of his knitted washcloths.

She smiled and said something to him. Probably *eskerrik asko,* which meant "thank you." Bernard blushed and moved back to his post behind her. Marie looked at the washcloths with a perplexed expression, as if she didn't quite know what to do with them. As if they didn't solve her problem of wanting to feel frothy and free.

After a while, Marie got up and took the washcloths inside the house. She didn't reappear.

The next time we saw Marie was at her wedding, a couple years later. Her betrothed was some white guy she'd met at college, who had nothing to do with Merritt. I imagined her wearing her filmy bathing suit outfit nightly, much to her husband's eternal delight. I hoped that was the case, anyway.

We ran security for the wedding. Bernard had brought a wedding gift: more washcloths. He'd been knitting them furiously leading up to the wedding, and had about fifty completed, in different colors, with different embedded nubby patterns that he'd invented. It was a lot of washcloths. I thought maybe it was a little too many, but I didn't say anything.

After that, he kept on knitting washcloths, though not quite as furiously. It had become a habit, and it was better than smoking—he'd stopped smoking shortly after we arrived from Spain. He had said in explanation, "The air does bad things here." He usually donated the washcloths to the annual clothing drive sponsored by the Church of the Deaf.

Many years had passed since Marie's wedding. We never saw her; she lived in the North Valley and to my knowledge, never visited Merritt. She had no reason to, really. I heard she'd had a couple of children. She probably couldn't get away to help her mother at Catholic benefits, nor to vote illegally for her father in Merritt elections.

After giving Bernard a moment to recover from his shock at hearing that he'd be seeing Marie again after all these years, I said, "Is there a problem?"

He shook his head no.

"Great," I said. "Pick Meredith up at 10 tomorrow morning. I'll let her know to expect you. And thanks."

He nodded and lumbered out, a big, sad man who deserved a lot more than he'd settled for.

The next day I met with Ochoa and the LAFD arson investigator. The investigator said, "We're trying to locate Raymond Grillo and Meredith James, tenants of the destroyed structure at 214 N Landis, Atwater Village. Cell phone records indicate the woman was in Merritt eight days ago."

Ochoa said nothing.

I said, "I see. What can we do to help?"

The investigator said, "You only have like, what, fifty residents? It shouldn't be too hard to check around, see if someone fitting her description has turned up."

I said, "There are over one hundred residents in Merritt. This can certainly be accomplished; however, we are short-staffed. It will take some time."

The arson investigator looked miffed. "Short-staffed? Since when? I know for a fact that MFD has the best salaries in the entire county if not the whole state of California. They're never short on firemen. Everyone I know would jump at the chance of getting hired into MFD."

Ochoa said nothing.

I shrugged. "Ochoa, aren't many of your staff on a holiday?"

Ochoa corrected, "On vacation. Yes."

I continued, "It's August. Several MPD officers are also on vacation. I would like to add that MPD has the joint regional operations agreement with LAPD. When an investigation involves both cities, the paperwork is complicated. And time-consuming."

The investigator said, "Like that silver Prius fleeing the scene of a robbery, ending up in Merritt? I saw it on the news."

I said, "Exactly. But we want to help you. The male and female. Do you have photos of them?"

The investigator slid two photos over to me, apparently pulled from the DMV. In one, a bald male looked angrily into the camera as if to issue a rebuke. I recognized him as the person formerly in possession of the body we'd disposed of back in Atwater. In the other photo, a beautiful woman wore her hair long, to her shoulders, and though her eyeglasses were different, my beloved Cutiecups peered back at me, smiling tensely, like she was very late for a meeting and the DMV was making everything worse.

The officer said, "We also have a partial license plate that appears to match a Merritt city-owned vehicle."

Ochoa said nothing.

I looked surprised. "How unusual."

"I'd like permission to inspect your city-owned vehicles."

"May I suggest we give you a list of our vehicles' license plates?"

"I prefer to physically inspect the vehicles myself," he said.

Ochoa said nothing.

I said, "Understood. I suggest you coordinate a date and time with Ochoa."

We wrapped up the meeting and left.

Outside LAFD headquarters, Ochoa said in parting, "You're not off the hook, Vasco."

I looked at him with a bored expression. I said, "Do your job."

I turned my back on him and walked away. He sent me a text.

I find way to bring u down. ull b sry.

HANCOCK PARK

As Bernard and Meredith drove through Merritt on their way to Hancock Park, they passed Topa Café. Meredith said, "It's too bad that Topa Café closed."

Bernard shrugged.

Meredith said, "A couple of times I went there with my husband Grillo. We'd joke about how, any minute now, Barbarella would storm through the front doors and shoot up the place, in her vinyl low-cut pantsuit and platform thigh-high boots."

Bernard raised his bushy eyebrows and said, "Barbara Ella?"

"It was a silly movie made in the late '60s. Grillo didn't know much about Basque culture. I told him a little. I used to know someone in elementary school who was Basque-American. I'll never forget the costume she wore to school one year for Halloween. She said it was for folk dancing. She'd practice at recess. I thought it was dorky."

Bernard nodded. "Pretty dresses."

"Yes, I suppose her outfit was pretty. She thought so. I guess it's good to have hobbies. Do you have any hobbies?"

"I knit."

"How wonderful! What do you like to knit?"

He tilted his head toward a bag sitting between them in the front seat. Meredith looked inside.

Meredith exclaimed, "These are wonderful potholders!"

Bernard frowned.

Meredith amended, "I mean...washcloths?"

He nodded.

She said, "I love the geometric pattern on this one. I have a thing for nubby fabrics. Anything with texture. Pom-poms, fringe. When I was a kid, I had this brown suede vest with a long fringe. My mom bought it for me at Olvera Street. Have you been there?"

Bernard shook his head.

"It's very touristy. I loved my suede vest. I liked to spin around so that the fringe flared out and when I stopped, it slapped me across the belly." Meredith laughed to herself.

They drove through streets bordering the Garment District.

"Ohh! Santee Alley," said Meredith. "It's been ages since I've walked through there. It's a crazy, giant bazaar, with merchants selling anything and everything, from knock-offs to dollar-store junk. But the t-shirts are on another level. Small t-shirt entrepreneurs sell shirts that they think represent what Angelenos care about. But because LA is not coherent, neither are the t-shirts. They're often these slightly unhinged collages. My favorite design depicted Marilyn Monroe wearing a midriff Dodger's shirt. A chola-style tattoo of a teardrop adorned her cheek; a tattoo of a hand tattooed with the Ace of Spades was placed on her exposed belly."

Bernard said nothing. After a pause, Meredith said, "It's nice that you have a hobby. I guess I don't really have any, myself. I aspire to hobbies, which isn't the same thing. But don't you think that's almost as good? To have goals?"

Bernard shrugged.

"I always hoped that I'd find the time to learn how to sing. I love the jazzy baby voice of Blossom Dearie. Have you heard of her?"

Bernard shook his head no.

"In between TV shows after school, *Schoolhouse Rock* would come on briefly, instead of a commercial, teaching basic math and grammar concepts with songs and funny cartoons. 'Figure Eight' still gives me goosebumps. This little girl with earmuffs is ice-skating while singing about math." Meredith laughed. She sang in a high soprano, "*If you could make a figure 8, That's a circle that turns 'round upon itself. Place it on its side and it's a symbol meaning Infinity.*"

Was Bernard smiling under his beard thicket? Meredith couldn't tell. She looked out the window as they passed LA Trade Tech.

She said, "My husband took a welding class there. For one of his art projects. Then he had to drop out because of his asthma."

Meredith rubbed the nubby surface of one of Bernard's washcloths. She said, "Art was more than a hobby for him. Maybe it would have been better if it was just a hobby. What did you like best about Basque folk dancing, Bernard?" She felt like she was talking too much. Maybe it was fine. She felt safe around Bernard.

He said, "Fireworks."

She laughed. "They danced with fireworks, or do you mean, Basque festivals had fireworks too?"

"The last one."

"It's a totally weird coincidence. Just a few days ago I found out that the girl I knew in grade school who loved her folk dancing outfit is actually Mayor Mendebal's daughter. I had no idea!"

Bernard almost ran a red light and braked hard. The nose of the car slightly protruded into the intersection.

Oncoming cars veered around them, honking in outrage and flipping them off.

Meredith commented, "People are so rude here. Give me a break! So what if you misjudged your stop? Can't they be, I don't know, a little more gracious? Anyway, what was I talking about?

"Oh yeah. I always worried about Marie getting teased. I suspect she never did? I'm not sure. It was tough all around back in grade school. You had to be careful with what you laid claim to. It was OK to brag about your new skateboard, going to Disneyland, getting *Dig Dug* for your Atari. Folk dancing was not something to brag about. But Marie was really proud of her Basque heritage. But. Almost all the kids' parents were from somewhere else. It didn't make you special. The kids who really had something to brag about, like if their parents were famous—which was often the case where I went to school—never would mention it."

Bernard gripped the steering wheel with both hands, and said nothing.

After Meredith knocked on the stately door of the Mendebals' Hancock Park mansion, it was opened by their housekeeper, who ushered the two of them into a spacious formal living room.

Bernard stood awkwardly by the doorway, gripping the bag of washcloths in both hands as if he was still at the steering wheel of the car. Meredith looked out the den's picture window. The coiffed landscape with its mature trees seemed like a mirage. Hearing footsteps behind her, she turned to see two women, one older and one younger, and introduced herself, saying, "Meredith James, pleased to meet you. This is Bernard—" Meredith realized she didn't know Bernard's last name.

Leonata said, "We know Bernard. Hello. You remember Marie, of course." Bernard nodded vigorously.

Leonata said, "I meant you, Meredith. You went to school with Marie, I believe."

Meredith smiled and said, "Yes! I'm impressed that you remember me! It's been ages. We took the bus together..."

Marie said, "You skipped grades. Later that year, the school canceled bus service."

Leonata said, "Yes. I remember how inconvenient that was for me. I was managing Topa Café at the time. I could not possibly do that and pick you up from school every day, so I had to quit." She paused, then said, "Of course I do not regret it—my family comes first."

Meredith was intrigued that Leonata appeared to have some lingering nostalgia for her years spent working in Merritt, of all places.

Leonata and Marie sat in easy chairs facing Meredith, who sat on the couch. Bernard stood by the door. No one thought this was strange, except for Meredith. Then again, she didn't really know why he had come with her to the interview, to begin with. She liked his company, though, and hadn't objected when Linda had called the night before to let her know he'd be going with her.

"What would you like to know, Mrs. James?" asked Leonata.

"Your husband may have already told you about my project to improve Merritt's image."

"Yes, of course."

"It's fantastic that the State Senate vote on Merritt's charter was postponed by over a week, isn't it?"

"Yes, my husband played golf with Senate Speaker Westmore in Huntington Beach yesterday."

Meredith wasn't quite sure what to make of this. Was Leonata insinuating that a round of golf allowed Mayor

Mendebal to procure an extension on the charter vote? If so, Meredith thought she'd need to reprioritize her hobby goals to include, first and foremost, golf.

"I see. You own a beach house there, correct?"

"Yes, that's where my husband is staying; he'll be back later today."

"How often is he at home here in Hancock Park?"

"He stays in Merritt all week and comes here most weekends unless there's golf, or we want to go up to the mountains."

Meredith proceeded to ask Leonata a few of her standard citizen survey questions. After Leonata answered them enthusiastically—even though she didn't seem to be in Merritt much, she certainly had a strong emotional attachment to it—Meredith got down to business.

"I'm sorry to ask but, what's your take on the charges brought against you?"

Leonata's pallor looked a bit moldy. She said, "Ah, that will go away. It happened before, with my husband, some years ago. Why would it be different now? They made a mistake. You'll see."

Turning to Marie, Meredith asked her, "What's your involvement with Merritt, Marie?"

Marie smiled. "I've always thought my father made the best mayor. He's Basque-American, you know."

Meredith laughed. "Of course! As are you. You really loved that folk dancing costume."

Marie said, "That's right!"

"It does strike me as a little strange that your brother participated in Merritt affairs more than you did?"

Marie shrugged. "My father loved us both equally. But he always wanted Michael to take over when the time came. I don't like being in charge. I like to lend my hand, help out behind the scenes. Unless there are costumes to wear. Then it's a different story." She looked at her mother, who smiled back.

Marie continued, "I teach kindergarten. I have kids. I help out my mother. It's enough, you know? When I can, I make costumes for the kids' school events. I make sure they know about their heritage. I'm still proud of it."

"Lovely," said Meredith. "And you're living in Calabasas, is that right?"

"Near it."

"Calabasas was actually at one time your, let's see, your great-great uncle's ranch?"

"That's right. Mama, show Meredith the knives." Marie turned to her and explained, "Family heirlooms."

Leonata brought out some kitchen knives with wood handles darkened with age. As they looked them over, the older woman said, "Still sharpens up well." Meredith thought it was too bad that Linda wasn't there for the knife viewing. Thinking of her triggered the memory of their knife-throwing expedition and their kiss. She tried to stay present, oohing and ahing at the damn knives. Now was not the time to decide whether she had been a lesbian all these years, but hadn't known it.

After Leonata returned from putting away the family knives, Meredith said, "Well, I won't keep you any longer. Thanks so much for taking the time to meet with me, Mrs. Mendebal. And Marie, be sure to email me when you next perform at a festival. It would be fun to see you dance for real!"

Marie shook her head. "I blew out my knee on the wine glass dance. Now I coach my kids."

"Well, either way, here's my card."

Meredith starting following Leonata to the front door. Halfway there, she turned and noticed that Bernard hadn't moved. It appeared he was trying to give Marie his bag of washcloths, but Marie had put her hands behind her back, as if she'd been kidnapped and they were bound by a rope.

They stood facing each other in mutual mortified paralysis. Meredith said quickly, "Marie, have you seen Bernard's hand-made washcloths?" She casually took a few out of the bag.

This didn't penetrate Marie's awkward trance, but Bernard followed Meredith's movements with his eyes. Encouraged, Meredith said, "Bernard, do you mind if I have a few?" He nodded.

Leonata still stood in the large foyer over by the front door, holding it open. She looked at her watch, and called to Marie, "Marie, stop dreaming and say goodbye."

This appeared to break Marie's trance. She reached out and took the bag from Bernard, saying something Meredith didn't recognize. Perhaps she was speaking in the Basque language. Bernard bowed slightly, then followed Meredith out the door.

On the car ride home, Meredith tried to dispel the mystifying gloom surrounding Bernard. She was unsure how, until she picked up one of Bernard's washcloths, which was pink. She smoothed it out on her knee, running her hands over the soft cotton yarn.

She said, "The color of this washcloth reminds me of 'pink slime.' Have you heard of that?"

Bernard shook his head no.

"That's how I was fired. It happened so fast. No warning. This food product called 'Lean Finely Textured Beef,' was renamed by social media as pink slime. A histrionic chef from England videotaped himself dumping household ammonia on some chicken and running it through a food processor on a reality show about obese kids in West Virginia. He wanted Americans to see how unprocessed food was better than what they were eating. He got the idea from some mom blog. Yeah. Some housewife in Houston had posted about school lunches, how it was all derivative food. She's the one who came up with 'pink slime.' Hello? Kids don't want to eat real food. They want all their food to taste like dessert or french fries."

"I like french fries."

"Who doesn't? So do I. There was a surge of social media disgust, then newspapers and network TV picked it up—and it didn't help that pink slime looked different. It was nothing like the iconic raw steak, with its deep red color, rim of white fat, marbling. Did you know that vegetable-based ground beef was dyed to look the same color as ground beef? Red was OK, but not pink.

"Then there was the ammonia. In the processing plant, when they melted off the fat to get those last bits of beef, the heating process increased the level of bacteria, so they used ammonium hydroxide gas to kill it. Lemon juice would have gone over far better with the public and accomplished the same thing. But AFA Foods said it cost more than ammonia, and rejected it out of hand."

Bernard kept both hands on the steering wheel at three and six o'clock. He had pushed the seat all the way back. The top of his head was mashed against the upholstered ceiling of the car's interior. He looked extremely uncomfortable, and at the same time, completely familiar with the situation.

"Would you prefer if I drove the rest of the way?" asked Meredith.

Bernard said, "It is fine."

Meredith sighed and put the pink washcloth back in her bag.

"I was the head of PR for AFA Foods, you know. Yeah. Big fancy title, but not a lot of power. I had much more sway at my previous job, where I didn't even have a fixed title. I was PR one day, advertising the next, pinch-hitting branding and marketing, you name it, I did it. But I was effective. People listened to me there. I gave all that up for a simple title that sounded super fancy. And it meant nothing."

Through the window, Meredith could see up a side alley, where the back doors of various businesses were all labeled with "Emergency Exit."

"I'd tried so many times to get AFA's Vulnerability Audit approved. The stakeholders kept blowing it off. That's why there was no PR Crisis Plan, which was like an emergency evacuation plan, but for PR."

She continued, "AFA Foods had an emergency evacuation plan, because it was required by OSHA, but no PR Crisis Plan, because it wasn't required by OSHA. Since I didn't have the power of the US Department of Labor behind me to mandate a PR Crisis Plan, when Lean Finely Textured Beef became Pink Slime, I couldn't save them from their PR nightmare."

Bernard said, "What is PR?"

Meredith laughed. "What is it, indeed! Communication is at the heart of it. The main problem at AFA was that their preferred terms, like *exposure, placement,* and *soft returns,* didn't refer to anything real, but they insisted I use them. Even the industry term *Value-Added Beef,* which I despised, was coined for businessmen to understand, not consumers. The term reeked of 'stuff we added to meat to make it taste good under difficult circumstances.'"

"Is it something to eat?" said Bernard. He looked confused. Meredith supposed this was an improvement over looking sad.

Encouraged, she continued. "Yes. Pink slime was used to create AFA's Value-Added Beef product, which was something you ate. In restaurants. Pink slime was the result of separating and using every last bit of meat from various parts of the cow, bits that were comprised mostly of fat. Imagine the friendly local butcher whistling opera in a white apron, right? He could never accomplish the transformation that industrial food could, and it *was* an accomplishment. It was technically quite sustainable. If you're going to kill an animal, why would you waste any edible part of it, if you didn't have to? It was a lot like how the dairy people separated cream from milk, but no one ever freaked out about that."

"Too close to bone," said Bernard.

Meredith laughed. "No pun intended!" She shook her head. "You know the worst part? The worst part was when I was fired, I told myself that I was just leaving early. 'Leaving early,' instead of 'being fired' was an example of PR at its worst: adjustable truth that wasn't a complete lie, but not exactly true either. And you know what? I am really tired of doing that. This PR campaign for Merritt is going to be very different."

As Bernard pulled into a parking spot in front of their Merritt apartment building, Meredith said, "I should have checked to make sure your favorite meal wasn't a hamburger before going on about this."

Bernard shrugged. "There's no problem."

Meredith said as she got out of the car, "Thank you for the washcloths. They're really beautiful."

While Bernard unfolded himself from his jackknifed position in the car, he said, "Hand wash in cold water. Dry flat."

ABOUT MICHAEL

When Meredith returned home from Hancock Park, she updated The Model with Leonata's interview answers, then she reviewed her notes from the phone call she'd had with Girron the day before. Girron had insinuated that she may have missed some important details about Chuck Peck, so she reread his articles on Merritt's irregularities one more time, along with anything else she could dig up online. Girron hadn't answered her follow-up email she'd sent after their phone call. She pinged him again, letting him know about the charter vote postponement.

In one article, Girron had reported that Peck had hired limos for his commute to Merritt from Huntington Beach. The city had reimbursed him. He'd also expensed gifts and groceries, and to top it off, he'd assigned himself an oversize pension and salary. All this was leaked to Girron via anonymous tips from someone at Merritt City Hall. A disgruntled employee might have been a little free with the hyperbole; nevertheless, Meredith realized she should immediately try to gain access to the city's archives to look for evidence that backed up the allegations. She'd ask Linda for help.

There was one other article by Girron online that wasn't contained in the stash of articles Vern had given her. It was about Michael Mendebal. It reported that Michael had been indicted for voter fraud along with his mother and father—which she already knew about. She didn't know, however, that he'd also been convicted for child abuse and child pornography, and was now in prison. Peck, when reached for comment, had simply said, "That unpleasant business has nothing to do with Merritt."

Meredith rolled her eyes and said aloud to no one, "Seriously?"

Vern should have done more to punch up Chuck Peck's response. He should have made it clear that the City of Merritt took a strong stance against crimes of this nature. He could have listed the steps the city's police had taken to protect underage residents from harm. Maybe Vern had, in fact, drafted a more useful statement, but Peck had ignored it.

While Meredith wrote up a summary about the allegations against Peck so that she could be on point when she interviewed him in a couple days, she wondered what was worse: raiding government coffers for your own gain, or stuffing the ballot box to stay in power? They were both bad. She had no personal knowledge of the city manager, except for the possibility he wasn't exactly kind to his admin, who had been nothing short of hostile when Meredith had made her appointment. Linda had also warned her about Peck's temper.

She expected Peck to be the bad cop, to Mendebal's good cop. She still couldn't help liking Mendebal. What had he said? "The truth of your heart is important." She closed her eyes and said the phrase several times out loud, like a mantra.

When she opened her eyes, she noticed feeling simultaneously better and worse. Better, because she felt less tense; worse, because sadness and loss had arrived. They had climbed onto her lap and clung to her, whining, like tired, hungry toddlers.

She decided to make herself lunch, since it was already 3:00 p.m. Then she took a nap.

She awoke around 5:00 p.m., then got up to make two kalimotxos, the ratio leaning more towards Coke than red wine this time, following her vow to cut back on alcohol. There were several reasons to feel celebratory, and if she acted like she was optimistic, maybe she would actually feel that way. The charter vote had been postponed; Vern had allowed her to keep working; and she'd finished the citizen survey. There was a lot to be happy about. Wasn't there?

Linda knocked on her door at half past. She smiled when Meredith let her in, ready with her kalimotxo. "Sorry," Meredith said in greeting. "I started early," gesturing to her own glass, which was almost empty.

"I heard you had an intense meeting with Vern yesterday," said Linda, sipping her drink.

"He seemed to think that The Model is all you guys need to turn Merritt around. It was totally insane."

"Didn't you read through all the articles about Merritt already?" Linda glanced at Meredith's laptop screen, where a browser was open to the *LA Times* article about Michael. The headline read: "Merritt mayor's son is sentenced to eight years in prison."

"Yeah, Girron thought I'd missed something. I was checking online to see if there was anything else. I was looking specifically for info about Chuck Peck." Meredith followed Linda's gaze and added, "Isn't it awful, what Michael did?"

Linda looked confused. "I don't know much about Michael."

"For the voter fraud investigation, the DA seized Michael's home computer. They found all these photos and videos of boys compiled while he was dean of an all-boys high school in LA."

"What kind of videos?" said Linda, downing her kalimotxo.

"Kids taking showers naked? Apparently shot at the Mendebal beach house in Huntington Beach. It's too bad that Merritt leadership didn't do more to make it clear where they stood on all of it. Chuck Peck then made a public statement that was worse than saying nothing, if you ask me."

Linda slammed her coffee cup down on the kitchen counter. She gripped the counter with both hands. She asked the cup slowly, "Michael was abusing kids?"

"Um, did you want another one?" said Meredith nervously.

"No. What about Michael?" Her breathing was labored.

Meredith answered, "I'm sorry, I thought you knew? Unfortunately, yes, he was grooming them, at the very least. Honestly, I didn't read that article in detail because, well, gross." Linda was silent. Meredith went on, assuming Linda was impatient with her, which made her feel anxious. "Of course, Michael also voted for his dad in Merritt illegally, because like the mayor, he doesn't live there. But Marie, his sister? She never voted in Merritt elections. Not one of these articles mentions her. Isn't that weird? I mean, if everyone else was voting illegally, why didn't she vote too? I asked her about that in a roundabout way. She said her father wanted Michael to be the next mayor, not her. But maybe it's neither here nor there. My PR strategy is still sound."

Linda sat down on the bed.

"Linda?" said Meredith. "Are you OK?"

Linda said, looking at the palms of her hands, "I didn't know about Michael."

"He's in prison now. He got eight years."

"That's all?"

"I guess he had a good lawyer? No prior convictions? I don't know what the normal sentencing is for something like this, sorry."

"I have to go," said Linda.

LINDA: MY UGLY REFUGE

The layout of my studio apartment mirrored that of Meredith's studio, one floor up, one apartment over, and though I'd lived there for over twenty years, it looked almost exactly the same as hers—as if someone appeared to live there, but didn't, really. I stripped off all my clothes and I sat on my bed, letting the AC blow all over me. I raised one arm and then the other to cool my armpits. Next, I lifted my breasts up, letting the air blow on the sweat accumulating just below each one.

Fat and gravity had slowly crept up on me all these years, while I wasn't looking, partners in crime, conspiring to create this middle-aged body. I didn't care about my body. It was animated meat. But grief? This hit me out of nowhere. A huge smackdown, like that time when I was a kid. I had taken my dad's favorite hunting knife and messed up the blade trying to open a can of beans. He smacked me hard, so hard I peed myself. But I didn't blame him. It was a good knife, and I had abused it.

Abuse. Knife abuse, child abuse. I couldn't think straight. It had something to do with the crushing sorrow I felt, laced with shame, regret, and stupidity.

Michael Mendebal. I never dealt with Mayor Mendebal's kids, who were adults by the time I was Merritt's special employee. I didn't deal with them because they didn't create trouble, unlike stupid Cousin Jerry, my former idiot-boss.

Michael and his sister Marie never officially worked for their dad, nor for Merritt, either, that I knew of. They had their own gigs somewhere else. I didn't inquire. I vaguely remembered seeing Michael standing in the voter line behind his father and mother, during Merritt's city elections. That was it.

The undersides of my breasts were dry finally, so I changed position. As I lifted up a leg and set it on my bed so that the cool air from the AC hit my inner thighs, I thought about how all of us at the polling place knew each other: security, the people in line, the voting administrators. I thought about how Merritt's set up was exactly like *caciquismo* in the old country. Dammit. How had this not occurred to me before?

My father told me once that caciquismo was one of the reasons why the first Basque nationalist movements were formed (pre-ETA), in an attempt to dismantle the *caciques'* corrupt feedback loop of local voter fraud, and at the national level, payoffs and arranged favors that kept the caciques, the local thug-bosses, in place. This was before Franco hijacked all of it, and coopted it under a national network of henchmen. Franco was from Galicia, where caciquismo corruption was deeply entrenched. He spread that system throughout the entire country, and at what cost? 400,000 people had died or disappeared because of him.

Goddamn Galicians. And that fucker, José the Galician—the megalomaniac in my last ETA cell. I tried to squish Barcelona memories between my upper thighs while I changed position again. The cool air of the AC brushed against my backside. I focused on Franco. Over twenty years, ETA had killed around eight hundred people—a tiny percentage of Franco's mass murder. I'm not proud of ETA's role in the bloodshed, but how else were we going to disrupt post-Franco caciquismo? Even though Spain reinvented itself as a constitutional monarchy, and in the '70s wrote a shiny new constitution guaranteeing cultural autonomy for the Basques and other "autonomous regions," all the original thug families still lined their pockets just like before. The roads sucked, the schools sucked, there wasn't any money—but there should have been money for all of it, because Basque folks worked hard and paid their taxes. But it didn't mean we had freed ourselves from the old caciques.

In the darkness of my studio apartment, the AC's air smelled like dirty socks. It mingled with my nervous sweat and kalimotxo breath. I sat down, facing the unadorned wall above my bed, and cooled off my neck and back. It was finally clear to me. Merritt was a little mini-caciquismo transplanted to Los Angeles. Mendebal's grandfather came here, founded Merritt, wanted it to be just like Bilbao—industrial. Then sixty, seventy years later, Mendebal hired Bernard and me, former ETA. He hired us to protect Merritt's town council, a cacique that represented everything we had fought against in the old country. It was so cynical. And I was such a dummy not to connect the dots before now. It shocked me, realizing just how much of a deep fog I had been in all these years.

In the voter line, who else did I see? The parking tickets cashier, the receptionist at City Hall, the gardeners, the janitors. Their cousins, their nieces, their nephews, all adding up to the same one hundred people ready to vote for Mayor Mendebal, again and again. I knew. But I shrugged and looked away.

Michael Mendebal, the son, was a child abuser all along. I felt my heart racing, then beating irregularly. I collapsed on my bed, the AC blowing on the bottom of my feet. I spread my toes to get air in between them. I usually ran election security, making sure there were no hijinks or interlopers, like that year when those East Gate thugs tried to stage a coup. Otherwise, Merritt was pretty quiet, an efficient, well-oiled machine. Everyone got mostly what they wanted, and those that didn't get what they wanted? Bernard and I handled the discontent. I worked for Vern, and Vern worked for Mendebal, and then later, Vern worked for Chuck Peck when Mendebal started slowing down, getting older. The old man delegated a lot of responsibility to Chuck. Maybe too much.

I always thought Mayor Mendebal was a sweet old man who took care of things quietly. Unassuming. Maybe he was better than the caciques back home: with the money overflowing his coffers, Mendebal reinvested some of it back into the city infrastructure. Look how he'd pulled off high-speed internet, far more advanced and reliable than what was available in the rest of LA, without even really knowing what high-speed internet was, exactly. My God. He probably didn't know how to use a computer, otherwise he would have known about Michael's disgusting proclivities. I installed the security cameras in their Hancock Park home and in their beach house. Did Michael use those same security cameras to record kids taking showers?

I ran to the bathroom. I threw up in the toilet. I came back and paced back and forth in front of the AC. Mendebal knew about everything that happened in Merritt. How could he not know about what Michael was doing? Did he know? His own *beach house*? Sorrow became pain in my knees and wrists. It made my ankles swell. I was getting a crick in my neck. An old gunshot wound in my right clavicle started to throb. Sorrow was spilling out of my pores, sad sweat that became clammy in the mildewed air of the AC. I couldn't do anything to stop my feelings. The AC was not enough.

Merritt had always felt like a shitty abandoned garden with more trash in it than plants, a cement garden with barbed wire vines, lead-laced earth. I didn't mind its ugliness, its significant health hazards. I liked it. Beautiful vistas were a lie. My homeland, the Basque country, had gorgeous rolling hills. Pristine. Everyone knew each other. Everyone spied on each other, everyone hated each other, everyone loved each other. Everyone completely missed what my uncle did to me right under their noses. Did I really think that an ugly landscape would therefore prevent this from happening? Did I really think that? I have no idea what I was thinking. I just went along with it. I accepted that people were just interested in grabbing as much cash as they could for themselves, but I had to admit it, finally. I must have believed in an absurd fantasy that greed would surely crowd out child abuse, that there was no room for both. What a chump.

Merritt. A smelly, ugly, confined, so-called city full of white boxy buildings, gridlock, manufacturing, slaughtering, processing—and let's not forget the murals of pigs. This so-called city was perfect for me to live in, when I had no choice but to flee the old country. It could never remind me of home and it never did. It was a goddamn refuge. My ugly refuge. I thought I had mastery over my feelings by not having them. Until now. Now Merritt reminded me of home. In the wrong way.

CAT FOOD

Sunday, August 30, 2009
Senate charter vote in 10 days

The closest thing to either a drugstore or a market in Merritt was the convenience store at the gas station. Since it was Sunday morning, it was completely dead. Residents were at church or sleeping in. Commuters were at home, far away from Merritt.

A buzzer went off when Linda and Meredith walked in the door. The cashier nodded to them behind bulletproof glass. The store's AC was on the fritz, and though the front door was propped open, it was stuffy inside. It was already 85 degrees out, and it wasn't yet ten in the morning.

Meredith wandered the tiny aisles with Linda, who carried a basket. The bathroom at Meredith's temporary digs had been stocked with some sample-size toiletries, but now Meredith was out of everything. She gathered up toothpaste, shampoo, lotion, and sunblock from the quarter-shelf devoted to personal grooming and tossed them in the basket. Linda picked up a box of bandages, examined the label, then put it back. She did the same thing with several other first-aid items. They wandered up the next tiny aisle, where Meredith grabbed olives and ramen from the wee grocery section, tossed them in the basket, and topped it off with twenty powerbars of various brands. An entire aisle was dedicated to powerbars. Linda held one in her hand as if estimating its weight.

Linda said, "What's so powerful about it?"

Meredith said, "I know. Talk about marketing hype. Though I do find them convenient. Over the years it's as if I've perfected an unhealthy lifestyle that's unassailably healthy. They're not really food, yet you never hear of powerbars being bad for you, unlike candy bars. High fructose corn syrup was always the enemy, not whey protein. Even pink slime, though highly processed, is technically healthy."

Linda didn't seem curious about pink slime, so Meredith didn't go into more detail. Linda sighed and dropped the powerbar onto the shelf, like she wanted to arrest it for its crimes but there wasn't enough evidence.

They continued on together until Linda stopped abruptly in the last aisle, in front of a few offerings of pet food: Ruff Kan, Frilly Feast, 99 Lives. Linda picked up a can of dog food, then tossed it back. She still hadn't placed any items inside the basket, and certainly didn't have a dog. Her face looked crumpled. Maybe she hadn't slept well.

Meredith said as if to herself, "There was this cat that adopted me. In Atwater Village. It didn't really want me, it wanted to get inside my house. Then, when I let him in, he wouldn't leave me alone, wanting constant attention—he'd head-butt my hand until he received the required amount of stroking, petting, and scratching behind his ears. He was extremely demanding, a lot like my husband. In the end I had to kick him out of the house—the cat, I mean, not my husband. Nevertheless, I continued to feed the cat nightly, outside the kitchen door. I think he'd adopted several families in the area, because he gained a lot of weight."

Meredith stopped talking and watched the cashier leave his station behind the bulletproof glass, disappearing through a doorway to the stockroom.

"Grillo never minded the cat," Meredith finished, as she picked up a can of 99 Lives. A large tabby with emerald green eyes peered haughtily from the label. The photo was fake-signed in thick black writing, *Ferris™*.

Linda picked up a can of Misty Cats cat food. This label featured a headshot of a gray cat with yellow eyes, its head cocked to one side, resting on its forearm, like it was straining to hear the can opener.

Linda said, "This is made here, in Merritt."

Meredith ignored the Misty Cats can and said, "Grillo. You know, my husband? Grillo never minded how much time I spent with the cat, nor how much I spent on cat food. It liked 99 Lives. He really only minded how much I worked. At home, it didn't matter to him what I was doing, as long as I wasn't working. As long as I listened to him. But that's the thing. I never listened enough to satisfy him. I did listen, but it was depressing. He always wanted me to completely agree with his unrelenting, morbid view of what was or wasn't happening. It wasn't enough for him to have opinions. He needed an audience. He needed a congregation of the devoted, the devout. Sometimes I'd think it didn't matter who it was, as long as someone was listening. His other friends didn't stick around. They all let him down. I guess I can't blame them. I let him down too. It wasn't like I didn't agree with him. Yes, the world is a shitty place, yes, the environment wasn't healthy, yes, it all needed to be burned to the ground." She paused, and looked at the cat on the 99 Lives label. Ferris stared back, defiant.

Linda said softly, "It *was* burned, actually."

"What was?"

"Your house. We had to get rid of evidence. We staged it to look like electrical failure. For an insurance claim."

"We rented." Meredith felt dazed.

"Oh." Linda still held the Misty Cats can. She no longer looked crumpled. She looked like the cat on the label: overly alert, ready to react, edgy.

Before speaking, Meredith paused, staring at Linda in shock. As she spoke, her voice started out as a low mono-tone then gradually increased in volume and intensity. "The house burned down. The house burned down? Wow. OK. I'll just—I don't know, I guess I'll just file that away for now, along with all the other stuff I can't really process."

"Understandable."

Meredith clenched her fists then stretched her fingers, as if she was warming up for a piano concert or a bare-fisted fight. She said, "Now would probably be the right time to tell me where the fuck you took my husband's body."

Linda couldn't look her in the eye. She put down the bas-ket, and fiddled with the Misty Cats can, rolling it around in her hands.

"Where did he go?" said Meredith.

"He's here," said Linda. She held up the Misty Cats can. "Maybe here too," and she pointed to the 99 Lives can in Meredith's hands. "And maybe here, and here," said Linda, pointing to a row of Frilly Feast, and next to that, a row of Ruff Kan, for dogs. "Hard to say exactly," said Linda.

"I don't understand," said Meredith.

"Vern didn't want an investigation of your husband's death to get in the way. He needed The Model. LAPD would investigate your husband's death too slowly. They always do. It would take weeks. We had no time to waste, because of the charter vote. If you got involved with the investigation, Vern said Merritt would be out of options. Goodbye to The Model. Goodbye Merritt."

Meredith folded her arms across her chest as if trying to contain her fury. She said, "Unbelievable."

Music came on abruptly, piped at high volume through the overhead speakers. It was a song by Duran Duran from the '80s about a woman dancing on the beach. The nasal whine of the vocals made Meredith clench her teeth. The cashier came out and resumed his vigil behind the bullet-proof glass.

"I'm still waiting," said Meredith. "My husband?"

"Bernard and I took your husband's body to Best Coast Rendering over on Bandini Avenue."

"Best Coast Rendering?"

Linda nodded.

"Grillo was *rendered*?" Meredith's voice changed its timbre. It was not unlike the sound of worn-out brakes seizing up just before a collision. Her voice slashed across Duran Duran's strained, thin tenor. The young cashier looked up from his magazine, confused, as if he was trying to remember the protocol for disruptive patrons. He was distracted by two people entering the store in their Sunday best. The man walked over to the cashier, and the woman crossed to the refrigerator section along the wall opposite Meredith and Linda.

Linda cleared her throat uneasily. "I know what you're thinking. How could anyone do such a thing? I know. I was following orders. Complete the task. Do not think. Before this, I was a soldier." Linda sighed. "Not thinking is stupid. I see that now." She dropped the Misty Cat can on the floor and kicked it down the aisle. It slid over the linoleum like a hockey puck, coming to rest just beside the thirsty church lady, who looked over at them suspiciously. She went back to evaluating the sugary drinks, selecting a peach Snapple. She moved on to the caffeine drinks.

The song's saxophone solo chased away the whiny vocals.

Meredith watched as Linda rubbed her face in her hands, squeezed her eyes closed, then dropped her hands, letting them hang by her sides like weights anchoring an unsteady ocean buoy buffeted by choppy waves. She opened her eyes, stood up straight, and leveled her gaze at the base of Meredith's throat. Standing at attention.

Meredith threw the 99 Lives can at her. It bounced off Linda's bosom and clattered to the floor. Linda winced. The church woman looked over and backed away. Perhaps she didn't need any caffeine after all. She whispered in the ear of the man, who was finishing up buying Scratchers from the cashier. The couple left the market quickly.

Meredith pulled another can of Misty Cat off the shelf. "He could be in here, you said?"

Linda nodded. Meredith almost beaned her with Misty Cat, but Linda shielded herself with her arm and it bounced off her bicep.

"What about this?" said Meredith, holding up a can of Frilly Feast.

"Maybe not?" said Linda.

The cashier shouted from behind the bulletproof glass, "Everything all right?"

Linda gave him the thumbs-up sign.

The cans came faster now; one clipped Linda's thigh, another whizzed by her ear. "Meredith—" said Linda in a small voice. "Can you please stop throwing cat food at me?"

Meredith threw three cans of cat food up in the air, in a poorly executed juggling act: Oceanfishy Delite, Chicken & Beef Dinner, Salmon & Shrimp Flavor. They slid through her hands and fell to the floor. She stared at them. She looked at Linda, thinking. She turned around slowly, surveying the tiny market. The cowering cashier had taken cover behind the counter. She said, "It's the most definitive conceptual art piece of his life, actually."

"Conceptual...what?" said Linda.

"It's mainly tallow that comes out of rendering, and it goes into everything." Meredith crouched by the basket and pulled out the toothpaste. "He could also be in this toothpaste. Imagine that. Bits of Grillo all over my teeth. He'll help prevent cavities."

Meredith pulled shampoo and sunblock out of the basket then stood up. She held them behind her back. "Pick a hand, any hand!" She laughed and then started to cry. She turned and swanned up the aisle, throwing the shampoo and sunblock over her shoulder as Duran Duran climaxed. Linda dodged them.

Meredith pushed more items off the shelf: cat snacks, dog kibble, dog bones. She ran up the next aisle, taking items off the shelf, holding them up, saying, "Here he is, and here too," then throwing them down.

The cashier continued to wisely shelter behind the bulletproof glass, but shouted, "You break it, you buy it!"

"We wanted to help," said Linda, trying to catch up to Meredith.

"Grillo made it into the crayons! Ahh—he would have especially loved that!" said Meredith as she beaned Linda with children's art supplies. "Look around! Rendering plants supply ingredients for a good 80 percent of the products in here. The plastic bag for your purchases? Coated with Grillo."

Meredith opened her arms wide, and turned in a circle. The aisles were so narrow that as she turned, her hands pushed canned beans, boxes of macaroni-and-cheese mix, and cans of chicken soup off the shelf, and onto the ground. "It's all coated with Grillo, or made from him, or contains him. Like God. He's everywhere." She collapsed next to some cosmetics near the end of the aisle. "He's making every woman beautiful," she said, throwing mascara halfheartedly in the air. "And he's feeding all the animals. He's carrying your burdens for you," she said. She held up a bag of marshmallows. "And even *better* than God? He's s'mores."

Duran Duran started to fade out. Tainted Love took its place.

Meredith laid down on the floor of the aisle and placed the bag of marshmallows over her eyes like a sleep mask. She could hear the cashier's footsteps, then his voice floating above her, mixing with the song's ineffectual and plaintive lyrics.

"I spent three hours cleaning up this place this morning before you destroyed it in five minutes flat. I only make minimum wage, you know—"

"Come on," said Linda, who pulled off the marshmallows, helped Meredith up, then tossed a wad of cash toward the cashier. She put her arm around Meredith's shoulder and ushered her to the door. The trembling cashier, still muttering about the mess, picked up the cash from the floor.

Linda said to Meredith, "Let's get you home."

"Home," said Meredith, laughing mirthlessly. "My Merritt home. God help me."

LINDA: BOB'S YOUR UNCLE

I had no idea Cutiecups was so well-informed about rendering, but I guess it makes sense, since she worked for AFA Foods. I had to visit AFA Foods every so often, for a quick meeting with the COO, a pasty white guy named Bob, in order to pick up cash for the Merritt "Fund." Thankfully it was only four times a year. Fuckers like him always stared at my breasts, regardless of how well I had them camouflaged, and he stared at them without any regard for the fact that they were attached to a real person who disapproved strongly of this rude behavior. He leered with abandon, as if it was a private affair, as if my boobs were depicted on a photograph at one end of a stereoscope viewfinder, and he scrutinized them from the other end, hypnotized by false perspective.

I didn't see Meredith when I visited AFA Foods, I'm sure of it, because I would have remembered her. She was the most beautiful woman I had ever seen; tall and willowy. Her delicate boobies—well. I knew her boobs didn't light up Bob's viewfinder like my boobs did, but if I had a viewfinder, you can be sure that Meredith's blushing, retiring boobs would have made it glow like it was radioactive.

Inside her white business-casual work-shirt, her boob outline was made consistent, sanitized by her underwire bra; her boobs were like little soldiers, facing forward, de-nippled by silicon and elastic, the outline a perfect but unnatural curve. A tiny bit of bra-lace peeked out near an unbuttoned shirt button, slightly above her cleavage (not that she has any cleavage, really).

Then when her boobs were trapped within a sports bra, they rearrange themselves into a different topography: softer and flatter, her boobs blurred together into one unanimous curve, unbounceable, armed against all possible disruptions caused by the intensity of running. I myself didn't run. I did enough of that during hectic moments while serving in ETA. I did, however, wear a sports bra daily, one that had four hook enclosures stacked up on the back strap, and it had wide shoulder straps, because my boobs were heavy and I needed them to be secured well.

Meredith's best boob outline of all was when she got up in the morning and hadn't dressed yet, and she was still wearing a soft oversized t-shirt she liked to sleep in. *Ziggy Stardust* was screen-printed across the front of the shirt. Small holes lined the edges of the sleeves, and the hem was frayed. I remember when I first saw this shirt, that night Bernard and I had to do the cleanup operation in Atwater Village. I grabbed it from its resting place along with other pieces of clothing and stuffed them all in a duffle bag. It was pretty easy to make my selections, because her clothes were all basically the same: white dress shirts, navy slacks. Running clothes. The *Ziggy Stardust* shirt was different. Soft from many launderings, faded—I could tell it was like a security blanket.

I guess we kind of kidnapped her and maybe ruined her life. I didn't wonder extensively at the time whether we had ruined her life, because I didn't care. Since then, though, I've had moments of doubt; but I've also heard so many things about her husband, with his "concept art" and so-called health problems...maybe we did her a favor when we took her away. I liked to think so.

In her sleep shirt, Meredith's boobs were loose and soft, not bound by anything, the faint outline of her nipples teasing me when I hazarded a little peek out the corner of my eye. Her boobs nestled lower on her torso than when she wore a bra, and they were wider apart, like they were looking both ways before crossing the street. Of course I wasn't a thug like Bob, and never stared. Just a brief glance here and there was all I needed, when her attention was on her phone or her computer. If I let my gaze rest on them too long, I was sure my eyeballs would melt.

Bob wouldn't understand any of this. I'm sure he wrote off Meredith's delicate beauty as nothing more than boring corporate androgyny. Which was probably a blessing, really, because I wouldn't wish his creepy stereoscope ogling on my worst enemy. Guys like that ignore most of the female population, zeroing in on us unlucky few with cup sizes bigger than double D.

AFA Foods' processing plant always passed inspections, but not without a few greased palms along the way, an operation that Vern coordinated. It didn't matter if it was a city, county, or state inspection. Even the federal inspections—Vern had the contacts and could get to the right person via plenty of middlemen, each without knowledge of the other—like a terrorist network. Cells of corruption.

Merritt bent over backwards for the Fortune 500, no questions asked, just pay up and Bob's your uncle. I love that expression. I got drunk with a British girl back in Spain years ago, during a furlough from ETA. She was pretty loud when I made her come, and that's what she said, over and over. "Bobsyourunclebobsyour Oh Oh OOOH!!" Heh. I miss those days sometimes. It's been a long time since I made anyone come, and vice versa. I stopped thinking about it. I stopped needing it. Until now. Cutiecups awakened me, like I was Sleeping Beauty, but without any dwarves handy. You could hardly call Bernard a dwarf. The guy was over 6'5" even when he was slouching.

That hot British girl had freckles on her arms like Cutiecups does. I wonder what Cutiecups shouts when she comes, or if she shouts at all.

It took every ounce of self-control that I possessed, but after that amazing kiss down by the train tracks last week, I backed off. I knew I had to wait for Meredith to be ready, to get used to the idea, and also it wouldn't hurt, if we ever did get together, to be totally sober. That way I'd know that what she felt for me wasn't colored by rebound, grief, or booze. That way I'd know it was the real deal.

When Meredith was done with her meltdown, I took her outside, sat her down on a bench in the shade, then returned inside to collect the items she had originally planned to purchase. The cashier flapped at me about the mess, but I ignored him, paid for the items, then left. I helped Meredith up and we walked home together in silence.

I wasn't hurt when Meredith threw all that stuff at me. Meredith didn't have a strong throwing arm, I'm well-upholstered, and I don't bruise easily. I was relieved. When I told her what happened to her husband's body, I think it caused her to defrost a little from the shock of his death. The sooner she defrosted, the sooner she could consider how she felt about me, about us.

Back at the apartment, Meredith took a shower. I stuck around. I turned up the A/C. I made her a kalimotxo. I pulled out some sleeping pills I'd swiped from Narcotics earlier, at work—I hadn't been sleeping well since I'd heard the news about Michael Mendebal. I put one of the tablets on the table next to a glass of water.

When she emerged from the bathroom wearing her Ziggy Stardust t-shirt and some boxer shorts, it was clear that I should go, though she looked adorable. Her dewy skin glowed from the heat of the shower, and her severely short hair was wet and spiky. I nearly swooned but kept my cool. She knocked back the kalimotxo and went to the kitchen, looking through the cabinets. "Is there any Advil here?" she asked.

I said, "Perhaps an Ativan?" gesturing to the table. She considered for a moment, said, "Why not?" and then swallowed it with the water. I turned out the lights and closed the blinds. She mumbled, "Sorry," from the bed. I shushed her and closed the door.

Everything I'd heard about Meredith's husband to date sounded like he was very useless, but when I reflected on her observation that his death was an act of art, it floored me. Imagine that? The world was a strange and disgusting place.

After I told Meredith the truth about what we had done to her husband's body and her house, I felt like I was on my way to disengaging myself from my years of service to Merritt. It was the first step. I was going to take Merritt down, fast. Because I was done. Next, I had to ensure that Meredith had every last piece of evidence she might need to get to the truth behind how Merritt really operated. To do that, it was time to contact all the businesses who were members of Merritt's donation fund. I would start with Bob at AFA Foods (I couldn't wait to harass Bob in particular). I'd make them all attend the meeting Meredith had planned. Even if they didn't want their buildings converted into giant hot dogs, they could still be shown that current Merritt leadership needed to be removed. Without some coaxing, though, these powerful businessmen might try to use their connections to help the current leadership, and I wasn't having that.

Next, I was pretty sure that if Meredith had all the dirt, then she'd very likely turn it over to Girron. I surmised that he would in turn publish it, and then Merritt would never recover from what would be a PR nuclear explosion.

Then Meredith and I could get the hell out of here and go somewhere far away. Like they do in fairy tales. I stopped dreaming years ago, but it was time to start again. Time to have a life.

BE NICE

Meredith's eyes were full of crud when she woke up the next morning, as if she had cried in her sleep. One eyelid was stuck shut. She threw some water on her face and dried it with a towel, then looked in the mirror. Her lips looked like little transparent earthworms and her eyes were bloodshot. How charming, she thought. How very nice.

She had no idea how she felt about anything anymore. She suspected this had something to do with her upbringing, but she couldn't connect the dots. And last night at the 7-11? It hadn't felt real. It was like someone else was throwing cans of cat food at Linda, someone else was raving about rendering, Grillo, and God.

The news of her home burning down had shattered her defenses—she could no longer circumvent her guilt and grief around Grillo's death. She wondered if her landlord had tried to contact her about the fire, so she pulled out her Nokia to check her voice mail, but it was still dead. She'd forgotten to replace the battery. She logged into her Yahoo mail account and saw previous emails from her mother, still marked as unread, as well as two new emails, also from her mother, their bolded subject lines varying on the same theme of perceived abandonment masquerading as concern. It was odd to see emails from her mother, who normally preferred the phone. Meredith imagined there were several voice mails that'd show up on the Nokia once she replaced the battery.

Her mother, her destroyed home, and Grillo. She closed her laptop and picked up the Blackberry. There was a new message from Gil Girron. She played it back. "Meredith, I heard the news about the charter vote. I'm very curious to hear how that came about. Also, I took a look at the Power-Point. I'd like to discuss it further. Please call me Monday at 2:00 p.m."

How promising!

She wanted to prepare. She wanted to have a clear head for the call, but her mother's unread email messages were like like invisible mosquitos dive-bombing her with their high-pitched whine.

She knew that her mother would be furious if she simply emailed her back. Her mother expected a phone call. Her indecision as to whether she should call her mother now, instead of later, was like water circling a drain, getting tinier and more compact, as she put on her clothes and ran her fingers through her short hair. As she drank a glass of water, she thought about the subject lines of the emails that had marched down her screen. The last one, in particular, had stood out because it shouted in all-caps, "VERY CONCERNED."

She told herself to stop being a baby and keyed her mother's number into the Blackberry. Her mother answered on the first ring. "Hello?"

"Hi, Mom."

"Meredith? I didn't recognize the number. You're alive?"

"Um. Yes?"

"I went by your house because I wanted to drop off some things I thought you'd want." Meredith's mother always gave

Meredith clothing cast-offs that were best suited for Goodwill. Meredith then turned around and dropped them off at Goodwill. This was tedious but it helped her mother. Did her mother dislike the idea that her worn-out clothes might adorn strangers who were poor? *Be nice*, Meredith chastised herself in her head. She remembered her grandmother talking about the Depression, when every last worn-out skate key, glass bottle, and empty can was worth keeping, just in case. The fact that her mother wasn't a packrat was the most evolved thing about her. *Be nice.*

"Oh!" said Meredith. "You saw my house?"

"What's left of it," said her mother. "I had no idea if you were even alive, and you didn't call—why didn't the hospital call me?"

"I wasn't in the hospital. Remember that project I told you about for the City of Merritt? They wanted me on-site, so I've been living here temporarily for the last few days. I completely missed the fire. I guess I was lucky." Was it a few days? Or was it more like ten days? She'd lost track.

"I'm so relieved you're both all right. I've been going out of my mind. But Merritt? That horrible, smelly town. How can Raymond stand it, what with his asthma?"

"The fact is, Mom, he isn't—" Meredith took a deep breath, and started again. "He died. He died, okay? He died and I didn't tell anyone because—"

"Wait a minute. Raymond is dead? He died in the fire?"

"By the time I came home, it was all over with. Mom, I'm really sorry, but I must go back to work. There are these hideous deadlines and—"

"Meredith, don't do that. It isn't nice. Be nice. You have a responsibility to Raymond's parents, to let them know. To let *me* know. You have no idea what it's like to have a child who has disappeared and might be dead. It's incredible to me that you're still, even now, hiding behind work. Stop being like your father. Look where it landed him—in an early grave. You can't just pretend as if nothing happened, after your husband died and your home burned down!"

Meredith said, "You're right, you're right. I'm really sorry I didn't call. But I couldn't call. I just couldn't. It's all my fault."

"You burned down the house?" Meredith could hear the clatter of the phone dropping onto the floor, then her mother's voice. "Did you say it was all your fault?"

"No, I mean, I should have been home earlier that day. I was late again, I'm always late, and usually he's angry about that—was angry." Meredith stopped. She wanted to hang up. She remembered Linda from the weekend before, gesturing to her, and knocking loudly on the inside of the front door. She had tried to help Meredith extract herself from her mother.

"Someone's at the door!" Meredith said. "I'll call you back." She hung up.

As if she was in some kind of screwball comedy, she then heard a knock on the door. It was Linda, looking like she had been sent to the principal's office.

"Come in," said Meredith. "I just got off the phone with my mother. Or actually, I just hung up on her. I can't believe I did that. Who am I?"

Linda followed her in, but hesitated just inside the door, which stood open. She said, "You are a very good person."

"Aw, thanks."

"I am checking on you." Linda said, standing with her hand on the doorknob, as if she fully expected Meredith to kick her out.

"Sure, come in. I haven't made coffee yet."

"I will make some. Did your mother want something?"

"She knows about the fire. And that Grillo is dead." Meredith sat down at the kitchen table. Linda started making some coffee.

"Do you want to talk about it?" Linda said.

"I suck. I just totally suck. Poor Grillo."

"You are grieving his death."

"We had a terrible fight the night before he died. Maybe that's why he—did it. I had said things that I couldn't take back."

"I have difficulty believing this."

"It's true. We'd fought about his shrink, Dr. Stein."

Linda looked confused. She turned and got two coffee cups down from the cabinet.

Meredith said, "I mean his psychiatrist."

"I see."

"I'd had a horrible day. I'd just been fired over pink slime."

"Pink slime?"

"It's a long story. When I came home, I found Grillo pacing back and forth along the foot of our bed." She slumped back against the chair. "He was angry, but it was hard to take him seriously because he was still wearing his pajamas."

"Why was he angry?"

"Something about Dr. Stein. I didn't understand what his problem was. I had a splitting headache."

"Was he a bad doctor?"

"Dr. Stein? He'd probably saved Grillo's life countless times. That's what Grillo had often said—in the past. It was a pattern. One day Stein was a godsend, next day, he was a quack."

"I love these expressions."

"They can be weird, right? I don't know how 'quack' went from the sound a duck makes to the name for an incompetent doctor."

"Maybe incompetent doctors talk a lot but don't do anything helpful."

"You're probably right."

Linda brought coffee to the table and sat down. She asked, "Why did your husband want to stop seeing his doctor?"

"That's what I asked, too. Grillo said I knew already. That I was playing games. My brain felt shaky and I couldn't concentrate. I was really hungry. My head pounded. I hadn't eaten all day, running from one crisis to the next. I wasn't up for playing games."

"You are not that kind of person."

"I remember how pale Grillo's skin was. He didn't go out very much. He kept following me around while I tried to find the Advil, then hovered while I poured myself a glass of water. He ranted about a message from Stein on the answering machine. We still have—I mean had—an answering machine, even though only senior citizens use them nowadays. It was barely limping along—like our marriage."

Linda had made some plain toast and placed it by Meredith's elbow. Meredith didn't touch it.

Meredith said, "I wonder if the natural end of my marriage could have been calculated in advance, the way one can determine the diminishing radioactivity levels of plutonium. Something you could figure out with math."

"Marriages are the opposite of math. This has been my observation."

"You're probably right. He would always say, 'you're not listening,' but if you can't ignore a person's tone, then that's not really true, is it?"

"No, it's not. You cared."

"He said I didn't care. It's just that, he usually talked about the same cheerless things over and over. It was hard to take. That night he said, 'You and Dr. Stein are like the Politburo, conferring about me behind my back, discussing the sick fuck who can't manage anything. Admit it.' Then he pulled a spatula from this pewter mug I have—I had. He brandished it at me like we were about to have a sword fight. I wanted to say, "You killed my father, prepare to die.'"

"He killed your father? When?"

"No, no. I was making a joke, quoting a silly movie we both liked. Stupid. Jokes never diffused Grillo's rage. They just made it worse. Anyway. He said, 'I think I have Stockholm Syndrome. It explains why I'm still married to you. You're holding me hostage.'"

"But Meredith," said Linda. "Think. Was he the hostage, or you?"

Meredith shook her head. "It was mutual, obviously." Linda sat down with two cups of coffee. They both sipped from their cups without speaking for a few minutes.

Linda said, "I still don't understand. What did the doctor say on the message machine?"

"Grillo had told Stein in their last session that he was going to kill himself. That wasn't new—Grillo often talked about that, which was terrifying by itself. This time though, he said he planned to kill me first."

Linda took Meredith's hands in hers. Linda's hands were warm. Meredith's own hands were ice cold. She started crying. At least she wasn't crying while she was asleep—was that progress?

Linda leaned forward and gave Meredith a hug. Hugging anyone in a sitting position is awkward, and this hug was no exception. It would normally have made Meredith laugh. But it just made her cry more.

"Don't comfort me," said Meredith, pushing Linda away. "See? I was to blame."

"Please let me participate in your dark feeling," said Linda. "I too have felt this way. Let me tell you what happened in Barcelona."

LINDA: MISCARRIAGES

After I had coffee with Meredith, I went to work. I usually gave Vern an update on Mondays, but he wasn't in, so I sent him a text. Bernard wasn't in, either. I was accustomed to seeing Bernard almost every day, but that had changed when Vern assigned me to tailing Meredith.

After I made arrangements to allow the LAFD investigator to inspect Merritt government vehicles, I filled out paperwork for the silver Prius chase. There was still no sign of Bernard. I missed the big lug. Besides our shared history, he was also the only person I could speak at ease with in Euskera.

Mayor Mendebal, like Shitbird and other second-generation Basque-Americans, only knew a little Euskera, though they always pretended they were fluent. This was beginning to bother me. Ten years ago, after I had installed Mendebal's security system at his Huntington Beach house, I had stopped by Mayor Mendebal's office to give him the temporary code. I refused to give it to his secretary because I take security very seriously, so I gave it directly to Mendebal in Euskera: 1234, *bat, bi, hiru, lau*. He had nodded and repeated the code back to me. I then continued, in Euskera, to explain that it was imperative he change the code to something else as soon as possible. He nodded again and I took my leave.

Two months later, when I had to go back again to Huntington Beach to supervise an installation of a new automatic gate for the driveway, I needed to add the gate to the security system. No one was home and I didn't have the new security code, so I tried using the original code to disarm the alarm, 1234, and to my surprise, it still worked. Either Mayor Mendebal was too lazy to change the code or he wasn't fluent enough in Euskera to understand what I had said, or he was too proud to admit he needed the instructions in English, or all of the above.

I thought about how Bernard, through his connections, had saved us all those years ago when things had gone wrong in Barcelona. When Mrs. Mendebal was a teen living in France, she had babysat Bernard's cousin, who had, like many Basques, moved to France from Spain. They had emigrated in order to flee from Franco, whose solution to the Basque nationalist movement had been to kill them all. Later, Franco adjusted his tactics when he realized he needed Basque manufacturing prowess and money, and if he didn't stop killing all the Basques, Spain would become even more broke than it already was. But I digress. Through the ETA network, Bernard's cousin got in touch with his former babysitter, Mrs. Mendebal, who by then was living in Merritt, and that is how we got out of the fire and into the stewing pot. I wondered how Mayor Mendebal and his wife communicated when they first met, if neither of them were fully fluent in a common language, but I guess you don't really need to speak the same language to know when you have the hots for someone.

I decided to go home for lunch. As I drove home, I watched my thoughts chase themselves around a central point that I was avoiding. I realized I felt responsible for what Michael Mendebal had done to those young boys. I had indirectly facilitated it. Why didn't I set that security code to be something more difficult when I had the chance, when I realized Mendebal hadn't changed it?

Maybe it wouldn't have made any difference, whether the code was 1234 or changed to something more complicated; Mendebal probably would have given his son the new code, because his family was close. I still felt guilty.

Once when Cousin Jerry, the drug addict, was stoned out of his mind at a benefit that the Mendebals threw one night (Bernard and I ran security for it, of course), he screamed in Euskera, "Goat-fucker!" repeatedly. It wasn't clear who he was calling a goat-fucker. Bernard and I just shook our heads, embarrassed for him. Mrs. Mendebal became very pale and agitated. I escorted Jerry out, and put him in a taxi.

A good Catholic lady, Mrs. Mendebal. Very Catholic. Always volunteering for the Catholic Church. I thought about how Michael Mendebal had been dean of a Catholic boy's school. Maybe the Church was the source of the rot. After all, it wasn't exactly smelling like roses these days, what with all the child abuse scandals that kept coming out every year. An avalanche. At any rate, Mrs. Mendebal seemed very devout. She wore a big gold cross, and she was Basque—all the Basques were very Catholic.

I myself never partook of the Catholic Kool-Aid, even though I was forced to learn the Catechism when I was young. I have always been an atheist, even before I knew the word. Why? First of all, my mother died having me. Her pregnancy was difficult and when her water broke, our small country village's midwife was off delivering some other brat. I don't think the other baby lived, because no one shared my birthday in school. It was probably stillborn, a regular occurrence back then, unfortunately.

In the absence of the midwife, my brother, who was eight at the time, delivered me. My father fainted at the sight of blood, so he held my mother's hand. Later, when my brother was just fifteen, he joined ETA. He was arrested by the Guardia Civil when he was twenty. We never saw him again. My father died when I was ten. That's why neither of them could stop my uncle from molesting me—they were both gone. I had no one to protect me from my uncle, who was, ironically, my guardian.

Anyway, the story my brother liked to tell me as soon as I was old enough to understand, was that my mother bled to death because of me. He said I clawed her vaginal canal with my fetal fingernails when I came out. I believed that for years, but in retrospect, maybe she bled to death for some other reason. After all, an eight year old had delivered the baby. Maybe it was my brother's fault my mother bled to death. How much harm can tiny fetal fingernails do, exactly? I didn't know. At any rate, my mother died giving birth to me and I lived; I was pregnancy number eight, but my brother was her only other child because her other pregnancies resulted in miscarriage or stillbirths; I concluded, therefore, that an abortion would have benefited my mother tremendously, instead of giving birth to me. After hearing what an amazing person she was from my brother, when he wasn't telling me it was my fault she died, it seemed to me that it would have been better if my mother had lived, and I had not. It would also have been better if she had access to contraception. Catholics weren't on board with that, of course.

To a large extent, Basques are self-saboteurs. Their Catholicism mixed with their genes meant tons of pregnancies and tons of problems giving birth—problems that had something to do with a blood incompatibility—the Rh factor. The birth survival rate started to improve soon after I was born; I guess the drug invented to head off Rh disasters had finally reached my hometown, because in school, there were double the number of kids in the classes below me than in the classes above me.

At any rate, though I have never been pregnant, I cannot imagine the level of physical agony one might suffer from stillbirths or miscarriages, as well as whatever other emotions a woman might feel, all because of a pregnancy that didn't need to happen in the first place. I am an atheist for many reasons, but this reason is central to my non-belief.

I heard a knock at my front door. Through the door's peephole, I could tell it was Bernard because his chest filled the entire view. After I let him in, he stood by the kitchen table, instead of sitting, because the chairs were too small for him.

He looked at me sideways as he always did. When we first started working together back in Spain, he looked at my breasts instead of my face while I was speaking to him. I'd considered having them cut off, these damned boobs of mine, since they didn't really do much but weigh me down, aside from their usefulness in private moments that I allowed myself occasionally. I eventually concluded that cutting them off was too drastic a solution. I'd considered cutting the breast-starers' eyes out; but that was drastic too. So I simply punched Bernard in the face and broke his nose. I made sure he knew why. He had no idea what he had been doing. It didn't excuse what he did, of course. People get hurt all the time because of some dickhead behaving without awareness. You should know what you are doing, always, and also, *why* you are doing it. You should always ask yourself, is the reason a good one? A fair one? Does it harm anyone? Otherwise, bad things happen that otherwise could be avoided.

From then on, Bernard was careful not to look directly at me. My colleagues in ETA were careful around me, too, after rumors spread about Bernard's broken nose—rumors that I spread, just to make sure no one messed with me.

Bernard said to the wall, "My mother is sick."

I said, "I'm sorry to hear that, Bernard."

He nodded and didn't say anything for a while. I made a salad. I knew he had something else to say, but it would take him a while to gather the words together.

He said, "Perhaps a visit?"

Bernard and I had been over this many times. I was deeply suspicious of the periodic offers of pardon from the Spanish government to members of ETA willing to give themselves up. Not once was I convinced it was safe, so I didn't take them up on their offers, and I made sure Bernard didn't either. Both of us were deeply sad about what had happened in Barcelona, but we also didn't want to spend the rest of our lives in Spanish prisons, not to mention being tortured.

My answering silence told Bernard what he knew already. We couldn't go back.

Bernard persevered, saying, "They disbanded ETA."

I said, "I hadn't heard." I didn't keep up with any of the old country's news. Bernard produced a folded-up newspaper from his back pocket and pushed it across the table. It was *El País*, published out of Madrid—every week, Bernard drove across town to the international newsstand on Fairfax to buy it as well as *El Correo,* one of the Bilbao newspapers. Under the headline, "ETA Announces its Complete Dissolution," was a quote from ETA's formal statement: "ETA was born from the people and now it dissolves back into the people." That sounded a little like a miscarriage. How very Basque.

I raised an eyebrow and stirred my coffee. "And?" I asked.

We enjoyed the silence of another long pause. He finally said, "We have American identities."

I read the article, then pointed to a paragraph near the end. I said, "Listen to this. 'ETA won't find a glimmer of impunity for its crimes. It can announce its disappearance but its crimes will not disappear, nor will the work of justice to track them down and punish them.'" I sipped my coffee, swallowed, then said, "The Guardia Civil never forget. Why would they stop now?"

"My mother is dying."

I sighed. I thought about it. Was it safe to go back? I found it improbable. Did I want to go back? That answer was always a resounding no, but maybe I felt differently now? Would I go back, for example if Cutiecups went back with me? Even then I wasn't sure. It would be nice to take her away from Merritt. My ugly concrete garden. The refuge that was a lie.

Bernard's hair was turning gray, and he had a stoop. He wasn't getting any younger. Still, he was huge. He was unmissable. He would easily be flagged at Spanish customs and immigration. But, as he pointed out, we did have American citizenship now, with new names. Maybe they wouldn't look twice at him because of the US passport. What's more, maybe he could avoid the obvious points of entry, like Madrid, and instead travel across the border from France, entering the country via a remote mountain pass.

I said, "I still don't think you should, but if you must, maybe you could go back—if you were careful." I proposed a strategy. "You'd need to use a wheelchair. Wear sunglasses. You can't use your legs and you're blind. That's what you tell them. In English. No Spanish. No Euskera. You're American. No walking."

He nodded.

"I wouldn't stay long," I added.

Bernard nodded again.

"So what else is going on?" I said, while I made some sandwiches for lunch.

Bernard shrugged. "Papers to burn for Peck."

"What papers?"

Bernard shrugged again. "Lots of papers. In boxes. In a storage unit. To shred. It will be a small bonfire."

I laughed. Bernard enjoyed estimating the size of things in terms of how big the bonfire would be.

I asked, "So only like, two or three boxes?"

He nodded.

I said, "Hold off on the bonfire, will you? Just tell Peck it's done. Give me the address and the code to the storage unit."

Bernard nodded and appeared to be much lighter in spirit. I served the sandwiches and we ate in silence.

He stood up and said, "After this job, I go to my mother."

"Sure. I'll deal with Peck's boxes. Buy your ticket." He nodded goodbye and left.

BIG SAD LYING EYES

Tuesday, September 1, 2009
Senate charter vote in 8 days

On Tuesday, Meredith woke up feeling tired again. She'd
missed going on a run because she'd stayed up late the night
before, going through the treasure trove of papers that Linda
had dropped off. Papers that apparently Chuck Peck didn't
want her to see.

In her call with Girron the day before, Meredith had
thanked him for the piece he'd ran that morning about the
charter vote being postponed. He wanted to know more
about the transparency campaign she'd mentioned in her
PowerPoint. She told him that she couldn't go into detail,
because she wanted buy-in from businesses first. It would
strengthen the plan. The City Council would have no choice
but to approve it, if their real constituency, industry, was all-
in. The business roundtable was in two days. She told Girron
she'd provide better details after the meeting.

As she got ready for her meeting with Peck, putting on
her Seventh Day Adventist business attire and some light
makeup, she had to admit that the vision she preferred for
Merritt's future—a surreal wonderland of giant everyday
objects, propane canisters, plush toys—was unlikely to be
realized to its fullest extent. She wasn't stupid. She knew

how phobic businesspeople were about scrutiny. But it would be fun to watch them squirm, and it was a bargaining chip. She wasn't worried.

In the meeting, Peck's opening gambit was to try to toss out Meredith's whole campaign plan. He said, "I was surprised that Vern bothered to hire you, honestly. We've had this sort of problem before, and it always goes away, case dismissed, etc. I don't see why it would be any different this time."

While he described Merritt's PR crisis and its similarities to ones in the past, talking down to her as if she had never heard of Merritt or PR, as if she was some kind of ingenue who had just walked in off the street, Meredith was transfixed by his big sad eyes and the way he used them in combination with his soft pleading voice, a voice that sounded manipulative and inauthentic, but was, at the same time, hypnotizing and persuasive. This guy was good. This guy should be a spokesperson. But he wasn't Merritt's spokesperson. He was the city administrator, finance director, redevelopment director, city clerk, city treasurer, and head of the municipal light and power operation. In other words, he was in charge of far too much already to also be an effective spokesperson. Vern, who was Merritt's spokesperson, also held many roles, roles that weren't on the books, so Meredith couldn't identify them properly. She had tried. Obviously, from what Linda had said, Vern also had a lot of responsibility, but he didn't have the same clout as Peck. And maybe Vern's other mysterious responsibilities were too overwhelming. Vern hadn't returned any of her calls. He had looked unwell at their last meeting. She hoped he was all right.

She wondered if Vern had hired her because he thought the situation was hopeless, and he wanted her to be the fall guy. Did they really expect results, or was it a giant set-up for failure? But no, Vern had clearly thought The Model was the answer. How absurd. It was just a souped-up Excel spread-sheet. People always thought their PR problems could be solved easily and quickly, when in fact, success was always achieved by plain old hard work, by paying attention, crunch-ing data, doing the analysis and research, being persistent and strategizing. Of course, all that work was for nothing without full commitment of the stakeholders. Also, being truthful helped a tremendous amount. Lying, along with not backing, or outright lacking, a PR Crisis Plan, always doomed the client. Meredith wished she had the deviant mind to exploit Merritt's desire for PR snake oil. But it wasn't who she was.

Chuck Peck was still talking. He was a few years older than Mayor Mendebal, but exhibited more vitality. Meredith tried to focus. He continued, "This is what we need, a clean sweep, open the windows and let the fresh air in." He chuck-led and said, "Except on Thursdays." Chuck could make his big sad eyes twinkle when he chuckled. Meredith figured if he was ever arrested for countless irregular and extra-legal choices he had made while helming Merritt, he might consider a new career doing hypnotic relaxation videos on YouTube.

She chuckled back. She thought about Linda's eyes, which were also big and sad, and brown, like Chuck's. Lin-da's eyes weren't manipulative. She used her big sad eyes to actually see Meredith—then, act on what she saw, by giving Meredith a hand when she needed it, to catch her before she fell. She used her big sad eyes to observe that it was time for a martini or time to watch the sunset or time to make coffee or time to listen, trust, and collaborate with Meredith. Linda helped, and she did it without fanfare, unobtrusively. Efficiently.

Because of Linda, Meredith had arrived at Peck's office with more confidence than she might have had otherwise.

The archive boxes had been a godsend. Just like that, Meredith had at her fingertips all the data a rescuer of a messed-up city could possibly ask for. As he talked about the city's improvements, history, and its close relationships with businesses there, Meredith knew exactly what was a lie and what wasn't. She'd chomped her way through the materials Linda gave her like a whale eating a school of minnows. She also knew what Chuck's hidden agenda was for the meeting: to deny and obfuscate his mismanagement and pure greed, and pretend like everything was on the up and up.

Linda had told Meredith to be careful, that Chuck was volatile. Meredith, however, didn't scare easy. Grillo had been volatile; it permeated the atmosphere of her home life for over a decade. Going along with it had been a mistake. Where had her compliance gotten them? Nowhere.

"As you can see, there's no real need for your services," said Chuck.

Meredith was ready. She said, "With all due respect, I'd have to disagree. Vern knows PR well, but one person isn't enough to battle this crisis."

His eyes lost a bit of their hypnotist's glow.

Meredith continued, "In order to make sure my PR campaign for Merritt is fact-based, I'd like to see records for the pension plan for all city employees. Can you tell me where I'd find those documents? Are they digital, by chance?" This was a test; Meredith had already seen the pension records. Chuck's pension was $550,000 a year, far more than any any other city official's pension in the state of California. Meredith had found other evidence of misappropriation: reimbursement for groceries, country club memberships, Christmas gifts for his family, homeowners association dues, massages, haircuts, and personal property taxes.

Peck cleared his throat. "Pension plans have nothing to do with PR."

"I'm simply pursuing your best interests. There's nothing to hide, is there? We need to approach your image overhaul without being on the defensive."

"No one is being defensive," said Peck defensively. "You're hardly like any PR people I've known. You're like some kind of widget-counting wonk. Was that a winning strategy for AFA's pink slime meltdown, I wonder?"

It impressed Meredith that Peck had researched her as much as she had researched him, even if his comment was clearly meant to put her on the defensive. She ignored it and said coolly, "Assuming that Mayor Mendebal is indicted for voter fraud—let's hope that doesn't happen—but if it did happen, how would you go about recovering from the negative PR?"

"I doubt he'll be indicted—I just spent a great deal of energy explaining why."

"You really doubt it?"

"It's purely political. LA just wants to get its hands on Merritt. They always have."

Meredith cocked her head to one side and said nothing. Chuck went on, "Mendebal has an excellent civil lawyer, too."

"What about the criminal case, though?" Meredith felt like she was pointing out the obvious. Did this man not read the *LA Times*? No one cared about the civil case. It was the criminal case that mattered.

Chuck scoffed. "Depending on the evidence, which sounds circumstantial at best—if it really was that serious a case, then we'd have to hold an election for a new mayor."

"You might want to consider doing that anyway, just to improve Merritt's image."

"Perhaps," said Chuck, tapping a signet ring he wore on the desk like he was sending a Morse Code message.

Meredith pushed farther. "And you might want to consider holding new elections for the city council—as well as appoint a new city manager."

"Now you've really overstepped—"

"Merritt needs to show that it wants to clean house and just because the kitchen is clean, it doesn't mean that mildew isn't still coating the bathtub curtain, as it were."

Chuck pushed back from his desk, stood up, and started pacing the length of his large office. He asked, "So what exactly is your PR strategy?"

"The best strategy, honestly, is total transparency, total honesty. Look at Tylenol—"

"Ah, Tylenol! I remember that! I was actually in Chicago when it happened! I took some Tylenol the same night all these people were dying. The news reported they couldn't figure out who the serial killer was, or how he did it. When I found out he'd poisoned random bottles of Tylenol, I couldn't believe I wasn't already dead."

"That must've been very strange for you," Meredith said. "But the fact is, the only way that Merritt can get out of this mess with some semblance of dignity, is to show your cards. I mean Merritt's cards."

After a pause, Chuck said flatly, "I do not approve."

"Vern Page already approved it." This was sort of true. He had allowed her to proceed with gathering info to back up the PowerPoint, but he hadn't specifically approved the roundtable and other tactical details. She was sure that it was only because she hadn't been able to get ahold of him.

"I don't care. Vern works for me, and what I say, goes. I don't approve of your damned plan at all. Or you." Peck stopped pacing, changed direction, and approached her as he said, "Get the hell out of here. I don't want to see your face inside this building ever again. Gina! Make sure this woman is barred from entry. GINA!"

Meredith stood up as Peck continued to shout at her as well as Gina, who had appeared in the doorway. He was becoming a cartoon. Red in the face, eyes bulging, fists in the air. It was ludicrous.

When Peck paused to take a breath, Meredith said simply, "You need a time out." Then she left.

Peck didn't worry her. He was knee-deep in scandal, and it was only a matter of time before he was indicted, himself. Though Vern had tried to fire her, he hadn't yet, officially. She took the stairs down to the next floor and stopped by the general admin's desk to ask after him. The admin said he was out sick.

Outside City Hall, Meredith made for her car, got in, and turned on the air conditioning. She drove to McDonald's and parked, keeping the engine running with the AC on full blast. The heat was giving her a headache. She saw a woman walking by who looked like her mother, which reminded her of the call she'd had with her the night before. She realized her mother had been right. Meredith needed to get the paperwork done for Grillo's death certificate, she needed to call her landlord, and she needed to file a claim with renter's insurance for the loss of all her belongings. She probably needed a new marriage certificate too, since she doubted she could do much without proof she was the spouse. It was a lot. She called Linda instead, who picked up on the first ring.

"Officer Vasco."

"Linda! I'm so sorry to bother you, am I interrupting?"

"No. It is only some paperwork. Where are you?"

"McDonald's," said Meredith. "I just met with Peck. It sort of ended badly."

"Are you safe?"

Meredith thought that was a strange question. "Yes. Sorry. I just wanted to ask you, do you know how to get a death certificate?"

"I'm confused. Did Peck threaten you?"

"No, well…sort of. I'm not worried about him. It's for my husband."

"I have it," said Linda.

"What? Really? But how?"

"I have connections. I can drop it off later. Anything else?"

"Would you call my mom back for me?"

"Your—mother?" Linda asked.

"I'm kidding! It's just that you seem to always know what I need, before I know it! I'm not used to it! It's like an uncanny superpower."

"My pleasure," said Linda. "I have a copy of your marriage certificate as well."

Meredith felt like she was going to cry. She whispered, "Thank you."

"It's nothing. I have other news. I followed up on your invitations to the meeting Thursday."

"What's the ratio of yeses to nos?"

"They're all coming."

"All—? That's…remarkable."

"You will have your meeting. You will make your presentation. It will be successful. I'm sure of it."

"It's all because of you."

"I am helping. That is all."

"Thank you, Linda."

"I must go. See you later."

LINDA: AMERICAN SAYINGS

Bob Hawley perspired a lot. He was perspiring now. Perhaps it was because he was surprised that I had unexpectedly visited him at AFA Foods. I wasn't due for another visit until the end of next quarter, technically. He stared at my breasts while he said, "We're paid up, I thought."

I thought of my spatulas. Spatulas are better than gonads, I said to myself. I said to Bob, "I'm not here for the usual reason."

"What, then?"

"Things have changed, unfortunately," I said. "Your involvement in Merritt payoffs will come to light soon. Unless you can help with a meeting we're planning." Bob stopped breast-staring and finally looked at my face.

"We're due to file Chapter 11 any minute now," said Bob. He had a tie on. Who wears ties anymore? Bob did. There were food stains on his tie, stains that blended in with the rest of the tie's blue paisley pattern. The top of his balding head was sunburned and peeling. He gave off a tangy unkempt smell, not unlike the smell of fearful livestock up the street at Farmer John.

I said, "It is my understanding that a business can remain open after a bankruptcy. Is this correct?"

"Yes, but—"

"Your business will not remain open if it is revealed that inspections were faked. Now. About the meeting—"

"What meeting?"

"Merritt would like to hold an emergency meeting with Merritt businesspeople in two days to discuss the upcoming charter vote. Our PR crisis consultant will make a presentation. We have reserved the conference room at Trattoria Pazza. Thursday at 1:00 p.m. Here is a list of people to contact." I pushed a list across the desk. "I believe you know these people. I propose that you contact them and inform them of the mandatory meeting. Can I count on you?"

He looked at the list, then pulled his calendar book toward him and opened it to Thursday, as if to buy himself time.

He said, "But it's on Thursday."

"Yes."

"Thursdays in Merritt—"

I gave him a look. He sighed and wrote down the details in his calendar.

He said, "It's not going to be easy to persuade the others to attend. It's a holiday weekend."

I stared at Bob blankly. Then I remembered it was the American holiday for Labor next Monday.

I said, "I believe a weekend begins on Saturday, not Thursday. Do not feel that it is torture. There will be sandwiches."

Bob loosened his tie and picked up the list of names I'd given him. He scanned it, then said, "At least one of these people might be a problem."

"Which one, exactly?"

"Gordon Jeffries. He left Best Coast a month ago. Marigold McCartney took his job."

"I don't know her," I said.

"That's what I'm trying to tell you—she's new and doesn't know about the various arrangements in place."

"I'll deal with her. I'm sure you can handle the rest. We're looking for 100 percent participation. Let them know that it's in their best interest. If the city loses its charter, you'll find your business suddenly situated in the middle of Los Angeles, instead. Many regulations, many obstacles will be introduced, yes? Invite anyone I may have missed. Colleagues with ties to the State Senate would also be helpful."

"How would I know who has that kind of power?"

"Is this my problem?" I asked.

"I guess I can try."

"Cross your I's and dot your T's."

Bob looked at me with confusion. Dammit. Maybe I got the saying backward. I said, "You know what I mean. See you Thursday. Don't be late."

"Fine."

Gordon Jeffries at Best Coast Rendering had always been extremely easy to work with, which wasn't surprising. Best Coast's operation would have been shut down for safety violations long ago if they hadn't subscribed to Merritt's Donation Fund. There was no time to bring his replacement, this McCartney woman, up to speed. I'd have to find another stooge at Best Coast to go in her place. I decided to head over there to remediate the situation.

When I arrived, I talked to Jeffries' boss, Horowitz, who was familiar with the Donation Fund, having worked at Best Coast for many years. I explained the situation and requested that he attend the meeting, instead of Jeffries' replacement. He agreed immediately. I thanked him and left. Walking down the hallway, I passed framed photos of executives, along with one Employee of the Month photo. Apparently if you were an executive, you didn't have to do anything to get your photo on the wall, but everyone else had to work for it, and even then, it was only temporary.

I noticed that among the executive photos, Gordon's photo had been replaced with that of a blond woman in her late thirties. I stopped and looked at the photo closely. I could tell she exfoliated. But that wasn't it. She looked familiar, but I couldn't place her. I gave up, left, and drove back to City Hall. Before going to MFD's headquarters, I took a detour to Vern's office to see if he was over his cold. His office was dark and his door was closed. When I walked on, past Chuck's office, I realized why McCartney looked familiar. She was the woman in high heels that I'd seen getting kicked out of his office, the week before.

LOOKING FOR FACES

When Linda and Meredith went out for dinner that night, they practically had Trattoria Pazza to themselves. A Dodgers game was broadcasting on one of the TV screens mounted high up on a wall, sports-bar style, even though it wasn't a sports bar, it was an Italian restaurant. Meredith thought she'd be annoyed to be facing the screen, but found the players' tightly-wound elegance fascinating.

Switching to the third person, Meredith elaborated silently to herself, *Meredith thought she didn't like eating in front of the TV because her mother didn't like it, but hadn't actually tried it herself to find out if this was her own preference.*

The most recent email newsletter she'd received from Spouses of the Suicidal (SPOT), suggested a SPOT could "get unstuck" by changing one's internal monologue from first to third person. Meredith had unsubscribed from the email newsletter that afternoon, but not before reading this tip. She had never tried any of the SPOT tips she'd read in the newsletter, because she had always been afraid of "getting unstuck." But now, she felt less afraid. This, by itself, was a shift. Meredith doubted that thinking in the third person would make a difference, but she was willing to try. For Grillo's sake. No. For Linda's sake? No. For her own sake.

It felt weird to consider doing anything for her own sake. Meredith thought about how Grillo never seemed to care about how well she was doing at work. She switched to third person: *Grillo never cared about whether Meredith did a good job at work.*

She added on: *Poor Meredith.* That surprised her. She couldn't recall a time when she had ever felt sorry for herself. It was easier to feel sorry for anyone and everyone else. She was conditioned to do so, and it made sense to her. She wondered if she was just a cloud of a person without any definite beginning or end. Again she restated the thought: *If Meredith felt like her identity wasn't fixed, if she was just a cloud of being that had no definite borders, it made sense that anyone else would be more solid, more definite, and therefore more important, than her.*

Light slanted through the black plantation blinds that covered a series of large windows. Some blinds were closed, some were partially open. This created a feeling of disarray, but the light was beautiful.

Trattoria Pazza's interior designer had made several odd choices, the wall of black blinds being one of them. The blinds reminded her of the stacks of enormous wooden pallets piled in the dirt of a stockyard next to the railroad tracks off of 35th Street. She'd driven past them once when she attempted to do an end-run around gridlock, back when she had to deal with rush hour. That was only last week, but it felt like years ago. She had been trying to get home from work, but had ended up right where she began.

Another prominent design feature of the restaurant was the exposed ductwork that crawled across the ceiling. The ductwork was painted gray, the same color as the ducts that hugged the sides of the Farmer John plant, wrapping around the building like rope binding a hostage to a chair. Opposite the television, an enormous framed photograph depicted a giant cup of coffee. Meredith conjectured that the restaurant had previously been an office space leased by a coffee distributor who may have been forced to leave hastily.

She was hungry and ordered the first thing that appealed to her on the menu: pasta with vodka sauce. Linda ordered the same thing.

They had decided to have dinner at Trattoria Pazza to check on the quality of the food, and to take a look at the private dining room that they planned to use for the roundtable. Meredith trusted Linda on these points, but it had been a while since either of them had eaten a decent meal.

Meredith told Linda about the call with Girron. She'd given him some anecdotes about meeting citizens during her survey. When she'd told him about the Latino man who reminded her of The Big Lebowski, Girron had laughed and said, "So when is Latino Lebowski running for mayor?"

"What was your answer?" asked Linda.

"I was taken off-guard. It's a brilliant idea, but it was several steps beyond the timeline I'd established! I hedged, and said, 'New elections? They're working on it.' Then I turned it back on him, and asked him what qualities he'd want in a mayor."

"Smart. What did he say?"

"He said, 'Usually journalists ask other people for comment, not the other way around.'"

Linda said, "Were you able to get him to answer the question, though?"

"Yes. He thought a good mayor was someone who cared about health and safety."

"I enjoy hearing how you handled Girron. I don't have this ability to do it nicely, in your way."

Meredith said, "I don't think that's fair, Linda. It's never easy to get the upper hand in a conversation if it isn't conducted in your native language."

Linda nodded. She tore a piece of bread apart and dipped it in olive oil. She sprinkled some salt on it and popped it in her mouth.

Meredith continued, "Then Girron said he'd run a piece about the roundtable. We already have it lined up for the Friday edition. I'm going to call him right after the meeting on Thursday to give him a recap. He asked if he could attend but I told him it was a private meeting."

The waiter came and took their drinks order. On the TV behind Linda's head, the Dodgers' pitcher stared at a point off-camera, squinting for the catcher's signal. His attention felt intimate, even if it was purely strategic. Meredith sighed, and said, "It's all going really well. It's hard to believe that if it weren't for pink slime, I'd still be at AFA Foods. I'd have never met you, or Vern. Though I guess Grillo would have died, either way."

Meredith felt tears well up in her eyes.

The busboy approached to top off their water glasses. Linda asked him to turn down the volume on the base-ball game. She said to Meredith, "What you said just now. I couldn't hear you well. It sounded like 'pink limes?'"

Before Meredith could answer, the waiter served them.

Meredith cast an eye over the plates of steaming pasta in vodka sauce. It was the exact color of pink slime. She said, "Maybe it's not a great time to explain pink slime? Sorry."

"I'm not scheme-ish."

"You mean—squeamish?"

"Right! Squeamish. I'm not. Tell me."

Meredith then went on to explain pink slime, Lean Finely Textured Beef, and the lack of a PR Crisis Plan at AFA Foods.

When Meredith was finished, Linda laughed again and said, "I love it!"

"Really? What's there to love about pink slime?"

"When I was young, before I came here, I worked at a fake baby eel factory!"

"A fake—what?"

"You see," said Linda, "It was a regional dish. Baby eels. Very tiny, smaller than anchovies. They're about an inch long. They're good on toast."

"Pintxos?" asked Meredith.

"Yes. Pintxos, you know, are sold at the same price as the Spanish tapas, but are half the size."

"Oh, that's funny," said Meredith. "Grillo hated going to tapas restaurants because he said they charged the price of an entree for a dish the size of an appetizer."

"Yes," said Linda. "The Basques know how to make money."

"Are you like that?"

"No," said Linda. "Let me tell you about the baby eels. They're just like your pink slime. At a company I worked for, they specialized in packing and freezing baby eels for restaurants. The dish was very much in demand. But the eels disappeared from the rivers because of pollution and overfishing. We then devised a method to create fake baby eels from white fish. How do you say it? Poland? *Pollack.* That's it. My boss asked the Japanese to explain how they made the fish cakes—"

"Surimi?"

"Yes. We learned the method, then changed it. We pushed the pollack through a pasta machine. Out came fake baby eels. This too is typical of the Basque: master it, then adapt it. It worked. 'Bob's your uncle,' as they say." Linda chuckled to herself.

"Oh my God," said Meredith. She looked at her tangled pasta drenched in pink vodka sauce, then back at Linda. "That's so weird!"

"The people insisted they must eat baby eels on toast because they have always eaten baby eels on toast. But word got around, so people started checking their pintxos for faces. If the eels didn't have faces, it meant they were fake. So my employer added a machine, like an ink stamp, that made the eyes. But of course then people started looking for a mouth. The mouth is very small, too hard to see. Eventually they gave up, and accepted that baby eels had to be fake, because the real ones were gone. My boss named the fake baby eels *gulas*."

"Gulas. That's a nicer name than 'pink slime,'" said Meredith, still unsure how she felt about eating baby eels, real or fake.

"It means 'greedy' in Spanish—like eating-too-much kind of greedy."

Meredith said, "Gluttony?"

"Yes! You have to admire the idea, yes? The fake eels are so good you will eat too much. Be gula! Eat lots of gulas."

Meredith smiled. "But how do they taste?"

"Like fishy pasta?" Linda shrugged.

"It sounds like...an acquired taste."

"Yes. One year, the baby eels appeared in the rivers again—no one knew why. My employer investigated. He had the real eels tested. They were so toxic from the pollution in the river water, it was much healthier to eat the fake ones."

"Or maybe not at all?"

"Right! But the people must have their pintxos just like always."

"It would have been a real win if I had managed to turn pink slime into a regional delicacy," said Meredith. "The regional delicacy of Merritt!"

Linda raised her glass, and said, "*Topa!*"

"Like the café?"

"That's what we say when we toast."

Meredith raised her glass. "To Linda! Topa!" They drank and smiled at each other. Meredith tried out the third person again, saying to herself, *Meredith felt happy making a toast to Linda. Linda was kind and helpful.* She added, *Meredith loved her.*

Meredith decided not to over-analyze where this last sentence came from. Because it was in third person, it felt like she was talking about someone else. It was almost like looking into a mirror that faced another mirror, the reflected image duplicating itself into infinity.

If Third Person Meredith loved Linda, she was happy for her. "Topa!" repeated Meredith. She looked at Linda affectionately. "To Linda and everything amazing about her."

Linda blushed; a rosy glow started at the base of her throat and went up her neck to her face. She fake-sneezed into her napkin.

LINDA: SALAD COOLS
ME DOWN

Wednesday, September 2, 2009
Senate charter vote in 7 days

Meredith called me first thing Wednesday morning. "I was told that Vern wasn't available, and there's no word on as to when he would be available."

"Who told you that?"

"The general admin at City Hall. She wouldn't provide any details."

I told her I'd check into it and hung up. My SMS plan was practically maxed out from all the text messages Vern had sent in the last couple of weeks, but there had been no new messages since last Friday morning. I sent him another text: *Are you out sick?* Vern was never sick. I frowned at the cursor on my tiny phone screen. It just sat there, blinking.

My worst suspicions were confirmed thirty minutes later when I went into work. I dropped by Vern's office, but the door was locked. I knocked. No answer. I opened it with my master key. His office was totally cleaned out.

I checked with HR who told me that Chuck Peck had fired Vern the Friday before. I felt sad on Vern's behalf. He had been an excellent boss all these years. I would miss him.

I was angry at Peck, too. Peck may have thought he'd gained control by firing Vern. Unfortunately for him, this PR project had taken on a life of its own and there was no stopping it. I was going to make sure there was no stopping it.

I called Meredith. "What did you talk about in your meeting with Peck?" I said.

"It was just a bunch of chitchat. Power games. Manipulation. Oh—he did have a little tantrum at the end? I wanted to look like I didn't know anything, so I asked if I could have all the pension files."

Holy crap. The pension files? That was right up there with Chuck's petty cash irregularities. I said slowly, "I see. That does seem odd he wouldn't be concerned. About the pension files."

She may have detected a note of sarcasm, because she said defensively, "Maybe tantrums seem normal to me, because my husband had them all the time. It seemed to me it's how he thinks he gets things done. I ignored it. Why do you ask?"

"It appears that Vern has been let go."

"Oh no! Do you think it had anything to do with my PR campaign?"

I said, "Peck is probably trying to shut you down."

"If Vern was fired, does that mean I'm fired too?"

"Perhaps Peck is worried about how much you know and that is why you are not fired. Vern, on the other hand, had too much involvement—blood on his face. I mean his hands. I'm sure his yellow sky-diving package was generous."

Meredith asked, "His golden parachute?"

"Yes. To keep you quiet, there's nothing Peck can do. But you must be careful."

"Peck is just a big baby. He doesn't scare me in the least."

I was impressed. Most people were terrified of Chuck's tantrums. But Meredith was acting like it was no big deal.

Meredith said, "Vern didn't deserve to be fired. Ugh. I feel terrible."

"Did you send an invoice yet?"

"An invoice?"

I said, "Are you worried about getting paid?"

"Paid? Oh my gosh! No, I haven't billed at all, yet. I wanted to have something to show for the work first."

I murmured a sound like a shrug. "I get paid every two weeks after I submit a timesheet. I get paid even if I haven't finished a project. Why would it be different for you?"

"I've been so busy, it was the last thing on my mind, honestly. If Vern's gone, who would I send an invoice to?"

"Send it to MPD care of Linda Vasco, I'll make sure it gets paid."

Meredith didn't answer right away. I could hear her soft breathing, which bobbed like a hummingbird hovering over a flower: elegant but hyper. She said, "Peck may know about the roundtable by now."

"When I personally checked in with people you invited, they all appeared quite willing. Besides, he has other problems. Even more reason to submit your invoice now rather than later."

"OK, you're right again," said Meredith. There was another silence, then she blurted out, "Linda, you make everything easy! One of these days you'll ruin me! You know what they say."

"What do they say?" I was excited to hear another weird American expression.

"Spare the rod, spoil the child!"

"What?" I was horrified. It sounded like domestic violence. "That sounds terrible."

Meredith said, "I think it just means something like, one shouldn't do too much for a person, they have to do it on their own."

I watched her filter her thoughts, consider her words. She reminded me again of a hummingbird suspended mid-air. A few seconds of hesitation required hundreds of wing-beats. I asked, "Does it bother you, my help?"

"No! Sorry, I was just thinking."

I asked, "About what?"

Meredith said, "Maybe I did too much for Grillo. He always complained that I wasn't doing enough. He also said that it was my fault that he was messed up. He said I should have never offered to support him so that he could do his art. That it was my fault he couldn't work. Maybe he was right."

I wanted to shake her. "Let me try to understand," I said, trying to keep my voice even. "You supported an artist so that the artist could produce art. Then when he could not produce art, he blamed your support as the reason."

Meredith said, "He didn't mean to, probably. It was only on bad days. On good days he was different."

"But Grillo was not a child."

"What?"

"Do not use an iron bar on the child, this causes the child to be spoiled, is the saying, correct?"

"A rod. Yeah."

"It seems to me that this saying is for the parents of children. A caution. So that their children can learn how to grow up without everything being easy. I am not sure about this rod business. I do not think beating the child is better than not beating the child. My father beat me when I did something bad. I do not know if that was good or not. Then he died."

"Oh Linda, I'm so sorry."

But I was on a roll, and wasn't going to stop to assure her that there was no need to be sorry. It all happened long ago. My father, may he rest in peace, did the best he could, I suppose. I said, "This is a strange country, with strange sayings.

What does this rod look like? Is it for a curtain? It would be difficult to use a curtain rod to beat a child. My father used his belt, much easier to access. But this business about rods doesn't apply to adults. You were married to an adult man, who was not a child. Correct?"

"Right."

"It's none of my business, but it seems to me that an artist not making art while someone else pays for everything, this is for himself to blame, not the person who is helping him."

"I don't know. Maybe you're right. Thank you for saying so."

"I mean it." Just then, I saw Peck coming back up the hall to his office. If he saw me, he'd probably give me yet another illegal task to complete. But I'd lost my enthusiasm.

I said to Meredith, "I have to go. Let's get lunch at Rage Café in an hour." I liked their salads, mainly. Salad cooled me down.

I ducked down an opposing hallway and stopped at what looked like a supply closet. The placard above the door noted that it was the permanent location of the Merritt City Library. I unlocked the door and slipped inside. The closet was just barely big enough for me to stand up; it was lined with shelves holding about a hundred alphabeticized books. The books were worn and well-used, like they'd all been sourced from Lost and Found. Most were romance novels, judging by the florid book covers depicting passionate tanned couples in various states of disarray. I slipped one of the books into my back pocket. Maybe I could get some seduction tips from it, just in case there was an opportunity. One always had to be prepared, and I was out of practice.

I listened to Chuck's footsteps until they receded and a door slammed, then made my exit.

OVERCOMMITTING

Meredith prepared for the business roundtable scheduled the next day. First she re-edited her presentation, adjusting the wording and adding animation to transitions. She searched for and placed stock-art photos to bring the mimetic architecture idea to life. It had to be perfect. Then she reconfirmed the reserved room at Trattoria Pazza. The restaurant was thankfully aware of the meeting. She compared the attendee list to Merritt's data on businesses operating there, to make sure it was sufficiently representative. She drove to an office supply place in Huntington Park to purchase name tags, pens, and notepads for roundtable attendees. When she returned, she realized she was an hour late for lunch with Linda.

Grillo got angry when Meredith was late, and rightfully so. He had no friends, felt lonely and isolated, and he looked to her for company. Though she felt bad for him, whenever he called her out on her lateness, she became defensive. The fact was that her employer's outsize demands upon her own meager resources crowded out attention and energy in her personal life. Even now, she found herself feeling defensive, though no one was attacking her. After all, a PR crisis on this scale required a large team, but she was doing it all without any support except for what Linda provided. But Meredith hated asking for help. She always worried that people would think she was incompetent.

Poor Linda. Had she really waited at Rage Café alone, for over an hour? It wasn't Linda's fault that Meredith had too much to do. It wasn't Linda's fault that Meredith couldn't budget her time better and hadn't asked Vern for more resources. Considering Vern's obsession with The Model, the skittish City Council, Chuck's overblown hostility, Mendebal's carefree attitude—even if she had asked for more help, she doubted that it would have been approved. But how much more time had she continued to waste while she put together this defensive story to assuage her guilt?

She may not be able to ask for help easily; she may not be able to say no; but she was always ready to apologize. She texted Linda: *I am so sorry. I lost track of time. Are you still at Rage Café?*

While she waited for Linda to reply, Meredith tried to believe that the lack of an immediate text response wasn't because Linda was angry with her, but was due to some other pressing concern that had nothing to do with her. She wondered what she could do to make it up to Linda; she was so insular and complete. Nothing seemed to faze her.

Meredith texted her again: *Can I make you dinner? Maybe one of your favorite Basque meals?*

Meredith googled "Basque recipes" and found one that seemed manageable in the tiny kitchen of her Merritt apartment. It was a basic tomato soup recipe, except the tomatoes and garlic were roasted and pureed, warmed with stock, then finished with some jamon iberico and idiazábal—a type of Basque cheese. It would be almost impossible to procure real jamon iberico before dinnertime, likewise the idiazábal. There were many wholesale food distributors in Merritt but almost no markets, and certainly not any that stocked imported specialty items.

Los Angeles had everything imaginable for sale, but the barrier of rush hour prevented easy transportation to points farther than a few miles, unless the time of day was within a narrow window of lesser congestion. You had to plan ahead. But Trader Joe's had pretty decent prosciutto which was similar to jamon iberico, and Trader Joe's also stocked their eponymous "Trader Joe's Basque Cheese." Maybe this was similar to idiazábal. She raced over to the Trader Joe's near USC in order to pick up the ingredients, but she'd have to be quick, otherwise her return trip would be mired in traffic molasses. She leveraged her interpretation of yellow stoplights as most Angelenos did. A yellow stoplight meant, "Go faster and get the nose of your car into the intersection before the light turns red." She perhaps took this too far at a couple of intersections, judging by the honking of horns that she left in her wake.

Meredith still hadn't heard from Linda by the time she returned. She started cooking anyway. She cut the tomatoes in half and put them on a sheet pan, then separated a head of garlic into cloves, scattered them around the tomatoes, then drizzled olive oil over all of it. She liked to cook. It gave her a sense of control, and provided a tangible outcome. There would be dinner at the end of the work, and regardless of how well it came out, it was still dinner.

She opened the oven door, and found that although the oven had been preheating the entire time she was prepping, to her dismay, it was no hotter than the rest of the apartment. It was broken.

She finally faced the fact that she needed Linda's help in order to make up for missing lunch with her. What would she say? "I was really rude at lunchtime, and now can you help me make it up to you?" There had been too many times in the last two weeks where Meredith had been completely at a loss, and Linda made it all right again, and all Linda got in return was getting stood up. She went upstairs and knocked on Linda's door, but there was no answer.

She called, "Linda, it's me Meredith."

She waited again. She was pretty sure Linda was home. Her car was parked out front.

Meredith called through the door, "Linda, I'm so sorry about lunch. Are you OK?"

She knocked again. "Linda," she called. "I do this a lot, but that's no excuse. I didn't mean to hurt you. It took too long to confirm with Trattoria Pazza; I was finishing the presentation; then I went to get name tags. I fully admit I am an asshole. It's terrible that you had to eat lunch alone. I would love to make it up to you."

"Make it up to me?" said Linda as she came down the steps from the upper floor.

Meredith jumped and said, "Oh my God! I thought you were inside. Did you hear all that?"

"Is this about lunch?" said Linda, walking past Meredith and unlocking the door. Inside, she switched on the air-conditioning unit, then sat on the edge of her bed and closed her eyes, letting the cold air blow on her face.

Meredith unspooled a lengthy apology. It lasted several paragraphs. By the time she was done, Linda looked visibly cooler. Meredith finished with, "I thought I could make you dinner. To make amends. But then my oven—"

"Oh, yes," said Linda absently. "Your oven is broken. Your apartment is for show. Like the mayor's apartment is for show. You saw his house in Hancock Park, yes? It's been in his family for years. I'm glad Merritt could provide a home for you. It's the least they could do."

"Linda. What's going on?"

"Did you know that two families owned all the land in Merritt, originally? The Mendebals and the Mallories. The Mallories made dishes. Ceramics. They had to close down because it was so toxic. Sold off their other properties. Did you know that lead was used in ceramics until the 1970s?

The entire town of Merritt is full of lead. When that battery recycling plant moved in, it didn't get any better."

"I read about Exodus! There were lead icicles on the bottoms of their delivery trucks!"

"Exodus was caught. Now they're in trouble. Boyle Heights is unhappy about the lead in their soil, spillover from Merritt's exclusive industry. Girron is from Boyle Heights," said Linda.

"I know."

"A while ago I looked into Girron for Vern. His reporting was quite accurate, considering the lack of, how do you say, 'those who blow a horn to sound the alarm?'"

"Whistleblowers?" said Meredith, leaning awkwardly against the inside of the front door.

"Whistleblowers. Very few whistleblowers in Merritt, that I can remember. It's not surprising, when you think of the corruption, how it works, how it has many heads. Like Smack a Rat."

"Whack A Mole?"

"Yes. Whack A Mole. You whack and whack, and another mole is there, it never ends."

Linda drew her arms close, hugging her abdomen. The air conditioner teased the baby hairs growing at her hairline into an aurora.

"What's going on, Linda? Why were you on the third floor?" said Meredith.

"Don't drink water from the faucet," Linda said, opening her eyes. "Did you want to use my oven since yours is broken?"

"No and yes. I don't drink the tap water. It always tastes like chlorine in LA anyway. Even if it's supposedly safe, it's like drinking swimming pool water. Blecch! I have a case of bottled water in my trunk, even though it ruins my gas mileage, and plastic is terrible for the environment."

Linda had closed her eyes again.

Meredith said, "I don't know why I'm babbling. Anyway, yes, if you don't mind, I'd love to use your oven. I'll go get the pan. It's all ready to go. I'll be right back."

Back in her apartment, Meredith paused on her way to the kitchen to look out the west window. She stared at the view, whose principal feature was a large rusting steel apparatus supporting a transformer about three stories tall. No security fencing surrounded it. A sign warned of high voltage. The apparatus sat in a lonely field of weeds. Beyond it, she could see other nondescript power company buildings—small one-story boxes painted white, clustered behind a long fence topped with barbed wire.

The forlorn scenery, its blunt utilitarian disregard for any embellishment in the name of beauty, disrupted Meredith's tunnel thinking about getting dinner ready. She realized that Linda had again managed to evade a direct question. Something had upset her. Meredith didn't mind that Linda didn't answer her questions. After all, if Linda didn't want to answer, she didn't have to.

Unlike Grillo, Linda didn't weaponize her sadness nor try to conquer all other sentient beings within her presence. She didn't campaign until there was one hundred percent buy-in that her despair was legitimate and that everyone else should feel as she did.

Meredith felt bad again about blowing off lunch, especially since Linda was clearly not herself. She said this to herself in third person, but it became something else again: *Making dinner might make Meredith feel better, and that was more important to her than the person she had hurt.*

It was an epiphany to realize that her relationship with her own guilt was a form of control. It suspended and postponed a real connection with someone else. She knew then that this was, in essence, what Grillo was complaining about all along. She sighed and picked up the pan of tomatoes and garlic glistening with olive oil. She went back to Linda's apartment with the pan and other ingredients. She would try to stay focused on what mattered. But she was done with the third person.

LINDA: TORTURE

I cranked up the AC more. I hoped it wouldn't blow a fuse, since the oven was on, too. I preferred not to use the oven in 90-degree weather, but I would do anything for Meredith, even though I was out of my mind with grief. I was still reeling from the news.

Bernard had left for Spain soon after our last conversation. That had been two days ago, and we hadn't been in contact since. He had promised to check in with me after he'd arrived safely at his mother's house, using a burner phone. But there had been no word. He always followed protocol, so I felt sure of the reason I had not heard from him. I wasn't an idiot. They had caught him. When he had to cross over the mountains from France into Spain, part of the mountain pass was nothing more than a rough narrow path through the woods. It wasn't exactly wheelchair-accessible. I suspected that's where they caught him, just inside the Spanish border, not far from Hendaye, France.

I had doubted that Bernard's mother was actually sick, and now I really didn't believe it.

"He didn't get to see his mother," I said aloud, by mistake. My internal thoughts were jostling each other, like a panicked crowd storming the exits. I couldn't keep them contained in my head.

Meredith looked up from from the fresh basil that she was de-stemming. "Who?" she asked.

I shook my head. "It's nothing." Meredith stopped what she was doing and sat down at the table. She started to say something, but decided not to. She waited. I repeated a Goop mantra in my head to calm me down. "Nourish your inner aspect." This made me hungry.

Meredith said, "I'm here. Like you said before—'let me share your dark feelings.'" Her close proximity was comforting.

I tried again. The mantra in my head shattered into, "Nourish your—why did I—inner aspect—allow him to go—fuck the haters." The founder of Goop had said that once in an interview. *Fuck the haters*. It's what got me hooked on Goop to begin with. All the other mantras were useless. I let my thoughts ooze like black tar around my grief. I had many potholes to fill, many cracks.

I said, "Bernard is in prison. And there, he will be tortured."

"Bernard?"

I nodded. "Did you know his last name, 'Leher,' means 'explosion' in Euskera?"

She shook her head no.

"Bernard loved explosions. I met him when he taught a bomb seminar for transfers and new recruits. He brought the various parts of a real bomb with him and demonstrated how to assemble one."

Meredith shook her head in wonder. "A bomb seminar?"

"Yes. I was an ETA librarian at first, then I asked to be transferred to project management. I attended his seminar as part of my training."

"Were you bored as a librarian? It sounds like a safer job."

I shook my head. "No. I liked the work. But I felt it didn't take me close enough to ETA's mission. I thought project management would be better, but it was a terrible mistake. I didn't understand, until too late."

"Understand what?"

"ETA's true purpose was not to obtain freedom for the Basque people, but to make sure ETA continued to exist."

"It wasn't always like that, though? You joined for good reasons. Sorry. I don't know much about it."

"It ended in horror. This is often the result of pure ideology. It's like the veil a bride wears. You are joined in union but only because you are blind."

Meredith regarded me thoughtfully. "That is really insightful. There are so many things one could apply it to." She sighed. "Tell me how you and Bernard ended up in Barcelona together."

I shook my head. Regret about Barcelona crossed with guilt about Bernard—it was too much. My throat closed up. Meredith sensed I needed some space and moved back to the kitchen. She put the pan full of tomatoes in the oven to roast. She shredded cheese. She sliced a baguette.

Her busywork made me think of how busy I'd been in ETA. How dedicated I was. I said, "When I joined up, I was old enough to remember Franco. Did you know that his thugs were never punished for making 400,000 civilians disappear?" I hoped to console myself by talking about Franco, whose atrocities by far outweighed my own. It was better than any mantra, hating Franco.

"Four hundred thousand?"

"Yes. Franco's thugs never went away when he died. They became the Guardia Civil."

She looked at me blankly.

I clarified. "The Spanish Civil Guard. Everyone hated them. ETA would ask prospective recruits, 'Are you for the police or against them?' We were all opposed, of course. And yet. Look at me. Look at what we became, Bernard and I. Police officers."

"But you had no choice."

"True. We had no choice. I had training in library systems, but Merritt had no library back then. And today it is only a closet! Anyway. We went where Mendebal wanted us to go. With our background, where else would we go, but to MPD?"

"What would you have preferred?"

I looked at her blankly. "For work?" I asked.

"Yes."

"No one ever asked me that. I have no idea."

Meredith opened the oven door to check on the tomatoes and garlic. They were done. She pulled out the sheet pan and placed it on a dishcloth so that it wouldn't melt the laminate counter. She put another sheet pan in the oven to toast bread topped with cheese slices. Using a spoonula—the same spoonula I had retrieved from her house before we burned it down—she transferred the roasted tomatoes from the sheet pan to a saucepan where she was sautéing garlic and onions. She added some chicken broth and stirred the soup. I watched her as she examined the spoonula with a quizzical look on her face, like she was having a déjà vu moment. But she said nothing and continued cooking.

I said, "By the time I went to Barcelona, I'd been in ETA for ten years. By then, ETA had evolved into something else entirely; at that point, they spent all their time harassing businesses for cash payments. In return, ETA would not attack them."

"It sounds like the Mafia."

"Yes. They became the very thing they said they were fighting against. Bullies. That's what Bernard and I became, too."

"You're absolutely not a bully!"

I didn't answer. The cozy aroma of tomato soup and melting cheese began to fill the apartment. It took me back. Memories kept resurfacing. Between stirring soup and checking the oven, Meredith glanced at me every so often, as if I might boil over or burn to a crisp if she wasn't vigilant.

I was telling her things in a disorganized fashion, but I couldn't help it. I said, "Bernard made building a bomb fascinating. Tiny pieces became a small metal box. A small metal box that could destroy a building, if placed correctly."

"I love Bernard's deep voice," said Meredith.

"Yes. He had a lovely voice."

"Had? But he's still alive, just not in the best place, right? I mean…"

"Maybe he is still alive. Some people survive. Torture is the great decider of who is strong and who is not strong. I hope that he tells them everything he knows, quickly. It's better that way." I thought about how I should have reminded him of that before he left, just in case. Then I felt worse.

Meredith shook her head. "I'm so sorry." She pulled the sheet pan out and slid the cheese toasts onto a plate. She turned off the oven. "He was so easy to talk to." She glanced at Linda, as if embarrassed. "I found myself telling him all sorts of dumb things. His silence was like a safe house. Did you have safe houses in ETA?"

"Bernard *was* remarkable. In the bomb class, he managed to convey paragraphs of explanation with just one or two words." Meredith placed the plate of cheese toasts on the table, and peeled the skins off roasted garlic cloves. I continued, "After the seminar was over, I asked Bernard where he was from. His hometown was just a few miles north of Guernica. My town was south of it."

"The same Guernica in the Picasso painting?"

"Yes. The same Guernica that the Germans bombed in World War II, destroying it. Killing everyone. A slaughter. Franco was behind it."

"I didn't know that."

I ruminated silently about Franco's awful reign, his crimes against his own countrymen, ETA, and the Guardia Civil. I wanted Franco to take the blame for Bernard. But it was ridiculous. Franco had been dead for decades. Meredith ladled the soup into bowls, brought them to the table, and sat down beside me. I realized how far away I was when she asked, "Linda, does it need salt?" Meredith's shoulders were tense and narrowed like little bird wings. She hunched over her bowl, uncertain.

"It's perfect," I said, making an effort to eat. I couldn't remember the last time someone had made me dinner. But I had no appetite. The soup was good even if it wasn't authentic. This so-called Basque soup, with the ham wanting to be jamon iberico, the cheese masquerading as idiazábal. Meredith had made it for yours truly, Linda Vasco. But I was still depressed.

Meredith asked, "Linda, are you very sure that Bernard has been arrested?"

I nodded.

She asked, "Couldn't we contact the US Embassy, or like, Amnesty International?"

"It is too late for that. Confirmed terrorists do not have options."

"Poor Bernard."

"Poor Bernard," I agreed. I pulled out my handkerchief and blew my nose. I said, "You know how everyone is guilty?"

Meredith looked stricken. She said in a quiet voice, "I'm so sorry that I stood you up for lunch, you didn't deserve that at all."

"Yes, I suppose you did. I forgive you. I received the news about Bernard while I was waiting for you at Rage Café. Eating wasn't possible after that."

I watched Meredith take dainty bites of her cheese toast and little sips of soup. I drank some water. The Goop lady said to always drink lots of water.

I said, "This town. There's nothing more to Merritt than the ruthless drive for profit. But I am not political anymore. I believe that if you know everyone is guilty, it should mean that you can see clearly."

"I don't know, it's a lot to unpack." Meredith looked away. She looked trapped. Indeed, if she wasn't unique in being a guilty person, what did that mean? Guilt hid her soul. Certainly I'd lost track of mine ages ago. And if you can't sense your own soul, you don't know where you start or end.

Meredith said, "I can't imagine the terrible loss you must be experiencing. I'm sorry. That sounded fake. But I really mean it."

"You have also experienced terrible loss. I am sorry for being the cause." I got up from the table and put my dishes in the sink. As I washed dishes, I thought about the future. It didn't look good. I said, "Now my days are numbered."

"What? Why?" asked Meredith.

I said, "The Guardia Civil trained under Franco. They developed very advanced torture techniques. Everyone confesses."

"Everyone?"

"Everyone. All ETA personnel are prepared for this. The PLO trained ETA, you know."

"The—Palestine Liberation Organization?"

I nodded.

Meredith tweedled her hair between her index finger and her thumb. "That's so weird."

I shrugged. I said, "The PLO taught ETA organize into small cells that didn't know anything about the other cells or the organization as a whole. When the Guardia Civil caught one of us, they only got a little bit. The information they'd squeeze out of Bernard would be about me—my American identity and my location. I must leave here, and soon."

"Oh my God!"

"I'd like to help with the meeting tomorrow. Then I will go."

"Go where?"

"Good question," I said. "Where? I need a new identity. That's no problem. But where do I go? Anywhere but here. Out of the country."

"There's a town in Canada named Merritt," Meredith said absently, mopping up the last of her soup with some sourdough bread. She stared at the bread, stained dark red from soup. She put it down and pushed away her bowl.

"Another Merritt?" I asked.

"It's north of Washington. About a three-hour drive. It's in Canada's Gold Country. There's like, two hundred lakes and streams there! It sounds pretty. Also, they host an important country music festival."

"How do you know about this other Merritt?" I asked. I took the rest of the dishes to the sink.

"I set a Google Alert for Merritt, and included 'CA,' the abbreviation for California. Every so often, results for the same town in Canada cropped up, because 'CA' is also the abbreviation for Canada. I didn't bother adjusting the filter, because it was kind of nice to hear about small-town Canadian news. I'm Canadian, originally."

"That's right, I remember. Your father made toys."

She laughed and said, "He was an executive. He made spreadsheets about toys. Did they have Barbies where you grew up?"

"No," I said. "I had a doll once. My aunt gave it to me. It was made out of fabric, with buttons for eyes."

"How sweet. Barbies are weird, really. Long legs with feet in a permanent arched position, for high heels. I liked the tiny shoes more than the Barbies, come to think of it. I had a lot of Barbies, naturally."

She continued talking about toys. I had probably made her nervous with all this talk about torture. I was amazed she was speaking to me at all, after everything I'd told her, about Barcelona, and the rest. I couldn't focus on the ugly dolls she described. I was consumed with the desire to ask her to come with me, but I was afraid of the answer. I never thought of myself as a coward, but when it came to love, I had no courage. I took her bowl to the sink and washed it.

Meredith spoke of other toys: a head made out of a potato; toy logs named Lincoln. It was a jumble.

She ended with, "No one in my family actually became a US citizen. Weird fact: I carry my passport around like a driver's license. See?" She rummaged in her bag and pulled out a Canadian passport.

"I see," I said, not seeing.

"Anyway, I wouldn't need anything special to emigrate, because I'm already a citizen."

I wiped my hands on a rag for longer than I needed to. I asked, "What are you saying?"

"I'll come with you," she said. She looked back at me, smiling, with those blue eyes, those dark eyelashes. Then she made a face and shook her head. "Oh no! I forgot dessert. Major fail. That was dumb. What's your favorite? I'll run out and get it."

I looked at her, speechless.

"I know—I'll get some ice cream. Back in a jiffy. Why don't you lie down?"

She left. I sat down again at the kitchen table. Objects were losing their dimensions. Their relative distances became uncertain. Was my glass of water close to my hand, or far away? I reached toward it and knocked it over. Water spread across the table and dripped onto the floor. I felt faint. I would feel embarrassed if Meredith came back to find me passed out on the wet floor, so I stumbled to my bed. I quickly fell asleep with the lights on.

Very early the next morning, I woke up and I found myself covered with a blanket. The lights had been turned off. I still felt sad about Bernard, but I also felt hopeful. Because of Meredith.

BULLSHIT CASTLE

Meredith arrived at Trattoria Pazza early to make sure that catering had set up everything for the business roundtable. The private room was at the back of the restaurant, with a separate entrance that opened directly onto the parking lot, where Linda was setting up traffic cones and signs, despite the Thursday stink. She had insisted that it didn't bother her.

Meredith was pleased with how the meeting had come together so quickly and easily. It was a small miracle that every single invitee had committed to attending, even with Labor Day weekend just around the corner. She set up the nametag table just inside the door. In prepping the room, restaurant staff had pushed several tables together and covered them with a cloth to form a makeshift conference table that could seat twenty-four people. Sandwiches, chips, and sodas were arranged on a sideboard.

Meredith wasn't completely sure that asking for help from the private sector was the best way to handle Merritt's problems. It felt somewhat fascist, though she wasn't sure what fascism was, exactly. She was more comfortable with setting up the citizen survey, interviewing people, and gathering data. That had made sense to her—citizens giving input on their city. Businesses, on the other hand, were not citizens. And yet, Grillo had often reminded her that a corporation had the same legal rights as a real person. He always said that when he complained about her employers, whom he felt took her attention away from what was more important—his health issues and his art. She could easily hear Grillo ranting in her head, starting with how corporate restaurants were destroying his health with those damned pizza ovens spewing smoke everywhere, how corporations had caused climate change and that was why the rat mites had gotten out of hand, then concluding that these were the end days of Earth. She wondered if she had relied on Grillo to be angry for both of them. Well, obviously. That's how it had been.

She had tried to separate Merritt's business goals from ethics because business and ethics didn't really mesh well. Once you started wondering about ethics, it's likely that you were already deep in unethical territory. After all, if a business was doing well, then its employees' jobs were more secure. That was good, right? On the other hand, nothing was baked into capitalism that guaranteed job security. And the alternatives to capitalism were extremely faulty too. Maybe she was overthinking it. Back in college, she had barely passed her political science class. She tried to focus her attention on finishing up the tasks at hand. She put out pens next to nametags and set up a sign-in sheet.

The first attendee arrived ten minutes early. She was in her thirties, garbed in neutral business attire that mirrored Meredith's own outfit of slacks with a simple blouse, but this woman also wore extremely high heels, in contrast with Meredith's customary black flats. The woman was very short, for which her high heels did little to compensate.

"Welcome!" said Meredith, extending a hand and introducing herself. "I'm Meredith James, the roundtable coordinator. I'm so happy that you could join us today," she said, and then glanced at the conference table, which wasn't round. "I love your shoes," said Meredith automatically.

"Thanks. Marigold McCartney, Best Coast Packing Company."

"Nice to meet you! Please make a nametag. Oh! I have to make one for myself. Ugh. I'm already behind," Meredith laughed nervously as she handed a nametag to Marigold and then wrote her own name on one. Below it she wrote, "Consultant, City of Merritt." The sticker had "Hello, My Name Is" preprinted on it, which Meredith thought was quaint, though obvious and redundant. As if a label stuck to your lapel with a name written on it would not have the signaling needed for people to understand that it was a nametag. As if the nametag needed accompanying instructions. As if American businessmen were indigenous islanders in the South Seas meeting outsiders for the first time. Yet here it was preprinted on the label: *Hello, My Name Is.*

Marigold wrote her name and company down on her nametag in large round block letters, "MARIGOLD MCCARTNEY, BEST COAST PACKING." Meredith's lettering, on the other hand, was small and pointy.

"Tell me, Marigold—" Meredith started to say as they both awkwardly tried to get their nametags to stick to their blouses. "Dammit!" said Meredith, giving up. "I hate nametags!" she said. "Either they don't stick, or the adhesive is impossible to remove! But sometimes you need them, right?"

"It's a necessary evil," said Marigold matter-of-factly. "I understand from Bob at AFA that you used to work there?"

"Yes, until recently."

"I heard there was a RIF," Marigold said. Meredith nodded. She hadn't been laid off, she'd been fired. But close enough.

"Pink slime, right?" asked Marigold. "I read about it in NAMI's newsletter this month."

NAMI stood for North American Meat Institute—and it also stood for National Alliance on Mental Illness. Meredith was familiar with both definitions; the former from her career at AFA Foods, and the latter from trying to cope with Grillo's chronic depression. She had gone once to a support group for families of the mentally ill given by a local NAMI chapter, and was surprised to see that she was not alone— that other people had the same difficulties that she did. In some cases, they had it much worse. This made her feel like she had no right to complain. She didn't return.

Marigold said, "Very tough. And I don't mean LFTB, of course." Marigold was making a joke. LFTB or Lean Finely Textured Beef was not tough, it was very tender. Meredith appreciated the joke, although she didn't feel at ease. Was Marigold trying to be kind, or was she deliberately putting Meredith in an awkward conversational position? It felt like things were already going badly and the meeting hadn't even started yet.

"Always very tender, good ol' LFTB," said Meredith, then she tried to deflect the conversation away from AFA Foods. "What's your role at Best Coast?"

"I just started there about a month ago, I'm the CMO." That explained everything, thought Meredith. Marketing people were always so complicated.

"I'm so glad that a marketing executive is here today. Merritt could definitely benefit from your perspective." said Meredith.

Marigold nodded. She observed the attendees streaming in through the door as if she was taking inventory, then turned back to Meredith, saying, "That's what I thought, too. My predecessor had been invited originally, but he left the company fairly recently. My boss planned to come instead, but when I got wind of it, I argued that cross-functional concrete deliverables were already suffering from schedule slippage, and it would impact OKRs if he was away for even one minute to deal with this, um, situation you have here."

OKRs. Meredith hadn't heard that term since she left AFA Foods. It stood for Objective and Key Results. It was one of Bob's favorite terms. He had wielded it like a baseball bat during status meetings, berating his direct reports about his disappointment at their failure to achieve impossible goals.

Meredith had been hanging out with Linda so much in the past couple weeks that she had forgotten how corporate people talked—the way they avoided calling things by their real names. In the case of layoffs, those that still had jobs hid behind Reduction in Force, and when that became untenable, they built up the signifier fortress with a further retreat behind its acronym: RIF. Hiding behind acronyms allowed those responsible to distance themselves from blame. Had she been doing that too, when she had tried out SPOT's third-person trick? That seemed so long ago. Was it really just yesterday?

Marigold continued, "And I felt that marketing should be involved at this meeting anyway, not sales. Sales is dealing with a customer satisfaction nightmare due to Operations' overdue subtasks and dependencies. They're multiplying like rabbits, and the end of Q3 is looming."

Meredith responded in kind. "KPI trumps sidebars of this kind, totally agree," she said. "I'm so sorry if the time to attend this meeting impacts your own OKRs. But hopefully it will benefit everyone in the end. We're expecting 100-percent participation, in fact. I can't get over the positive response!"

"The thing is," said Marigold, "I was surprised at your methods."

"I know," groaned Meredith. "I hate email blasts! But we didn't have a lot of time—"

"I'm not talking about the email blast," said Marigold. "I'm talking about dialing in on our pain points."

"Pain points?"

"You know. Service fulfillment of contract payments, Merritt Fund donations—?"

Meredith was too stunned to answer.

Marigold continued, "What nonprofits are they funding, exactly? For what purpose? To maintain that pile of boulders in front of City Hall? There aren't any other landmarks here, except for that plaque near the freight train terminal. Merritt doesn't have any parks or libraries, either."

Meredith stuttered, "I think there *is* actually a library at City H—"

Marigold cut her off. "You didn't earmark the payments as 'marketing fees,' did you? That's why I had to put my foot down. I am so sick of everyone putting that garbage under marketing."

Meredith was taken aback and looked around, trying to collect herself. Several attendees were making their way silently toward the nametag table. Marigold and Meredith drew back to make room for them.

Contract payments and marketing fees. Meredith had seen some of these phrases in budget meetings at AFA Foods. She hadn't thought about it much because she wasn't in procurement or marketing. But Marigold seemed to be implying that these were labels for something more nefarious. *Dialing in on our pain points.* Could she be referring to bribes? It was the first time Meredith had heard of this, at least in connection to her own work for Merritt. Even in her research of Chuck Peck's checkered past, she hadn't come across any mentions of corrupt payoffs between Merritt government and businesses. It reminded her of what Linda had complained of the night before, when she described late-stage ETA behaving like the Mafia.

But not only that. Marigold was suggesting also that the existence of bribes had been used against the other silent attendees filing past them, in order to coerce them to attend. Meredith cast her mind back to the citizen interviews. The woman who had lost her amona had been angry—at Linda. Some of the other interviewees had been scared—of Linda. Meredith envisioned the City of Merritt's nametag: *Hello, My Name Is Extortion*.

It was a lot to think about, and it was neither the time nor place to get into it. Meredith pretended she misunderstood Marigold. "Bullshit Castle, right?" Meredith said. "I hate that too, but I especially hate it when they blame PR when other departments' DRIs ignore their dependence on data curation and think they can just make shit up. Excuse my language," said Meredith, hating that she was swearing, but feeling a little out of control. Swearing usually helped her feel calmer.

"No problem," said Marigold, looking at Meredith thoughtfully. Marigold seemed to make a decision, as if she'd been testing Meredith, and Meredith had passed.

Marigold took her leave, saying, "I'm glad I met you. I think we're on the same page, and all I can say is, anything with poor process behind it is not scalable. It isn't scalable at all. Sure, you got more headcount here than you expected. We can iterate about it later, and find out how best to package the outcome—whatever it might be. But I just wanted to make sure you knew how I felt. It's not scalable. Are any of these sandwiches vegan?"

As Marigold walked away, Meredith turned to watch Linda checking people in at the door. Powerful executives who usually took up too much space, expected special deference from others, and basically mowed everything down in their path with assumed privilege, these same people blanched when they saw Linda and wouldn't look her in the eye. They visibly shrank before her. It was pretty clear who was behind the "poor process that wasn't scalable."

Meredith sighed, and as she helped various executives with their nametags, filling them out for those whose hands were shaking too much to do it themselves, she thought about Linda.

Despite the many thoughtful, helpful things Linda did for Meredith, she often failed to communicate important facts and, too often, dodged direct questions. It wasn't just that Linda had a creative understanding of ethics, but it was also concerning that she had such an extensive criminal reach. The worst part of all was Linda's comfort level with her criminal reach.

Or was it the best part of all?

Where had Meredith's strong sense of guilt, of taking responsibility for anything and everything, gotten her? Was Meredith too mired in knowing right from wrong to ever be completely free of guilt? But if she could be a little more like Linda, wouldn't that be better? Linda was a wonderful person. Except for certain outrageous deeds that couldn't be undone. Couldn't you still be a wonderful person, despite your past? Meredith admired how direct Linda was, how unapologetically authentic. Wasn't extortion basically taking advantage of the need to cover up what was illegal or wrong in the first place? So, did that make it as bad as the original wrong thing? Nice try, Meredith thought. You know the answer. A wrong on top of a wrong was just remodeling the bullshit castle.

She went to set up the AV equipment. When she hooked her laptop up to the projector, she configured the screen-saver to display Merritt's city crest, which bounced around the screen like a large ping-pong ball. The city crest depicted two men in the foreground: a chemist holding a test tube, and a butcher, who was holding a mallet. She tried not to think about what slaughterhouses did with mallets back in 1905, when the city was founded. The crest's background depicted a train and a factory's smokestacks, both spewing smoke. A bridge hovered next to the factory, and above it flew a light aircraft. It was all detached from the earth, floating in the sky behind the two men in the foreground. Encircling it all was Merritt's tagline: An Industrial Paradise.

If Meredith wasn't getting the hell out and starting anew in Canada, a top priority would have been to redesign the city crest. She looked forward to doing something different when she got to Canada. Something that was not PR or related to government.

Most of the attendees had arrived, quietly sitting at the conference table, some eating their sandwiches, while others just sat and waited, looking gloomy. Meredith watched the door, to see if there were any more arrivals. There were a couple of empty seats because she'd put out extras, just in case. She saw a man walk up to Linda outside the door, who didn't have the same air of defeat and fear as the others. Linda asked him a question, and he answered. Linda picked up her phone, talked to someone briefly, hung up, then told the man something. He nodded and came inside.

As he approached the nametag table, he said hello to Meredith, looked at her nametag, smiled, then wrote on his own nametag, "Gil G, GULA Inc." He looked pointedly at Meredith while he affixed the tag to his polo shirt. "It's very nice to meet you in person, Meredith." She recognized the company name, GULA. It was that place Linda had worked for, back in Spain, that made the fake baby eels. She recognized the man's voice. It was Girron from the *LA Times*.

LINDA: THE MEETING

Meredith gave me a look after I checked in Girron, a look that was like a laser she beamed at me from her cohesive, clear conscience, targeting my lack thereof.

When Girron walked up to my check-in table, I didn't recognize him. I'd never met him and his name wasn't on the list. He introduced himself and said, "Vern Page suggested you call him and he'd explain."

I hadn't spoken to Vern since before he'd lost his job. He picked up on the first ring.

"Vern Page."

"It's Vasco."

"Girron tell you to call?"

"Yeah."

"Give him full access to the meeting Meredith organized."

I looked at Girron. He was standing off to the side, eyeing the activity in the conference room through the open doorway. He wore his thick, dark hair a little long, had regular features, and an olive complexion. If I liked guys, I'd have been smitten.

"Vern," I said into the phone, "Is this a good idea?"

"I'm off to Puerto Vallarta to join Sharon," he said. Sharon was his wife. "I Skyped her last week and promised I wouldn't leave my socks on the floor, plus a few other vows that in the scheme of things seem pretty minor when it comes to one's safety as a whistleblower. My flight leaves in ten minutes. I've filled Girron in on everything."

"Everything?"

"Everything going back fifteen years. Let him into that meeting. It's the coup de grâce."

His California accent mangled the original French; I was momentarily baffled. I asked, "The Grass?"

"The final blow, Linda."

"Thank you?" I felt confused. I wasn't sure this was actually a good thing. Maybe it was. Wasn't it?

"It'll be on the *LA Times* website and feeds by tonight. Then in the print edition tomorrow morning. You best get the fuck out of there. Hasta la vista." He hung up.

I decided to let the chips fall where they may. I used to think that "chips" referred to potato chips, but I now think it is actually poker chips. In other words, I decided to accept fate. It was the least I could do for Vern, who wanted to go out in style, and I approved. What did I care? I was leaving too, it's just that now my departure date would be much, much earlier than planned.

I told Girron he could go in, but first advised him to use GULA for the name of his company. In this way, Meredith might understand that he was a special guest. I watched her grab a soda and drink it like some parched desert creature. As Girron approached the nametag table, she looked past him at me. It wasn't a look of love, unfortunately. It was something else entirely. She knew about something I had done, but I wasn't sure which of my questionable actions had come to light. There were more than a few choices, unfortunately.

Maybe it was that Marigold lady. I'd noticed Meredith speaking to a small blond lady who looked a bit like the photograph I'd seen at Best Coast Rendering, except now she had a sunburn and her hair was closer to platinum than dirty blond. They had spoken at length. I had thought

Horowitz was coming, not her. I wondered if she had complained to Meredith about the Donation Fund. Maybe even blamed Meredith too; that would be even worse. I smiled in response to Meredith's piercing gaze and cupped my hands in the shape of a heart. She made a rueful expression, one that I couldn't read, and turned to start the meeting.

Closing the door behind me, I leaned against the wall and surveyed the occupants of the room. Twenty-five attendees sat at the large conference table: all were men, except for Marigold, Meredith, and me; all were white guys over the age of fifty, except for Girron. It gave me a sense of great satisfaction to observe that for the most part, the executives wore fearful, tense expressions. They gave Meredith their full attention, something truly rare in men of this age group, when it's not about what they want or what they are taking without asking. Having that much control over so many powerful men in one place gave me a feeling of immense satisfaction.

When I thought about how Meredith might view my method of achieving perfect attendance, I felt uneasy. I hadn't thought about it when I coerced and threatened these men into coming today, and maybe I should have. I wasn't sure whether I had any more free passes with Meredith. I worried that she might change her mind about Canada. I didn't know if I could survive that.

While Meredith was queuing up her first PowerPoint slide to display on the monitor, Peck stormed in. Red in the face, he yelled, "This meeting isn't sanctioned by the City Council and I'm immediately adjourning it." No one moved, though some of the stiffs looked a little hopeful.

"This is a rogue operation! You can all go!" repeated Peck. A few of them started to rise from their seats.

I stepped forward and stood just behind Peck. "Please sit down," I told the scared attendees. I held my gun discreetly against Chuck's back. I didn't want any difficulties, and these guys looked like prime candidates for cardiac arrest. I smiled and said, "Meredith, please begin." I put more pressure on the nuzzle of my gun pressed against Peck back. "Come with me, Peck," I said, as I started steering him toward the door.

Like most people who have amassed a great deal of power illegally, Peck had a hard time accepting reality. The gun digging into his back couldn't be more real. But did that stop him? Nope. He lunged for Meredith's laptop and yanked out the cords, then he raised her laptop over his head and threw it hard at the fake wood floor, where it bounced a couple of times, lost a few keys, and came to rest next to a sandwich someone had dropped near the catering table. The AV overhead projector screen went black. The words "No Signal" bounced around it.

Nobody moved. Girron appeared to be observing my weapon with interest. The others looked quite dazed, like they had no idea what to do without a PowerPoint presentation to guide them.

The fact is, I knew Peck would try something like this. He was stuck in the past and mired in denial, making him unable to see that he no longer had control of anything, anymore. I was sure he thought he could just fire the whole State Senate before they voted on the charter, the same way he'd fired the Merritt Fire Department when they tried to unionize many years back.

To prevent Chuck Peck from attending the meeting, I had made some adjustments at City Hall early that morning. I knew his habits well. He always arrived at City Hall at six am, before anyone else. He made himself a pot of coffee and drank four cups by the time his admin, Gina, arrived two hours later. Gina didn't drink coffee. She was a Diet Coke gal.

I went to City Hall around four am. I loved Merritt at that hour. It was peaceful and quiet. The constant roar of freeways, compressors, and machines was mostly at a standstill. At City Hall, in Chuck's private kitchen, I rejiggered the coffeemaker's water supply so that it was connected to the sewage line. I hooked in a fresh water line as well, to make sure the coffee's taste wasn't a tip-off. I figured the crappy coffee that City Hall Procurement insisted on buying would mask any lingering off-putting flavors. I used his private bathroom to test my work, seeding the sewage line with fresh sewage.

There were easier ways to slow Chuck Peck down, but I like a little creativity in my sabotage. How else do you get through life not believing in anything? I got the idea for bespoiled coffee when I was flipping through the files on Meredith's computer a few days ago. There, I found a folder full of plumbing repair videos. Meredith must have produced them for some other client about ten years ago, judging by files' the creation dates. In the videos, a slightly overweight white man with a tenor voice and fat fingers explained in impressive detail what backflow was, how to prevent it, why you prevent it, and how to fix the thing that prevented it, which was something called a backflow valve. Because they kept everyone safe, the valves had to be tested periodically to make sure clean water was always kept separate from the dirty water.

I loved watching these videos. The backflow expert wore a bland button-down shirt and dress pants and stood in front of a bookcase full of plumbing manuals. Framed pictures of his wife and kids smiled at me over his right shoulder. I watched him taking the pieces of the valves apart, putting them back together, all the while explaining every movement. "The check spring has to be inserted before the O ring and don't forget the diaphragm." His methodical explanations made me feel very peaceful, like I was learning something that completed me. The videos reminded me of Bernard's bomb seminar, although the instructor's style couldn't have been more different. Poor Bernard.

If I made it to Canada, I resolved to become a plumber in my new life there. I loved the idea of safeguarding clean water and keeping it separate from dirty water. It was a wonderful idea. In my life, clean and dirty had always been mixed together—everything was polluted. The idea that you could keep the filth out, forever, as long as you tested and calibrated? Sign me up.

I had expected that the effects of my coffeemaker sabotage on Peck would have kicked in long before the meeting started, so I was surprised to see him walk in the door with such gusto. By now, he should have been feeling very sick. Very sick indeed. I wondered if my plumbing work had been faulty. But just then, in the middle of his tirade, the color of Chuck's face went from red to white, then back to red, and a strong smell arose, one that was emanating from inside the room, distinct from the stink of Merritt on a Thursday. A dark stain slowly spread across the seat of Chuck's pants. He abruptly scrambled over the broken pieces of laptop at his feet, shoved past me, and ran out the door of the meeting room into the restaurant, a putrid odor trail lingering in his wake.

I hid my hand holding the gun behind my back and said, "Go ahead, Meredith. I'll open some windows."

Everyone protested that idea. Instead, I went to fetch a fan. When I returned, Meredith had restarted the meeting. She acted like nothing unusual had just happened. She had to wing it without the PowerPoint, but she had it mostly memorized. She was a pro.

After plugging in the fan, I wanted to make sure Peck was fully indisposed so I headed to the men's bathroom.

Listening at the locked door, I could hear a lot of groaning and other impressive noises of extreme digestive suffering. I figured he'd be tied up for a while, so I grabbed some air freshener from the other bathroom, and returned to the meeting room.

It didn't smell too bad, all things considered. I stationed myself next to the door of the meeting room, spraying the air every so often with some air freshener, and listened to Meredith continue her presentation.

"…So it seems to me that you, too, can be constituents of the City of Merritt, just like the voters. After all, if the city keeps its charter, you stand to benefit more than anyone else. But what we need are some options, some fresh ideas. Mimetic architecture is a big idea, with big returns. Go big or go home, as they say."

The businessmen were leaning forward in their chairs. They were engaged, but they weren't pleased. They all started talking at once.

A man with puffy eyes and a wattle under his chin said, "There's no way So-Lite Lingerie is turning its facade into a giant bustier. In no time, we'll have those feminists permanently camped out in our parking lot, protesting the patriarchy, or whatever. We're just trying to run a business. This is absurd."

Other complaints along the same lines rose and fell.

Finally, a balding, fat white guy to Meredith's left said, "But we can't stay in this location if Merritt is absorbed into the City of LA."

Directly opposite him, a slightly more fit white man with a crew cut of silvery hair said, "Can you imagine? The bureaucracy, the absurd environmental regulations, the difficulties in making any kind of innovative changes to our plant, all of it would be catastrophic to our profit margin. We'd have to shut down."

"Huge hit to the bottom line."

Marigold spoke up. "Pivot it—" she said, but the others talked over her. They were too involved in their whining.

"Pivot it," she said louder. Meredith had heard her, but she couldn't tamp down the rising wave of complaints. The white men were on a roll.

Marigold rolled her eyes, stepped onto her seat, then jumped from there onto the conference table. She did all this in one fluid movement, like she was a gymnast mounting a balance beam. This shut everyone up. Her high heels were at the executives' eye-level; their gaze followed her shoes back and forth as she paced up and down the table.

Marigold said, "The solution is obvious. Unions. Get the unions involved. They have huge political sway in California. Isn't Speaker Westmore completely in their pocket? They'll get him to stand down, stat. Unions will also unequivocally oppose this absurd architecture idea." She nodded to Meredith. "No offense. We have to solve this in a more mature, effective way. One that doesn't involve turning our businesses into a surreal sideshow. But we have to do it together."

And with that, she calmly stepped off the table, onto the seat of her chair, and sat down, as if she dismounted from conference tables in high heels regularly. She looked across the table at Girron and gave him a little wink. He smiled back and tried to look more serious by covering his mouth with one hand and coughing. It was clear he was trying not to laugh.

Meredith smiled. She looked luminous. She wasn't disappointed or sad about her mimetic architecture idea getting tossed out the window. I realized that Meredith had planned this outcome, all along. She had staged a ruse! By being unanimously opposed to the idea, the twenty-four businessmen (and one woman) were now willing to work together for a common goal. Her ruse had worked.

Meredith said, "Thank you so much, Marigold. You make many good points. Does anyone here have union reps they can reach out to? Like, immediately? How about a show of hands?"

Almost everyone in the room raised their hands.

"Fantastic! There's only one other thing. What happens when we get to the other side of this crisis? I mean, obviously we don't want to go back to business as usual."

The businessmen looked at each other blankly, as if they didn't understand what she was getting at.

"Right, Marigold?" said Meredith pointedly. "It's not scalable, is it?"

Marigold smiled. "Not at all."

Most of the executives now looked confused. Meredith continued, "It would be great if we could also, I don't know, find some kind of consultant or auditor, someone who knew how cities should be run, to sort of, you know, clean things up around here. You'd get what you want, what everyone wants, right? There would be no need to shut down operations. The complex codes and permits required by the City of Los Angeles could be held at bay. Eventually an overseeing entity could bring Merritt governance up to a higher standard of accountability and ethics, and you could still receive the excellent city services and low taxes to which you are accustomed."

The executives absorbed this info, nodding in approval.

"Any ideas as to who this auditor could be? Or should we just leave it up to the State Senate?" said Meredith.

"Van Decker," said Marigold. Did none of these men ever have any ideas of their own? I guessed not.

Meredith said, "Van Decker! Blue windmills and hot cross buns."

Marigold said, "Yes, he's from the same family that owned the bakery chain, but he went into politics. He's retired now but he might be willing to take this on."

Several of the others nodded and smiled. "Great," said Meredith. "Does anyone know him?"

A few people raised their hands.

"Perfect. My suggestion? Form a business task force. Marigold, I hope you can lead it?" Marigold nodded. Meredith continued, "Those who raised their hands, please be sure to sign up over at the nametag table. I strongly suggest you cancel your holiday weekend plans and convene a meeting to define tactics and delegate responsibilities." There were some scowls from the crowd, but no one voiced objections.

Marigold said, "What about you? Do we need approval or input from Merritt on the plans we develop?"

Meredith laughed, gestured toward her banged-up laptop on the floor, and said, "I think we've had enough input from the City of Merritt. By saving yourselves, you'll save the city too."

Some attendees thought that the meeting was done and started to rise, but Meredith put up both hands like she was stopping traffic. She said, "I believe in transparency when it comes to crises of this nature. But I understand that this might undermine business goals, so I'm holding off on that in order to give you a chance to save the city in your own way. I'm sure you understand what I mean." I was intrigued to watch how Meredith motivated her audience. Was this the difference between professional and criminal behavior? It wasn't just the fancy business language and free sandwiches; Meredith had something else in play, something more elusive and elegant.

Girron nodded, and jotted a few notes down. The other men looked worried. Marigold smiled.

Meredith continued, "I'd prefer not to exert undue pressure, but there's a lot of ways this could go. Change can be accomplished without burning the place down." I looked at her guiltily, but she didn't meet my eye.

She ended with, "We don't want to create more harm—harm and profit don't need to go hand in hand. Well, I've gone off topic I suppose." She laughed. She was beginning to sound like the early ETA leaders that I'd found so inspiring when I was young. It was dazzling. "Let's try to get back on track, work cross-functionally. Reach out any time. Thank you so much for attending, everyone! Have a great day!"

LEARNING TO SWIM

Meredith and Linda shared a pizza in silence late that evening. They were both exhausted. When they were finished, Meredith stared at the remains of the pizza in the box on the table, mentally tracing the archipelago of grease stains scattered across the cardboard. Linda worked on deleting data off her phone and beeper.

Though the meeting had gone better than Meredith had expected, she was bothered by Marigold McCartney's insinuations about bribes and payouts. Meredith couldn't excuse them away, no matter how hard she tried. She knew she had to talk to Linda about it, especially if she wanted to preserve the fragile, tender connection she felt for her.

She rose and dared to open a window. The foul air didn't bother her as much as it normally did on Thursdays. Apparently, you could get used to anything after a while. It was like when she ate too much garlic and a little later, a rank odor bloomed unbidden from her pores. She couldn't smell it, even though it enveloped her like a putrid yellow cloud. Grillo would gag and act like he couldn't breathe before leaving the room. It was overly dramatic, like everything else he did. He himself couldn't eat garlic. It gave him gas.

There had been a lot of powerful people at the roundtable, who had collectively agreed to work together on a solution. Yet the accomplishment felt like a mirage. She couldn't really take any credit for the positive outcome if the whole thing had been a set-up.

She was beginning to sound like Grillo. Get it together, she thought to herself. That cut short the onslaught of her self-pity, making it retreat back into the swamp where it belonged. Emotions turned everything into a garish cartoon. She strategized about how to start the discussion she needed to have with Linda.

With conflict involving either Grillo or her mother, it was rare that Meredith was able to achieve a tidy consensus when it came to rehashing the past. She doubted that broaching the subject with Linda would be any different.

Meredith cleared the pizza remains off the table and went to get more water. She stood at the kitchen sink, gazing out the open window at the swimming pool visible beyond the back fence of the apartment building. The fire station's back windows were dark. The color of the pool was beginning to deepen from turquoise to midnight blue. Soon it would lapse into shadow, though its outline would still be easily discernible, because at night Merritt lit up like a five-mile-wide Christmas tree. The power station, the substation, the factories and warehouses—all of them made heavy use of security lights mounted on buildings, cranes, and fences. Except for the minority using security robots, of course.

Meredith said, "That pool is so inviting."

"I don't know how to swim," said Linda, still looking at her pager. The awkwardness between them expanded.

Meredith sat down at the table again. She said, "I was just fantasizing. It's not like we can actually get access to the pool. It's for the firemen, right? Except I've never seen anyone using it."

Linda said to her pager, "I still have master keys. I must turn them in with my phone and pager tonight."

Meredith said, "That must have been strange for you, quitting after so many years with MPD?"

"Twenty years."

Silence drew up a chair and sat between them like an unwelcome dinner guest.

Meredith wanted to start off on the right note. Be positive. Communication was supposed to be what she was good at. What did she want from the conversation, anyway? An assurance that Linda was no longer corrupt?

"Even if everyone is guilty, the ends don't justify the means," Meredith said, as if to herself.

"I knew it," said Linda. "You changed your mind. You're not coming with me."

"What? No. I didn't change my mind. I just…you need to—" Meredith took a breath. "I mean, you helped me tremendously. There's no way I could have pulled off 100-percent attendance. It couldn't have been easy, dealing with all those muckety-mucks."

"It was necessary under the circumstances," said Linda. She stared at her nails, and started chewing on a cuticle.

Meredith thought about all the couples therapy she'd had over the years with Grillo, and she remembered the term "nonviolent communication," something the therapist had tried to get them to adopt instead of arguing. You were supposed to make statements based on how you felt, delivered gently and neutral in tone, like reporting the weather, instead of a blasting of cannons. For example, "I felt sad when you accused me of ruining your life," was better than, "You always blame me for your own failures, which is terrible and you're terrible." Nonviolent communication did seem to help their marriage a little, but only during therapy sessions. At home, they reverted to old habits.

"Linda," Meredith said, "I felt betrayed and scared when I realized that those executives had attended out of fear instead of enthusiasm."

Linda squeezed her eyes shut. "I am a liar and a criminal, and it's hopeless."

"Why didn't you tell me?"

Linda rubbed her ear so hard it turned red. She opened her eyes and said, "I always choose the shortest path. What's efficient. It's how I was trained. It's extra work, and it's more risky, you see, to also make sure it's legal. And maybe they deserved it."

"Nobody deserves to be threatened or extorted or whatever it was you did..."

Linda pushed her phone and pager away from her and finally looked at Meredith defiantly. "Even Bob Hawley at AFA Foods? The man who fired you, unfairly, without warning?"

Meredith sighed. Bob had barely acknowledged her at the meeting.

"Even Bob doesn't deserve that," Meredith said gently. She realized that this was the crux of Linda's problem. Her loyalty and devotion, when combined with a confused sense of right and wrong, led her down the wrong path. That's it, thought Meredith. Linda is just confused. And who wouldn't be a little confused, if one was an ex-terrorist? It was an extraordinary story that Meredith was still trying to digest. As for Linda's job working for the City of Merritt, it seemed to Meredith that Linda was nothing more than a cog in a corrupt machine. It wasn't Linda's fault, was it?

Meredith said, "You've been through so much. Maybe we're alike. We both want to get things done. We think we have to do it all ourselves."

"You shouldn't give me any sympathy," Linda said. She got up and went to the front door.

"Where are you going?" said Meredith.

Her back to Meredith, Linda said quietly, "You don't deserve to live a life where you're always looking behind you to see who is chasing you, who will find you out. You don't need such a life. You deserve better than that. You deserve more."

"But—"

Linda cut her off. "I never learned to swim, but I can learn. I can learn to swim. Nevetheless. This isn't what's good for you. You already know how to swim." She unbolted the front door.

"Wait!" said Meredith. "I can teach you how!"

Linda's hand hesitated on the doorknob.

Meredith said, "We should check out that pool. I could teach you how to swim."

Linda turned, her voice catching in her throat. "You would do that? For me?"

"Of course."

They stared at each other, not moving. Meredith said, "Let's go."

Meredith put on running shoes and picked up her bag. Linda followed her out the door. They walked around the block to the fire station, which was dark. Linda unlocked the gate to the back area, and they quietly made their way to the swimming pool.

"I forgot," whispered Meredith. "No bathing suits."

Linda rolled up her pants to her knees. "My feet don't need a swimming suit," she said tiredly. She sat heavily on the side of the pool, swishing the water around with her legs. Meredith dropped her bag a good distance from the pool so that it wouldn't get wet. She sat down beside Linda. Some water splashed on Meredith's blouse.

"Oh phooey," said Meredith, taking off her top. "I am so fucking sick of business casual."

Linda made a small smile, and took off her shirt too. "Is it hard, to learn to swim?"

"No! It's not hard," said Meredith. "First you blow some bubbles, they have all the little kids do that first."

"Blowing bubbles? Like this?" Linda let out a Bronx Cheer. Meredith laughed. "Noooo...like this." She slid into the pool, and pulled Linda in with her. The water was only three feet deep, but Linda looked alarmed.

Meredith bent her knees until just her head and neck were above the surface. She gestured for Linda to do the same.

Meredith said, "Take a breath, then blow out under the water. Make some bubbles, like this." Meredith demonstrated. She came up for air and said, "Now it's your turn."

Linda tried it, but forgot to take a breath first, coughing on the water she'd inhaled. "Oh no!" said Meredith. "Don't forget to take a deep breath first." She patted Linda's back until Linda had recovered.

Determined, Linda tried again. Imitating Meredith, she inhaled, dipped down just below the surface of the water, and blew bubbles. She resurfaced and rubbed water out of her eyes, saying, "I am happy that I didn't drink the water that time. The bubbles sounded like little explosions—so loud! How does the water do this to the ears?"

"You did great!"

Meredith held Linda's hands as she pulled her across the shallow end of the pool. "Kick out your feet behind you. I've got you," she said, but Linda's pants got tangled and weighed her down. She starting sinking. Meredith helped her up.

"Ugh," said Meredith. "I'm so sick of pants, too." She took off her pants, squeezed out the excess water, and lobbed them over to the side of the pool, the garment thwacking the concrete on contact. Linda followed suit, with a slow throaty laugh.

"Fuck it," said Meredith. She took off her bra and threw it at a disheveled shrub growing against the fence. The bra caught on a branch and hung there like an ornament.

She turned to Linda. Seeing that she wore a sports bra, Meredith said, "Let me help with yours. A wet sports bra sucks. I should know—they're always such a pain to pull off after I go for a run. A stinky sweaty torture device." She turned Linda around in the water and unhooked the back of her bra then tossed it at the shrub. It missed by a wide margin. "Damn, I was never any good at sports," said Meredith. She said, "Let's try blowing bubbles and kicking at the same time."

She turned Linda around and led her across the pool, saying, "Kick out your feet. Kick! Kick! That's it!" At first Linda was able to stay afloat, but then she grew anxious, froze, and started to sink. Meredith pulled her up close, and whispered, "I got you," until Linda's breathing steadied.

"Maybe I'm too old for this," said Linda.

"Maybe we're too young for this," said Meredith.

"I am serious," said Linda.

"I regret to inform you that I hereby refuse all requests to be serious," Meredith said. She blew a raspberry on Linda's neck, then kissed her.

LINDA: FLOODLIGHTS

Inside the bright darkness of Merritt's night, standing in the shallow end of the pool, we embraced. Meredith tasted like chlorine and pepperoni. But in the next moment, we broke away from each other, temporarily blinded by the scalding glare of floodlights.

Squinting in the light, Meredith sank down under the water to hide her naked upper half as best she could.

I heard a male voice that said, "Vasco in the pool kissing a lady! Wait till I show this to the guys."

As my sight returned, I could distinguish a dark figure backlit by the lights mounted to the corners of the fire station roof's end caps. It was Bill Ochoa. He was holding up his phone and taking pictures.

"Please stop taking pictures, Bill," I said with a false calm I didn't feel. I heard Meredith gasp behind me, huddling in my shadow.

"That's what she said!" Bill laughed far too long at his stupid joke.

"Ah, good one," I said, considering my options. "Do we need the floodlights, Bill?" I asked.

"Oh yes we do, Vasco. We definitely need the floodlights. I can't wait to post it on the station's Facebook page. You're finally going down, Vasco. This shit is going viral. And it's about time!"

Apparently, he'd already heard that I had quit MPD, and I was fair game. News moves fast in a small town.

This was going to be tricky. I had vowed to myself that I would, from now on, always do the right thing. I vowed it when I realized that Meredith had forgiven me for my horrible transgressions. You don't teach someone to swim if you hate them. You don't kiss them either.

I eyed our dry shirts a few feet in front of Ochoa. Next to the two shirts were my wallet, keys, knife, and phone, arranged in a neat pile.

I said, "How about some towels, Bill?"

"You forgot towels? Can this get any better? Let me figure out the video on this thing. Stupid phone. How about some naked water ballet, a little wet T&A? Come on, girls, let it all hang out."

He laughed again. I was offended for Esther Williams. I used to watch her movies with my dad before he died. I was enchanted by the roses on her swimming cap, her structurally immobile bathing suit. Water ballet was a dance performed upside down and under water. I loved it because it was both ridiculous and beautiful.

While Bill was still focused on his smart phone, I thought about escape routes.

I said, "What would the Chief say when he finds out about this? I'm concerned about your professional ethics."

"Give me a break. Like that ever stopped you."

I tried a different tactic. "The lady here has diabetes. If she can't get out, get dressed, and gain access to her insulin, it would be very dangerous. You are a first-responder. Didn't you take a oath?"

"No way, José."

I watched him fiddle with his stupid phone. I said, "You seem to be having trouble. Isn't there a professional camera inside the station? For training?"

"Nice try. I'm not going anywhere. Let's see those jugs. The guys all have longstanding bets on how big they are. I told the guys, triple D for sure. Sports bras are misleading. I can't wait to cash in. Photos are better than nothing. Let's go, Vasco!"

I shrugged. I turned and heaved myself out of the water, moved up the shallow end's steps and stood in the main thrust of the floodlights a few feet in front of Bill. Dripping wet, arms akimbo, I watched while he snapped his photos with the delight of a young child opening a birthday present. When he finally looked up from his phone at my body, he got that hypnotized look in his eyes that I have seen many times in my life.

I addressed Bill from my right breast, pointing it at him like it was doing the talking. I might as well have been headless anyway, for he was unable to look at anything else. I should have learned ventriloquism. I missed my calling.

I said, "I respectfully request some towels. Where can we go, after all? Our clothes are wet." I gestured to our wet pants clumped in disarray near his feet. I shivered for dramatic effect.

"No pants? You can't go anywhere! Fuck the towels. I'm getting the video camera. And the rest of the guys! They're not going to believe this." He ran inside.

"We must move quickly," I said to Meredith, who didn't need to be told twice. We still had our underwear on—mine were more like shorts because I wore boxers; Meredith was wearing bikini bottoms, unfortunately. At least our shirts were dry. We threw them on, grabbed our stuff, and got the hell out of there.

We sprinted down the deserted street to the shared lawn of two duplexes huddled near the front of the power substation. I whispered to Meredith, "We need to dry off a little so Ochoa can't follow our trail. The dripping water, the wet footprints. Not good." I rolled sideways on the grass like I was a dog. Meredith was taken aback for a minute but silently did the same. I could hear Bill shouting. He was still far enough away, but gaining ground. At night in Merritt, residential homes were little dark spots, while everything around them was lit up by security lights. It was like a photo negative of stars in the sky. We edged our way around the hurricane fence that bordered the lawn, moving toward the power plant grounds next door where, with my master key, I opened a locked side gate.

We hid just inside the gate in the dark to see if we had lost Ochoa.

We heard Ochoa shout close by, "Vasco, you bitch! You're gonna pay for this! You think you're free of me? You have no idea. MPD is on their way now. They're gonna arrest your ass for trespassing and loitering with intent." Vern's leak of Merritt's crimes, which included my crimes, was probably already online; if I was arrested, they'd have me right where they'd want me. I'm sure I'd become the lightning rod for all of Merritt's misdeeds, regardless of whether I had been carrying out orders or not. It was clear that the plan to leave soon had become a plan to flee immediately.

He continued, "You might as well surrender. I know where you live. There are security cameras everywhere! Olly Olly Oxen Free!"

Ollie? Who was Ollie, and what was this business about oxen? Bill had clearly lost his mind. I steered Meredith to an underground tunnel that took us under the substation, running across the property to the other side, careful to not touch converters or anything else that was live with thousands of kilowatts of electricity coursing through the lines that ran along the tunnel's ceiling, because that would be an unfortunate way to die.

We made it to the adjoining block where our apart-ment building was. Meredith started to walk toward it, but I stopped her. We had to steer clear, though we were still in need of pants.

I thought of Mayor Mendebal's apartment. I knew my master key fit his lock; it was Thursday night, and he was rarely there on Thursday; it was just a few blocks away. We set off carefully, hiding when there was a passing vehicle, and sprinting when there wasn't. From dumpster to newsstand and back again, we zigzagged our way to Mendebal's place.

We snuck in through the back entrance of the building and went up the stairs. As expected, the apartment was empty. While Meredith took a shower to rinse off the chlo-rine, I rummaged through the bedroom. I found some of Mendebal's suits from the 1950s in his closet. A pair of pants with a belt would fit me fine, because Mendebal's size in the 1950s was the same as my size, today. But Meredith was taller, so that was a problem, until I found some pajamas from the 1960s that I thought would work. The Basque crest was silkscreened onto the pajamas in a pattern. They appeared to be brand new. After Meredith got out of the shower, she tried them on. She looked great in them, of course, though the pants hit her mid-calf because of her long legs.

While I took a shower, I silently thanked Mayor Men-debal for his reluctance to throw out stuff from previous decades. Though the place wasn't stuffed to the gills, it didn't really have belongings that would make it something you'd call "home." The closets contained nothing else besides the sixty-year-old suits, and the drawers contained nothing else besides the fifty-year-old pajamas. Who knew why he kept them around? People were funny.

Meredith poured two glasses of water and gave me one. "Linda," she said, "I can't believe you got us out of that. It was just amazing. Also embarrassing. But amazing."

"Thanks," I said.

"And I know, I just know that you could have made it easy on yourself. Because you had something on him, didn't you?"

"Yes, I did."

"I knew it! I'm so proud of you."

I was embarrassed. "But I lied. You don't have diabetes."

"A little white lie is OK, sometimes. That was an extreme situation."

We looked at each other and smiled. It was all I could do not to jump on her right then and there. But we had to get going.

It was on her mind too. We said it in unison: "We have to get out of here." I laughed.

I said, "Check under the sink will you? All the way toward the back. Is there an envelope taped there?" She checked and looked up at me, nodding. "Great," I said. "Hang onto it."

After Meredith opened the envelope and found a thick stack of cash, she said, "Isn't this stealing?"

"Yes, it is," I said. Then I demonstrated that I could collaborate. We were partners now. I said, "What should we do? It is very likely that Mendebal forgot about it. Check the dates on the bills."

She checked and sure enough, none of the one-hundred-dollar bills in the envelope had dates later than 1988.

I said, "It's also very likely that the cash was not properly obtained."

Meredith rubbed her eyes. I could tell she was tired. It was getting to her, all this fleeing, lying, and now stealing.

"Just this once, I guess," she said. "We can pay it back anonymously, later, right?"

"Of course," I said, although I hoped she'd forget about it. We didn't need the paper trail.

We'd ditched our phones in the underground tunnel of the substation, so I used Mendebal's landline to call a cab, which took us to Union Station, just ten minutes away. On our way out of Merritt, we passed Mallory Place, where Shitbird and his wife lived. They were the only people left in Merritt that I might actually miss.

At Union Station, when the newsstand opened at 6:00 a.m., I purchased two burner phones, some snacks, and two cups of coffee. We then boarded a train going north. Despite the holiday weekend, it wasn't crowded.

No one checked our ID on Amtrak, which is why I'd decided we needed to take a train as opposed to an airplane. We found two empty seats in the last car. We didn't relax until we left the state about ten hours later. The train would take us all the way to Washington, where I could make contact with some ETA brethren who'd hook me up with a new passport. Then on to Canada.

I leaned close to Meredith and asked, "Will you miss it?"

"LA? Gosh. Good question. I've lived there all my life, not by choice, just, you know, that's how it worked out. One thing led to another and…but that's not what you asked me, is it? Would I miss it? No. No, I don't think I will. And you know what? I don't think it will miss me, either."

I smiled. I loved her perspective. I took her hand and held it to my heart. I could feel my heart better that way.

———■-■-■———

ACKNOWLEDGEMENTS

Historical material used to develop character background as well as the novel's fictional setting mostly came from *LA Times* articles as well as *The Basque History of the World: The Story of a Nation*, by Mark Kurlasky (New York: Penguin, 2001).

Thanks to my family for their endurance and support. I have endless gratitude for Nancy Agabian's writing classes, where the seeds of this book were born. Thanks to Chris Lastovicka, whose revenge idea allowed the character of Linda to fully form. Posthumous thanks to Tommy Gillilland, who provided the idea of citizen interviews. I have tremendous appreciation for Carrie Frye, who is a brilliant editor and who suggested in many large and small ways how I might consider elegance instead of brute force to tell a story. To Courtney Hudak, my writing partner: how lucky I was to meet and collaborate with you. You sustained me. Thanks to all early readers—you know who you are. Your sacrifice was vast and your input was invaluable.

Thanks to Carla Green, for layout genius as well as for putting up with tedious late-breaking edits. Thanks to Paolo Skyrus for the terrific cover design. Thanks to Matt Levine for permission to quote him, though please know that at the time of printing, he has neither read nor has he endorsed this book. Lastly, as General Oleksandr Tarnavsky said, "I want to thank even the skeptics, their criticism also influences our task's success."